HE TOOK A STE
but she did not move ~~...~~ ~~...~~ ~~...~~uld
have, for she had the reactions of a trained
warrior. Yet she didn't. Rather she lifted her
head, waiting, inviting.

His mouth came down on hers fiercely. Dax
took her lips with an intimacy that would have
been an insult but for what had just passed
between them in the guise of simple song. And
her response had nothing to do with the collar
that bound her.

She swayed and felt his hands grip her shoulders to steady her. At least, it began that way;
in the next instant he was pulling her to him,
holding her tightly against his chest. . . .

ANNOUNCING THE

TOPAZ FREQUENT READERS CLUB
COMMEMORATING TOPAZ'S
1 YEAR ANNIVERSARY!

THE MORE YOU BUY, THE MORE YOU GET

Redeem coupons found here and in the back of all new Topaz titles for FREE Topaz gifts:

Send in:

 2 coupons for a free TOPAZ novel (choose from the list below);
- ☐ **THE KISSING BANDIT**, Margaret Brownley
- ☐ **BY LOVE UNVEILED**, Deborah Martin
- ☐ **TOUCH THE DAWN**, Chelley Kitzmiller
- ☐ **WILD EMBRACE**, Cassie Edwards

 4 coupons for an "I Love the Topaz Man" on-board sign

 6 coupons for a TOPAZ compact mirror

 8 coupons for a Topaz Man T-shirt

Just fill out this certificate and send with original sales receipts to:

TOPAZ FREQUENT READERS CLUB-1ST ANNIVERSARY
Penguin USA • Mass Market Promotion; Dept. H.U.G.
375 Hudson St., NY, NY 10014

Name_____

Address_____

City_____State_____Zip_____

Offer expires 5/31/1995

This certificate must accompany your request. No duplicates accepted. Void where prohibited, taxed or restricted. Allow 4-6 weeks for receipt of merchandise. Offer good only in U.S., its territories, and Canada.

THE
SKYPIRATE

by

Justine Davis

A TOPAZ BOOK

TOPAZ
Published by the Penguin Group
Penguin Books USA Inc., 375 Hudson Street,
New York, New York 10014, U.S.A.
Penguin Books Ltd, 27 Wrights Lane,
London W8 5TZ, England
Penguin Books Australia Ltd, Ringwood,
Victoria, Australia
Penguin Books Canada Ltd, 10 Alcorn Avenue,
Toronto, Ontario, Canada M4V 3B2
Penguin Books (N.Z.) Ltd, 182–190 Wairau Road,
Auckland 10, New Zealand

Penguin Books Ltd, Registered Offices:
Harmondsworth, Middlesex, England

First published by Topaz, an imprint of Dutton Signet,
a division of Penguin Books USA Inc.

First Printing, February, 1995
10 9 8 7 6 5 4 3 2 1

Topaz is a trademark of Dutton Signet
a division of Penguin Books USA Inc.

Printed in the United States of America

To Dale and Mark—

Not for treating my virus-ridden computer,
Not for replacing it with one that made this book
seem to come at light speed,
Not for building me a new one that makes life even easier,
But for becoming that rarest of all good things:

True friends.

Tyche is indeed the goddess of good fortune.

Thanks, guys.

Chapter 1

I don't mind dying, but I'll be damned if I'll do it here.

Not here, not now, and not by the likes of the men who guarded this grim place, Dax Silverbrake thought. No, the way out of this fix was guile, and he'd learned the craft well.

"I swear," Dax muttered under his breath as they walked down the grim, narrow hallway, "if Rina wasn't the best navigator I've ever seen, I'd—"

"—still go after her." Dax gave his first mate a sideways look; Roxton was grinning at him despite the danger. "And don't be trying to convince me otherwise, Cap'n." The grizzled older man, disguised as a servant, tugged on his beard as he went on in a whisper, "Not that I'd blame you, mind, even though she is like your own blood sister to you." He shook his head in disgust. "Of all things. Gettin' caught rigging a game of chaser!"

Dax's jade green eyes narrowed in warning, and Roxton quieted as the guard ahead of them, who had slowed his pace, came too near to risk further talk.

They continued down the stone corridor, their way lit only by the guard's cellight, the dank walls making Dax glad of the heavy, hooded cloak of his disguise. The rustling he heard from the floor made him glad of his knee-high boots; being nibbled at by Carelian muckrats was not his idea of fun. Blast Rina anyway, how could she let herself get caught rigging the dice for chaser? A child could—

"Here we are," the guard said as they turned right and stepped into a wider corridor, no less dark, but lined on each side with barred cells that were even danker and colder than the hallway they'd come through. "You'll find one here to warm even this chilly night."

Chilly? Dax didn't want to know what the man thought was cold. Carelian nights were bleakly cold this time of year, something to hide from, not go wandering about in. The cold made the byways and main concourses virtually deserted, which was both good and bad from their point of view; once they got out of here they could be reasonably certain of going undiscovered, but if they were, they would have a difficult time explaining why they were out on this freezing night.

"Take your pick, friend," the guard said.

Friend? Not likely, Dax thought. But he answered mildly enough. "In the dark?"

The guard sniggered, a lewd, nasty sound. "Why not? That's where you'll be with her anyway, isn't it?"

Dax restrained the urge to bury his fist in the man's round, leering face. He knew the sale of Coalition prisoners, no questions asked, was a common practice among the more unsavory of their guards, but he still found it repugnant. He reined in his distaste; Rina's freedom could depend on how well he played this part.

"Not necessarily," he answered, putting as much of sordid anticipation as he could manage into his voice.

The guard laughed, loud and ribaldly. "I forgot. A man who's spent a season mining in the caverns of Boreas wouldn't want to spend any more time in the dark, would he? Well, I've a few worth looking at, even in the light. Come along."

Dax followed the man, resisting the urge to straighten his shoulders to relieve the ache. Every crystal miner he'd ever seen walked hunched over from years of working in cramped quarters; if he'd realized what he was letting himself in for, he would have picked another disguise for his tall frame. Not for the first time he wished for a bit more anonymity; he might have been able to simply buy Rina's way out by paying off the officer she'd tried to bilk.

He heard the mumble of voices, some rambling crazily, some wailing pathetically, and some strident with anger. The only consistency was that they were all female. The males, equally subject to sale if the price was right, were obviously in another wing. Dax smiled wryly in the shadows. Perhaps it was a good thing that it had been Rina who had gotten caught; he doubted he could work up a credible show of enthusiasm for Roxton. He wondered briefly if the guards ever had to account for the prisoners who were never seen again.

Not likely, he thought again. There were so many Coalition prisoners that the loss of a mere hundred or so here and there would hardly be noticed.

The guard stopped, turning the ray of his cellight through a set of bars. "Now here's a nice one, if you'll be wanting it a little . . . rough."

Dax frowned as a gleam reflected from eyes that looked decidedly pink. "She looks Carelian." Hard to believe; the natives of this world were known not to survive captivity.

"She is, but don't worry. We've declawed her. And after a long season on that ice planet, you must be . . . eager."

If you only knew, Dax thought wryly. But this was not the time to dwell on his own mating problems. "Not that eager," he said. "What else have you got?"

Several cells and rejections later, the guard was becoming irritated. Dax knew it was only a step from irritation to suspicion, and he tried to ease the man's mood.

"You were right, you know," he said unctuously. "After a season buried under tons of ice, mining crystal, I've a preference for sunlight. Have you any with that coloring?"

Placated by the flattery, the guard's face was split by a grin, distorted evilly by the angle of the cellight. "Ah, so that's what you're after. I have just the thing for you. A young one. She just came in today. A Coalition officer caught her cheating at chaser. I warn you though, she's a bit stubborn. We haven't had time to work on her yet."

Dax's amusement at the understatement—Rina, only a bit stubborn?—was tinged with relief at the last words; they hadn't hurt her yet.

"I'm not averse to a little spirit," he said casually.

"Oh, she's got that, all right," the guard crowed. "And except that it's short, she has gold hair, like a Triotian."

Dax was grateful for the dim light then; he was sure his sudden fear must have shown in his face. He felt Roxton stiffen beside him. It was a moment before he trusted his voice enough to tell the man to lead them on. Roxton held back, and Dax slowed his steps to match the older man's.

"Do you think he guessed?" the first mate asked in a hushed whisper.

"No."

It was flat, certain, and Roxton lifted a bushy gray brow. "So sure?"

"If he knew she really was Triotian, she'd be dead."

"True enough," Roxton agreed after a moment, but Dax was already ahead of him, striding after the guard.

They came to a halt at the last cell. Only a tall, solid metal door remained between them and the end of the corridor. The guard directed his light through the bars. It caught the face of a female, barely more than a girl, who blinked in the sudden brightness. Her face, although dirty, was that of a pixie, a legendary creature of the Triotian woodlands. Big eyes nearly the same vivid green as Dax's own, and a tiny, pointed chin were topped by a short, tousled cap of hair that was indeed the uncommon color of a Triotian, the same shade as the golden steeds of Arellia. Only the shortness of her hair and the sun-browned color of her skin masked her true origin; with few exceptions, Triotians were the golden children, both in hair, which they never cut, and skin.

For an instant Dax was unable to speak, his throat tight at the sight of her, safe. Roxton hadn't exaggerated; this girl was as precious to him as a blood sister. Perhaps more so, since he'd lost his own true sister.

"She'll do," he said, his voice tight with emotion. He heard the husky sound of it, and hoped the guard would take it for the arousal of a long deprived man.

The guard laughed, pleased, but under the sound Dax heard Rina whisper his name in tones of utter relief.

"Well, now," the guard drawled, "this one may cost a bit more than we agreed on. We haven't had a chance to examine her yet, but it's quite possible she's untried."

Fury rose in Dax. He heard Rina's outraged exclamation and motioned her to silence. He knew damned well she was untouched; he'd fought on occasion to keep her that way. Rina had a hard-learned dislike of most men except the *Evening Star*'s crew, and none of them would even think of laying a hand on her. The thought of some man the ilk of this grinning knave intimately examining Rina made him want to pull his flashbow right now and put an end to this farce. But with a patience that had been long fought for and hard won, he reined in his naturally hot temper.

"Fine," he said to the guard, with a blitheness he was far from feeling. "But if your examination proves her not virgin—quite likely, if she's been long on her own and running games of chance on the streets—the price is halved."

"Halved?" the guard sputtered.

"Fair enough, for my time and patience. As you said, it has been a very long season."

Dax's tone brooked no argument. The guard gulped, then swallowed as he stared up at the broad, hooded figure that, even hunched over, towered above him. "But you'll take her as is, at the price agreed?"

"Only if I take her now."

The man made his decision quickly. "Then take her." He reached to his belt and removed his code key, which he aimed at the lock as he punched a series of buttons. With a click that echoed in the damp darkness, the lock opened. He turned around and held his hand out to Dax.

Reaching into the cavernous pocket of his cloak, Dax grasped the bag of coins, a motley collection of Arellian Novals, Carelian Ducas, and two rare Romerian Withals. Different coins, from different worlds, but similar in two ways; they were all accepted at face value or more throughout the system, and all had been liberated from their original owners. They clinked satisfyingly as he drew out the pouch. A small price, to walk out of here without—

"So"—the voice came out of the darkness, clear and ringing—"you will escape, just as you said."

Startled, Dax's gaze darted to the blackest corner of the cell, from which the voice had come. His instincts were slipping, he thought. He hadn't even realized there was another prisoner here in this gruesome place that was the possible—probable, he amended grimly—future for them all.

"And here I thought all your bragging about your rescue merely talk."

Dax's gaze shot back to Rina, who looked away, but not before he saw her chagrined expression. Damnation, couldn't she keep her mouth shut, even here?

"Silence!"

It took a split second for Dax to register that the guard had not voiced his own thoughts to Rina, but had barked an order to the as yet unseen female. As he spoke, the man moved the beam of the cellight to the dark corner.

Dax's brows furrowed. There, standing with a proud, straight posture that surprised him, was another female. At least, he supposed it was, since all others in this wing of the Coalition prison were. But this one was filthy, the kind of grime built up over time, not the surface dirt such as Rina had acquired during her short stay. This one had hair cropped even shorter than Rina's, hair that was either dark unto black, or so dirty it didn't bear thinking about. Her face was almost as dirty; he had no idea how old she might be. Her eyes gleamed in the cellight's glow.

They were blue, a startling pale blue, the color of the purest ice on the mining planet Dax was pretending to be from. They were fastened on him with a steadiness that made him long more than ever to straighten his aching, hunched shoulders; a man shouldn't face a stare like that without whatever advantage his superior height might bring.

Who was she, this prisoner who held herself so proudly? Who was this, holding his intense stare with a coolness he'd not seen in even his fiercest opponents? She was slender, he guessed from the shape of her face, since it was impossible to tell in her grubby, baggy clothes. She was tall. She was—

She was a slave.

He hadn't noticed before, with his fascination with those unusual eyes, but now he focused on the dull glow of gold at her throat. A collar. The collar of Coalition enslavement. He'd heard of them, even seen some of the lower levels, but never a gold one before. It looked almost ornamental, with the sheen of the precious metal and the three jewel-like lights. He supposed that helped the citizens of the almighty Coalition pretend they weren't truly slaves.

He'd heard they were referred to merely as "gold collars" or "bronze collars," or whatever level they were, as if the collar itself was the being. He hoped this was as close as he would ever get to one.

She didn't wear it well. It was at odds with her proud carriage, with the force and intensity of her eyes. And most especially, at odds with the ringing tones of her voice.

"When you told me about the man who would come for you, I didn't realize you spoke the truth." Dax caught his breath. Just how much had Rina said?

"Silence," the guard roared again, apparently too angry—or too thick—to be suspicious, "or I'll get the controller and quiet you permanently."

"I think not," the female said. She was, Dax decided, either incredibly brave, or incredibly stupid. Or, he thought suddenly, she had a token up her sleeve. Something to bargain with. Something with a worth of which she was very, very sure.

"From your bragging of his strength and beauty, I didn't expect a broken-down hunchback," the female added scornfully.

As the guard gaped at the prisoner's effrontery, Dax's gaze flicked to Rina once more. Was she bluffing, or had Rina, in her youthful excess, let slip the identity of the rescuer she expected? There was a healthy price on his head—dead or alive—in this and more than a few other sectors. Perhaps even enough to buy freedom for a collared slave.

Rina met his gaze, and for the first time since he'd pulled her out of that cave on Daxelia, he saw fear there. And anguish. His jaw clenched. How much did this female know? Only that Rina had expected rescue from her crew, or had the girl let slip his name? Even if she knew only that this was indeed a rescue, not a purchase of a female prisoner for carnal purposes, she could get them all killed. He would have to move fast, or this whole thing could disintegrate on them.

"She's not very pleasant, is she?" Dax said in an amused tone.

"She's been nothing but trouble since she got here," the guard grumbled. "She's on her way to Ossuary, but if they'd turn me loose on her, I'd show her fast enough what we do with crippled Arellian slaves who don't know their place."

"Better men than you have tried, you Carelian blowpig." Her voice rang with defiance, and Dax felt a grudging admiration for her courage, if not her fool-hardiness.

"They've clearly been far too easy on you, Arellian bitch," the guard snapped, whirling back to glare at her. "It's time you learned your place, and what that controller is really for."

"You won't dare," the Arellian said. "Not when I tell you what I know about—"

"As I said, I'm not averse to a little spirit." Dax cut in quickly, putting a hand on the guard's shoulder and leading him away from the female who was apparently about to play her bargaining token—him. "And if one woman is good, two is better, hmm?"

The guard blinked as they came to a halt out of ear-shot of the cell. "You want both of them?"

Dax shrugged as if it were of no import. "I would pay extra, of course. Not that she's worth it, unless you cut her tongue out first."

The guard gave a low chuckle. "She's already marred," he warned. "Lame. Left leg."

Dax grinned, a deadly imitation of the guard's lewd expression. "It's not her leg I'm concerned with."

The man returned the grin, but then his eyes narrowed. He abruptly shook his head. "No. I can't. Not a gold collar."

"Oh? Are they so valuable, then?"

"The most valuable of all Coalition property. My life would be the price for misplacing a gold collar. And I hear they have special plans for that one, once she's broken."

Which is nothing, Dax thought grimly, compared to the special plans they have for me.

"You're sure?" he asked, hoping to avoid what his gut was telling him was rapidly becoming inevitable. "Perhaps you could just say she escaped?"

The guard snorted. "Hasn't been but one gold collar *ever* escape. A lot of people parted company with their heads over it. More just plain disappeared." He shook his head, more definitely this time. "Coin's worth nothing if you're dead."

"How true," Dax muttered.

Then he let out a sigh as if giving up, and walked back to the cell. Rina met his gaze, apology—a bit late, as usual—in her green eyes. But Dax merely glanced at her; his attention was fastened on the other occupant of the cell. Still, she held his gaze unflinchingly.

"You're sure you want to do this?" he questioned softly, too low for the guard to hear.

She didn't pretend to misunderstand. "I have no choice."

As the guard came up to stand beside him, Dax drew in a deep breath. "I guess I'll have to give you one, then."

The Arellian looked, for the first time, startled. The guard's forehead creased. "What was that?"

"I said 'Too bad, she's a live one,' " Dax improvised.

"Hmph," snorted the man. "You're better off with the younger one. The Arellian'd probably freeze a man's nether parts off."

"Hmm. Perhaps."

Dax reached down to tug at his cloak, as if it had caught on the uneven floor. The guard's eyes instinctively followed the motion of his hand. The moment his field of vision was diverted, Dax grabbed the unlocked cell door and swung it open in a swift, powerful arc. The bars caught the guard at the temple, and he went down heavily.

Rina was out the cell door in an instant. The Arellian, while not quite as quick, was only a step behind.

"They've got my disrupter in that locker over there," Rina said, pushing thick blond bangs out of her eyes as she ran to the metal door they'd seen before. "It's locked," she exclaimed in frustration.

"What did you expect?" Dax asked mildly. He glanced at his companion. "Roxton?"

The older man nodded, keeping a wary eye on the Arellian as he walked toward Rina. Dax, too, was watching the Arellian, who had followed close on Rina's heels, and was showing her first sign of tension as she stared at the locked cabinet door as if the sheer fierceness of her gaze could melt it.

Roxton pulled out his disrupter, and aimed it at the lock on the metal door. At the piercing sound, a rumble of voices began echoing down the corridor.

"Be quick about it," Dax muttered as the door swung open. "The guests are getting restless."

Rina reached in and grabbed an armful of weapons, tossing a couple to Roxton, three more to Dax. He caught them and stuffed them into the pocket that had held the coins—

The coins. He was bending to retrieve the pouch from the unconscious guard when a movement by the Arellian brought him sharply upright. He suppressed a groan of relief at standing full upright for the first time in what seemed like aeons, but barely had time to savor it; he leapt forward, slammed the metal door shut, and trapped the Arellian's hands in his. He felt her pulse leap beneath his fingertips.

"You'll pardon me for not arming the person who was so very eager to hand the Coalition my head," he said dryly.

"I had no choice," she repeated. "Besides, I wasn't going for a weapon."

"Oh?"

He released her hands, but kept hold of both her wrists with one hand as he pried open her fingers with the other. She resisted him with a strength that surprised him, but eventually she had to give way.

What she held was like no kind of weapon he'd ever seen. It was palm sized, adorned with buttons, a knob of some sort, and three crystals, one each of red, yellow, and blue. No, not crystals. Lights. His gaze flicked to the collar that banded her slender throat. The matching lights were there. This must be the controller the guard had mentioned. He hadn't the slightest idea how the thing worked, but knew he wouldn't like it if he did.

The racket increased down the long corridor of cells as the prisoners began to guess that something was going on. The shouts were starting to ring off the damp stone walls. Dax bent to remove the code key from the downed guard's belt.

"Better move, Cap'n," Roxton urged. "They'll soon hear all the noise."

"If we go back that way," Rina whispered, staring down the long, dark corridor, "we'll run right into them as they come down."

"Give me a weapon," the Arellian snapped. "I can help you fight them."

Dax lifted a brow. "Fight? Four against ... what, forty? Sorry, that's not my kind of odds."

She glanced down the hall, then turned back to Dax, contempt rife in her eyes and voice. "In a few moments, you'll have no choice."

She didn't call him coward, but Dax heard it as surely as if she had. It didn't matter; he'd been called that and worse. He'd called himself worse. But it made him wonder about this female, and why she was prisoner here.

"Quiet," he ordered. He turned to look at the stone wall that was the dead end of the corridor. Then he spoke to Rina. "Did you pay any attention when they brought you in here?"

"Of course," the girl answered indignantly.

He gestured toward the wall. "What's on the other side?"

The girl closed her eyes for a moment. It was a familiar action to Dax; he knew she was pulling up the memory. And when she did, it would be, as it was aboard the *Evening Star,* as accurate as any star chart. But the sound of shouts and distant running footsteps overhead told him they were running out of time.

"The cliff," she said a second later. "About twenty feet high, here. Above the main path."

"Good." He reached beneath his cloak once more.

"Good?" The Arellian gaped at him. "What's good about it? That wall's so thick even the strongest disrupter would barely scratch it."

Dax gave her a look suitable for a pesky insect, then ignored her as he turned to face the blank wall, pushing his cloak back with one arm. He now held a lethal-looking yet beautiful gleaming silver weapon. Its short stock was etched with an intricate design that ended at a heavy oblong cube, which in turn gave way to an arm's length half cylinder with a wide groove hollowed out of the upward-facing flat side. Near the far end of the long cylinder was a curved crosspiece, bent back and held with a strand of some material that shone as silver as the weapon itself.

"The flashbow," Rina breathed, her eyes widening.

The Arellian glanced at her recent cellmate, then turned her gaze back to Dax. He bent for a moment, reaching for something beneath the cloak, then stood once more, pushing the hood back. With his free hand he slid what looked like a handsbreadth-long bolt of an oddly colored material into the groove, moving it back until it butted against the metal case. He pulled the metallic string back until it slid into a slot in the case, behind the bolt. He moved a lever on the metal portion, and an odd, low-pitched hum began. The bolt began to glow. He raised the weapon to his shoulder, ignoring the staring Arellian as he concentrated, focusing on the spot he'd chosen on the wall. His right hand curled around the stock, his finger slid over the trigger.

The sound of the footsteps above were growing fainter, which only meant they were closer to the stairway at the far end that would lead them down here. He heard the Arellian say something, urgently, heard Rina hushing her, but he blanked it out. It had been a while since he'd used the weapon, and he needed all his concentration.

He expelled his breath slowly, mentally closing out his surroundings. He closed his eyes, focusing all his energy on the feel of the silver, until it grew warm beneath his hands. Then he opened his eyes, sighting down the groove to the place on the wall he had instinctively chosen.

Only when all he could hear was the steady thud of his own heart and the hum of the flashcharger, when all he could see was that spot on the wall, so clearly he could count the nicks in the stone, when he had no breath left in his lungs to strain to hold, he moved that one finger.

The glowing bolt shot down the groove. A split second later the corridor was lost in a flash of blinding, fierce light and a sharp, deafening crack of sound that made their ears ring and their balance waver. Dax stood frozen as the others lowered the hands they had put before their eyes at Rina's warning.

Before them, the wall that had been the dead end of the corridor had vanished, leaving nothing but a few settling motes of dust. They stood on the edge of open air, nothing but the drop of the sheer cliff in front of them. Only Rina seemed capable of movement; she stepped toward the motionless Dax. He didn't react. She reached upward, taking a lock of thick, dark hair in her fingers and tugging.

"Unh!" Dax grunted. Then he shook his head sharply, as if coming out of a daze. Slowly, he lowered the flashbow from his shoulder.

"Eos," the Arellian breathed, her eyes wide as her gaze flicked from the gaping hole to the man who had done it.

"Come on," Rina urged, releasing Dax's hair and pushing her own bangs from her eyes. "They'll be here any minute."

Dax blinked, and shook his head again. Roxton moved then, taking a long, thin cord from under his own cloak. He looped one end around the base of the bars of Rina's former cell and knotted it, then tossed the other end over the drop. Gingerly, he leaned forward to look.

"Have to scramble the last few feet, but it'll do."

"Go ahead," Dax said, back with them now.

"But—" Rina began.

"Let Roxton go first." The flashbow disappeared beneath the voluminous cloak once more. "We don't know how visible we're going to be going down that line. There could be somebody waiting for us by the time we hit the bottom."

"Just why I should go first," Rina said. "I'm a smaller target."

"While you're wasting time arguing, *I'll* go down," the Arellian snapped.

"No," Dax ordered firmly. He nodded at Roxton, who disappeared over the side without hesitation. Dax moved to the edge and looked over. After another long, silent moment broken only by the clang of the metal door at the far end of the hall, he nodded at Rina. She scrambled over the side with youthful agility.

Dax turned to look at the Arellian. With an elaborate bow, he gestured to the taut line.

"You expect me to dangle there in the open, unarmed?"

Dax shrugged. "Or wait and meet the guards, unarmed."

She looked at him sourly. "Are you sure you want me below you?"

With a movement so swift it made her blink, Dax swept the controller from her hand. "As long as I have this, it won't bother me a bit."

She swore, an Arellian oath he'd heard but didn't know the meaning of, then swung over the edge. Dax noticed the slightest stiffness in her left leg, but she didn't let it slow her down once she'd begun; she was down the line and out of sight before he heard the sound of running footfalls at the far end of the corridor.

He took out the code key he'd liberated from the guard. There was no way he could open the other cells; the possible combinations were nearly infinite. But given time . . .

He ran back to the cell that held the Carelian. She was at the door, her hands curled around the bars, obviously aware something was up. Dax winced when he saw the twisted scars at her fingertips, where they had removed—none too carefully, it appeared—the retractable, curved fingernails. He held out the code key.

"I'd suggest you keep it hidden until you have all the combinations," he said lowly. "You'll have a better chance if you all stay together."

She took it, quickly, then tilted her head back to look up at him, her eyes looking eerily pale in the shadows. "Why?" she asked, her voice harsh with the effort to lower her species' normally loud tones.

Dax grinned. "Why not?"

She leaned closer, peering at him. Then she gasped. "Dax!"

Blast it, he hadn't realized he'd become so easily recognizable, even here. He backed up a step. The guards were getting closer, he could hear them. Was this fanciful gesture going to cost him his life? If she gave him away—

"Skypirate or no, your name shall be held sacred in the house of my clan," she hissed. "Go, and Eos be with you."

"Good luck," he whispered. He spun on his heel and took off running back to the opening he'd blasted.

He reached for the line, then stopped. He knew that as soon as they made the turn into the cell area, the guards would see the gaping hole at the end of the corridor, streaming sunlight into this place that hadn't seen it in aeons. They'd head straight for it, instinctively. Hurriedly. With a crooked grin he moved back a few steps, swiftly adjusted the course of the line, then went back to the edge and over the side.

The adjustment he'd made had cost him in the cord's length, making the final drop at the end nearly eight feet. Hoping that he wouldn't break a leg, he let go. He hit at an awkward angle, sending a sharp pain shooting up from his left ankle. He slipped, then rolled, biting back grunts of pain as sharp-edged rocks—and the bow—dug into him.

"What in Hades took you so long?" Rina whispered through clenched teeth. "And what happened to the cord?"

"I'm fine, thanks," Dax whispered back wryly as he limped out of sight behind the large outcropping of stone that hid Roxton and the Arellian.

Roxton looked him up and down before, apparently satisfied that he would live, he said, "What *did* happen to the line? It was long enough—"

"—to wrap around the bars of the opposite cell."

Roxton blinked. "Huh?"

"Across the corridor. At about ankle height."

Roxton blinked again, then grinned. "Son of a whisperbird, that's what you—"

A scream cut him off, and they looked up in time to

see first one, then a second prison guard cartwheel out of the opening above them and plummet downward, arms flailing uselessly.

As one, the four of them turned and took to their heels.

Chapter 2

"You're an idiot, you know that?" Rina stood in front of Dax, her hands on her hips, glaring up at him with more ferocity than anyone of that size and age should have been capable of.

"I believe you've mentioned it on occasion," Dax said amiably.

"Going back like that, they could have caught you—"

"They didn't, little one. Let's go."

"But they could have! One of these days you're going to take one chance too many—"

"It won't work, Rina."

She blinked up at him. "What?"

"You're still in big trouble, and trying to divert all the attention to me isn't going to change that."

The girl colored, looking away. But after a moment, she looked back at him, all the ferocity gone from her face and voice. "I wasn't just trying a diversion. You scare me, the way you take crazy chances, and—"

"I know, little one," Dax said softly. "But now is not the time. We've got to make it to the shuttle and get out of here before they regroup."

"Shuttle?" The Arellian reached out and grabbed Dax's arm. "You have a ship here?"

"I did when I left it," Dax said in a wry tone, turning to look at her.

He realized his mistake as soon as he'd made it. The Arellian's eyes widened as, for the first time, she saw his face in full light. Her gaze lingered a moment, as if assessing the jade of his eyes, then flicked to the long, thick mane of hair that gleamed darkly in the sunlight.

"Dax!" she exclaimed, the same way the Carelian had.

He let out a compressed breath. So she hadn't known

who he was, until now. She'd bluffed him. He shrugged
it off; it had been a risk he hadn't dared take, for
Rina's sake.

"I'm getting too damned recognizable around here,"
he muttered.

"The infamous skypirate known by just one name,
with a face that's on reward placards all over the system?" the Arellian asked. "What did you expect?"

"We'd best move," warned Roxton, who had spent
most of their lengthy run along the back paths of the
outer city looking back over his shoulder.

"No." It came from the Arellian firmly, with a snap
that made Dax look at her curiously.

"No?" he asked, his voice giving away nothing of his
rapid speculation.

"I thank you for the rescue, but I'll be on my way. If
you'll just give me the controller?" She held out her
hand, palm up. Her fingers were long, slender, and ele-
gantly tapered, Dax saw. And she was older than he'd
thought. Woman, not girl. More his age than Rina's.
He'd be very interested to know where she had developed that air of command.

"Just how far do you think you'll get on your own?"
His tone was light, one of idle curiosity.

"Farther than you'll get," she snapped out, as if irritated by his tone, "with half the planet after you for the
reward, and the entire Coalition looking for the glory of
bringing your head on a stake before Legion
Command."

Dax lifted a brow. "I think you're forgetting
something."

He reached out to touch the gold collar that banded
her neck. She recoiled, he wasn't sure if it was from the
reminder of her status, or the fact that he'd inadvertently
brushed her skin with the backs of his fingers.

"No," he said, "I think this will likely get you caught
long before any of us."

"I'll take my chances. Just give me the controller."

"I think not."

"Damn you to Hades," she ground out.

After the last six years, Hades would be an improve-
ment, Dax thought. But he merely shrugged.

"Sorry." He didn't sound sorry. "I don't want you left here to advertise my presence. You'll be coming with us."

"But they'll think I helped you—"

"You should have thought of that before you opened your mouth back there." He started forward, leaving Roxton to chivy along their reluctant company. Then he stopped, turning back to look at her pityingly. "Did you really think you could bargain with the Coalition and win? That they would free you once you'd given us away?"

The Arellian's head came up sharply, and Dax knew he'd struck a nerve.

"If you believed that, then you belonged in that cell. Anyone who trusts the Coalition is a fool."

The woman's proud posture failed her; she slumped as if in exhaustion. She shifted her stance to take the weight off her weaker leg, a favoring she had denied herself until now, forcing herself to keep up with them despite the stiffness of the wounded leg. Defeat, Dax thought, sat no better on her than the collar of subjugation. He felt a pang of regret that he had done that to her. He took no pleasure in seeing spirit crushed. If she'd been in Coalition hands for any length of time, surely she had already suffered enough.

Without another word he bent and tore a wide strip of cloth from the bottom of his cloak. He straightened and handed it to her.

"Wrap it around your neck," he said quietly. "It will cover the collar."

She hesitated, looking at him suspiciously, then took it. She wound it around her throat until the attention-drawing golden band was hidden. It made little difference that he could see; she looked every inch the slave, now.

"What shall we call you?" he asked, avoiding asking who she was; it was an ill-advised question in his world.

"I . . . Califa. Just Califa."

Her voice sounded as defeated as she looked. Perhaps that burst of spirit had been momentary, induced by the chance for escape. Or perhaps it had been a flash of what she had been before being captured and caged like an animal. Whatever the case, the sound of her now brought the pang he'd felt earlier back even stronger.

"Named after a Triotian legend?" He made his voice light with an effort as he said the rarely spoken words.

She lifted her gaze to his face then. The pale blue eyes, so icy before, had gone flat, hollow. "My mother," she said slowly, "was an even bigger fool than I."

He didn't know what to say to that, so said nothing. And when they began to walk again, she followed without a word. Like, he thought, a well-trained slave. The thought made his stomach churn. He wondered how many of the prisoners in those cells had a collar in their future. He hoped the Carelian found the door codes soon.

"Welcome back, sir!"

Dax stepped out of the small craft, checked that the shuttle bay door had closed and locked behind them, then nodded to Larcos, the tall, lanky man who served as the *Evening Star*'s engineer in flight, parts scavenger when aground, and as the most ingenious inventor Dax had ever seen all the time.

"Brought the little rapscallion back, did you?" Larcos asked, grinning at Rina.

"Against my better judgment, yes," Dax returned dryly. He felt the *Evening Star* begin to move, following the orders he'd given from the shuttle before they'd docked; get them out of this sector, and fast.

"Eos," Rina said, a distinct note of disgruntlement in her voice. "It was just a little game of chaser. How was I supposed to know the mark was a Coalition Officer?"

Dax whirled on the girl. "Just a little game? You could have gotten all of us killed. Risking your own life is one thing, but did you really want Roxton to die for you?"

The girl paled. Dax knew it was a harsh blow; Roxton was one of the few men Rina trusted. She'd seen past his gruff exterior and gone straight for his heart, and the old man had treated her like a daughter since the day Dax had brought her aboard three years ago, a shaking, frightened child who'd witnessed horrors no child should ever see.

"I didn't mean—"

Dax cut her off. "You never do. If you want to rig a game, that's your business. But getting caught, for God's sake, at something you've been doing for years!"

"I was distracted," Rina protested. "That officer was talking about how he was going to be the one to capture you, take your head and present it to General Corling on a pikestaff—"

Rina broke off as Dax went utterly still. He thought he heard a smothered sound from, oddly, the Arellian, but he didn't look at her.

The name of the man who had destroyed Trios was never mentioned aboard the *Evening Star,* by anyone, let alone by Rina, who had more reason than most to abhor the man who had wiped out her world and her people. It had been an unspoken rule for so long that most of the crew had forgotten that it had begun long before Dax had brought the young Triotian aboard, and attributed the ban to her presence.

"I'm sorry," Rina whispered. "It just slipped out, I—"

"Never mind." His voice was low, flat, and much harsher than when he'd been lecturing his young navigator. He looked at Califa. "Take our . . . guest. Clean her up, and find her something"—his nose curled expressively—"else to wear."

None of the spirit he'd hoped for—he wasn't sure why—flashed in the Arellian. But Rina was quick to yelp, "But I'm needed on the bridge—"

"I think I can manage this time without your help."

Rina glared at him. "Is this my punishment? Playing maid to a slave?"

Dax's eyes narrowed. "If you hadn't earned it before, you just did."

The girl flushed. "I didn't mean that," she said, sounding chagrined. "Not that way. It's just—"

"What it is," Dax said, his tone severe, "is time for you to learn how to think before you speak. As you should have in that cell."

Looking chastened, Rina nodded quietly. Cheeks flaming now, she led the unprotesting Califa away.

When they'd gone, Dax let out a long breath; he felt exhausted. He felt someone's gaze, and looked up to find Roxton grinning at him.

"Easy to humble them when they think the universe of you, like she does," the old man said.

"She doesn't," Dax corrected. "She just knows she was wrong. Tell me, old man," he added ruefully, "why in Hades do people have children?"

The grizzled first mate's smile faded. He tugged at his beard. When he spoke at last, there was no trace of humor in his voice.

"Hoping for one like you, I suppose."

On the last word, the first mate turned on his heel and strode out of the shuttle bay. Dax gaped after him. Roxton was as stingy with praise as Ansul, his old tutor had been. He forced his mind away from those memories; Ansul, like all others from his past, was dead, long dead.

That must be it, he thought. The old man must have really feared him dead in those moments before he'd come down the cliff, to shake that kind of compliment out of him. And how like Roxton to fire this salvo, and then retreat before Dax could react. Before he could tell the old man he was crazy, that no parent anywhere would want a son like him. And that Rina, of all people, couldn't possibly think the universe of him. Because Rina, alone of those aboard the *Evening Star,* knew the ugly truth about him.

"Sir? Will you be going to the bridge now?"

Yanked out of his grim reverie by the words, Dax looked up to see Larcos standing in the doorway of the shuttle bay. Where, Dax realized suddenly, he'd been standing for some time, waiting.

"Sorry," he muttered. "Let me get out of this thing."

He shrugged off the heavy, enveloping cloak, tossed it over his shoulder, and then strode past Larcos into the companionway.

The *Evening Star* was a brigantine class ship, built as a light cargo carrier by the Clarion Starworks. She had been built for maximum capacity and speed; Dax had made some renovations to up the capacity, then handed her over to Larcos, who had turned her into the fastest thing in five sectors. Able to run, thanks to some computer adjustments Dax had made, with a crew of twenty rather than the usually requisite fifty, she was the perfect ship for his purposes.

Not bad, Dax thought as he came onto the bridge, for a ship won on a role of the dice.

He stopped for a moment to replace the flashbow in its case. It was left unsecured; everyone aboard knew it would do no good to take it; only Dax could fire it. He tossed the cloak over the back of the command chair, and asked for a position report from the navigational computer. The report came back instantly, but no faster than Rina could do it. And without her usual flair.

"Looks like a clean getaway, sir," Larcos said. "Easy, with us parked on the dark side, away from the checkpoints."

"We nearly didn't make it," Dax said with a grin at the engineer. "Shuttle came in on vapor, after all that low level flying to get out of range of their sensors."

Larcos frowned, his brows lowering on his long, thin forehead. "Did it malfunction? You should have had exactly enough fuel."

Dax's grin widened. He'd known that engineer's brain would immediately take over. "Relax, Larc. You figured perfectly. Don't forget, we had some unexpected extra weight. There may be only a hundred and twenty pounds or so of her, but it made a difference."

The engineer's brow cleared. "Of course. I should have made allowances."

"It was already fueled to the maximum," Dax assured Larcos, beginning to wish he hadn't tried to tease him; the man had absolutely no sense of humor about his precious equipment. Which, Dax reminded himself, has saved your ass more times than you can count.

"I could have rigged something, temporarily, to—"

"Cease and desist," Dax ordered with a laugh. "We made it. Let's just concentrate on making sure nobody's on our tail, all right?"

"They're probably still trying to figure out that hole in the wall," Roxton put in with a grin. "I'll never forget the look of them two, flapping down that cliff like a pair of crazed rockfowl. 'Course you weren't exactly grace itself after you ran out of—"

"Dax!"

Rina's shout came across the ship's comlink with no lessening of its fervor. Dax spun back to the command chair and hit the button.

"What's wrong?"

"She's gone crazy!"

"What?"

"We were just walking along and all of a sudden she went demented on me."

Dax saw Roxton tense, and waved the older man back. "Did she hurt you?"

"Yes—no, not really." Rina sounded confused. "She just stopped and refused to move. When I tried to grab her she did . . . something. It didn't really hurt, but—"

"Where are you?"

"On the gangway from the sub-one deck."

"On my way. Stay there." He raised his voice. "Califa, you hurt her and I'll sell you to the lowest bidder."

He snapped off the comlink. It was a bluff, but the Arellian didn't know he'd sell himself before another human being, such was his distaste for the whole system of enslavement. He just hoped the threat would hold her long enough for him to get there.

He grabbed his hand communicator, motioned to Roxton to follow him, and headed off the bridge at a run. Once clear of the bridge, he activated the small device.

"Nelcar! Meet me on the sub-one deck gangway. Bring something—we may have to sedate an Arellian."

"Yes, sir."

The snappy reply was a holdover from the young man's days serving as medical officer aboard a Clarion transport, about the same time the *Evening Star* had been built on the industrious planet. But Nelcar and his ship had fallen to the Coalition just as his home world had, and the bloody process had cost Nelcar an eye, making him worse than useless to his conquerors. They had given him the choice of immediate execution or slave labor, and sent him off to die a slow death in a labor camp.

It was there Dax had found him, and despite the campmaster's incredulity, had paid enough for the man to look the other way as he led the gaunt, half-blind young man out of Hades. He'd never regretted it.

Except when Nelcar's deference brought back memories Dax would rather keep buried. And buried deep.

When they reached the gangway, Dax slowed to a walk. The woman he knew only as Califa was leaning against the bulkhead, nonthreateningly, submissively slavelike, yet radiating a stubborn determination that reminded him of the fire he'd seen in her in the prison. For a reason he didn't understand, since it was clear it meant nothing but trouble for him, he was glad to see it again.

Rina stood to one side, watching the Arellian warily. "It's not my fault, Dax, really, we were just walking—"

"She speaks the truth," Califa agreed. "She did nothing but try to follow your orders."

Dax eyed her, one dark brow raised. "But?"

"I can go no further."

His eyes narrowed. "Why?"

She crossed her arms across her chest, saying nothing. Dax noticed a faint sheen of sweat on her brow and upper lip, as if she were under great strain. Yet she would not speak. He smothered an exasperated sigh; females, he thought.

"You began willingly enough," he pointed out.

"I can go no further," she repeated.

Dax's temper, always on a tight rein, snapped. "I should just dump you right back where I found you!"

"You cannot do that without risk to yourself."

"It might be worth it to get you out of my way."

"I can go no further."

Dax swore. Nelcar joined them then, a boyish-looking young man on whom the eye patch he wore jarred. "Will you be needing this, sir?" he asked, gesturing with the medicator he'd prepared to Dax's order.

"So it seems," Dax said with a grimace. "Looks like we'll have to carry her—"

"No!"

For the first time, Dax saw real fear in Califa's eyes. Even when she had seemed beaten, defeated, there had been no fear. To see it now struck a deep, hidden chord in him. A woman afraid stirred up hideous thoughts, images that haunted his dreams far too often.

He forced his voice to steadiness. "Give me another choice."

"You don't understand—"

"Believe me, woman, I've been downwind, and you *need* a good soaking."

She lowered her eyes. Had he embarrassed her? It didn't seem possible, not the woman who had virtually forced him into helping her make her escape. Or had that woman been born only of desperation? Was this, the compliant slave, all that was really left?

"I know," she said, so low only he was close enough to hear it, "but I—"

"—can go no further. So you've said. Why?" he asked again, this time in the voice of the commander, a voice he used rarely but to great effect.

Califa looked around a bit wildly, then turned her gaze back to him. "I . . . I'll tell you. But only you."

Roxton protested immediately. "Don't do it, Cap'n. We don't know who she is, or why she was in that stinking place. Could be she's a murderer, or worse."

"Puts her right on the level of the Coalition's best, then, doesn't it?" Dax remarked. "I think I'll be safe enough."

"Dax, no," Rina put in. "She did something, pushed right here"—she gestured at her neck—"and I couldn't move."

Dax's brows shot up once more. "The Daxelian clamp hold? This becomes even more interesting." He looked at the others. "Go." When they protested, he added, "I'll yell if I need help."

"By then it may be too late," Roxton grumbled.

"Then you'll own the ship at last, won't you, my friend?"

When they realized he was serious, they reluctantly left. Dax turned back to Califa. She was back in nearly the same position she'd been in when he'd arrived, but he got the impression that this time she was leaning against the wall for its support, not as a statement of her unconcern.

She closed her eyes, and Dax could have sworn she suppressed a shudder. Was he so frightening, then? Or was it merely helplessness that made her shake? He had a feeling it was an emotion foreign to her. Had they all felt so helpless, his mother, his sister, all the women he'd known, when the end had come?

He recoiled from that line of thought as a muckrat dodges the kick aimed at its head. Don't think of those women, think of this one, he ordered himself. You can do nothing for them, so deal with this one; she is the problem now. How long had she been a slave? What had she been before? Who was the woman he'd seen only glimpses of, tough, reckless, and brave to the point of foolhardiness?

"Well?" he said, folding his arms across his chest in an action that mimicked her own.

"I ... can't go any further." She held up a hand at the look he gave her at the repetition yet again of that phrase. "Because of this," she said, gesturing at her throat, at the strip of his cloak that wound around it.

Dax's brows furrowed in puzzlement. In response she tugged the cloth free to reveal the collar.

"The yellow light is glowing," he said, certain it hadn't been that way before.

Califa laughed, a short, harsh sound. "I know."

His gaze went back to her face. "Which means?"

"It's activated when I reach my limit."

"The light?"

"The yellow system." She gave him a twisted, sour smile. "The pain system."

Dax blinked. "You were right. I don't understand."

The smile, for the briefest instant, became a real one. In the moment before it faded, Dax caught himself starting to smile back instinctively.

"The collar isn't just worn ... Captain." She sounded as if she wasn't sure what to call him, but he waved her to continue. "It's implanted. With probes directly into the brain."

Dax winced at the thought. "Probes to cause pain?"

"For control."

He stared at her for a moment, nausea churning in his stomach at the evil simplicity of it. Her desperation, her fear made sense now, as did the sweat of pain on her face.

"The controller," he said softly. She nodded. "That's what you meant by your limit? Your distance from it?"

She nodded again. "It has a range. It was set for the length of the prison wing."

"That's why you had to take it with you."

"Yes."

"And why you can't go any farther now. Because it's on the bridge, in my cloak."

She nodded.

"Can't you change the range?"

"No. It takes a special seal to activate that system. Only Coalition officials have them."

"What are the other two systems? The red and the blue?"

"You don't know?" Her eyes widened in apprehension, as if she were afraid the question would anger him. "I'm sorry, I didn't mean to question you, I—"

Her fear irritated him. "Stop looking like you think I'm going to beat you or something."

"It is the usual punishment for a slave who questions the master."

His stomach knotted at her words. "I'm no one's master," he ground out. "I merely asked about the other crystals."

"You truly do not know," she said, and he wondered if that, too, would have been a question instead of an observation had she not been afraid—or too well trained?—to make it one.

"Forgive me for not being familiar with the details of Coalition enslavement," he said, his repulsion at what had been done to her making his voice sharp. "I've been gone a long time. Please explain."

At his tone, the wariness, the fear, reappeared in her eyes. She hesitated, studying him. Suddenly, he understood. And his irritation faded away.

"Never mind. If I don't already know, you'd be a fool to tell me."

She gaped at him, clearly startled once more. "But if you order me to tell you, I must—"

"It would give me a power no one has the right to have." He tried to shrug off his distaste for what she had told him, and said lightly, "I'm just sorry you didn't explain this before. You're lucky Rina didn't try to knock you out and drag you the rest of the way. You are a little ... pungent."

"If she had," Califa said, her tone grim, "it wouldn't have mattered. We'd all be dead."

Dax stared at her. "What?"

"I told you there's a set limit. When you reach it, the pain system activates. If you go past it ... it blows up."

Dax's gaze shot down to the collar. "It's explosive?"

"Very. The core is photon propellant igniter." Dax whistled, long and low. Califa's mouth twisted into that acid smile again. "Yes. They call it permanent discipline."

"Permanent is right," Dax muttered. "It would take your head off, along with the top of this ship." His gaze lifted to her face. "How long have you been ... ?"

"A slave?" She laughed, that harsh, humorless sound again. "Nearly a year."

He sucked in his breath. For her to have withstood this for a year and still have any spirit left at all, amazed him. She must have been a most amazing woman, before they began to try to break her. His gaze flicked to the collar once more.

"How do you get it off?"

"You don't. Unless you happen to have a good laser surgeon handy."

Dax shook his head. "Nelcar's good at what he does, but he's no surgeon." He might have become one, once. But the Coalition had put an end to that dream.

"Captain," she began hesitantly.

"Dax," he corrected. "Only Roxton calls me Captain, and only to irritate me."

"Does it?"

He drew back a little, surprised by the question. She looked equally surprised that she'd asked it. "Yes," he said after a moment.

"I wonder why," she said.

It was a rhetorical enough question—or another question safely phrased as an observation—that he didn't try to answer. That he didn't deserve that or any other title was not something he wanted to discuss with this woman, a stranger. When he didn't speak after a long moment, she did.

"Dax ... would you ..."

She stopped, biting her lip, her eyes lowered. He wanted to snap at her, to tell her to show some of the spirit he'd seen before. But he restrained himself, and kept his voice even.

"Am I so frightening that you can't ask a simple question?"

As if unconsciously, her hand crept to her throat, to finger the gold band. Her eyes met his. "It is ... the first thing they train us in. A slave never questions, never looks, never thinks ..."

Train. Not teach, but train, Dax thought. Like an animal. "I am no one's master," he repeated. "Ask what you will."

"I ... would you ... give me the controller?"

His first instinct was to say yes, to show her he meant what he'd said, that no one should have that kind of power over another being. But he had more than just himself to think of. He had a ship, and a crew. He might not deserve the title, but he knew that crew looked to him as they would a captain. And trusted him.

He let out a long, weary breath. "I can't, Califa. I don't know you, or what you were in there for—"

"The usual Coalition assumption of guilt by association," she said bitterly.

"I'm sorry. But I can't. I can't risk the safety of my crew."

For a long moment she just looked at him, and he had the oddest feeling that he had somehow hit upon the one argument that would work with her. Why it did, he didn't know, but she only said stiffly, "Then you'd better stay upwind."

"I didn't say we couldn't compromise. This is the range? From the bridge to here?" When she nodded, he did some quick figuring. "I'll move it to my quarters."

She inhaled quickly, her eyes widening.

"Something wrong with that? It's just forward of amidships. You'll have to share quarters with Rina, but you'll be able to go anywhere forward of the weapons stations, and aft of the bridge. You get half the ship and I get to sleep at night."

She relaxed, as if she'd misunderstood what he'd

meant at first, although he didn't see how. But then, he was still trying to figure out why his reference to the safety of his crew had quieted her arguments.

"All right. I . . . Thank you."

He had the feeling that hadn't been easy for her to say. "Wait here. I'll send Rina back when I've moved the controller." He gave her a sideways look. "You will take a soak, won't you?"

"With pleasure," she said, giving him a real smile that echoed the glimpse he'd seen earlier. She could, he thought in surprise, be passable looking under all that grime.

He turned to call for Roxton, who was, if he knew him, waiting just out of sight beyond the next bulkhead. Before he could, Califa spoke again softly.

"Dax?"

It sounded quite different from the first time she'd said his name, besides just the volume, but he wasn't sure exactly why. He looked back over his shoulder at her.

"I . . . Thank you for taking me with you."

His mouth quirked. "Did I have a choice?"

"No, I suppose not. But neither did I."

"So you said."

"They were going to ship me to Ossuary. Because I wasn't . . . cooperating." He saw the shudder again, and her instant effort to control it. "I know what happens there."

"So do I," Dax said softly.

He had seen the place, when he'd taken Nelcar out of the labor camp next to the infamous prison. Huge, hulking, dark and ugly, the screams echoed from its walls day in and day out. It was where those worn out or useless to the Coalition were sold, where the stubborn were broken, the proud crushed. He'd never been so glad to leave a place in his ion trail.

"I had to do it," she said.

"I suppose you did."

"I knew if you were half the man the girl said you were, you would pull it off."

He lifted a brow at her. "Was that a compliment?"

"If you wish." She raised a brow at him in turn. "I've never seen a weapon like that crossbow you used."

His face lost all expression. "And you probably never will again." He turned his back on her then, and shouted for Roxton. As he'd expected, the man popped out from behind the next bulkhead, grinning.

"Stay with her until Rina gets here," he ordered, and walked away without looking back.

Chapter 3

Califa studied herself as best she could in the small mirror—Rina apparently didn't worry much about appearance—and decided that while the red flight suit was far from the luxurious gowns she'd once worn, it was decidedly better than the baggy, filthy clothes she'd been trapped in for weeks.

Red. Despite the way it accented her dramatic coloring she'd never worn red, preferring the black that made up most of her wardrobe. Or had, she thought bitterly, in another life.

Stop it, she ordered. Self-pity accomplishes nothing. Hang on to the anger, if you must waste your time in emotion.

She fingered the sleeve of the flight suit. At one time it would have been tight on her, the girl being so much smaller than she, but she'd lost considerable weight in the last year, so although a bit short, and snug across her breasts, the garment fit well enough.

Looking at her reflection, she almost wished she'd left the dirt untouched, except that she didn't think she could bear it another moment. So she'd washed her face as well as the rest of her—thankfully including her hair—only to now face the reminder of one of the Coalition's less subtle methods. The bruise that marred her cheek was now turning an ugly shade of yellow, and stood out starkly against her naturally pale Arellian skin. And no amount of washing would make the collar that banded her neck disappear.

"Eos, you look different."

Califa turned to Rina. The pixielike blonde seemed to have gotten over her disgruntlement with the quickness of the young, and had apparently decided that if they were going to have to share quarters, they might as well coexist peacefully. She'd even let Califa be first to use the soaking spray, and had gingerly disposed of her filthy clothing in the ship's trash atomizer. More important, Rina apparently hadn't the slightest notion of how one was supposed to treat a slave; she spoke to her as an equal, if not a friend.

Califa looked at the girl for a moment, waiting for some comment on the bruise. None came.

"Are you hungry? I'm starved. Let's go raid the galley."

Califa blinked. It had been a long time since she'd been asked what she wanted. Imperious commands had been the pattern of her life for what seemed like forever. At the thought, the dark, consuming cloud that hovered over her heart and soul threatened to descend; she fought it back, knowing she could not face it, could not confront the ugly self-knowledge it held.

"Yes," she said quickly, more to divert her mind than from the undeniable hunger that made her stomach cramp at the thought of food. "I am hungry."

Rina flashed a smile at her, a smile that reminded her of that moment when she and Dax had been alone, when he had very nearly smiled at her. Were they related, the skypirate and this pixie-child? she wondered as she followed the girl down the companionway. He was too young to be her father, but there was a resemblance noticeable despite the disparity of the girl's golden blondness and the skypirate's long mane of dark hair, despite her deep brown tan and his golden skin. It was in the vivid green eyes, mirror images except for the girl's pale lashes, and the pirate's thick, dark ones.

They were obviously close, but Califa sensed no sexual overtones in their relationship; besides, the girl was very young. If she'd seen her eighteenth year, Califa would be surprised, and rogue though the skypirate might be, she doubted his taste ran to children, despite his performance in the prison. No, it was more what Califa imagined a brother to sister relationship might be. She couldn't be sure; she'd never had either.

Was that their connection? she mused. Then a shocking idea occurred to her: why not ask?

The realization that she could simply ask a question nearly took her breath away. Even Dax had allowed her that. The girl had not treated her like a slave, either, not even in the cell they had shared. She had talked freely—too freely, Califa thought, remembering Dax's lecture and her thought at the time that, as stern as the words might be, they lacked the heat of true anger— to her cellmate, as if she were just another unfortunate prisoner, not a gold collar doomed to a life utterly and completely controlled by others.

For nearly a year she had lived with no right to speak or even move unless ordered to, and then only to follow those orders, knowing if she did not—and sometimes even if she did—pain unto agony would follow. But now . . . Did she dare? She swallowed heavily, the motion of her throat making her all the more conscious of the golden band.

"Have you a surname, Rina?"

The girl looked back at her. "Carbray," she said, smiling as if the question was of no consequence. And it wasn't, Califa supposed, to her. And the girl had no idea what it meant to her companion, to be able to do a simple thing like ask a question.

"And . . . Dax?"

The girl's smile vanished. "Dax is Dax," she said simply. "He needs no other name."

That was true enough, Califa thought. The man was the most legendary skypirate in the system, with a reputation for daring, fighting skill, and absolute mercilessness when it came to his preferred Coalition targets. It was for this last reason that the Coalition's Triad Commission had raised the reward for his head to an astounding level.

From what she'd heard, no one knew where he came from, but his name alone was enough to strike terror into the most seasoned Coalition pilots, and word of his presence in the vicinity made even the most well-guarded of Coalition colonies nervous.

"He is . . . notorious," Califa ventured, choosing her words carefully in view of the girl's obvious devotion to the man.

"Yes," Rina answered, pride ringing in her voice. "He

is. With reason. But he is more than a skypirate, you know. To some he is a hero. To those who welcome him, those who live under the Coalition's heel."

Califa winced inwardly at the girl's words. She herself had, literally, felt the pressure of that crushing heel, and she still bore the marks to prove it. Turning away from a memory that was bitter for more reasons than physical pain, she made herself think of the rest of what Rina had said.

Even before her enslavement, she had heard the murmurs about the larger than life Dax; afterward, when she was among those who had the most reason to hate the Coalition, the murmurs had taken on the aspect of legends. She had heard many reasons for his seeming crusade, from the theory that he was seeking vengeance for some Coalition injustice, to the simple conjecture that since the Coalition had practically all the assets in the system, it made the most logical—and profitable—target.

It was said that honest people had nothing to fear from him; it was the Coalition and its direct supporters who had best watch all flanks—and their backs. She had once dismissed the stories as exaggeration—and near treason. Now that she'd met the man himself, she wasn't so sure. Just as she wasn't sure she knew what treason was, anymore.

"And you, Califa? Do you have a surname?"

Too late, she realized she should have expected this. She had no wish to offend the girl, but nor did she wish to take the chance some member of this crew might recognize her name. Their feelings about anyone connected to the Coalition had been more than clear, and she didn't dare take a chance that there would be any quarter given for her circumstances.

"Slaves have no need of surnames, Rina."

The girl's forehead creased in puzzlement beneath the thick, blond bangs. "But you weren't always a slave, were you? And you're no one's slave here."

No one's slave. The very words made her heart leap. What had Dax said? *A power no one has the right to have.* Eos, there had been a time when she would have considered that kind of thinking treason as well.

The sudden increase in noise brought her out of her

thoughts, and saved her from having to answer Rina's
questions. They had come to what obviously served as
both galley and gathering place for the crew. There were
half a dozen men there, including Roxton and the man
she'd seen in the shuttle bay, the man Dax had called
Larcos. Tall and lanky, he reminded her of a man she'd
once known, in another life. Yet somehow she sensed
there was a lively intelligence in this man that had been
lacking in the other.

The silence that fell upon the room as she entered
gave Califa a powerful feeling of remembrance. This was
no strange experience to her; she had often brought silence to a noisy room by her mere presence. In that
other life.

Again she fought down the bitterness that thought
roused in her. Bitterness was a worthless emotion. Anger
was much more productive. It enabled you to stay sane
when your mind was on the verge of snapping. It kept
you from breaking to another's will. It gave you a reason
to live, when all other reasons were gone.

Slowly, talk began again as Rina led her across the
room to a table where food was set out—surprisingly
good food, Califa thought, recognizing rockfowl,
sloeplums, and a decanter of lingberry liquor among the
dishes. No prepackaged, zap-heated meals for this crew.
The pirates ate well, but then, why not? They raided the
best Coalition galleys and pantries with regularity.

She wondered if the cook, who stood to one side of
the table, his eyes fastened on her collar, had been pur-
loined along with the food, or if he, too, was a pirate by
choice. She wished she'd kept the strip of Dax's cloak
wrapped about her throat, hiding the golden band.

She filled a plate, trying not to betray her hunger by
tearing into the spicy rockfowl the moment she had it
in her grasp. She had some little bit of pride left. She
passed by the liquor, thinking if there was ever a time
when she needed her wits about her, it was now. Water
would suffice, or perhaps some of the sloeplum juice.

Rina, fortunately, was hungry as well, and not disposed toward conversation as they took seats near the
door. Califa bit into the rockfowl, thinking nothing had

ever tasted so good. Her stomach growled loudly; Rina merely grinned at her while chewing industriously.

Califa remembered the story she'd heard about Dax's bold foray into the storehouses on Alpha 2, where he'd snagged a shipment of brollet steaks headed for Legion Command itself. No one in the Coalition had believed the rumors that Dax had distributed the steaks among the labor camps, and they knew there was no way he could have used the entire shipment himself, even had he and his crew eaten the meat three times a day for a week. So the Coalition had seen the raid for what it was: a slap in the face. And the Triad had promptly doubled the price on his head.

Enough to tempt even the most loyal crew member, she thought, gazing around at the gathered group.

As if she had conjured him up by her thoughts, Dax strode into the room. He was greeted by a chorus of good-natured jibes about his less than graceful descent down the last few feet of the cliff, a story which had obviously quickly made the rounds. Califa waited for him to explain that what he'd done had quite probably been the only thing that had given them enough time to get safely away, but instead he merely grinned back at them and made an elaborate bow, which was greeted with a raucous round of applause.

He didn't need to defend himself, she realized. Not to these men, who looked at him with a respect and admiration that fell little short of worship. Perhaps that reward wasn't high enough after all, she thought. Perhaps no reward would be high enough to induce one of this group to betray him.

She knew what it took to inspire that kind of feeling in a crew, especially a motley bunch like this one. She'd never been able to do it, herself. Fear, yes, she'd been able to induce that, and swift obedience, but never this kind of affectionate, almost loving respect. Shaylah had, but—

She purposely bit down on her lip, hard. She hadn't willingly allowed that name into her mind for nearly a year. But that was when she had had the misery of her existence to distract her; what would be strong enough to take her mind off that old pain now?

Involuntarily her gaze went back to the man who had just entered the room, as if he held the answer. She remembered the odd feeling that had come over her, standing there on the gangway, when he had first come striding toward her.

The voluminous cloak and hunched posture he'd assumed in the prison had been a better disguise than she'd realized. He was tall, straight, broad-shouldered and narrow-hipped. Strongly muscled without bulk, he moved with a quick grace that put her in mind of some of the wild creatures she'd seen in cinefilms—mainly the lethal ones. The thick mane of hair, which was nearly as dark as hers but much longer, tumbling past his shoulders, did nothing to allay the feral image.

He had been clad then as he was now, in a loose white shirt, laced at the throat, a belt that held both a hand disrupter and a dagger that looked almost too ornate to be of much use; she had wondered where—or from whom—he'd stolen it. Snug dark blue trousers clung to the lean muscles of his thighs before they were tucked into knee-high boots.

Odd boots, she realized now, studying them with interest. From the top of the right one, within easy reach, protruded the handle of what looked like a much more functional knife. That was not so strange. It was the left boot that was different. Around the top were stitched several small pockets, narrow and only a handsbreadth long. Each one held a length of odd-looking material, appearing to be not quite metal, not quite stone, and blunted on the protruding end. Like some kind of huge nail or bolt—

Bolts.

It hit her then. These were the ammunition for that amazing weapon he'd used, the thing Rina had called the flashbow. The weapon that had blasted a hole in a wall she'd have thought would have taken a fusion cannon. The weapon that had glowed at his touch, that had come alive as if with the energy of the man himself.

The weapon that had made him close up against her like a curlbug at her mere mention of it.

He spotted her then. His eyes widened, flicked up and down her slender frame, as if he was as surprised as

Rina had been, but in a different way. Then he started toward her.

Slowly, unwilling to give the appearance of nervousness, she set down her glass. As he approached, she held his gaze, feeling his stare was a test of some kind. The vivid green eyes bored into hers, and she felt as much a captive to them as to the collar she wore. This, then, was the legend, the man who struck terror into the hearts of the Coalition's finest, the man who needed but one name.

He came to a halt in front of her. "You look . . ."

"Different," Califa suggested, as Rina had.

"Quite." His gaze flicked downward, and Califa was suddenly aware of the snugness of the borrowed flight suit over her breasts. His dark lashes lifted, and she lowered hers so that he wouldn't see her unexpected response to his perusal. "Those rags did you no justice."

"Thank you." Eos, was she blushing? She couldn't believe it; she never, ever blushed.

"You've eaten?"

The mundane question relaxed her. "A little," she said, discomfited at having to crane her head back to look at him. She was a tall woman, and unused to feeling small beside a man. "You dine well."

He grinned, and Califa sucked in a quick breath. Instead of hunting him down, she thought, the Coalition should convince him to join them; he would be a walking, breathing recruitment placard it would be hard to resist. Especially for women, she added with a rueful honesty.

"That we do," he said. "But we're hardworking men. And girl," he added, his grin widening as he glanced at Rina.

"Honestly, Dax," Rina sputtered. "You'd think I was still a child, the way you talk."

Dax looked at the girl, his amusement gone, something dark and pained taking its place. "No. It's been a long time since you were a child, Rina, though you should still be."

The girl looked distressed, as if she had somehow caused his pain. "Dax, don't. If you hadn't rescued me—"

He raised a hand to quiet her. "Sorry, little one. It's old ground that should be long forgotten." His mouth twisted into a wry smile. "*This* rescue, however, will take some time to forget. At least until the bruises fade."

Califa looked at him sharply. The green eyes flicked to her face, to her bruised cheek. She knew he had to know by the color of it that it had occurred long before their trip down the cliff. But he said nothing about it, only letting his smile and his tone change to one of pure self-mockery.

"I'll be eating standing up, it seems."

The crew roared with laughter, then began their teasing anew, and the moment of odd tension abated.

"I've a question for you, sir!"

Dax turned to look at who'd spoken, a man with bushy hair the sandy color of Omegan soil. Califa thought he had the look of an Omegan as well, stocky, with muscles thick enough to cope with the big planet's heavy gravity. When away from their home planet, Omegans possessed strength that was, by comparison, extraordinary. Califa had found that strength had interesting uses, in that other life she'd once led.

Dax grabbed a piece of the savory rockfowl, then sat with one hip gingerly on the edge of the table, facing his questioner. The crew laughed again, saying they now knew exactly where he was bruised, but Dax merely grinned.

"Out with it, Hurcon," he said with a nod toward the stocky, bristle-faced man who had spoken.

"What do you plan to do with the Arellian?"

Califa stiffened as the others chimed in, echoing the question. After the brief moments of being treated like a normal being, the reversion to slave status, to being talked about as if she weren't there, or was too stupid to understand, stung more than she would have believed possible.

"Her name is Califa."

Dax's voice was cool, and the tone of it quieted the room in an instant. He took another bite of the rockfowl before turning to look at Califa again, as he chewed thoughtfully. After a moment he swallowed, and Califa found herself watching the muscles flex in his throat, found herself wondering what it would feel like to trace the taut, strong cords of his neck with her fingers.

She nearly gasped aloud at the incongruity of her thoughts. She had never allowed such things to pop into her mind unsummoned before. She controlled her desires, not the other way around. Eos, had this damned collar affected her so much? Was there some level of the blue system always active?

"Sorry," the chastened Omegan muttered to Califa. "But the men, we were just wondering . . . we don't know who or what you are. Or why you were in that prison."

"They do have a point, you know," Dax said casually. "You know a lot more about us than we do about you."

Califa's head came up then. "Just let me go. Then I won't be your problem."

"Ah, but I'm afraid I can't do that. Not yet anyway. Not until we're well out of this sector, and sure of no Coalition warships on our trail."

"I wouldn't tell anyone—"

"Do you really think your image isn't on as many reward placards as mine by now?"

She hadn't thought of that. Eos, would they put her history on it, too?

"Not to mention that lovely necklace of yours," Roxton put in from a far table. "Marks you to anyone's eyes as good for a big reward."

Had she thought things had changed? Califa wondered, stunned by her own foolishness. She had no hope of escape, not as long as she wore this collar. And if this crew ever found out the truth about who she was, her life wouldn't be worth the price of the igniter in the collar's core.

"If she has to stay," Larcos put in, "how do we know she won't get in the way?"

"Aye, sir," Hurcon agreed. "And how do we know she won't betray us to the Coalition the first chance she gets? They'd pay dear enough to put us all in Ossuary, for what we've cost them in the past three years."

Dax stood up then. He covered the distance to Califa in two long strides, those green eyes once more staring into hers. In that instant, as he stood there, if someone had told her he had some magical power, some method of reading her deepest thoughts, of seeing through to her dark, shriveled soul, she would have believed it without reservation.

After a long, silent moment during which it took all of her will to hold his powerful gaze, he reached out and once more touched the gold manacle that bound her.

"I don't think," he said, "that a woman enslaved by the Coalition is going to betray us to that Coalition."

"She would have handed you over easily enough to that prison guard," Roxton pointed out.

"She was just scared," Rina put in. "They were going to send her to Ossuary. I heard them taunting her about it. About what would happen to her there."

Califa glanced at the girl, startled by her defense. Or was it just that it had been so long since anyone had come to her aid that she didn't know how to deal with it?

"Califa?"

His voice was soft, low, and she nearly shivered at its impact. What in Hades was wrong with her?

"I . . . You saved me from Ossuary. I would not intentionally betray you."

One corner of his mouth curved upward. "A wise woman, who sets limits on her promises."

Eos, he was so close, too close, she couldn't think . . . "I merely do not guarantee that which I cannot control."

He was silent a moment, his gaze still fastened on her. Yet there was a difference in his searching look this time. It was no less intense, but somehow gentler. And laced with a bitterness she somehow knew had nothing to do with her.

"A lesson all of us must learn, I suppose. Why do I feel you learned it sooner than most?"

For an instant Califa was back on Darvis II, amid smoke and flame, her leg pinned and broken, watching the raging inferno march toward her. It was then that she had learned the lesson he spoke of. Until that moment, she had been secure in the colossal confidence of youth in its own immortality. Until that moment, she would have admitted nothing to be totally out of her control. She had often wished she had died there, rather than survived with her leg crippled for life. If not for Shaylah, she would have.

Again she veered off the mental path that bore the name of the woman—the only woman—she had ever called friend.

"I suppose you'll be wanting a vote," Larcos said.

"No," Dax said, never taking his eyes off Califa. She heard the murmurs of surprise, telling her his decision was unusual. "I think this time I'll exercise my privilege as owner of the *Evening Star*. She stays."

Califa expected a protest, but none came. The crew seemed to shrug unanimously, and return to their meal. Such was the power this man held, and though he disdained the title, she knew he was their captain in the truest, finest sense of the word.

But as she sat back down to her own meal, she wondered if the crew's acceptance of her would last if they knew the truth. She wondered if Dax would have made the same decision.

You're a fool if you think he would, she told herself. Worse than a fool. This was the skypirate who had been hunted to the end of the system by the Coalition. If he'd known the truth he would have cast her out to the Carelian jackals. If he'd known the truth, he would have put an end to it back in that cell, with a disrupter blast to her head. Or perhaps he would have stood her in front of that wall he pulverized with that incredible, impossible flashbow of his.

Any one of the grim scenarios seemed possible, even probable to her. And she wondered how long she was going to be able to hide the fact that this Coalition slave had once been a decorated, honored, and utterly loyal Coalition Officer.

Chapter 4

He needed his mind probed, Dax thought as he leaned back in the chair in his quarters, for whatever blank spot there was that had allowed him to make that ridiculous decision.

He swung his booted feet up onto the table, and took a sip from the glass of Carelian brandy he held. He'd been holed up in here all night and most of the morning, intending to rest yet getting little. He had been preoccupied, a state he thought he'd long ago given up as profitless. Preoccupied with an icy-eyed Arellian, whose transformation from a tatterdemalion barely recognizable as female to a tall, curved woman with translucently pale skin and sleek ebony hair had shaken him in a way he'd not felt in a very long time.

He should have left her back there. Not in that cell, he wouldn't have done that to anyone short of the Coalition High Command, but back on Carelia. The only decent things to be taken off that planet were Ducas to spend, and this brandy to drink. But he'd been seized by this temporary—and he'd make damnation sure it was temporary—aberration and decided to keep the Arellian woman aboard the *Evening Star*.

But he'd been right, he told himself. He couldn't just leave her behind, to spread the story of his presence there. His instincts told him the Carelian prisoner would keep quiet about who he was, so only Califa could tell who had really broken them out, and he couldn't let that happen. More for Rina's sake than his own; he was already far too recognizable in this sector, but no one knew who Rina was, or would connect her to him, unless someone spread the story around.

And it had to stay that way; he lived in constant fear

of someone seeing past the surface camouflage and realizing the girl was Triotian. If that happened, the Coalition would hunt her down as fiercely as they hunted him.

No, it was a good thing Califa had come with them. With her gone as well as Rina, no one could be sure who he had really been after in the first place. He might know little about the details of Coalition enslavement, but he did know that gold collars were the highest, most valuable rank of slaves. They might think he had just taken this one to sell.

His musing considerations came to an abrupt halt. The thought of selling another person, no matter what they'd done, filled him with repugnance. It went against everything he'd ever been taught, everything he'd ever believed—

He laughed aloud, a sound full of rueful self-knowledge. His entire *life* went against everything he'd ever been taught, everything he'd ever believed.

"God, Rina was right, you are an idiot!"

He downed the last of his drink in a gulp, set down the glass, and locked his hands behind his head. He was near to exhaustion, that bruise he'd developed on his backside made him want to reach for another dollop of brandy, and he still felt the lingering effects of the flash-bow. It had been a long time; he was out of practice at maintaining the high level of energy and concentration it took to fire the weapon. He'd taken it along only because he'd known he couldn't pass up any option when it came to Rina's safety.

He let his eyes start to drift closed, knowing only sleep would rid him of the fuzziness that remained at the edge of his consciousness. But then his gaze, narrowed by the lowering of his eyelids, focused on the shelf over the table.

His eyes came open. His boots hit the floor a second after the front legs of the chair. He reached up to the shelf and picked up the controller. It was barely as big as his palm, and sat there serenely, the three colored crystals dark, giving no hint of purpose. Had he not known, it would seem no more malevolent than the communicator on his belt.

It wouldn't take much, he thought, to find out what

the other two crystals meant. He knew how to prod the telerien, that underground network of communication that consisted mainly of gossip layered over a grain of truth, much like the Omegan perlas he'd smuggled on occasion. There were many in that network who felt they owed him, and he knew he could quickly have more knowledge than he wanted about the Coalition's system of controlling their collared slaves.

The problem was, any knowledge was more than he wanted. He supposed that was foolish, since there was a good chance he might someday be wearing one of those collars himself, if they didn't just kill him outright. He would prefer that, he realized as he truly confronted the idea for the first time. He would kill himself before he would let them collar him.

Assuming, of course, he had the chance. Somehow he couldn't see Califa submitting meekly to a collaring. Not a woman with her spirit, a spirit they hadn't been able to totally crush even in a year of enslavement. How had they done it? Had they overwhelmed her with force? Had they captured her by trickery? Had she been betrayed?

The usual Coalition assumption of guilt by association.

Her bitter words came back to him through the brandy haze. What had she been? Why had she given up her argument so easily, at the mention of his concern for his crew? Where had she learned, of all things, the Daxelian clamp hold? And why had it been his words about trusting the Coalition that had brought her down, defeated her?

The image of her, slumped and beaten where once she had defied them all, came to him with a vividness that startled him. He suppressed the urge to simply take this hellatious device and go hand it back to her. Instead, he sat staring at it, reflecting on who was the more evil, the ones who had created it, or the ones who used it.

"—and laughed when they did it. Took his land, raped his woman before his eyes until she died, screaming. Larcos was shipped to Boreas, to a crystal-loading gang. That's where Dax found him. Then there's Qantar. All three of his children dead, two years after his woman died aboard a passenger shuttle blown up by the Coalition. Dax found him outside the Coalition headquarters on Clarion, getting ready to charge it with only a small thermal gun. He talked him into coming with us, instead."

Califa glanced over her shoulder at the man Roxton was referring to, a tall, thin shape that sat in the far shadows of the room, apart from the others who were eating firstmeal. These were but two of many stories she had heard this morning. All grim. All bloody. And all something she would have once shrugged off as the necessities of maintaining system rule. Now she couldn't shrug off the horror of them.

Now she couldn't even shrug off the feeling of freedom it gave her to just be able to ask questions.

"And Nelcar?" she asked as she shifted her gaze to the younger man seated at the next table. He wore a protective goggle over his empty eye socket, and was animated compared to the grim countenance of Qantar.

"He wound up in a labor camp on Daxelia." Roxton shifted his gaze to Califa as he added, "Just outside Ossuary."

Califa's breath caught; the very name still had the power to disturb her. Then the implications of Roxton's words hit her.

"Are you saying Dax dared to get that close to Ossuary?"

Roxton shrugged. "He dares anything he pleases."

She stared at the older man for a moment. While her faith in her own judgment of people had been severely shaken in the past year, she knew she hadn't mistaken this man's love for the skypirate he flew with.

"And you let him?" she asked softly.

Worry flickered in the old man's eyes, the worry of a father for a much loved son. He tugged at his beard. "It would take a stronger man than I to stop him," he said at last. Then he abruptly rose and left, and Califa wondered how many times he had tried to do just that, stop Dax.

It was odd, Califa thought, her sudden fascination with the history of the people on this ship. She had never spent much time thinking about people before, why they did what they did, why they were the way they were, how they did, or didn't get along. She had decided long ago she didn't much care for people in general, and made exceptions only for those who had won her respect in one way or another.

So why, now, was she so drawn to find out their stories? It was more than just being free to question for the first time in so long; somehow she had developed an urgent need to learn as much as she could about them all.

One thing she had found early in her unpleasant existence as a slave was that if you kept quiet and listened, you sometimes learned more than if you pushed for answers. So she did just that, picking up a piece of information here—Roxton was from Clarion, as was Nelcar—and a bit more there—Dax had, it seemed, won the *Evening Star* on a single roll of the dice in a game of chaser, and an honest game at that—and wondering if any of it would ever do her any good.

A burst of laughter that had a ribald tone to it, a tone that reminded her uncomfortably of the prison guards, drew her attention to a conversation in a far corner. Her hearing, always acute, picked up the lowered exchange she obviously wasn't meant to hear, whether out of suspicion, or consideration for her gender, she wasn't sure.

"—after him like a Carelian in heat."

"Aren't they all? Seems every female in the system wants to be able to say they've mated with the most celebrated skypirate of them all."

"If he's half as good as they say he is, it's no wonder."

"Wish he'd send some of the overflow our way," Larcos, the only one of them she'd actually met, complained.

"Eos," one of the others hooted, "no female who's after Dax would look twice at you, Larc."

The talk reduced to howls and taunting jests for a moment before Larcos said, "Remember that little Daxelian? The one who worked in that taproom back on Carelia? The one formed like"—he made an expressive gesture with his hands near his chest—"that?"

"You mean the one telling the whole planet the next morning that Dax was as smooth as old Triotian silkcloth, as big as an Arellian steed, and as hard as crystal?"

The raucous, bawdy laughter broke out again, and for the second time in as many days, Califa felt herself blushing. She turned away, trying to tune out the men. And trying not to wonder if she had blushed because of the crudity of it, or because they'd been talking about Dax.

The connection of Dax with the salacious conversation brought back the problem that was uppermost in her mind during her waking hours, and most of her few sleeping ones as well. The controller. She had to get it back.

If it was true Dax had no idea what power it gave him over her, or how to use it, then she had nothing to fear. But if he was lying . . .

No. Just as she was sure of Roxton's love for Dax, she was sure Dax hadn't been lying. His distaste for the device had been too real, so real it had been almost tangible.

But if he were to learn, by intent or even by accident, would he use it? He had not looked at her with the sexual assessment of those who had used the controller on her before, yet he had looked. But perhaps he would take no pleasure in using a machine to make a female willing.

She nearly laughed out loud at herself. Eos, you've heard them talking. And you've seen him. Do you really think he'd have to force anyone? In any way?

Even you?

The thought appeared out of nowhere, and Califa wished it had stayed there, forever. Along with the traitorous thought that followed it; even with the controller, would it be so horrible, if the man were Dax? Not the soft, bloated officials of the Coalition, not the dregs that came into the prison, but a bold, fit, beautiful man like Dax?

Rage filled her, and no matter that she tried to tell herself it was at the idea of not holding the controller that was capable of turning her mindless with machine-induced passion, she knew part of her fury was at herself. For the first time in her life, she was letting thoughts of a man cloud her thinking. Even in mating, she had always been in charge, had been the instigator—and later the intimidator. Never had she had—or allowed herself to have—feelings like this. And she couldn't blame this on the controller.

Realize this, then, she told herself acidly; why, when by his own crew's admission he could pick from the beauties of the entire system, would a fit, beautiful man like Dax want a woman who was maimed?

True, her limp was barely noticeable unless she was tired, but the scar was all too visible, twisted, and ugly down the outside of her left leg. The *Brightstar*'s surgeon had been killed in that same explosion, leaving only a green medical officer to tend her, and his inexperience marked her from midthigh to knee. When she had been the person of power, it had been easy to assume it went unnoticed; now, it merely lessened her value as a slave.

A hail of greetings signaled Rina's arrival. Califa and the girl had spent a great deal of the night past first edging around each other warily, then speaking with formal politeness, and at last, after Rina's ingenuous declaration that she was very glad to have another female aboard, in tentative conversation. To her surprise, Califa had found herself enjoying talking to the girl; something about the wide-eyed pixie charmed her. Or perhaps she, like Rina, had been too long without the companionship of her own sex.

Rina had been asleep when Califa, after a restless night peopled with strange thoughts and dreams, had left their quarters. It had been stranger yet to walk down the ship's companionway, knowing that she was, within the limits set by the controller, in essence free to go where she wished.

She returned the girl's wave now, and was once again struck by the resemblance of those green eyes to another vivid pair. And she suddenly had the answer to her earlier question: she was drawn to learn about these people, because each story told her a little more about the man who, whether he admitted it or not, commanded them. The man who, whether he realized it or not, owned her body, mind, and what was left of her soul, as long as he held the controller.

And she *had* learned, she thought. She had learned that Dax had gathered them over time, from defeated worlds, from Coalition prisons, from far-flung labor camps, using some standard for selection that none of them quite understand; there seemed to be no consistency of traits among them. Yet it had worked; they functioned as a well-chosen team.

She had learned they thought him the best pilot in the system. She'd seen for herself he refused to take himself too seriously, had no pretensions of being better than the crew who followed him, and they knew it. He was tough, fair, and generous, they told her; they could ask no more of a leader.

And they all swore Dax would protect them unto death—and in turn, every last one of them would fly into Hades for him.

Which, she supposed, told her a great deal about the man himself. The kind of man who could inspire that kind of loyalty was not to be taken lightly—had she ever been fool enough to take a man that looked and moved as he did lightly.

"—sleep very well, did you?"

Rina's words jerked her out of her musing. "What?"

"I heard you tossing around. I know that cot is not comfortable, but—"

"It's fine," Califa said quickly. She lowered her gaze. "I'm sorry if I disturbed you."

"Stop that," the girl said, a little sharply. Califa's head came up. "I noticed you doing that yesterday, when we first came aboard. Avoiding my eyes, apologizing for no reason, acting like—"

"—a slave?"

"Yes," Rina snapped. "I don't like it."

"I don't care for it overmuch, myself," Califa said, smiling in spite of herself, as she hadn't in a long time.

No, not so long. She had smiled yesterday, smiled and meant it, for that brief moment on the gangway. At the man who held her life, literally, in his hands.

"Is it really true that slaves aren't allowed to speak unless spoken to?"

"Yes," Califa answered, stifling another smile.

She liked this girl, she thought. She was irreverent, headstrong—just as she herself had once been. But Rina had a generosity of spirit that, if she'd ever had it, Califa had smothered long ago. Generosity, she had decided early in life, got you nothing and nowhere but taken advantage of.

"No wonder Dax keeps threatening me with it. He always says I talk too much. And too fast."

Eos, Califa, you can talk at a few knots above light speed.

The memory spun into her mind before she could stop it, words spoken in teasing affection, probably the last true affection Califa had known.

And you killed it.

No, by Hades, it wasn't my doing. Damn you, Shaylah Graymist, Califa swore silently, quashing that tiny voice of conscience with a ferocity that turned her expression harsh.

"Are you all right?"

Rina's words brought Califa out of her suppressed fury. The girl was staring at her, eyes narrowed in concern. Genuine concern, Califa realized. She'd been right; the girl was far too generous for her own good.

"I'm fine," she muttered.

"You looked very fierce."

"I was ... remembering."

Rina lifted a brow as her mouth curved into a wry smile. "That's what Dax always says, when I catch him looking as if he'd like to blow up an asteroid. That he's remembering."

Califa looked at the girl. "Remembering what?"

"He never tells anyone. After we make a looting run, or he talks somebody into fighting with him, it's all right again."

The more she knew, the better. That was the reason she pushed Rina for more, Califa told herself. If the girl seemed willing to talk to her, she'd be a fool not to take advantage of it. Information was power, and she had little enough.

"Does it happen often, these moods?"

Rina shrugged. "No. Not a full-blown mad, anyway. But that's better than when he gets ... I don't know, sad, I guess. That's worse," the girl said, remembered pain darkening her bright eyes, "because it hurts just to look at him."

"Is he like that a lot?" Califa asked quickly, this time without even thinking about her quest for information.

"I don't know. He tries to hide it. But once I walked into his quarters to get something. I didn't think he was there, but he was. In the dark, all alone. When he talked, his voice sounded funny, all thick, like he'd been—"

Rina stopped abruptly, and Califa could almost read her thoughts as they skated across the expressive young face; she'd suddenly realized she was pouring this out to a virtual stranger.

"Eos, if Dax ever found out I was tattling to you about him, he'd have me on galley patrol for a year!"

"You mean like you were tattling to me in the cell?"

The girl brushed those words aside. "That was different. I was just talking big because I was scared."

It wasn't talking big, Califa thought, when the rescuing hero you were bragging about not only appeared, but lived up to his advance notices. Was he also a rescuing hero fighting his own hidden torment? A rescuing hero who sat alone in the dark and . . . cried? Was that what Rina had been about to say? It seemed impossible of the powerful, cool, sometimes flippant man she'd seen. It seemed impossible of the legend.

But she only smiled at Rina. "I was scared, too."

"I'm babbling because I'm not used to having a female to talk to. You won't tell him, will you?" Rina begged.

Did she like this girl because she reminded her of herself, Califa wondered, reminded her of the girl she'd been, more than once letting her mouth get her into trouble? Or was it simply the novelty of, for the first time in so long, hearing that pleading tone of voice directed at her?

A sudden, raucous sound interrupted her thoughts. She turned to look for the source, and caught a glimpse of Rina's pained expression. She lifted a quizzical brow at the girl.

"It's Hurcon," Rina explained. "He thinks he can sing. He's awful, but he does it anyway."

That, Califa thought, was an understatement. The multitude of off-key notes would have been bad enough, but the man's voice was uncompromisingly flat and nasal, and was annoying enough in itself to warrant throttling.

"Sometimes," Rina told her, "we try and sing along, to drown him out. But if there aren't enough of us, he just sings louder."

"A frightening thought," Califa muttered.

Rina giggled. "Yes. But I think there's enough of us, today. Just watch Nelcar. He usually breaks first."

Smiling in spite of herself, and in spite of her urge to clap her hands over her ears, Califa did as Rina said. Nelcar's face was twisted into a grimace as Hurcon stomped flat-footed over an old Clarion melody that was supposed to have been sung with a light, airy touch— and usually by a woman, the rather bawdy, masculine twist Hurcon put on the words not withstanding.

Nelcar lasted only a few more seconds. Then, rather fiercely, he began to sing along. His own voice was much more pleasant, but still too masculine for the piece, at least to Califa's ear.

Gradually others joined in, volume seeming to be the main objective; Califa weighed the destruction of the pretty little song against the pain of Hurcon's voice, and accepted it as a necessary evil.

Rina joined in, her voice plain but at least in tune. After a moment she nudged Califa with an elbow, urging her to join them. Califa hesitated, then shrugged; amid the din, no one could hear anyone save the person right next to them. She began to sing, shaking her head ruefully at a sudden image of herself, singing along with a crew of rowdy skypirates. It was like one of the old Triotian myths about men who sailed the great oceans, bellowing out a sea chanty as they worked the sails that harnessed the wind to propel them across the water.

Rina had stopped singing and, her eyes wide with pleased surprise, had nudged those around her into silence, letting Califa's clear, pure voice ring out above the others who still sang. As it did, others stopped, turning to look at the newcomer to the ship.

It was a moment before Califa realized what was happening. Her voice faded away as embarrassment overtook her; she'd always loved to sing, had even, before entering the Coalition Academy, thought of seeking instruction. But the academy had quickly taught her that anything other than booming anthems to the glory of the Coalition was unacceptable, and that singing itself was far too foolish a pastime for an officer, and probably smacked of weakness as well.

"No, don't stop!" Rina exclaimed. "It was wonderful. Please finish the song."

Califa shook her head, wishing she'd never begun, never drawn such attention to herself, an unwise action for a slave. Yet the others were chiming in with Rina, urging her to begin again. Even Hurcon grudgingly admitted she "had a decent voice," and waved at her to go on.

To refuse now, Califa realized ruefully, would bring even more attention down on her. She wasn't being treated as a prisoner, yet she knew that could change easily if she angered them. And she found that she was enjoying this tiny taste of freedom far too much to risk losing it. So she sang.

She had learned the song long ago, from a Clarion shipworker who had visited her mother. He had been one of the few "visitors" her mother had had that had ever paid any attention to the child who lived in the same dwelling. He had been very kind, Califa had thought then, never realizing until later that his kindness had no doubt been merely pity.

But he had taught her this song and others, and had praised her voice in words she remembered to this day. And six-year-old Califa had wished mightily that this gentle man were her father.

She sang it for him now, the notes high and sweet and clear. In her voice, the song behaved as it was meant to; it soared, it danced and sparkled like crystal dust caught in a feather of a breeze.

When the last note died away, the crew broke into a boisterous round of applause and cheering. Califa blushed, pleased. But her color faded when she realized there was one among them, a latecomer standing near the door, who wasn't applauding, but was studying her intently, as a pilot studied an instrument that gave an unexpected reading.

Dax.

She didn't know when he'd come in. She'd been too intent on the music, and remembering the long-forgotten pleasure of letting her voice run free. She lowered her eyes, not looking at him, yet she was still aware of his every movement. He crossed the room slowly, nodding a greeting to all. The noise level in the room rose once more as conversation resumed. But not, Califa noticed thankfully, the singing. Perhaps the leader didn't approve of such frivolity, she thought.

"Please," Rina whispered, "don't tell him we were talking about him."

It took a moment for Califa to remember the girl's urgent plea. She gave her a reassuring nod, and the girl breathed a sigh of relief and turned back to her food.

Dax poured a cup of the strong, thick, Arellian coffee that Califa had been delighted to find on the table. It was a rare commodity these days; too many of the growers who had once specialized in producing the pods that made the reviving brew had become traitors, refusing to aid the Coalition.

At least, that had been the version Califa had heard; Larcos's this morning had differed. The growers were now laboring in Coalition camps, he'd said, or reduced to trying to grow enough food for what survived of their families after the Coalition slaughter and scorching of the landscape.

Califa felt a pang for her home world. Perhaps she should have asked for a posting there, when she'd been taken off active duty. Then none of this would have happened. She would still be free, a nobly injured Coalition officer retired with honor. She would never have taken the wolf into the fold, and Shaylah would never have—

Stop it! she ordered herself. But it was getting harder to keep her old shipmate from her thoughts, as she'd sworn to do. But she'd made that oath before she'd been collared, back when she'd been smugly sure she knew what treason was. Now, she wasn't sure of much of anything anymore. Except that she had more than fulfilled any obligation she'd had ever had to Shaylah Graymist. And that the decision to do so had cost her, in essence, her life.

A life given for a live saved, she repeated silently. It balanced the scales. Even if Shaylah had long considered them balanced, Califa hadn't. When they had served together on the *Brightstar*, Califa had merely observed the overload on a weaponry circuit, shouted a warning in time for Shaylah to get clear, and helped her escape after the ensuing explosion. On Darvis II, Shaylah had risked her life to come back for her trapped comrade, disobeying a direct order from the team leader not to go back into the blazing ordnance bunker. Although Shaylah had then called them even—for Califa's sake, she had said, since she felt such things needless between friends—Califa had never felt it so. Until now.

The hardest part was, deep in her soul, she knew Shaylah would not think them even. She would never trade her own life for a friend's life spent in torment and torture. It was a quality of mercy Califa had ridiculed in her friend before; now she wished she had treasured it.

She heard a laugh, deep, resonant, and flagrantly masculine. She didn't need to look to know who it had come from, but she did nevertheless.

Dax didn't look as if he felt much like laughing. He looked weary, his face drawn, his eyes dark-circled, as if he'd had no more of a restful night than she. But if he was as tired as he looked, he wasn't letting it affect his crew.

"—sector scan an hour ago, and still no sign of anyone on our tail," Larcos told him.

Dax nodded. "Good. We'll proceed as planned, then. Four nights from tonight."

A cheer went up, including from Rina. Dax grinned at her. "You'll have the coordinates and the course laid out by morning, navigator?"

Rina gave him a look that could only be described as smug. "It's been done for hours."

Dax lifted his cup of the Arellian brew to her in salute. Rina flipped a rockfowl bone at him; he dodged it, laughing. When the room had settled down once more, Califa looked at the young blonde quizzically.

"We're going to Boreas," she said in answer to the look.

"Boreas?" Califa's brow furrowed. "Why? What isn't ice year-round is impassable mountains and poisonous seas. There's nothing there but the crystal mines."

Rina nodded, unconcerned. "And a big Coalition Outpost."

"A heavily armed Coalition Outpost." This was no secret, everyone knew that the crystal mines were fiercely guarded except in the winter months, when it was impossible for anyone to get through. Only the minimum contingent of troops remained there then.

"Of course. They have a huge supply annex, for those who are stuck there through the winter. That means guards."

"Of course," Califa echoed, an odd tightness knotting her stomach. "So what in Hades is the skypirate wanted all over the system going there for?"

Rina grinned. "Simple. He's going shopping."

Chapter 5

He was crazy. That was the only answer. He was off his axis, he was jackaled, he had slipped his orbit. No one who wasn't would even conceive of attacking one of the best armed of Coalition outposts, let alone with just a light cruiser and crew of twenty. No one who wasn't would fly all that distance just to commit suicide. No one who wasn't could get what seemed like sane men to go with him.

No one except maybe a legend.

She rose and paced the floor of Rina's quarters again. It had been three cycles of the ship's days since Rina had casually dropped her news. Califa didn't know what planet the ship's chronometer had been set to, but she assumed it was Clarion, where it had been made. But perhaps not; Clarion seemed too small for twelve-hour breaks of dark and light. Not that it made any difference. No matter what the schedule, they were marching closer and closer to disaster.

Califa tried to tell herself that you didn't build a reputation like Dax's by being conservative. It would take daring, boldness, even recklessness. But there was a line between recklessness and carelessness, between boldness and foolishness, between daring and stupidity.

But Dax was not stupid. She had seen too much bright, agile intelligence in those green eyes to think that. So why would he risk a raid doomed to failure? If he was so concerned about his crew's safety, why risk them on a suicide mission? Was his hatred of the Coalition truly so great?

She knew the crew loathed the Coalition with a passion she'd rarely seen. While Dax was the force that bound them together, was this the unseen criteria of his choices? Was this the one thing, the one common trait in the crew that seemed so different, so varied? It seemed each of them had a personal grudge, some reason for vengeance against the power that ruled the system with an iron hand.

And having heard their stories, she wasn't sure she could blame them. It was painful, beyond painful, to face the dark, evil side of the calling she'd devoted her life to, but if the tales she'd heard in prison, if the accounts of the crew members were not enough proof, she had only to touch her throat and the cool metal band that proclaimed her slave to the system in which she had once held a place of honor.

The whoosh of the door brought her pacing to a halt. Rina came in, her color high, her displeasure clear in her quick, jerky strides. Now it was she who paced the small floor space of her quarters, made smaller by the cot Califa was sleeping on.

"He thinks I'm still a child. He treats me like a child. Sometimes I think he wants me to just stay a child forever!"

Califa had no doubt who the girl was talking about. *It's been a long time since you were a child, Rina, though you should still be.* Dax's words, the memory of his eyes, shadowed with pain, came back to her sharply.

"Perhaps he just wants you to have the chance to *be* a child again, Rina."

"Being a child is a waste," the girl snapped as she spun and strode back across the room. "Being a child means you're too young, too small, and too silly to know what you want."

She whirled and started back again. "It means everyone else thinks they know what's best for you. It means they don't care if you're perfectly happy where you are, they have to take you away, so you can be treated like a child."

Rina's vehemence would have been musing, if Califa had not also remembered the girl's answer to Dax, that time. *If you hadn't rescued me . . .*

"Is that what Dax did, Rina? Took you away from someplace where you were perfectly happy?"

The girl stopped midstride, her back to Califa. It was

a moment before she spoke, and her words were oddly muffled. "I was doing all right."

"Were you?"

Rina turned then, and Califa was shocked to see tears streaming down her face. "Eos, sometimes I hate myself," the girl choked out. "I say these awful, wicked things, and I don't mean them, I even know I don't mean them when I say them, but I can't seem to stop them!"

Moved by a feeling she didn't understand, something all tangled up with her recognition of a child so much like she herself had been and the wish that someone who understood had been there for her, Califa raised her arms and opened them. Rina ran to her, throwing her arms around her, sobbing.

It was very strange, Califa thought. No one had ever turned to her for comfort. For cool-headed advice, for professional assessment of a tactical situation, yes. But never comfort. Not even Shaylah, when she had been clearly tormented in those last days, had had faith enough to trust her supposed friend to comfort her.

And had Shaylah been wrong? Califa wondered as she patted the girl's shoulders as the wrenching sobs continued. The woman she had been then would not have been at ease with such emotions, even from Shaylah. Perhaps especially from Shaylah. She certainly would not have welcomed a weeping child into her arms, nor would she ever have felt—or at least admitted to—this odd sense of fulfillment that someone had come to her like this.

"I—I d-didn't mean it," Rina stammered out again.

"Sshh," Califa soothed. "I know."

"Dax saved me. I would have died there, in that cave."

"Cave?"

"On Daxelia. My . . . my parents had been there, looking for a friend. They were killed by the Coalition."

Califa's arms tightened around the girl.

"My father fought them, but there were too many. Then he made them chase him, led them away. Only two stayed with my mother and me. She distracted them from me. So I could get away. She— They were so intent on her, touching her—" Rina gulped back another sob.

"Rina, you don't have to tell me this."

"I do, to make up for what I said. Dax would never, ever hurt me. But I seem to hurt him all the time. Sometimes when he looks at me it's like ... something's tearing him up inside."

"Does he know? What happened to your parents?"

She nodded. "I told him. When I realized he was—" Her words broke off suddenly, and when she went on, Califa knew it wasn't with what she had almost said. "After he found me."

"In that cave?" She nodded again, a tiny movement Califa felt more than saw. "I'd been hiding there. At night I went out and tried to find food. One night Dax saw me. He followed me to the cave. I fought him, because I thought he was one of them. It took him hours to talk me into coming with him."

He had taken the time to talk to a terrified child, Califa thought. He could have just taken her, for her own good, but he had not. Even to a child, he gave a choice, or at least the appearance of one. As one who knew all too well the pain of having no choice at all, she could appreciate such a simple thing, a thing most took for granted.

"Your parents?" Califa asked gently.

Rina went very still. Then she straightened, not deigning to wipe her eyes. But when she spoke, her voice was no longer that of a weeping child. It was a voice far too mature for her years, a voice cold with remembered pain, and hard with fury.

"They hung my father at the gate to Ossuary. I never saw my mother again. Dax went back to try and find her. I made him. I was only twelve. I was afraid, I made him promise to find her, never realizing I was asking him to risk his life for a woman he didn't even know, who was surely already dead. But he went, for me. A child he didn't even know."

With each awful word, Rina left the child farther behind. She drew away now, her arms withdrawing to cross over her chest.

"He let them catch him." Califa smothered a gasp. "For me," Rina repeated flatly. "He let them catch him trespassing on Coalition property, so he could try to learn what had happened to my mother. While they held him, he heard of a woman who'd been raped by the Coalition troops, then thrown to the prisoners until they used the life out of her. It was my mother."

"Eos, bless her soul," Califa whispered.

"They would have killed Dax, had he not pretended to be a simpleton. Instead they sentenced him to a public flogging. He could barely move, afterward. He still carries the scars. For me."

As she repeated the words a third time, her eyes, now dry, lifted to meet Califa's.

"He is not of my blood, but I would give my life for him. As would everyone on this ship." Her mouth tightened, and for an instant Califa saw the child there, young and frightened and weeping. "Because," Rina said, her voice husky now, "we all know he would give his for us."

For one of the few times in her life, Califa could find no words. There was nothing she could say in the face of such a horrible story, and such fierce devotion. Devotion to a man who, by all accounts, deserved it.

She watched as Rina walked to her bunk and sank down on the edge of it. She was clearly drained by the reliving of the ugly memories. Long moments of silence passed before Califa finally spoke again.

"Why were you so angry at him?"

Rina's head came up, guilt displayed clearly on her delicate, pixie-featured face. Her priorities were back in order, and she was feeling remorseful at having, at least temporarily, forgotten what Dax was to her. After a moment, she sighed.

"I'll have to go apologize now. I yelled at him."

Califa controlled her urge to smile. Such a paradox Rina was, at the same time so young and so very, very old.

"If your mood when you came in is any measure, I'm sure you did. Why?"

"He won't let me go on the raid."

"I should hope not," Califa said immediately, instinctively, horrified at the idea.

Rina eyed her, her expression rueful. "You look just like he did when I asked."

"You have no business on a mission like that," Califa

said sternly. "Eos, *he* has no business on a mission like that! Does he have any idea what he'll be going up against?"

Rina shrugged. "He's done it before. A couple of years ago."

Abruptly, Califa remembered. It had been the talk of the system, the rumors spreading like a firestorm. She had heard so many versions of how he had pulled it off that she had doubted anyone would ever know the real truth. The only thing that never changed, story to next exaggerated story, was Dax. The bigger-than-life, dark-maned skypirate who fought his way through Coalition troops like an avenging fury, leaving the Legion's best scattered like toy soldiers in his path.

He had become the scourge of the system—in Coalition eyes, at least. That he had become hero to many, and little short of godlike to some, she could no longer doubt. But she couldn't help thinking if he persisted in the folly of this raid, he would be dead. And that disturbed her more than she cared to admit.

She hadn't meant to spend the night in the crew lounge, wondering if any of the men were still alive on the planet below. It was no concern of hers, unless the *Evening Star* herself fell into the hands of the Coalition. And she had long ago decided on her course of action should that happen; she would never let herself be cast back into slavery alive.

No, she had no reason to be here, waiting, except perhaps to keep Rina company. The others left behind— far too many of them, Califa thought, although she could see the tactical advantage to a small, swift strike—were busily making room for the expected cargo; no one, it seemed, would admit the fact that Dax was leading his team into a death trap. Dax had always come through, and they refused to believe this time would be any different.

Rina had been pacing for an hour, clearly on edge. She had, Califa knew, apologized to Dax before the raiders had gone. Califa was glad, because although Rina had never even admitted the possibility of Dax never coming back, it would have been horrible if something happened and the girl had to live with the knowledge that their last words had been harsh ones. Califa knew too well that kind of pain; when Shaylah had gone, their parting had not been pleasant. But then, she hadn't expected that she would never see her friend again.

She watched the girl pace, brushing her golden hair back in a gesture Califa had come to realize was habitual. Once again she saw a resemblance to Dax there; they had the same air of barely contained energy, although the girl's came out in nervous gestures like that one, where the man's was controlled, giving the impression of a tightly coiled strength, just waiting to be unleashed.

She had seen a lot of that coiled strength last night, when she had, after two days of internal debate, gone to Dax's quarters. He'd looked startled at first, then rueful, and she wondered if there was any truth to the feeling she'd gotten that he'd been avoiding any contact with her; the *Evening Star* wasn't that big, and she'd only seen him half a dozen times since she'd been aboard. He seemed to hesitate for a moment, then moved aside to let her in.

The moment she'd stepped inside, she wanted to change her mind. There was danger for her here, in these close quarters. Every instinct she'd acquired in years of training and honed in Coalition service told her so. And the danger for her here was this man.

He was dressed as usual, minus the belt and its equipment. His shirt was unlaced, baring too much of the smooth, golden skin of his chest for her comfort. His pants clung faithfully to his lean hips and strong legs. His hair was tousled, falling forward over his shoulders, as if he'd been running his fingers through it in distraction.

She was seized with a sudden burning need to know what it would feel like, that thick mane of dark, gleaming hair, sliding over her own fingers. She clamped down on her spiraling senses. Perhaps she had been damaged in some way, she thought, when they implanted the collar. Or perhaps the collar was defective, the blue system active without any outward signal.

Eos, she thought suddenly, perhaps he had discovered

how it worked, and was using it to lure her to him. But why would he bother with subtlety, when it wasn't necessary? If he'd learned how to use it, he merely needed to increase the power and she would be what she was in fact, for as long as he held the controller: his slave. In any way he chose.

She couldn't reconcile the idea of him using the controller on her with what she'd come to know about him. But what else could explain the way she felt, the way warmth seemed to flood her and her pulse seemed to speed up, just at the sight of this man? It had never happened to her before.

He held a glass of amber liquid, Carelian brandy, she guessed. He gestured at the heavy crystal decanter that sat on the table behind him, as if to offer her some. She shook her head; the last thing she needed around him was to have her mind clouded by alcohol.

"This raid, why are you doing it?" she'd blurted out, her cool, reasoned approach forgotten. Amazing how quickly she'd returned to the freedom of asking questions.

He raised a brow at her. "I'm a skypirate, remember? It's what I do."

"But why here? There are hundreds of other places, other targets."

She knew she was treading a fine line, that one wrong word, one slip that betrayed too much knowledge, would expose her. And she knew what she was doing would be considered nothing less than treason to the system she'd once been a part of. She just wasn't sure she cared anymore.

"What's wrong with this target?"

She drew in a deep breath. "Rina told me about your raid here two years ago."

He lifted the glass of brandy. He sipped, then slipped his tongue out to taste the drop that lingered on his lips. Califa felt something hot and tight knot up in her belly.

"So?" he said, his tone as cool as she was warm. She fought to keep her voice steady.

"Do you really think it will be that easy this time?"

His mouth quirked. "It wasn't *easy* the first time."

"Then it will be ten times worse this time! Do you

really think they won't have increased security, that they won't have at least doubled the troops?"

"I'd expect nothing less."

"Then why? Think, Dax! The entire area around the annex is probably mined, and rigged with motion-triggered thermal cannon."

"Probably."

He was so unshaken, she wanted to shake him herself. "You only have twenty men—"

"We won't all be going. Fewer targets that way."

Califa smothered a groan of frustration. She would have sworn this man was not a fool, but to take on nearly a hundred crack Coalition troops ...

"But why Boreas? The most heavily guarded outpost in the system?"

"Is it?" he asked mildly, as if it was of no import.

"Of course it is. The crystal mines are the Coalition's most valuable resource. Except for Trios, it's their only source of crystal for the whole fleet."

The now empty glass hit the table with a thud. He spun around, all mildness vanished. There was something fierce in his eyes, a savage fury that made her back up a step. This was the man who had cut a swath through the Coalition's best. And he had turned on her, and she didn't know why.

"How in Hades do you know so much, Coalition slave?" He spat it out, in a voice matching the wrath in his eyes.

"I ..." She struggled to remember the answer she'd prepared, fearing this question. She didn't understand; she'd fought in pitched battles, she'd looked at death time and again, yet this man daunted her like nothing— and in particular no man—ever had.

"People talk," she said weakly. "In front of slaves ... they are less careful with their words."

"Perhaps you should be more careful with yours."

His voice was as icy as the planet below them. He turned his back on her in an obvious gesture of dismissal, but she summoned up nerve she hadn't been sure she possessed anymore.

"I was ... concerned. For Rina."

For a long moment he didn't speak. Then, at last, "I

told her she's not going. Even if I have to lock her up. She'll be safe."

"I didn't mean that," Califa said, fighting the trembling in her hands as she stared at his back; Eos, had she truly once been a warrior? In one year, had she been reduced to a woman who shook at a confrontation with one man? Or was it just this man?

Slowly, he looked back over his shoulder at her. The anger was still there, but it was banked now, controlled. She wondered how long it had taken him to learn to keep it in check. That had been a hard lesson for her, to harness her naturally short temper so that it didn't interfere with her job. She sensed it had been even harder for him.

"What did you mean?"

"I meant what she will do if you don't come back."

He had stiffened. He'd turned away from her once more. And after a long silent moment he'd spoken, his voice low and rough. And tortured. "She wouldn't be the first one."

The *Evening Star*'s sudden surge shook Califa out of her memories with a start. They had accelerated suddenly, and Califa wondered what was going on. She wondered if the lights had come on in response to a manual command, or if the hours of the ship's night had truly passed.

Rina leapt to her feet and ran for the far wall. She reached it just as the ship's comlink crackled to life. It was Roxton's voice; the first mate had reluctantly stayed aboard during the raid. Califa had wondered, when she'd learned it had been a last-minute and much-protested decision by Dax, if it had been a result of her visit. She thought perhaps it was. The choice of Roxton to stay was telling; he was the only other man Rina thoroughly trusted.

"I'm here, Rox," the girl said anxiously into the comlink receiver. "Is there news?"

"They're headed home, little one."

Rina sagged against the wall in relief. Watching her, Califa felt an echo of the same sensation.

"No one hurt?" Rina asked.

"One little scratch, nothing serious."

The girl's mouth thinned. "Dax, I suppose," she said resignedly.

"Now don't worry, Nelcar'll fix him right as sunlight."

"I'm going to the shuttle bay." Rina flipped off the comlink, then looked at Califa. "Coming? Watching Dax dock a shuttle at full speed on a moving ship is quite a sight."

Califa stared at her. Just the thought of the timing, finesse, skill, and sheer guts necessary for that kind of maneuver filled her with awe. "Are you serious?"

"Sure. He's done it a dozen times. Nobody does it better."

"If anybody else does it at all, I'd be amazed," Califa observed dryly.

Rina grinned at her. "So come watch."

"I can't."

Rina tilted her head. "Can't?"

"It's out of my range."

The girl blinked. Dax, it seemed, had kept her secret. "Never mind. Go, you can tell me about it later."

Rina didn't have to tell her. After their escape was assured, the entire crew did, including the four men who had gone down with Dax, who were telling their tale with the greatest of glee. Only Rina and Nelcar, who were with Dax in his quarters, and Roxton, who was busy on the bridge, making sure of their escape, were absent.

"Talk about a clean getaway," Hurcon chortled, rubbing a hand over his chronically bristly chin. "Dax disabled all six of their ships, and they never even knew he was there! I can just see them, trying to get those birds going while we flew right past them. By the time they can even start after us, we'll be in the next sector."

"That shuttle was so loaded down we barely got her off the ground," Larcos put in. "I had to use one of the portable thrusters we picked up just to get us airborne."

"And how about that on-the-fly shuttle docking?" Hurcon asked, sounding awed. "He never even had the *'Star* slow down on that pass, just open the shuttle bay and in we went. Then Roxton hit the throttle and we were gone before they could blink. I tell you, that man can fly loops around any pilot in the system."

"You encountered no resistance?" Califa asked in astonishment. She supposed it was a measure of how accustomed they had become to her presence—and perhaps a measure of their affection for Rina, who had made it clear Califa was in her good graces—that they answered her at all.

"Sure," Larcos said. "There was a squad of guards, but Dax kept them occupied while we loaded up." A frown flickered over the engineer's face. "That's when he got hurt."

She'd already heard from Rina that Dax had taken a blast from a disrupter to the left shoulder, but it had been at the extreme limits of the weapon's range, and so wasn't nearly as serious as it could have been.

"Anyway, that was about it," Larcos went on, grinning now. "Especially after Dax took that laser torch and welded the doors of the barracks shut."

Califa drew back a little. "He what?"

"I wondered why he took the thing," another man said. "But that's Dax. He thinks of everything. By the time they realized what was going on, they couldn't get out."

Califa had to smother the smile that threatened. Eos, that was the work of a true tactical brain, she thought. She had always admired the ability to improvise under pressure. *I was right, the Coalition should have recruited him. Except that he'd never do it, never sign on to fight for a system he so hated. And the Coalition had little use for independent improvisation these days. Perhaps that's why it defeated them.*

"Did you see him make that jump from the barracks roof to the supply annex?" Hurcon asked Larcos.

Larcos nodded, leaning his lanky frame forward, bony elbows resting on the table before him. "That was demented. That gap must have been fifteen feet."

"But it saved us ten minutes getting over that damned electrowall," the other man who'd spoken said.

Larcos gave an expressive shudder. "If he'd missed . . ."

"Ah, you know Dax never sets a foot wrong," Hurcon said with expansive pride.

"But the chances he takes—"

"He's blessed. Why, this is the worst he's been hurt

since that whipping on Daxelia, and you know that was
different, so it doesn't count."

"Invincible," the other man said.

They believed it, Califa thought. They believed that
Dax was invulnerable, indomitable. A valuable reputation for a skypirate to have, no doubt. But Califa knew,
perhaps better than any of these men did, that that kind
of luck didn't last. No warrior went forever unscathed.
Sooner or later, fate would catch up with him, and Dax
would pay the price for this long run of fortune. And
when he did, Califa thought grimly, who else would pay
with him?

Chapter 6

Califa heard the sound drifting gently down the passageway. She followed it instinctively, the soft, sweet music an inexorable draw to her.

The ship was dark, most of the crew sleeping after the tension of the raid and the relief of escaping Coalition pursuit. She herself was far too restless to sleep, and she didn't know why. She hadn't been in on the raid, so could not blame that for her disquiet. She was, apparently, in no danger from the people aboard the *Evening Star*. She had even, amazingly, found a friend in Rina. For all her youth, the girl's life had made her wise beyond her years, and their difference in age only occasionally interfered in their growing friendship. She treasured the feeling; she did not have enough friends to take acquiring a new one lightly.

She should be at ease, she thought, or as much so as it was possible for an escaped slave to be. Yet here she was, walking the passageways, too edgy to sleep. For a person who had spent most of her adult life keeping her emotions tightly under wraps, as befitted a trained Coalition officer, she was certainly in a muddle now, Califa thought. It amazed her that she could still feel any emotion at all.

The past year had stretched her control, had tested her discipline to the limit. Sheer determination to survive had often been the only thing that had gotten her through the humiliation, the degradation, the pain. Day after day, night after night, whether obeying commands that made her shiver with repugnance, or sitting alone in her slave's cell, she had fought not to lose that determination, knowing that if she did, it would all be over for her, that she would never, ever, be free again.

She couldn't give up, she had told herself. She wouldn't give up. Others had, those hollow, empty shells that had once been people. Those slaves who had died, yet still breathed, whose spirits had surrendered to their masters. She would never surrender. She would not be one of them, broken, beaten. She would be different. She would resist, no matter what they did to her. She would be, not like them, the quiet wraiths, she would be like—

Like Wolf.

An image had come to her then, of a golden, magnificent man. A Triotian, as dazzling as all of his people, chained yet not bound, enslaved yet not broken. The Coalition had done its worst to him, and yet he had never surrendered. She had held a grudging respect for him then; now, truly understanding what he'd done, she felt nothing less than an awed, nearly reverent admiration. And a growing dislike for herself, for she had been instrumental in the effort to break that proud strength.

She came out of the memory to find her fingers rubbing the golden collar, twin to the collar worn by the man she'd been thinking of. For the first time, she faced the wish she'd been suppressing for a time now, be it traitorous to the almighty Coalition or not: she hoped he had truly escaped. And Shaylah with him.

Be all right, Shaylah, she thought prayerfully, *please be all right.*

She tried to shake off the moment of softness, of tender feeling for the woman she should hate. Yet it lingered, wistfully, until she forced it out of her mind by turning her attention to tracking down the source of the haunting melody that was giving rise to a strange tightness in her chest.

Her footsteps began to slow as the slight increase in volume told her she was nearing the source of the music. Doubt warred with a sudden sense of inevitability; it didn't seem possible, yet she instinctively knew it was true. The delicate strains, the flowing, flutelike sounds, were coming from Dax's quarters.

She told herself to turn back, to leave, but the song wouldn't release her. It was an old Triotian air, one that she had heard in what seemed like a hundred variations on different worlds, adopted as so much from Trios had been adopted throughout the system.

She came to a halt outside his door, knowing she should leave. But it couldn't hurt to listen, just for a moment, could it?

That moment of indecision cost her. The music stopped, and the door slid open. Her breath caught, then released as she realized it was Rina who stood there. For some reason she felt relieved, oddly safe somehow; it must have been she who'd been playing.

"I thought I heard someone out here," the girl said.

"I heard your music," Califa said.

"Dax's, you mean," Rina said with a smile. "Isn't he wonderful on the dulcetpipe?"

Califa's sensation of safety vanished. "I . . . Yes. Yes, he is."

Eos, why did this knowledge alarm her so? Why was she fearful because the skypirate was a musician? And obviously a good one, on a delicate, ethereal instrument rarely seen, let alone played. And even more rarely played so well.

"Come in and listen," Rina said.

Califa shook her head, taking a step back.

"Please. Dax won't mind."

Califa doubted that, but Rina reached out and tugged on her hand, pulling her forward. She looked over her shoulder. "Dax, you don't mind, do you?"

She was inside and the door shut behind her before she could think of a way to deny the enthusiastic girl. Once inside, she instinctively glanced around the room, eyes searching. She found what she was looking for quickly; the controller was visible on an upper shelf, as if he wanted it well out of sight and reach.

His quarters were smaller than she might have expected, certainly smaller than any captain's on a Coalition vessel. The wide bunk, comfortably long enough for Dax's height, was beneath a viewport. A table that took up a sizable portion of space was cluttered with the remains of a meal for two.

Dax sat leaning back in a chair, his long legs, still encased in his boots, atop the table. He had stiffened slightly when she had come in, but he didn't move or speak as Rina dragged her further inside. And he was looking at her now as if he knew exactly what her hurried visual search of his quarters had been for.

He seemed well enough; if there was any lingering pain or stiffness in his shoulder from the disrupter strike, it didn't show. In his hands was a thin, long, silver tube, festooned with an intricate arrangement of levers, and with a mouthpiece at one tip. Califa had seen a dulcetpipe before, but had never heard its ethereal, haunting sound until now.

"I ... I'm sorry," she said. "I didn't mean to intrude. I'll go."

"You're not intruding," Rina insisted. "And stop apologizing all the time. I hate that submissive act, don't you, Dax?"

"That depends," he said, his gaze fastened then on Califa as he still sat unmoving in the tilted chair. "Is it an act?"

"Of course it is," Rina said. "She's had to do it, but it's not really her."

Califa blinked, startled at the astuteness of the girl's words. Rina truly was wise beyond her years.

"I think you're right," Dax agreed, his voice oddly soft. "She's like a Triotian snowfox, pale as the snow she's named for, eyes the color of purest ice against the sky, and who bluffs when she has to, merely to survive."

Califa stared at him, then swallowed tightly; she hadn't expected such gentle understanding.

"Here," Rina said, pulling out a chair from the table. "Sit down. Dax was just going to play—"

"Rina," Califa interrupted, "I *am* intruding. I'm sure Dax would prefer—"

"Sit down," Dax said. He sounded like he thought he would regret it, but he indicated the chair Rina had provided. Reluctantly—these quarters were far too small, she thought, when they were filled with a man as big as Dax—she sat.

She looked at her hands, then laced her fingers primly together. She looked at the table, noting that the leader of this crew ate the same meal as his men; no special cuisine such as was demanded by the captains of Coalition ships. She looked at the boots propped on the table, noticing that even now, in the relative security of his quarters, the knife was there. She did everything but look at his face, although the urge to do just that was compelling. She didn't dare; her mind became too snarled when confronted with those jade eyes.

In her effort to avoid giving in to that urge, she shifted her gaze to the silver instrument he held, trying to ignore the long, muscled length of leg above the boots, and the expanse of golden skin visible beneath the loosened laces at the throat of his shirt.

"I've seen a dulcetpipe, once," she said hastily, hating the way her composure, hardened to what she had once thought an impenetrable shell by a year with the collar, seemed to disintegrate around him.

"Oh?" he said unhelpfully.

"Where?" Rina asked. "They're rare, outside of—"

"Yes, where?" Dax said, cutting sharply across the girl's words.

Rina's eyes widened, as if in realization of some mistake almost made, and when Califa glanced at her, she could have sworn fear flashed across the girl's face before she subsided into silence. Fear of Dax? Califa wondered, but then dismissed the thought as soon as it occurred. Whatever Rina feared, it wasn't Dax.

"In a museum. There was a carving there, too. I think it must have been of your snowfox. In that incredibly white stone. It was quite ... wonderful."

"Triotian white marble," Dax said softly.

She nodded. "It was an exhibit of recovered Triotian artifacts in the archives on Alpha Two."

Rina's head came up sharply, but Dax went very still. "Recovered?" he said. She was coming to know that deadly soft tone; it made her wary. "Some might say stolen."

Califa was used to that; ever since Trios had been inducted—those same people Dax referred to would no doubt say forced—into the Coalition, some had protested the raiding of that world that had given so much to other worlds. Triotian myths, legends, traditions, music, and instruments like that marvelous dulcetpipe, were scattered throughout all sectors, and many had felt they deserved to keep the neutrality they had declared to all.

Shaylah had been one of those. And although she had teased her friend about her affection for things Triotian, when she heard Shaylah speak of that world, with its beauty of land and water, and the talent and exuberance and beauty of its people, Califa had felt a tug of longing for such a life.

She had, of course, suppressed it immediately. She had all she needed as a Coalition officer, and besides, most of the stories about Trios were surely fables. But if they weren't, and the Coalition had indeed looted and destroyed such a world . . .

"Some might," she agreed finally. "And perhaps they're right."

Dax seemed to relax slightly, but didn't speak again. Rina rushed to fill the void.

"I have an idea. Let her sing to your playing, Dax. You heard her before, she's wonderful."

Califa cursed her pale Arellian complexion as she felt heat rise in her cheeks. The heat intensified when Dax said, "Yes. I heard. She is . . . very good."

"Play the song Hurcon was butchering," Rina said. "I'd love to hear her sing it again."

"No," Califa protested, "I couldn't."

She meant it. Singing was too personal to her, and in the company of this man, far too intimate to be shared.

"Please?" Rina begged guilelessly. "I don't get to hear music enough. Dax won't play very often, even though I love to hear him."

Califa's gaze flicked to his face then, but he was studying the instrument in his hands as if it were new to him. Why, when he was obviously so very good, did he not play? And how on earth had a skypirate learned such an elegant skill in the first place?

Suddenly his eyes shifted, pinning Califa with his gaze. "It's up to you," he said. "If Rina wishes it, and you will sing, I will play."

"Please?" Rina said again.

It was more than Califa could do to say no to the girl's entreaty. She was beginning to understand why the entire crew of the *Evening Star* so indulged her; the girl was nigh on to irresistible. Reluctantly, Califa nodded.

Dax didn't say another word, but lifted the dulcetpipe to his lips, his hands spaced evenly down the silver tube that extended in front of him. Braced by his thumbs, his fingers came to rest lightly on the levers on the top side of the instrument.

She had never realized before, Califa thought, how beautiful his hands were. She'd been so stunned by his sheer male presence that she hadn't noticed the smaller details, the grace of his hands, the fine, strong tendons of his long fingers, the gentle touch those fingers were capable of.

And then the music started, a bare whisper of sound, like a distant song carried on the wind. It was delicate, fragile sounding, as that old ballad had been meant to sound. It should have seemed incongruous, that light, airy tune played by such a big, powerful man. Yet it didn't, Califa realized. For what good was power if one could not harness it, to use as one wished?

That Dax chose to leash his considerable power to produce such beauty moved Califa in a way she could put no name to. Almost without thinking, when the music shifted to the lilting melody, she began to sing. Softly at first, tentatively. And as if he sensed her uncertainty, Dax played the melody alone, only the fingers of his right hand moving on the sweet-toned dulcetpipe. Then, as her confidence and her voice grew stronger, as if he knew she no longer needed his support, he began to play a counterpoint with his left hand, a lower-pitched harmony that made the higher notes—and Califa's voice— seem all the more clear and dazzling.

Inspired, she let her voice slip the bonds and run free, caressing each note as his fingers caressed the keys of the pipe. He answered her in kind, his fingers flying over the intricate levers, creating harmonies that made her shiver. She took the words and made them her own, as he took the music and made it his.

Between them the simple song became a weaving of two elements into a whole that surpassed the sum of both. It became an intricate, and somehow intensely inti-mate dance, a duet of more than just voice and instrument. It was more than just a peerless rendition of an old song, it was a joining, a declaration of feeling by the two beings creating it.

By the time the last notes died away, Califa was staring at Dax, her heart pounding, her blood pulsing through her in hot, heavy beats. Slowly he lowered the pipe, holding her gaze, his lips still parted slightly, as if he, too, was feeling the intensity of it, needing more air than it seemed there was in the room.

"That was glorious!" Rina cried, clapping loudly. Neither Dax nor Califa looked at her.

"Rina," Dax said, his gaze never leaving Califa's face, "go get me those star charts."

"Now?" the girl yelped incredulously.

"Right now."

Muttering a protest, the girl went. The moment the door closed behind her, Dax's boots hit the floor. He stood up. So did Califa, taking in short breaths as she tried to slow her racing pulse. He set down the dulcetpipe and took a step toward her. She meant to step back, she knew her brain had sent the command, but her legs refused to obey.

"You sing beautifully," he said, his voice thick, husky.

"You play better." Eos, she sounded like he did.

She saw him swallow tightly, saw, for a split second, the battle in his eyes. Then he closed them and let out a long breath.

"I ... have to," he murmured, lowering his head.

She had time to move. She knew she did; she had the reactions of a trained warrior. Yet she didn't. Rather she lifted her head, waiting, inviting.

His mouth came down on hers, fiercely. He took her lips with an intimacy that would have been an insult but for what had just passed between them in the guise of a simple song. And her response had nothing to do with the collar that bound her, she knew that; had she wished it, she could have fought this man and he would not turn to the controller. Somehow she was certain of that.

But she didn't wish it. Eos, how could she wish it, when the feel of his lips fired her in a way she'd never imagined?

She swayed, and felt his hands grip her shoulders to

steady her. At least, it began that way; in the next instant
he was pulling her to him, holding her tightly against his
chest. He was broad and solid and strong, and heat radiated from him until she moved her hands, caught between them, to lay flat against his chest to savor the
warmth.

His lips gentled then, the bruising force lessening, becoming a coaxing, cajoling thing. She felt an exciting,
wet warmth as his tongue stroked her lower lip, and a
dart of white hot sensation rocketed through her. Helplessly, she parted her lips, and moaned when his tongue
slid between and traced the even ridge of her teeth.

She heard a low, faint groan rise up from deep in his
chest. It was the echo to her moan, as surely as his hands
had played the echo to her voice. The sound compelled
her, as his music had compelled her, and she tentatively
reached for his tongue with her own.

At the first touch, flame shot through her in a rush.
His grip on her tightened, as if he, too, had felt the
shock of it, the heavy jolt of pure sensation as tongues
probed and tasted. Then, with another groan, he wrenched
his mouth away; Califa almost cried out at the loss.

For a long moment they stood there, staring at each
other. Califa tried to draw in enough air, but she felt so
. . . strange. She didn't know what it was, couldn't know;
she'd never experienced anything like it before.

What was wrong with her? Eos, it was only a kiss! So
why did she want to run as if the jackals of Carelia were
after her? Why did she feel as if she'd just discovered
the greatest danger to herself that she'd ever faced?

This couldn't be happening, she told herself fiercely.
Not to cool, composed, and ever indifferent Califa Claxton. *She* controlled her responses, not whatever male she
happened to be with. And certainly not this rogue of
a skypirate.

But that wasn't true anymore, was it? Others did control her. Whoever held the power unit for the collar
controlled her. She had lost her self-dominion, it had
been stolen from her by the people she'd once sworn
her life to.

Yet with one kiss, Dax had made her feel more than
anyone ever had, more than she had thought herself ca-

pable of feeling. And he'd never even touched the controller.

Somehow, that thought was more frightening than the controller itself. And Dax was staring at her as if he was as scared as she was.

The opening of the door made them both jump.

"I don't know why you needed these now," Rina groused as she came in, several holograph disks in her hand. "We're not going to— Uh-oh."

Rina gaped at them both. Califa knew the tension between them must be unmistakable, although she hoped the reason for it wasn't, at least to the girl.

"Er, you want me to leave?" Rina asked Dax uncertainly.

"No!"

It came sharply, instantly, and Califa wondered why he wanted the girl to stay, when he'd so obviously sent her away moments ago. The fact that he didn't want a replay of what had happened moments ago didn't occur to her for a moment; when it did she had to turn away to hide her face for fear her emotions were showing far too plainly.

Whatever those emotions were, she thought ruefully. Right now she felt so tangled up and confused she might well have been a bewildered child again, wondering why her mother's visitors never stayed. And the truth that would follow this foolishness would be as harsh as the truth that had followed that long ago folly, she told herself sternly.

Rina was looking from one to the other. "Did you two have a fight or something?"

"Or something," Califa muttered.

"Not exactly," Dax said under his breath.

Silence spun out as Rina studied them both. At last Dax spoke again to Califa.

"If you'll excuse us," he said formally, "we have some charts to go over."

"Gladly," Califa said, her voice tight.

She meant it, too. She needed to get out of here, away from this man. She glanced back only once as she walked to the door; Rina had already activated the holograph projector, inserted a disk, and the image of a star sector glowed in the space above the table.

When she was safely outside in the companionway, she felt a release of tension that reminded her of the aftermath of a battle. She had no idea if she'd won, or lost. What she couldn't rid herself of was the idea that somehow, she had been forever changed.

Chapter 7

"Tell me about mating, Califa."

Startled, Califa stared at Rina. Eos, had the girl guessed what had passed between her and Dax when she'd been sent from his quarters? Surely not; she was too young, and in a way too sheltered from the ways of male and female to realize what that scene she had walked in on had meant.

Califa's mouth twisted wryly: even *she* wasn't sure what it had meant.

The girl was sitting cross-legged on her bunk, apparently intent on cutting down one of the new equipment belts acquired in last night's raid so that it would fit her slender waist. But not intent enough, Califa thought, if she could ask a question like that.

"Why ask me?" she said, carefully keeping her own eyes fastened on the tear she was trying to mend in the borrowed flight suit; such work had never been her strong point. She had always had slaves to handle such menial tasks, she thought, the irony of her situation never ceasing to dig at her.

"Because," Rina answered simply, "you're a woman, and I have no one else to ask."

"You have friends among the crew—" Califa began.

"The men won't even speak to me about it. I hear them talking, joking about it, but the minute I get close they turn red and go quiet."

Califa didn't want to ask, but the words came tumbling out anyway. "What about Dax?"

Rina gave her a sideways look that spoke volumes. "He's worse than any of them. He'll answer, but with silly words. I asked him once why females always overheat around him, and he just said something about women who wanted wild creatures for pets, to show them off. It didn't make any sense."

Didn't it? Califa wondered. It did to her. She'd known her share of males who had thought to add her to the roster of females they'd mated with, as if her honored Coalition name on their list somehow improved their own standing.

"I mean I know what happened to my mother was something else. Dax said that was about power, and violence, not mating."

Unusual wisdom, from a man, Califa thought. Even more unusual from a skypirate.

"Some men feel that by overpowering a person who lacks their bulk and strength, they have proven themselves mighty," she said, then added coldly, "They are fools."

And didn't that apply to the Coalition as well? she thought suddenly. Wasn't that exactly what they—and she, as part of it—had done?

"So why do males and females mate?" Rina asked, distracting Califa from a rather disturbing revelation.

"Sometimes for children, of course," Califa began, stalling.

Rina gave her the look that comment deserved; if children were the intent of every mating that occurred, the entire system would be overrun with them.

"I don't think I'm the best person for you to ask, Rina," Califa said slowly. "I'm not ... I haven't ..."

When she hesitated, Rina's eyes widened. "You can't mean you haven't mated before? You're so old!"

"Thank you," Califa said dryly.

She knew the girl meant no insult. It was true no one in this age went far beyond maturity without mating regularly, whenever they chose. Sometimes, whether the other party chose them back or not. Or often, if no other choice was at hand, with whoever was available. So it was proclaimed by the Coalition; only a fool believed in anything more than gratification of a physical urge, anything more than the slaking of lust.

Shaylah, I swear you're from the Creonic Age.

Her own words, uttered in amazement at the friend she had once considered too sexually fastidious to be real, came back to her now, hauntingly. Shaylah had believed in more. She had believed in the old Triotian bonding myth, the joining of two beings not just bodily, but with mind, soul, and heart. And no matter how Califa had baited her fellow Arellian about believing in fables that were not even of her own world, Shaylah had remained steadfast in her beliefs, more than once making Califa question her own.

But it wasn't until she wore the collar, it wasn't until the simple act of choice had been taken from her, that Califa had seen the true ugliness of what passed for pleasure in her world.

"You know I didn't mean you're really old," Rina was saying hastily. "But you are older than me, you're almost as old as Dax, and Eos knows he's done his share of mating."

"So I've heard."

Califa didn't care to examine why that knowledge disturbed her. She'd done more than her own share of heedless mating in her life before; she could hardly judge this man for doing the same. But the memory of that kiss was seared into her mind as if with a laser scalpel, and she couldn't deny the image of Dax with any one of the women the crew had joked about troubled her.

"I just wondered what it was like," Rina said with a shrug. "I can't imagine ever trusting a male that much."

How could she tell this girl that trust had so little to do with it? Why worry about trusting someone you had never seen before, and would no doubt never see again? Why worry about trust in a contact that would last only as long as it took to slake the need, the only criteria for mating under Coalition rule?

Dax had not done Rina any favor by keeping her so isolated from the reality outside the *Evening Star*. She could not live aboard the ship forever, and she would be ill equipped to survive outside it, not in this time, in this system.

"It can be ... pleasurable," Califa said. "Intense, but momentary."

Rina's golden brows furrowed. "Hardly sounds worth the effort."

Califa chuckled humorlessly. "You may be quite right."

Rina looked troubled. Califa studied her, seeing this time a girl who had something she herself had never had, an innocence about mating, about the urges between male and female. Dax was wrong. Rina's childhood might have come to an abrupt, traumatic end, but she had had twelve years of innocence. Thanks to her mother, Califa had had none. Perhaps it was this that drove her to save, not destroy, that innocence.

"I've heard it said," she began, "that with some ... there is more. That there is a greater pleasure, more than just a mating out of lust. That there can be ..." She took a breath as she struggled to find the words to express something she had never believed. Then the memory of Dax's kiss intruded again, and suddenly she found the words. "That there can be a joining, they call it bonding, which makes the two together stronger than the two alone. A joining that creates a link so strong nothing can sever it."

Rina stared at her. "Ever?"

"That is what some accept. It is an old Triotian"—she hesitated on the word "myth"—"belief."

"So that's what Dax meant," Rina murmured, wide-eyed.

"What?"

The girl looked startled, then, oddly, frightened. As if she'd said something horrible. Like she had looked in Dax's quarters, when he'd cut off her words about the dulcetpipe.

"Nothing," she said hastily. She grabbed at the belt in her lap and scrambled to her feet. "I have to get another tool."

She was gone practically before Califa could blink.

Dax flexed his shoulder as he walked down the companionway, lit for evening now by the ship's computer. Nelcar had done his usual fine job; some residual stiffness that would be gone in a couple of days was the only reminder of this run.

He thought that the young Clarionite's order for him to stay in his bunk for two days was a bit extreme, but he'd dutifully stayed in his quarters; Nelcar, when it suited him, had the bedside manner of a Carelian jackal.

His only visitors had been Roxton and Rina. And, last night, Califa.

Califa. Little snowfox, with her pale skin and blue eyes. And a voice like the sound of spring coming to life. God, what had he gotten himself into?

He didn't want to think about it, tried to force it out of his mind.

He'd been headed for the crew lounge, but changed his mind and stopped at the narrow stairway that led up to the small observation deck. The bubble of anything-proof plaxan gave a full overhead and 360-degree-around view of everything—and all the nothing in between. It was one of the few places on the *Evening Star* where quiet was the rule, and right now he needed that, not the chatter of the crew. After each new raid, it seemed to take longer to come down, and the low after the adrenaline rush seemed lower.

He ran up the narrow stairs, then froze on the top step, cursing the urge had made him come up here. For up here, sitting in the circle of soft light from outside, was the very woman he'd been trying like Hades to avoid even thinking about.

She was alone, staring outward, in the direction they were headed, not back at Boreas. The soft light gleamed on her hair, an ebony cap that looked like spun silk as it brushed her ears. Tiny, delicate ears, at odds with her uptilted nose and determined chin. And her eyes were so darkly fringed, yet that extraordinary light blue color. The arched brows were as dark as her lashes, and stood out against pale Arellian skin. And that mouth . . .

Images from last night flashed through his mind. The way she had looked at him after the song was done, her wide-eyed expression telling him without words that she had been feeling what he had felt, that somehow that song had compressed time between them, that in those minutes they had learned more of each other than some people do in a lifetime. The way she had held still for his kiss, instead of dodging away as he'd half expected. The way she'd parted her lips for him. The feel of her tongue as it had brushed over his, sending a burst of blazing heat through him . . .

He yanked his wandering mind back to safer territory.

As if looking at this woman could ever be considered safe, he thought. At least for him.

The bruise was fading, he noticed. It was barely visible in the subtle light here. He wondered if there were other marks marring that exquisite skin, other badges attesting to Coalition cruelty. He had a sudden image of himself, laving every one of those imaginary bruises with his lips. Heat rocketed through him, hardening him in a rush.

She seemed raptly caught by the starry view, and Dax thought he could probably turn back and she might not even realize he'd ever been there. But he would know. He would know that he had turned and run, on his own ship, because he was afraid of the way an icy-eyed, ebony-haired Arellian made him feel.

And that was something he'd been avoiding as well, thinking about just that subject. He'd met many women he'd been very aware of as women, who had sent out subtle—and some not very subtle—messages of invitation. Some of those invitations had been tempting enough to accept, even though he was certain of the inevitable outcome. Sometimes he'd felt driven to discover if anything had changed, if perhaps this woman, or that one, would make a difference. They never did.

He didn't even care why they wanted him; he knew for most of them it was the thrill of the forbidden, a mating with the notorious skypirate, as if he gave them some kind of cachet that they could brag about later. He didn't understand it, but he didn't begrudge them, either. How could he, when he'd used them as they used him, in his effort to learn why his body always betrayed him?

But this was the first time a woman had ever made him so aware of himself as a man. He didn't know if it was her cool but undeniable beauty, so unexpected after his first sight of the grubby waif in that dank prison cell, or if it was the glimpse he'd gotten of a bold, fiery woman, who had clung to some shred of spirit despite the efforts of the massive machine of the Coalition to turn her into an automaton.

In either case, he'd known he was in trouble the first time he'd seen her in the crew lounge, wearing Rina's flight suit, the bright, crimson shade a dramatic contrast for her ebony hair and pale skin. And an altogether too vivid delineation of the feminine curves her ragged, filthy clothes had concealed.

For a while, he had wondered if he was going to have trouble with the men over her; he'd noticed more than one of them eyeing her with a surprise that hadn't been there when she'd come aboard looking as much a lost waif as Rina had that first time.

But perhaps that very connection was why the surprise had never turned into the hormone-driven haze he'd half expected in this crew that had been a long time without female companionship. Every one of them had come to look upon Rina as one of their own. Whether it was because she represented the families they'd lost, or now would never have, he didn't know, but he knew they all protected the girl. Perhaps some of that protective instinct had spilled over to the woman Rina had made her friend. It didn't matter, he supposed; he was just glad he wasn't going to have to face the problem of his crew panting after the Arellian.

It was bad enough that *he* was.

He waited until he had his body—his uselessly quickening body—under control. Then he went up that last step, reluctantly, yet feeling that if he didn't he would never be able to face himself again. She didn't react, even when she had to have seen him, and Dax realized that she had indeed known he was there all along. Grateful now that he hadn't retreated, he walked slowly over to where she was sitting, in one of a group of four chairs place for optimum viewing of the expanse of forward space. There were three other groupings facing other directions, empty now.

After a moment's consideration, he chose the seat opposite her, deciding that was the best compromise between appearing to avoid her and getting too close.

Silence spun out between them, yet there seemed to Dax to be a charge in the air, like the scent that lingered after the firing of the flashbow. He searched for something to say, to talk about—anything but that sizzling kiss—but before he could think of anything, she spoke.

"Do you wish me to leave?"

Her quiet question startled him, both in its unexpect-

edness and its content. As Rina had said, he hated this
submissive act of hers; it reminded him too forcefully of
the meaning of that gold band around her slender neck.
But perhaps it had been merely consideration that had
prompted the question. After time spent in a Coalition
prison, perhaps she appreciated the need for quiet. So,
although he wasn't entirely certain his answer wasn't yes,
he said, "No. Why would I?"

She looked at him then. "This seems a private place."

His mouth curved upward at one corner. "Not usually.
And usually not for long. But if it's quiet you want, this
is about the only place outside your quarters to get it."

"Even if it is fully occupied?"

He nodded. "It's the only rule, here."

"Your rule?"

He let out a compressed breath. He had wanted her to
drop that slavelike habit of phrasing questions as merely
observations, hadn't he?

"Yes. My rule."

He said nothing more, but after a moment she said,
staring once more out at the stars, "A quiet place is
necessary to sanity."

"Yes," he said after a moment of surprise at how exactly she had expressed his need for this one place of
calm amid the chaos of a skypirate's vessel.

She shifted her gaze back to him. "Your shoulder? I
neglected to ask . . . last night."

He answered hastily, feeling like a man dodging
through a field of saturation fire set down by thermal
cannon. "It's fine. Nelcar did a good job. And it wasn't
very serious to begin with."

"Rina was worried."

"She overreacts." His mouth quirked. "So does
Roxton."

"They would not, did they not care."

He let out a long breath. "I know. But they shouldn't.
Everything went well."

"So I hear. The crew talks of nothing but your great
success."

They had talked of none of this last night, he realized
in surprise. It was as if last night had truly been a magic

interlude, with nothing mattering except the music. And a kiss.

Once more steering himself away from memories of those few moments that so inexplicably alarmed him, he answered with a negligent shrug.

"It was a good run."

"And they talk of your own risk taking."

Another shrug. "You can't expect to gain without risk."

She looked startled, as if she hadn't expected to hear those words from him. He didn't know why, it was a common enough belief. He had even heard that it was a well-preached dogma of the Coalition, taught in all their schools.

"You take them ... excessively, it seems."

He looked at her consideringly. "There are those who would say that no risk is excessive if you succeed."

"You mean that your very success is proof that it wasn't?"

The corners of his mouth twitched as she used the very words he had so often used on Roxton when the older man chided him for his recklessness. "Exactly, snowfox."

Her eyes widened, and color tinged her cheeks. He could almost see her fighting back the blush. It was a moment before she spoke.

"Perhaps there is truth in that," she admitted, "but there are also those who speak of pushing your luck until fate pushes back."

"Is that what you did, Califa?" he asked softly, his gaze flicking to the gold collar.

She went very still. One hand crept up to finger the cool metal at her throat. "No," she whispered.

"So sometimes fate pushes first?"

He thought she wasn't going to answer. He couldn't blame her, really. One kiss hardly gave him the right to pry into her life. But then, in a voice so low he barely heard the words, she said, "Sometimes someone else pushes their luck, and you get caught in the backlash."

There was so much pain in her voice, and she was fighting so hard to hide it, that he said nothing. Had she been caught in someone else's fated backlash? Was that why she'd been so concerned about Rina being caught in the backlash of his pushing his luck?

He'd spent a long time mulling over that unexpected visit the night before the raid. When she'd first come in, he'd nearly choked on the brandy he'd been drinking at the way she had looked at him. He had seen looks of hunger on women's faces before, but had never expected to see such a look on her face.

He had wondered, because it hadn't been quite the same look he was used to seeing from other women. It had been more intense, somehow, fiercer, as if it was coming from the Califa he'd only seen glimpses of, not the compliant slave. And that thought had nearly driven him straight back to the brandy. Only the realization that he shouldn't add the heat of alcohol to his already too-quickly heating body had stayed him.

And then it had been gone, that look, gone as if he'd imagined it. He'd thought perhaps he had, that it had merely been urgency he had sensed; she had clearly become attached to Rina, and was worried about her welfare.

More likely, he'd thought wryly, it was the product of far too much wishful thinking on his part.

When he heard the sound of voices on the steps, he was almost grateful; he had no solution for the kind of pain she was in. If he had, he would have eased his own long ago. Up came Nelcar and Roxton, still consoling each other on having missed the raid. As was the custom, their voices dropped to a quieter level as they came onto the observation deck. As was also the custom, they did not intrude, but merely nodded before taking seats that faced back toward Boreas, and continuing their conversation.

When Dax turned back to Califa, she was looking at him with a hint of anxiety in her silver-blue eyes.

"I must ask you . . ." she began, then stopped.

She obviously wasn't assuming she had gained any influence over him with that kiss, he thought. He should be grateful for that, he supposed. So why wasn't he?

"Go ahead," he prodded. "You seem to have recovered the ability to question well enough."

Still she hesitated, as if gauging whether there had

been any sarcasm in his words. She either decided there wasn't, or that what she wanted to ask was important enough to outweigh it.

"Please, give me the controller."

He drew back a little. "This again?"

"Surely you see I am no danger to you—"

"What I see," Dax said seriously, "is a woman I know little about, except that she is a slave."

"You yourself said a slave to the Coalition would not betray you to them."

"Perhaps not. But would a slave be above selling her knowledge to those who might pay well enough for her to buy her freedom?"

Her mouth twisted bitterly. "I'm not sure anything short of your head would buy that."

He lifted a dark brow. "I'll endeavor to keep it on my shoulders, then."

"Dax, I swear to you—"

"The risks I take are my own, Califa. Would you expect me to risk my crew for the word of a woman who is a mystery to us? A woman who knows of many things I would not expect a slave to know?"

"I told you, people—"

"Talk. Yes, I remember. But talk of guards and troop movements, of thermal cannons and mines?"

"That was merely common sense." She was beginning to sound frantic now. Roxton and Nelcar were casting curious glances in their direction.

"Who are you, Califa?"

"Surely that doesn't matter. I swore I would never betray you—"

"Intentionally," Dax reminded her. "And I believe that, to the best of your power, you would keep to that. But if this controller you are so anxious about has the power that you claim, what is to prevent it from being used on you, to force you to break that very promise? Anyone will break—or die—eventually, under that kind of pain."

"You don't understand," she said, her voice rising slightly. "It's not just the pain, it's . . ."

She broke off. He saw her shiver, then fight to control it. Her fingers crept to the collar, then tightened, as if she wished to rip it away, implanted probes and all, regardless of the fact that it would no doubt kill her.

No, he didn't understand. He doubted that anyone who hadn't been through it, who hadn't known the sensation of being owned, controlled, by another could ever completely understand. But that lack didn't lessen his reaction to her anguish.

"What is it, Califa?" His voice was gentle, coaxing. "It's more than the thought of pain driving you. It's the other systems, the blue, and the red, isn't it?"

Her head came up then, and fury glowed in her eyes. Whoever or whatever this woman had once been, powerlessness had never been part of her life; her rage at it now was too evident, too fierce.

"Tell me," he urged. "Perhaps we can find a way to free us all of this scourge."

"There *is* no way."

The other two men were staring now. Dax ignored them. "There must be."

"You want an end to it?" she snapped. "Then use the red system."

"The red?"

"It's simple. Activate the controller with the key that's set in the bottom. Set all registers to the maximum. Then press the red crystal." Her words dripped acid as she recited the instructions as if teaching a beginner to open a code lock.

"And ... what happens?"

"Your problems are over."

"Califa," he said warningly.

"The same thing that happens when the collar goes past the controller's range."

Dax sucked in a quick breath. "It explodes?"

"As I said, your problems are over." She added bitterly, "And mine as well. Permanently."

Dax swore, a pungent, biting curse that condemned the contrivers and the builders of this system to an eternal life under its yoke.

"And the blue crystal?" he asked. "What charming function does it have?"

She leaned forward, fixing him with a fierce gaze full of anger, frustration, and a hint of desperation. The others on the deck shifted nervously, as if waiting for Califa to make some threatening move.

"Does it matter?" she asked urgently. "Just give it to me, Dax, if you meant what you said."

"I did mean it," Dax said, feeling ripped in two, caught between the horror of what had been done to her and the safety of his people. His heart, his very gut urged him to do as she asked. But he couldn't be sure his thinking wasn't fogged by his fierce, unexpected desire for her; his common sense told him he had no idea who or what this woman was, and keeping that device, no matter how evil or repugnant it was to him, was the only way to insure she was no danger to them.

The strain rang in his voice when he said, "I can't."

"Why, damn you?"

She was close to snapping, Dax could see that. What he wished was that he could see a way out of this. "Even if I trust you, I have no right to make this decision for everyone else aboard the *Evening Star*. If I'm wrong, I've jeopardized all of us."

"You're not wrong!" She leapt to her feet. So did Roxton and Nelcar, clearly not caring now that it was obvious they had been listening.

"Califa—" Dax began, standing up slowly.

Her fists clenched at her sides as she drew in short quick breaths, as if running some great race. "I'm no danger to you, any of you. Or to the *Evening Star*. I promise you."

He stared at her for a long moment, his quickened breathing matching hers. Only the truth of what he'd said before stopped him from giving in to her. "How do I know that?"

"You have my word!"

"And how do I know I can trust it?"

"It's the word of a Coalition officer, you—"

She broke off sharply, horror showing in her eyes. The echo of her involuntary shout hadn't even died away before the other two men moved in, trapping her. It was just as well; Dax found he couldn't move at all.

Chapter 8

Roxton and Nelcar were dragging her away when Dax at last found his voice and stopped them.

"You heard what she said," Nelcar exclaimed. "She's a Coalition officer!"

"Apparently so," Dax said.

"No!"

Dax whirled; Rina, eyes wide with shock, stood at the top of the stairs. She was staring at Califa, shaking her head as if in pain.

"Rina, go to your quarters," Dax ordered.

"No," the girl said. "I want to—"

"Not now."

Rina shifted her bewildered gaze to Dax. "But—"

"I rarely give you direct orders as a member of this crew, Rina," he said in a low, deadly calm voice that brooked no denial. "But I am now. You will say nothing of this to anyone, and stay in your quarters until I come to you."

Rina lowered her eyes, and Dax knew he had gotten through. She gave Califa a last, slightly wild look, then turned and ran down the steps. Roxton tightened his grip on Califa, who had paled a little herself at Rina's appearance.

"For that alone," Roxton said, watching the agitated girl go, "she deserves to die, and painfully," Roxton said. "As they all do!"

"Possibly," Dax agreed. "But not before I get some questions answered."

That seemed to placate them. They didn't loosen their hold, but they stopped trying to drag her toward the steps. Dax knew he would have to be very careful. Tempers were running high, and if things got out of hand, if the rest of the men learned of this, he wasn't sure he could stop them.

He wasn't sure he wanted to stop them.

A Coalition officer. The words caused a sickness in some deep, core part of him. Images flashed through his mind in rapid succession, destruction, death and blood, the legacy of the Coalition in every place he'd ever been. The legacy of his home, the place that no longer existed as he'd known it.

He veered away from memories too painful to linger on. He refocused on the present, to find Califa watching him, only him, not the two men who held her. Despite their grip, she stood tall, straight, and there was no trace of the slave in her manner.

But every trace of a proud, well-trained warrior. Who no doubt could have killed him that night they'd been alone in his quarters. He knew the question was unnecessary; the words that had broken from her under stress had been instinctive, a deeply ingrained response so automatic she hadn't been able to stop it. But he voiced it anyway.

"Is it true?"

"Yes."

No dissembling, no explanations, no denial. He hadn't expected any; his gut had told him it was true long before he'd heard her answer. This explained so much; her boldness in the prison, her interest in the flashbow, her knowledge of the probable defenses of the Boreas outpost. It also explained her fury at her own helplessness, and the glimpses he'd gotten of a different woman, a strong, fierce woman. They didn't come any fiercer than Coalition officers.

"So tell me," he said, his voice dangerously soft, "how did a Coalition officer wind up a Coalition slave?"

As she had on the gangway that day that seemed an aeon ago now, she said, "I'll tell you. But only you."

"In Hades you will!" Roxton bellowed. "You think we'd leave you alone with him?"

"If I wanted him dead, he would be so. I've had chance enough."

Dax was startled at her blunt words, but then realized she must think she had little left to lose.

"Arrogant bitch." Roxton backhanded her so hard her head snapped back against Nelcar's shoulder.

"Hold!" Dax ordered. "She speaks the truth."

"Dax," Roxton began, but Dax shook his head. He understood how his first mate felt, more even than the older man knew. Dax had seen what had been left of the capitol of Clarion, where Roxton's family had died. It had been his first sight of total Coalition destruction, and the realization that his own home no doubt looked much like that pile of rubble had made him shake inside.

Nevertheless, he restrained the man with a gentle hand on his arm. Nelcar he was not so concerned about; the younger man had as much reason to want any Coalition officer dead, yet his natural bent was to healing, and Dax thought that would curb him for the moment.

"I do not want her dead just yet. There is a great deal I want to know. I'll listen to her."

"Don't be a fool, Dax!" Roxton exclaimed. "Alone with a Coalition officer?"

"And a Coalition slave," Dax pointed out.

"The crew will not like this," Roxton said. "They believe once Coalition scum, always Coalition scum."

Dax's jaw clenched as his first mate confirmed his earlier thoughts. Were the crew to learn of this, there wouldn't be an undecided one among them; they would clamor for her death. He wasn't sure he didn't agree, but that cold, knotted-up place in his gut told him he had to have some answers. Her stance, her stubborn, determined expression, despite the blood trickling from her mouth after Roxton's blow, told him he would get them alone, or not at all.

He was at a loss about what to do when Califa's earlier words came back to him. He glanced at Roxton. "You heard what she said before, about the controller's red system?"

Roxton shifted uncomfortably, then nodded. Dax guessed the older man had felt as sickened as he had, and was now regretting wasting any sympathy on a Coalition officer. Dax looked back at Califa.

"We'll go to my quarters then"—the outburst from both men overpowered him for a moment, until he held up his hand for quiet—"and I will hold the controller."

Her eyes widened. She stared at him, then, after a moment, she nodded.

"But how do we know she's not a spy?" Nelcar protested. "Sent to lead the Coalition to us? Maybe that collar's not even real!"

"Oh, it's real, all right," Dax said. "She was much too desperate to get the controller back. Besides, Rina scanned it the first day she was aboard, and she spoke the truth. The core is pure photon propellant igniter."

Califa looked startled, and Dax gave her a sour look. "Did you think me a total fool, taking all you said at face value?"

"I still don't trust her," Roxton said.

"She is unarmed, Rox. Have you so little faith in me?"

"But a trained Coalition officer—"

Dax's eyes went frosty. "I've had some training of my own, here and there."

"Yes," Roxton agreed, "but do you have the stomach to kill a woman if you have to?"

The first mate's words threatened to bring on the visions of Dax's horror-filled nightmares. He fought them off. Would he have the stomach to kill a woman? Especially this woman, who had the strangest effect on him? No doubt he was a fool for even attempting this.

"Let's hope I don't have to find out," he said grimly, and gestured to Nelcar.

It was a slow procession down the companionway to Dax's quarters, since neither of the men were willing to leave. Dax guessed that no matter what he ordered, they would be outside his door, ready to burst in at the first sound of a fight. Knowing this, he didn't bother to order them at all.

Reluctantly they released their hold on Califa. When she didn't move, they shoved her inside. She stumbled, then caught herself. Dax jerked his head at the two men in the doorway. Unwillingly they backed away, and Dax shut the door.

Dax passed Califa without a glance, walked to the table, and picked up a carved crystal decanter of brandy. He poured some in a small glass, set the decanter down, and only then turned to look at her.

"Dare I give this to you, or will you try to cut my throat with the glass?"

Her gaze shot to the closed door, as if she, too, had guessed the men would be just outside. "I'd say it depends on who you ask."

He considered for a moment. "And I'd say you will not. As you said, if you'd wanted me dead, you had your chance."

She'd more than had her chance. He'd been so enraptured when he'd kissed her, she could have plunged his own knife between his ribs and he'd never have been able to stop her.

Kissed her. A Coalition officer. He wondered why that thought didn't make him feel sick. God, he couldn't think about that, not now.

He held out the glass. She hesitated, then took it. She inspected the contents. "Perhaps it is I who should be worried. Only one glass, and you not drinking?"

"My gut is on fire enough," he said with blunt honesty.

"Then you do not wish me dead, like the others?"

"I'm not really sure." His eyes narrowed as he looked at her. "Perhaps I'm just not in such a hurry."

"No," she said. "You want your answers first, don't you?" She downed the brandy in one gulp, then sucked in her breath as it hit. "I've been wondering how long I could keep it secret." Her mouth twisted in obvious self-disgust. "And then I'm the one to blurt it out to all and sundry . . ."

She held out the empty glass. He took it, set it down, then turned to lean against the edge of the table. He drew one leg up to brace his foot on the edge of the table. He rested his crossed arms on his upraised knee, but he didn't relax. It was a ready posture, and he knew she knew it; using the solidly fastened table as a base and his bent leg to push off, he could launch himself powerfully and instantly. It was the kind of thing a trained soldier would recognize.

"Aren't you going to get the controller?"

At her question, his eyes moved to the shelf beside him where the device sat. "It's close enough."

She gave him a long look, her eyes narrowed. "You're

not a fool, despite Roxton's words. I could get to it—"
She stopped, understanding dawning across her face. "I
see. You'd rather kill me . . . personally. Hand to hand."

He shrugged, giving nothing away.

"What's to keep me from detonating it and blowing
both of us to Hades?"

"How about my hands around your damned neck?"
he suggested grimly. "Enough of this game. I want those
answers, and I want them now."

Her eyes searched his face for a moment. Looking for
what? he wondered. Mercy? Forgiveness? Or was she
merely deciding how much she would tell him?

"I will have it all," he warned her, trying not to think
of other ways in which he might have meant those
words.

"Where do you wish me to start?"

"Your true name will do as a beginning."

"Califa is my true name."

"And your surname?"

"Claxton."

Dax's brows shot upward. "Claxton? *Major* Claxton,
of the Coalition Tactical School on Carelia?"

Califa gaped at him, but recovered quickly. "You
know of me?"

"What pilot doesn't? Your treatise on tactical strate-
gies for the Rigel class Starfighters is required reading
even for—"

Damnation, he thought as he cut himself off. She'd
almost startled him into very incautious words there. But
of all the things he might have expected, to find that this
woman who had so beguiled him was one of the fore-
most authorities on tactical situations in the system was
the very last. Any formally trained first-year flight stu-
dent knew of her, and that she had retired to run the
academy school after an injury. Her leg, he thought, still
a little dazed. It was so barely noticeable he'd forgotten.

"How in Hades," he said slowly, "did the pride of the
Coalition wind up"—he gestured to the collar—"like
this?"

"I . . ."

Her voice trailed off. She still seemed a little startled
herself. No doubt that an outlaw skypirate had heard of

her, Dax thought wryly, regaining his equilibrium now. Or, at least as much of it as he ever seemed to have around her. Odd how finding out she was one of his hated enemies had had little effect on that.

"May I sit?" she said at last. Dax gestured at the empty chair beside the table. She sat, looked at him for a moment, then lowered her gaze.

"They ... the Coalition hold me responsible for the escape of a slave. A gold collar. The only one to ever escape. They made me a gold collar to replace him."

Hasn't been but one gold collar ever escape, and a lot of people parted company with their heads over it. And even more just plain disappeared.

The prison guard's words echoed in his mind, giving credence to her story.

"Why you?" he asked.

"The slave was at my school."

"You ... owned him?" God, how ironic, he thought when she nodded reluctantly. "Did you help him?"

"No! I had sold him before he escaped."

"How convenient," Dax said, feeling his stomach knot at this casual talk of selling a man. "Why were you blamed?"

"Because I had owned him last."

Dax blinked. "Well, that makes a Coalition kind of sense I suppose. Could you not convince them it wasn't your fault?"

"I hoped to, at first. To regain my honor, I mean. But as they began to ... train me, I realized I could not buy back what had never existed."

That, Dax thought, is learning the truth the hard way. "Why were they so convinced you were guilty?"

She raised her gaze to his face. "They thought at first I had sold him to the dealer and then taken him back to sell him again in the underground market. To deprive them of both a slave and his value made them very angry. When they realized he had truly escaped, they assumed I had helped him. They were furious."

"Pleasant thought," Dax began, then, as what she'd said registered, he asked, "What dealer?"

She lowered her eyes again.

"What dealer?" he repeated, his voice deadly soft.

"Ossuary," she whispered.

He straightened up and his raised foot hit the floor. "Damn you to Hades," he spat out. "I should have let them kill you. Better yet, I should have left you there in that prison, so they could ship you there. It would be a small piece of justice for you to wind up in that abyss. Perhaps I can still arrange it."

Her head came up then. Her eyes were moist, the pale blue brilliant now, but she didn't shirk his burning gaze again. Whatever else she was, she had courage, he thought.

"I make no excuses," she said. "I was born to this system. It's all I've ever known. Slaves were always there, not to be thought about, any more than a child's pet. From the day I entered the Coalition Academy, I was taught how to handle them, and that we had the right to own them. It was as normal to me as firing thrusters to turn."

"And now?" His voice was still low and ominous, his gaze shifting to fasten on the collar that marked her as no better than those she'd once thought she owned.

"What do you want me to say? That I've learned my lesson? That a year as a slave has taught me the pure injustice of slavery? That now I know better, that no one should be able to own someone else? Would you even believe me if I said it, all of it?"

Dax leaned back against the edge of the table wearily. "I don't know."

He rubbed his temples, feeling an ache there to match the one in his shoulder. He didn't know what disturbed him most, that she had been a Coalition officer, or a slave owner. And seller. Or perhaps what was truly bothering him was that he had responded to a woman like her, with a heat he hadn't known in . . . ever.

"Couldn't you prove you didn't help him escape?" He wasn't sure why he was asking; the answer could make little difference.

"Does it matter?" She sounded as weary as he felt. "Haven't you already made up your mind?"

"We've gone this far. You might as well tell me the rest. Wasn't there some way for you to prove your innocence?"

"I have learned," Califa said flatly, "that guilt or innocence has little to do with Coalition justice."

"Congratulations," he said sardonically. "We've all known that for years."

"Perhaps it is easy to be right when you are not in the middle, looking out."

"Can't see the zipbugs for the swarm? Perhaps. Why were you found guilty?"

She hesitated, then seemed to make her decision. "Because I wouldn't tell them who was."

Dax went very still. "What?"

"I knew who helped him. At least, I had a good idea."

"But you didn't turn them in? To help yourself?"

"I ... could not."

"Why?"

"I ... It's a very long story."

"I've got time. But those men outside will be running short on patience soon."

It was a moment before she spoke again, and he could tell by her voice it was a painful process.

"I had a ... friend, a shipmate, when I was on active duty. Younger than I, but we got along well. We flew together for a while. We used to joke about who would get her own ship first. But then I got hurt, and was retired."

"You didn't want that?"

Her head snapped up. "Of course not! Would you like never to fly again?"

He had to give her that one. "No."

"They said I couldn't. That I wasn't ... fit."

"Your leg seems to give you very little trouble," he remarked.

"Enough so that you noticed," she pointed out, her voice bitter with loss.

"Actually," he said, "the guard at the prison told me, or I might not have been sure for some time."

Distracted, she looked at him quizzically. "Why did the guard tell you that?"

Dax coughed. "I, er, asked him if you were for sale, too."

He saw her swallow visibly. "You would have bought me? To get me out of there?"

"To get us all out of there," he corrected, irritated. Why did people always seem to think he was some kind of altruist, when there wasn't an altruistic bone in his body? "I wasn't doing you any favor, just trying to avoid a fight. So what does this friend of yours have to do with it?"

"Shaylah was . . . different. She only wanted to fly. She never really saw eye to eye with the Coalition."

"Sounds like my kind of woman," he muttered, and was surprised when Califa flushed. "If that was her attitude," he said, "she must not have gotten far in the ranks."

"Oh, but she did. She had her own starfighter at twenty-four. Shaylah Graymist was the youngest graduate ever to make captain."

Something tugged at Dax, some memory he couldn't bring to the surface. He wrestled with it for a moment, then gave up and gestured to Califa to continue.

"She collected medals like coins. She once destroyed three Romerian warships that had tried to attack Zenox."

That, Dax thought, would have taken some fine flying. And fighting. But he said nothing; something else about Califa's account, something in her voice, distracted him. There was pride for her friend there, but something else as well.

"And how did you feel about her flying to all this acclaim while you were relegated to teaching?"

She drew back sharply, and Dax knew he'd hit a nerve. He knew he should force her back to the point, but he found he wanted to know this, too, and he didn't understand why.

"Jealous, hmm?" he said, his tone mild.

"No!" The protest was immediate, and a little too fierce. "Of course not. Running the school is—was an honor."

She hadn't admitted it even to herself, Dax thought. "Go on," he prompted.

She took a deep breath as if to steady herself and went on. "That . . . slave, at the school, was a man. When Shaylah came to visit, she saw him, and . . . Eos, she was always such a fool, believing in love, and bonding, and all that ridiculous nonsense civilized people gave up on aeons ago."

"Bonding?" His voice was sharp.

"Yes. Her parents taught her about it. She even said they *were* bonded, although they weren't Triotian."

"A Coalition pilot whose parents were bonded?" It hurt him just to say the words, and he couldn't hide the edge in his voice. Califa looked at him curiously. Then she shrugged.

"I told you, Shaylah was . . . different."

"Was? Is she dead?"

"I don't know."

"But you're saying . . . What?" He began to pace. "That she fell in love with this slave? And helped him escape?"

"I know it sounds crazy, but she never, ever took a slave for mating when she visited. Her fastidiousness was legend. Yet she took this one. I don't know what she told him, but when she was recalled, he went berserk. Not even"—she swallowed tightly, as if only now realizing the full import of what she was saying—"Eos, not even the pain system could control him. I was afraid they would fry his brain with too much power through the probes."

"So you sold him."

"I had no choice! He was disrupting things, and if it had gone on, Legion Command would have learned of it."

Dax restrained himself from comment on that. "How do you know this Shaylah helped the slave?"

"When she came back from her assignment, she asked for him. I had to tell her he was gone. She was furious. But when she found out he was in Ossuary, she went crazy herself. She swore she would never fly another mission, fire another round, or do anything in support of a system that believed one person could own another. Nor would she . . ."

Dax wanted to cheer the unknown Shaylah, but he merely prodded Califa to finish. "Nor would she what?"

"Have anything to do with someone who did. Meaning me. She left without another word. I doubt she thought of me as a friend at all, by then." It was a harsh whisper,

tinged with the pain of loss. Dax told himself not to feel
sorry for her, she'd brought this on herself. It was harder
to suppress the sympathy than he would have expected.

"And?" he prodded again.

"And the next day, the slave was missing from
Ossuary."

Dax gave a low whistle. "She broke him out? Of Ossuary? That took some doing."

"Yes." Despite her distress, there was pride back in
Califa's voice. "She was always resourceful."

"And I suppose you, the great tactical strategist,
taught her everything she knows."

Califa's chin came up. "Yes, I did. She was one of my
best students in the advanced classes."

Then her original words came back to him, and it hit
him why he'd been having trouble painting her with a
totally black brush.

"You didn't turn her in," he said softly.

She lowered her eyes. "No. I told myself I should,
that she had betrayed both me and the Coalition, but I
couldn't. She was my friend. I owed her my life."

"Your life?"

"I was hurt on Darvis Two. My leg. She risked herself,
disobeying a direct order, to come back for me. I would
have died."

Dax lifted himself up to sit on the edge of the table.
He felt battered, pulled in so many directions at once
he wanted to let go and see which one won. He rubbed
at his gritty eyes, wondering what in Hades he was going
to do.

How could this woman, once a Coalition officer who
had owned and sold slaves, tear him apart with a story of
a rare loyalty? She could no doubt easily buy back her
position, her honor, and probably a glorious promotion
with the knowledge she had, that of a medal-winning
Coalition pilot who had committed what the Coalition
would unquestionably see as high treason. Yet she did
not, condemning herself to a life of the same miserable
slavery for the sake of a friend.

"They escaped?" he asked suddenly, seized with the
need to know.

"I don't know. I . . ."

"What, Califa?"

She looked up again, startled, perhaps that for the first time since they'd begun this, he'd used her name. Then she looked down again, staring at her hands.

"I hope so," she whispered.

"Because if not, your sacrifice was for nothing?"

"No." Her voice was hushed. "Because, foolish as it is, deep inside I . . . I hope she was right."

"Right?"

"About love. And . . . bonding. It's a beautiful thought, even if only fools and Triotians believe in it."

Dax fought down the rage and guilt that flooded him at the mention of that once-beloved and now-dreaded name. His laughter was harsh, bitter. "I thought the Coalition had decided they were one and the same."

Califa sighed, as if she were as weary as Dax. "If so, they were wrong. Wolf was no fool. He had us all convinced he was beaten. Except Shaylah. She found something in him she'd never found in any other man. I could see it in her eyes."

Dax was so tired it took a moment for the implication of her words to register. When it did, he went rigidly still.

"Who," he said carefully, "is Wolf?"

Califa stared at him. "The slave we've been talking about all this—"

Even more carefully, he said, "What is Wolf?"

She looked at him, bewildered. "We just called him that because when he was chained at the market on Clarion, he nearly sawed his own hand off trying to get free. The Triotians have a legend about a wild creature who has been known to gnaw off its own paw to—"

"I know." He couldn't stop the edge in his voice. "Why a Triotian name?"

"Because he was."

Though he'd been half expecting it, Dax's breath caught in his throat. When he went on, he spoke each word as if the fate of the system depended on its clarity.

"This . . . slave . . . was . . . Triotian?"

Still looking bewildered, Califa nodded. "I know there aren't many, and they're so valuable, I only had him because he'd permanently damaged his hand that time—"

"Who was he?" She blinked at the snap in his tone, and at this line of questioning she obviously didn't understand the reason for.

"I don't know."

He leapt off the table and into a crouch before her, his hands coming up to grip the back of the chair on either side of her, trapping her with the muscled strength of his arms.

"What *do* you know?"

"I . . . Only that he'd been taken at the fall of Trios, so a slave for five years. And a problem every day of it."

"He survived this"—he moved one arm and flicked a finger at the yellow crystal, then imprisoned her again— "for five years?"

"He was very strong. And stubborn. Marcole—the school's enforcer—had a very difficult time with him."

"The school's enforcer," Dax muttered venomously.

"I didn't build the system," Califa burst out. "I know that's no defense, I did my part to support it, but don't you see? The Coalition was all I had! It was all I ever had."

Something in her voice pulled at him, made him want to know of the woman who had had nothing in her life but a cold, monstrous machine. But something else was far more important now.

"What did he look like, this Triotian?"

Looking like she wished she had restrained that outburst almost more than the one that had given her away, Califa spoke slowly.

"Big. Your size. Strong. Golden, with a great mane of hair, all shades of blond. Like all Triotians."

Dax felt himself tense, and tried to fight it off. She wasn't exactly right, but close enough that it made no difference. There were far too many Triotians—or had been, he amended painfully—that matched that description for his imagination to skyrocket like this.

"In truth," Califa said suddenly, "if you had Rina's color hair, or she your color skin, you would have it."

He couldn't fight off the tension this time; she had to

be deflected from that idea. "His eyes," he prompted sharply.

Califa shrugged. "Green eyes, like yours but not ... We had a patch of Triotian grass at the school, in the garden. His eyes were that color. He carried himself well. Proudly." Her mouth twisted ruefully. "Too proudly, for a slave. He was ... quite beautiful, actually."

"Do you know where he was captured?"

Her forehead creased for a moment. "I ... Near the capital city."

"Triotia? You're certain?"

"Yes. I heard a rumor that they'd found him in the hills north of the city, and that if he hadn't been slowed by a woman, they might never have caught him."

"A woman?"

Califa nodded. "Not a Triotian, apparently. She was dark haired, and very small, they said."

He felt as if he'd been hit by his own flashbow. His stomach knotted anew; he wanted to ask if the woman was dead, but he already knew, knew in his gut, and couldn't bear to hear it aloud. And then she told him anyway.

"He nearly escaped after the woman died," Califa went on. "He knew the mountains well, they said. Only General Corling's direct orders made them keep after him."

Dax froze. "He gave specific orders to capture *this* man?"

"So I heard. One of my cadets came in on the ship that transported the Triotian. He was badly beaten, she said. Corling had ordered it. After he had ordered the prisoner dragged through the streets of Triotia, so he could see the body of the old king, hanging at the temple."

Dax swore, suppressing a shudder. "Damn him."

Califa was staring at him now. "It must have been something personal," she said. "I heard that Corling personally oversaw his banding, and was the first to test the collar's systems. He's never done that, to my knowledge."

Dax fought down nausea. "So this was ... a special prisoner."

"I suppose," Califa said slowly. "I never really thought about it before, but that is quite odd. Perhaps that's why they were so zealous when he escaped. Corling was more than furious, he was . . ."

"What?" Dax prodded when she trailed off.

"It sounds absurd, but I think . . . frightened? As if this man could hurt him somehow."

And who could hurt the man who had conquered Trios? Only one possibility came to Dax's mind, and it seemed far too extraordinary to be true. Yet his gut told him it was true, had been telling him since she'd begun the incredible tale.

"Why did he not just kill him, then?"

Califa was watching him steadily now, considering. "I heard—the Coalition has an effective telerien of its own—that Corling wanted him a slave. That he was seen screaming at the prisoner that it was a fitting punishment for him."

Fitting punishment. Dax was reeling now. All the pieces were there. The timing of his capture. God help him, the woman, the small, dark-haired woman in a world of golden manes. The description of the unwilling slave. His demeanor. His stubbornness. A determination and courage strong enough to risk maiming to escape. His proud carriage and the grass-green eyes that, in a world of green eyes, belonged only to one family. The family that owned the hills north of Triotia. The family that would be the only possible threat to the man who had conquered their world.

The royal family of Trios.

Dax's muscles went slack. He sank down onto the floor, sagging back against the base of the table.

"Dare," he whispered brokenly. "Dear God, Dare."

He was alive. Prince Darian of Trios. No, Dax thought numbly, king now, after the brutal murder of his father. No wonder Corling thought enslavement such a fitting punishment. And no wonder he was so enraged—and frightened—at the escape of the only gold collar to ever slip the chains of Coalition bondage.

"Dare," he murmured again, sickness at what had happened warring against a fierce, violent joy that Dare had proven himself a Triotian and a true king with his escape. "Our king is alive."

His hand had come up, instinctively wiping at his eyes, before he even realized his eyes were damp. He heard a soft, quick intake of breath, and instinctively raised his head.

Califa was staring at him, pale blue eyes wide with shock and wonder.

"Eos, preserve us," she whispered. "You're Triotian!"

Chapter 9

"It all makes sense now," Califa said. "Why only Coalition targets. Your reaction anytime Trios or anything to do with it is even mentioned. Why you were so furious when I spoke of Trios being a source of crystal for the Coalition."

Dax didn't react. He just sat on the floor, where he had been since the moment he had realized that the slave she'd known as Wolf was, incredibly, Darian of Trios. The hereditary royal prince, she thought, stunned. She stared at Dax.

When she had surmised he was Triotian, she had seen the truth of her guess in his eyes, but he had yet to admit it. She watched him for a moment, thinking. Then, slowly, she said, "I wondered if that was the link, if hatred of the Coalition was the tie that binds your crew together."

"Many have reason to despise the Coalition." His voice was distant, vague.

"So they go along with you, getting their revenge while they help you get yours, for the destruction of your world?"

"They don't know."

Califa blinked. "Don't know? That you're Triotian?"

He let out a long, slow, breath. "It is of no import to them," he said, admitting now the truth of his origin, in a voice that said he was too weary to hide it any longer. "They all have their own reasons for hating the Coalition."

But nothing to match the bloodshed and destruction the Coalition had visited on Trios, Califa thought. No wonder he had kept it secret; the Coalition's largest rewards were offered for surviving Triotians. If they ever found out the skypirate whose head they already wanted was also Triotian . . .

"So only Rina knows?"

He spoke quickly. "Rina knows nothing."

He was lying. She knew he was. She studied him as he sat there on the floor. Somehow their status had reversed. She was now the questioner. He looked drained, and her instincts told her now was the time to get whatever answers she could; he was too strong for this state to last long.

"Even Rina," she said slowly. "When we were alone, in quarters talking, she ran like a brollet when the word Triotian came up. And when she spoke General Corling's name, she couldn't apologize to you fast enough."

"It meant nothing. There are many people who don't wish to hear the name of the Coalition's most predatory animal."

His voice was a shade too insistent, his tone just a bit too sharp, as if he were hastening to divert her.

"But that night, in your quarters, when we spoke of the dulcetpipe, and Triotian artifacts . . ."

Califa's eyes widened as the truth, obvious now, struck.

"Eos, she's Triotian, too, isn't she? I should have seen it, that hair, and her eyes . . . She said that she told you her story after you rescued her, but she had started to say something else. She started to say she told you after she realized you were also Triotian, didn't she? That's why she trusts you so completely."

Fear flickered in his eyes. Califa caught her breath; that was something she'd never expected, to see fear there. It was a measure of how much he loved the girl, she supposed, that he would be afraid for her but never for himself. As if she needed any proof after Rina's story. Were the scars still visible, she wondered, from the brutal whipping he'd endured for the simple cause of putting a child's mind at rest?

She sat back down on the chair she'd left and leaned forward, resting her elbows on her knees as she looked at him. "You must know I would never do anything to hurt Rina. I . . . have come to care a great deal for her."

"I know that. She . . . cares for you, too."

Or she did. Califa heard the unspoken words clearly. Of course, she thought. Rina would hate her, as a representative of the brute force that had left her orphaned and homeless. That she had taken no part in the Trios campaign would make little difference to either of them.

Dax closed his eyes for a moment. Califa wondered if it was a sign of trust, or merely how exhausted he was.

You know which it is, she snapped to herself. Don't be a fool by wishing it otherwise. You saw how he reacted to what you've done, to who you are. She forced back the misery that was trying to rise up and swamp her.

"Is her skin dyed somehow?" she asked.

His eyes snapped open. He hesitated, then nodded slowly. "Something Roxton knew of. From a tree that grows on Clarion. Nelcar makes it up."

"Is that what you use on your hair as well?"

His mouth twisted into a wry expression that wasn't quite a smile. "You *are* a snowfox," he said. "Tenacious." He let out a long breath. "My hair," he said, "is my own."

"But I though all Triotians—"

"—were blond. The beautiful golden ones. I know. Most people think that. But there are—" He stopped, and let out a long, slow breath. "There *were* a few of us, one of every thousand or so, who were dark. Only born to those like us." His mouth twisted again, nowhere near a smile this time. "The sons and daughters of the evening star, they called us."

"The evening star? As in . . . ?"

He lifted his gaze to her face. "Yes," he said with a shrug, confirming her guess as to the source of the name of his ship. "Foolish sentimentality, I realize."

She shook her head. "I think most people name their ships after something that is special to them. Shaylah named hers the *Sunbird,* after a mythical bird of Arellia that legend says flew to the stars."

Dax drew back a little, his brow furrowing, as if he were searching for a memory. "The *Sunbird* . . ." He sat up sharply. "Shaylah Graymist. Graymist and the *Sunbird.*" He stared at Califa. "That's her?"

"Yes, why—"

"My God, the *Sunbird* is the ship that took out Cryon's *Wanderer* last year. One starfighter with a crew of—what, twenty?—against a Diaxin class cruiser with six fighters and a crew of a hundred!"

"Last year?" Califa asked.

"Yes, right after the last circuit of the Tarx comet, out in Sector Twenty-two. It's already become legend among us, how the *Sunbird* blew up her own shuttle while the *Wanderer* had a tractor beam locked on it. It damaged Cryon's ship beyond repair. I can think of only one other pilot who would have been able to pull off such a gambit."

He shook his head in remembered wonder. "The only way they knew the name of the craft that had destroyed them was by finding the name on a piece of the shuttle debris. That Shaylah of yours must be quite a captain." One corner of his mouth lifted quizzically. "Although what a Coalition starfighter was doing way out there is still a mystery."

"Hiding," Califa whispered, shaken as it came to her.

"What?"

"They were hiding," she said again. "That was ... after she left for the last time."

Dax went still. "You mean after she broke Dare out of Ossuary? They were together, then?"

She nodded. "And alone. Her crew was still on leave."

"They fought off that heavy cruiser ... alone?"

"I don't know how. On a Rigel starfighter, the con and the weapons station must both be manned in a fight," she said. "Shaylah could not have done both."

"Then Dare was flying."

Califa blinked. "Your prince is a pilot?"

Dax's voice went soft with regret, and his eyes dark with a pain that bordered on anguish. "The best I've ever seen, though I never told him so."

"He's that one pilot you mentioned?" Califa asked, her tone gentle in the face of his sorrow.

"Yes." He shook his head as if that would rid him of the pain. Then a smile, both sad and joyous, curved his lips. "I should have guessed sooner. That stunt with the shuttle had all the earmarks of one of Dare's."

"They must have ... survived that fight, then?" She couldn't control the sound of trembling in her voice. She remembered her silent prayer that Shaylah be all right; somehow, this knowledge had become more important to her than almost anything. Except the fact that Dax hated her.

"Yes, they did." His voice was jubilant, yet gentle, as if he saw and understood her compelling need to know. "Cryon saw the fighter take off like a bat out of Hades, while they sat there drifting, until a freighter came along and towed them in. For the price of their entire cargo, of course."

"Shaylah is the best pilot I've ever known," Califa said honestly. Then she looked at him levelly. "But I'm not sure even she—or your prince—would try to dock a shuttle at full throttle aboard a moving ship making a right-angle pass."

For a split second he looked pleased at the compliment. But the expression was gone so quickly she couldn't be sure.

"You learned to fly on Trios?" she asked.

He shrugged. "There is—was—a small school."

She knew that. That this was why he'd heard of her—and why he'd known of her treatise on tactics—seemed obvious. She also knew it had the finest school in the system, turning out pilots of amazing capability. Some said it was inborn in Triotians, that knack for flying. She didn't know about that. But now she did know something else.

"You can't expect to gain without risk," she quoted.

"So they taught us in flight school."

"So they teach everyone in flight school. Quark's axiom."

How many times had she heard it, in the academy, and later from superior officers? How many times had she said it herself, lecturing classes of cadets who looked at her with awe? But to hear it from this man, this rakish, reckless corsair of the far reaches? At the time, it had seemed the final seal to the irony that had become her existence.

But he wasn't that corsair, that skypirate. He was a Triotian, native of a world her world had destroyed. She tried to keep the trembling from spreading to her hands as she readied herself to ask him the question she thought she already knew the answer to. She doubted he would answer, but she couldn't stop herself from asking.

"You knew ... know Prince Dare? Personally, I mean?" It still rattled her, to know the man she'd used as a slave had been the son of the royal house of Trios. If he still lived, he was a king—if there was anything left to be king of.

For a long moment Dax had that distant, unfocused look of one lost in memories. "Yes," he said at last, softly. "We grew up together. Went to school together."

"You grew up with a prince?"

Dax looked at her reproachfully. "Royalty on Trios does not mean what it has on other worlds. There is no divine right to rule presumed. The royal family rules by consent of the people, and that consent can be withdrawn by a vote at anytime the majority of the people feel the family has not upheld their vows of service."

"And Darian's family ... ?"

"Has held the throne for ten generations, without so much as talk of change. And rightfully so."

She hesitated, but then asked anyway, thinking she had to know just how much he hated her.

"He was your friend?"

Dax's voice went low, harsh. "He was my *best* friend."

Califa's heart sank. There was no hope for her. He couldn't help but despise her. He would give his men their way, condemning her to whatever long, painful death they decreed a fitting punishment of a detested Coalition officer.

Fine. She would at least face it like an officer. The kind she'd wanted to be, the kind she had once thought she was. Perhaps she even had been; it was what she'd represented had been evil and worm-eaten beneath the glorious surface. She drew herself up, knowing that once she explained all to him, any chance she had for his forgiveness would be lost.

"I know that you will not believe this," she said. "But I am not the woman I was when ... your friend was in my power. And I did not know who he was, then. I used him, but even more viciously, I let others use him, in a way I have come to see no person should ever be used.

I regret that it took personal experience for me to learn that."

With movement so swift Dax couldn't rise quickly enough to stop her, Califa swept the controller off of the shelf and into her hand. She held it tightly for a moment, staring at it, as Dax slowly straightened and turned to face her.

"So what will it be, Major Claxton?" She winced at his use of her former rank. "Will you push that button and blow us both to Antares?"

She didn't look at him, just continued to stare at the small power unit in her hand.

"Do you know," she said, her voice barely a whisper, "what the most appalling part of a collared slave's torture is? It is not knowing that another claims to own you. It is not that they control you with pain. It is not even the knowledge that with the push of a button they can annihilate you at will, and you would never even see their face."

He said nothing, but she knew he was listening. And she guessed he was watching, warily, to see what she would do.

"I look at this device now and shudder. Yet I used it, to force a slave's will to my own. Or gave it to others, whose desires were often more depraved, more evil than anything I could imagine. To know that of myself, that I was capable ... it makes me wish to use it for my own destruction."

She sensed rather than saw Dax tense, could almost feel his muscles going taut, ready.

"But that would be too kind. Too lenient by far."

She looked at him then, not allowing herself to care that he would see the self-loathing in her eyes.

"Perhaps I can give you that little piece of justice you wanted. It is not enough to atone, there will never be enough, but it is all I have."

She cradled the controller on her palm. She looked at it for a long, silent moment, then held it out to Dax.

He stared at her. "You're ... giving it back?"

"It is what slaves must do. Hand the instrument of their torture to the one who will administer that torture."

She heard him let out a low, harsh breath. He hesitated, then reached out with one hand, all the time watching her as if he expected some trick. His fingers closed around the controller, in the process brushing across her palm. She tried to hide the shiver that rippled through her, and wondered if this was all part of some godly plan of retribution, that she should feel this way about a man who could do no less than loathe her.

Dax stared at the power unit he now held. Then he lifted his gaze to her face. "And this was what you meant by the most appalling thing?"

"To be forced to give your tormentor the means he will use to degrade, dishonor, and ultimately destroy you? Yes."

"You've forgotten one thing," Dax said, in tones laced with distaste as he stared at the device. "I have no idea how this works, therefore I have no power at all over you."

Oh, but you do, Califa thought. And you have no need of control units to exercise it.

"I have not forgotten," was what she said. "If you will listen, please?"

Dax's gaze shot back to her face. She had sounded as she must when lecturing a class, as if the material to be covered was abstract, safely contained on a history disk, or in the models she sometimes used in her tactical demonstrations. She had deliberately tried for that tone, knowing she would need the well-practiced, cool impartiality to get through this.

"You already know what the red system is for, and how it works. The yellow system works similarly. You just change the indicator"—she gestured at the button on the end of the controller, just below the yellow light—"there, set the level of pain with the same registers as the red system, and push the crystal."

"What in Hades—"

"The blue system is more complicated. It is the brain wave synchronizer."

"I don't care what—"

"Listen, please," she repeated, still in that same flat, emotionless tone. "The blue system produces a kind of hypnosis in the slave, an adjusting of brain activity that

is directed entirely by the holder of the control unit programmed for that slave."

She knew she sounded odd, talking as if the slave in
question were someone other than herself, but it was the
only way she could get through this without breaking
down.

"The holder of the unit literally controls the slave's
mind, including what the slave says, does . . . or thinks."

Dax didn't protest this time, he merely stared at her
in undiluted, unmasked shock. "Are you saying this . . .
thing is programmed to the specific brain waves of the
slave it was designed for, and whoever has it could alter
those waves in any way they wished?"

"Very good," Califa said, as if complimenting a stu-
dent on a correct answer.

"And they call us pirates," Dax muttered.

Califa went on as if he hadn't spoken. "You merely
set the system for whatever level of hypnosis is necessary, depending on how deeply against the slave's own
wishes your commands will be. The blue crystal will
blink. When it comes on steadily, you relay your commands to the slave, and your commands become their
thoughts. Synchronized."

Dax glanced at the controller, then back to her face.
"You could not only make a slave *do* anything you
wanted but actually think it, as well?"

"In certain areas, mating in particular, willing partici-
pation is more . . . desirable than passive cooperation.
With the blue system, your slave will not only do and
say what you wish, but will think it is their own desire.
Afterward, if you wish, for your own privacy, you can
erase all memory of your encounter from the slave's
mind."

"My God," Dax whispered, clearly shaken.

She could see what he was thinking. It was one thing
to order a slave to clean your boots or serve your meals,
quite another to use a machine to turn that slave into
your dream lover for the perfect mating, subjecting them
to whatever was your pleasure and making them think
they wanted it that way.

His gaze fell to the collar around her neck. Then it

shot back up to her face. She knew the question that was coming before he ever voiced it.

"Have you . . . ?"

"It is the lot of all Coalition slaves."

"Damn them to Hades eternally," he ground out savagely. "No wonder you were dismayed when I said I would put this in my quarters. You must have thought I would use it on you."

For a moment, she slipped out of her professorial detachment. "I did . . . wonder. I am, after all, your prisoner."

"I don't make a habit of raping women, and this would be no less," he snapped.

"Then you see why I was so desperate to get it back?"

"Yes." She saw him suppress a shiver as he bit out the words. "Anyone would be, who had been forced to . . . to whore against their will, been forced to believe they had wanted—"

He broke off, and Califa shivered in turn as she realized he had made the final, utterly damning connection.

"Dare?" he asked hoarsely, his fingers curling around the controller until his knuckles were white. "Dear God, you used this system on Dare?"

"*I* did not." She knew it would save her from little of his fury. "But I was ever . . . generous with my slaves."

"Others? Others did? You allowed it? He was subjected to . . . such degradation? Made to . . . act the whore, at the command of whoever you gave this to?"

She didn't answer; there was nothing to say. For a moment she thought he might strike her, but at the last second he whirled away from her.

"God, how did he survive it?" Dax walked over to the small viewport over his bunk, and stared out. "With all good reason, Dare is one of the proudest men I've ever known."

"As I have learned, pride is one of the things the Coalition takes greatest joy in destroying." When he looked back over his shoulder at her, she flicked the collar with her forefinger. "They obviously think nothing of enslaving one of their one."

Dax laughed, a loud, grim sound that held nothing of humor and everything of a harsh, biting hatred. "One of their own? They enslaved a *king*! They murdered the rightful leader of a neutral world that never raised a hand against any other people, and then enslaved his son."

He spun on his heel then, giving her a look that chilled her very blood. He held up the controller, and for an instant Califa fully expected him to activate it before her eyes, and blow her to pieces.

"Why did you give this to me? Why did you explain it, that perverse hypnosis system?"

She swallowed tightly, wondering where all her fine Coalition courage had gone, and why it always seemed to desert her when she had to face this man.

"It was the only way I could try to show you ... to prove I'm ... not that woman anymore."

He gave a short bark of disbelieving laughter. "You mean you've found you don't like being on the receiving end of what you've been dispensing, and now claim a metamorphosis, hoping for mercy."

She nearly stepped back from the rising wall of his hatred. She wondered how much of his fury could be credited to that night in his quarters, when he had yielded to a need she'd never expected him to have and kissed her. Now that he knew the truth, that memory must disgust him.

"I should throw you to the men, as they wished. Or perhaps use this wonderful hypnotic device. Shall you dance naked for my crew, Major? Or simply service them all?"

She felt herself go ashen; the sudden chill of her face was an odd sensation. With her pale Arellian skin, she must look unto death now. And perhaps, she thought as she forced herself not to cringe from Dax's rage, she wasn't far wrong.

"Or maybe I'll keep you to myself, chained here, to my bed," he spat out. "Oh, I forgot, I won't need chains, will I? You'll stay here of your own free will, and cast loving glances at me as I beat the Coalition conceit out of you before I take you. Shall that be it, *Major*?"

She drew herself up then. If this was the payment demanded of her, then so be it. And oddly, that image rose in her mind again, of the man she'd known as Wolf, shaky and weak after a night of Marcole's discipline, yet refusing to give in. Could she do any less than the man— Eos, than the king—she had once thought she owned?

She lifted her chin, and held Dax's furious gaze. "If that is what you wish," she said quietly.

He swore, low and fierce. "No, thank you. It would require me to touch you, and right now I don't think I could endure that." His expression changed to one of rank distaste. "How could I have ever thought—"

He broke his words off, but the memory of that instant when his fingers had brushed her palm, and those quiet moments when he had stood at the top of the observation deck stairs, simply watching her, made her think she knew what he had been going to say. The skypirate was wondering how he could ever have been attracted to the woman who had helped to degrade and debase his best friend. The woman who had let others do the same.

The woman who, for brief, foolish time, had thought she owned a man who was a king.

Dax lay in his bunk, staring at the slight glow coming in through the viewport above his head. Distantly, he could hear the sounds that told him shipboard activities were proceeding as usual. He didn't know how long he'd been in here, how long it had been since he'd told Roxton to get the esteemed Major Claxton out of his sight— but not to kill her just yet. And to keep quiet about what had happened.

Roxton had grumbled a bit, but his thirst for immediate blood seemed to have waned, and Dax was reasonably certain Nelcar could keep him from slitting her throat the moment they were out of sight.

What he wasn't certain of was why he gave a damn whether Roxton did or not. He told himself it was because, as a former Coalition officer, she might have knowledge that would be useful to them. He told himself that she had some worth of her own, as a salable commodity, trying to ignore the fact that that thought, no matter who the person was, made him sick. He told himself that she could be a bargaining token, should they have a run of bad luck and wind up in the clutches of the Coalition.

He told himself everything except the one truth he was avoiding; he wanted to know how the woman he'd admired for her spirit, who had tugged at him in ways he'd never known when she'd seemed defeated, the beautiful woman who had roused in him sensations he'd thought long dead, whose kiss had stirred him to a fire he'd never felt, could be the kind of woman to do the things she'd admitted to. By comparison, the fact that she'd been a Coalition officer paled.

What do you want me to say? That I've learned my lesson? That a year as a slave has taught me the pure injustice of slavery? That now I know better, that no one should be able to own someone else?

Her words rang in his ears. Could it be true? Was she truly not that woman anymore, the woman who could callously own another—dear God, Dare—and abuse him in ways Dax couldn't bear thinking about?

You are a damned, stupid fool, he thought, nearly snapping it aloud. You're just looking for an excuse for the fact that you went to afterburners the minute you laid eyes on her after Rina had cleaned her up. You want her not to be what she is because you can't stand the thought that you were attracted to—no, admit it, plain lusting after—such a woman.

So take her. She's a slave, and now you own her.

The thought floated up out of nowhere, created, no doubt, by the string of restless nights he'd spent trying to drive her out of his dreams. The thought also repulsed him; no Triotian of blood would ever accept the idea of owning someone. Even a Triotian as tarnished as he was.

He stifled a desolate laugh. Tarnished wasn't the word for it. Once the name of Silverbrake had been an illustrious one on Trios. Now, all who had carried it with pride were dead, leaving only he, who didn't carry it at all. He didn't deserve to. This ravening, growing need for Califa proved it.

He groaned inwardly. How in Hades had he gotten so tangled up, that his nightmares of the women he'd loved dying in agony had been traded for erotic fantasies featuring a woman who had been part of the instrument of their deaths?

He lifted one hand, to look at the controller. He'd barely been aware he still held it. He could use it, he thought. Use it, and make every one of those heated, erotic dreams a reality. He could begin with kisses that would make that one in his quarters seem tame, and then go on to every kind of sensual pursuit he'd ever heard of. His snowfox would become his dream lover, acceding to his every wish. Even now, after all she'd told him, his pulse began to speed and his body began to heat at the thought.

Dear God, why had she given this evil thing to him, and why in Hades had she told him how it worked? If what she said was true, he could have her in any way it was possible for a man to have a woman, and she would seem to revel in it. If what she said was true, she was his to use at the touch of a button. If what she said was true . . .

He would take no pleasure in any of it. If he couldn't take pleasure with a willing woman, he doubted very much that he could with one he knew was forced to seem willing, no matter how she fired his blood. And even though forcing her to submit in the way she had once allowed Dare to be forced seemed a more than appropriate revenge, he questioned his ability to cold-bloodedly carry out that revenge. Perhaps it marked him as weak, but he didn't think he could take his anger out on a woman in that way; rape was a subject that hit too close to home, too close to his nightmares.

Maybe he should just turn her over to the crew. They would have no such qualms, he imagined, except for Qantar, still frozen by the brutal murder of his woman, and perhaps Roxton, who had always declared himself as having better taste than to indulge in Coalition women. Now that, indeed, would be fitting punishment for what she'd done to Dare.

Dare.

God, he was alive. Or had been less than a year ago. The boy he'd grown up with, the youth he'd gone to school and trained with, the man he'd still called friend, even when the weight of royalty came between them.

The man who no doubt hated him now, as must any other Triotians who had perhaps been fortunate—or unfortunate—enough to survive the Coalition assault. At least none of his family were alive to hate him, to call him coward, to tell the tale of his desertion. He would never have to face them.

But he was going to have to face Rina. To tell her what she had heard was true. It would deeply wound the girl, he knew. She had come to care for the Arellian, to enjoy having a female to talk to, to make a confidant, something that had been sadly lacking in her life. It had been the knowledge that this was the one thing he had never been able to provide for Rina that had kept Dax from cautioning her against becoming too close to the unknown woman.

And now it was too late. Far too—

"Dax!"

The comlink came alive with Roxton's voice, his tone urgent. Dax rolled out of his bunk, dropping the controller unheeded. He crossed the room in two swift strides and punched the button below the speaker.

"Here. What is it?"

"You'd better get up to the bridge, Cap'n. Seems we've been picked up by a Coalition warship. We're under attack."

Chapter 10

"Is it true?"

Rina's words echoed Dax's, and Califa felt the same sickness in the pit of her stomach. The girl had somehow found her, and managed to open the small storage room they'd locked her in. She stood in the shaft of light cast from the companionway into the dark room.

And now, Califa knew, she was waiting for the miracle the young always seemed to expect, the miracle that would tell her this was all a mistake, that the woman she had come to like and trust, the woman she had confided in, was not her mortal enemy.

"All I can say, Rina," Califa said quietly, "is that I am the same person I was yesterday. The same person I was this morning. I felt we had become friends. How I feel about you hasn't changed." Nor, pitifully, has the way I feel about Dax, she added silently to herself.

"Then it is true?" Rina demanded.

"I am a Coalition slave," Califa said. "That is now the sum of my life. But I was—once—a Coalition officer."

The girl drew back, staring at Califa with those eyes so like Dax's, even down to the pain and anger that glittered now in the green depths. She could see that the girl was torn between running away and shouting her rage. At last, the need to vent her fury won.

"You lied to me!"

"I never lied to you."

"But you never told me—"

"I told no one, Rina. I didn't dare, in fear for my life. Everyone aboard the *Evening Star* made their feelings about the Coalition clear from the moment I came aboard."

"Because we trusted that a Coalition slave would feel the same as we do!"

"What makes you think that I don't?"

The girl considered that. Califa felt a trace of hope; at least she was listening. "But you were an officer—"

"I can't change my past, Rina, no more than you can, or Dax. But *I* have changed. I swear that to you, upon the graves of your parents."

Rina paled at the uncompromising words.

"Yes, I know what that means to you. That is why I chose that oath, to prove to you the truth of my words."

"But you're one of them." The girl's voice was laced with a bitterness far beyond her years.

"It is true," Califa answered slowly, searching for any words that would make this girl she had, so unexpectedly, come to care for, understand, "that I once belonged to the forces that made you an orphan, that took away your world. But those same forces have done the same to me, Rina. They've taken from me all I've ever known, they've made me wish for death as I suspect you must have when you realized you were all alone."

Rina's quick, shocked glance told Califa her guess had been accurate. "I . . . wanted to go with them."

She had the girl's attention now, and Califa pressed her advantage, without ever stopping to think why it had become so important to her to have at least one of the Triotians on board this ship not hate her.

"Do you remember yourself, Rina, before your parents' deaths? What you were like at twelve?" Slowly, Rina nodded. "What did you like to do? To play? Did you have a best friend, or a pet?"

"I was a silly little girl," Rina said sharply. "I thought everyone kind, my world beautiful, and that my parents would be with me forever."

"And now?"

"I know there is more ugliness than good everywhere."

"So do I," Califa said with heartfelt sincerity. "And I was as foolish as you to believe otherwise."

Something in her tone reached the girl before her. When Rina looked at her now, Califa could see a longing to believe that was poignant on her young face.

"So," Califa said, a little urgently, "you are saying you

are not the same person now that you were then? Before your parents were killed?"

Lowering her eyes, Rina shook her head, her distress visible.

"Neither am I the same person I was a year ago."

Had she gotten through to her? Could this woman-child do what Dax could not; believe that the woman Califa had been was as dead as this Rina's parents?

Rina lifted her gaze, not to meet Califa's eyes, but to linger on the golden collar.

"Why did they do that to you?"

Eos, help me, Califa thought, if I tell her it was because I once owned her king, she will never forgive me. Just as Dax never will. She didn't think she could bear the loss of them both. Then she jeered at herself silently; *you never had Dax to lose.*

Still, she chose her words carefully.

"They blamed me for the escape of a slave."

"So they made you one?"

Califa nodded.

"Was the escape your doing?"

"No."

She wavered, wondering if going on would do any good. It hadn't with Dax, but he had been so very angry, so horrified at the fate of his dearest friend ... For an instant she felt a pang of self-pity, an emotion she had denied herself since the age of nine; there had been no one to care when *she* had been cast into slavery. And in that moment of weakness, the words slipped out.

"But I did not help them to catch him, when I could have."

Rina considered this for a moment, her eyes fastened on Califa with that look that seemed incongruously ancient.

"Would it have saved you?" the girl asked at last.

"Perhaps not my position." She fingered the collar. "But it would have saved me this."

"Then why didn't you help them?"

Hadn't she asked herself that question a thousand times, especially in the nights after she'd recovered consciousness after the implantation of the collar's probes? Hadn't she cursed herself for her stupidity, the Coalition for its injustice, and Shaylah Graymist for her betrayal? Yet in the end, she had done nothing. She had been offered her freedom, the return of her honor and position, even a reward, for one simple thing: the name of her one true friend.

"I ... To help them, I would have had to betray a friend."

Rina's eyes widened. Her gaze went to the collar, then back to Califa's face. "It must have been a very dear friend."

Califa's mouth twisted wryly. "My only friend."

Shaylah had had many, Califa knew. She drew people to her. While she herself ... discouraged them. Only Shaylah had persisted, had insisted on calling her friend until Califa had let down her protective walls enough to let her in.

Irony again, Califa thought. How many times had she baited Shaylah with jokes about her belief in love and bonding in the face of the legislated reality of uninvolved mating that was the doctrine of the Coalition? How often had she indulged herself in that casual pleasuring, secure in her knowledge that since she never cared beyond the moment, she could never be hurt? And now here she was, shaking at the anger of one man, and devastated at the thought that he hated her beyond redemption.

She forced her mind to abandon that futile subject, and looked again at Rina. "Tell me, then, Rina. You were my friend yesterday. Do you hate me today?"

"I ... I don't know. I wish—"

The alarm that blasted down the *Evening Star*'s passageways was near-earsplitting. Rina leapt to her feet.

"An attack!"

Almost simultaneously with the words the ship jerked fiercely. The lights flickered, then came back on steadily. The sound of running footsteps echoed back to them. Rina ran to the door, shouted at someone passing. An answer came, short and sharp, and Rina voiced a curse that would have done the crude Hurcon proud.

"I'm not sitting here waiting it out," Rina snapped. Another blast shook the ship; again the lights faded and returned. Rina reached out to the door to the small room.

"Rina, please, no!"

The girl looked back at her.

"Don't lock me in here. If there's more damage, or a fire—"

"But Dax said—"

"I know. He's very angry with me. But I can do you no damage, not without risking myself. And I cannot reach the bridge, or the weapons or fighter stations." Rina looked doubtful. "I can't explain now, there's no time. But the collar limits me."

Still Rina hesitated. "I don't know."

"Do you really wish me to die before you make up your own mind whether I deserve to? Even Dax"—she barely managed his name—"is waiting to decide that."

Again the ship shuddered, and this time the lights flickered and went out.

"We'll all die if this keeps up," Rina said grimly, "so I guess it doesn't matter." Then she was gone, racing up the companionway toward the bridge.

Califa stood for a moment, unable to quite believe the girl had left her unconfined. Then she dashed out into the passage.

She could hear the distant shouts, and the firing of weapons. It had been a long time since she'd been in battle, yet the adrenaline rush was familiar and exhilarating. But she had no part in this battle, and if she tried to change that, she would no doubt be executed on the spot. At Dax's order. And, she grudgingly admitted, were she a captain faced with the same set of circumstances, she would do the same.

But at least she wouldn't die cowering in some dark, small closet of a room. If she were to die, she wanted to see her enemy. And that was one thing she *could* do.

She saw no one as she ran to the narrow stairway she had last seen as they had dragged her down them and to Dax's quarters. The *Evening Star* jerked again, staggering her, but the shields held. She knew the shields of a ship of this class would normally have given way on that third hit; obviously Dax had modified well.

She was halfway up the steps when they took another

hit. Sparks spewed across the passageway below her. She froze as two men, Larcos and another she'd never met, hurried past, never even looking up to notice her.

"—crazy! That's a Coalition cruiser out there!" the one unknown to her was yelling.

"Of course it's crazy, but try telling Dax that! He's damned well decided the fighter can help, and he's the only one who can fly it."

"He'll be fried before he gets off a shot—"

They had disappeared around a corner, headed, Califa realized from the layout of the ship—and the end of the collar's range—for the launching bay she had heard held two small fighters. She didn't know what kind, the crew was at least that cautious around her, but if they were the *Y*-class ships, long discarded by the Coalition, that other skypirates had been known to have, they were in trouble. The fighters were solid, and fast, but the price was maneuverability; their lack of agility was what had made the Coalition abandon them. And what had consequently made them available on the underground market to any skypirate with the funds.

And if Dax was going out after a Coalition cruiser alone in a *Y*-class fighter, he was worse than crazy. He was suicidal.

She scrambled up the last of the stairs and onto the observation deck. As usual it was not lit from the inside, to avoid becoming a bright and irresistible target.

She could see nothing. She checked again in all directions, but saw nothing but the reaches of space, a scattering of stars, and the distant sparkle of Boreas, a bit brighter than the stars, as if the ice there were collecting what light there was and sending it on.

Her mouth twisted wryly at the thought; she knew quite well it was only the planet's relative nearness that made it seem brighter than the more distant others. She'd never been given to such frivolous thinking, that had been Shaylah's domain. Her mouth quirked as she wondered if that, too, along with the gift of flight, was a trait of Triotian males: the subverting of logical thought into silly fancifulness.

The Coalition ship must be out of the line of sight of

the observation deck, she thought. If she just waited, at some point the angle would be right and—

No sooner had she thought it than there it was, just coming into view on the port side. They'd called it right; it was a Coalition cruiser, a lightweight warship, fully armed and approaching in an attack stance.

But it would do them no good. Dax would never surrender. He would fight to the death, because he knew, as she did, what would happen to these men, already so devastated by the Coalition, if they were captured. And Rina. She didn't want to think what would happen to the girl in the hands of a victorious Coalition crew. But she knew, and she knew that Dax knew.

As she pictured what was happening aboard the Coalition vessel, something occurred to her. It was standard on some smaller Coalition ships, Shaylah's *Sunbird* had been so equipped ... She turned and ran to the comlink panel on the bulkhead beside the steps. She tapped various parts of the panel until it lit up. She studied the markings for a moment. There were enough similarities to systems she knew that it took her only moments to find what she wanted. She raised the volume until she was sure she had the bridge communications tuned in, then ran back to her position below the curve of clear plaxan.

The cruiser might be larger, and more heavily armed—although she didn't know what armament the *Evening Star* carried—but next to the quick, agile brigantine, it would be a Daxelian slug. Even as she thought it, she heard Roxton's voice crackle over the comlink.

"So they think they can take us with a few cannon rounds, do they?"

Laughter, sharp and tinged with an adrenaline pitch Califa recognized all too well, came over the comlink. Dax. Her heart seemed to quiver for an instant in her chest, forgetting its natural function.

"Then they can join those who have tried before."

She heard a burst of noise, a cheer for Dax's bravado. But from what she knew of his reputation, it wasn't bravado at all, it was fact. She found herself smiling without knowing quite why.

"Give me fifteen seconds on my mark, Rox."

"Right, Cap'n."

A pause, then, "... two ... one ... mark!"

"Copy," came Roxton's voice.

Califa held her breath, waiting, wondering, watching. No matter that Dax had clearly turned the *Evening Star* into a very special ship that performed beyond her original design, there was no way anyone could turn a cast-off Coalition *Y* fighter into anything that could go up against—

"Eos," she breathed as something caught her eye to starboard, "what in Hades is that?"

She'd never seen a ship like it. The only two things she was sure of were that it could only be, at that size, a fighter of some kind. And that Dax was flying it. She would have known even had she not heard the two men talking; the very look of the craft would have told her it was his.

It was a long, slim delta shape of sharp, angular planes, with a power source at the tail that glowed oddly blue against the blackness of space. It had no markings, was just a pure, unrelieved black that would make it difficult to track by eye alone; only the fact that it had come into her line of vision silhouetted by the distant glow of Boreas made her sure she had seen it at all.

And it was moving faster than anything she'd ever seen.

The dark fighter rolled up and over the top of the *Evening Star*. At the same instant, the *Evening Star* herself fired; long-range thermal cannon, it appeared. The fiery nimbus of disruptive energy hit near the bow of the Coalition ship, then spread and leapt along the shields in a glowing display. Another round followed, then another, lighting up the cruiser's shape against the darkness.

"Three hits, Cap'n."

"Copy, Rox."

It would only weaken the shields, not take them down, Califa knew, unless they expended many more rounds. If they had nothing larger, they were in trouble, she thought; the cruiser normally carried a dozen of the same cannon, and a full complement of photon guns.

But if they did have something bigger, then Roxton was wise to hold back.

And then, belatedly, she realized that that had not been the sole purpose of the succession of blasts. They had also been a diversion, to distract the crew of the Coalition ship from the appearance of the fighter. And it had apparently worked; the cruiser hadn't changed position, but Califa could see the dark, wedge-shape closing fast.

"They've spotted you," Roxton warned Dax.

"Too late," Dax said.

She could almost see him grinning. Before his words had faded away, she saw a burst of light from beneath the dark fighter. It faded, but her trained eyes spotted the thin glow that arced toward the Coalition ship, headed straight for the weakened portion of the shields.

A torpedo. He had a photon gun aboard that lethal-looking craft. She saw it hit, explode, and the cruiser shuddered. When the debris cloud cleared, she saw that the cruiser had been damaged, just how severely she couldn't tell.

Without realizing it she tensed, leaning forward as she stared out at the battle scene. She had forgotten the reality of it. She had taught tactics for so long, had used nothing but models or computer-generated simulations for so long, that she had lost the edge, had forgotten the tension, the adrenaline rush ... That she felt it again now, in a ship going up against her old colleagues, seemed only another example of the travesty her life had become.

She could almost see them aboard the Coalition ship, shifting tactics, adjusting to a second flank. When the cruiser altered course, she instinctively nodded at the accuracy of her guess. They were playing this by the book—most of which she had written. They would maneuver until they were in position to—

Her breath caught in her throat. If the Coalition captain indeed took a page out of her own book ...

It wasn't a conscious decision, she just ran to the comlink and spoke into it without thinking.

"Roxton! They'll maneuver until you're both ahead

and then lay down an all-direction field of fire with everything they've got. Get out of here!"

"Who in Hades—"

"She's right, Rox!" Dax's voice came sharply over the speaker. "Full speed, head on! Full port thrusters at the last second! *Now,* Rox!"

Califa realized instantly what he was doing, and she couldn't stop the flood of pride that swept her. Without question Roxton followed Dax's orders; Califa felt the *Evening Star* accelerate powerfully. The Coalition ship loomed larger through the bubble.

Califa nearly laughed aloud. It was a stunt worthy of the wiliest of opponents, and with any luck it would take the habit-bound, regulation-choked Coalition vessel by surprise. To see their intended victim suddenly bearing down on them on a collision course at full throttle would no doubt freeze them into shock. Not for long, Coalition crews were too well trained, but those few moments gained could be the difference between escape and destruction by the rain of firepower about to be unleashed on them. All Dax would have to do was get clear himself—

He wasn't going to do it.

She saw the delta-shaped shadow, arrowing down at the cruiser. Lightning bright bolts from a thermal cannon erupted in a stream as constant as a laser tracer from the belly of the fighter; lighting the cruiser's weakened shields until the ship itself seemed on fire.

He was making sure the *Evening Star* escaped. He was making sure the crew of the cruiser had too damned much to think about to lay down that lethal field of fire for another precious few moments. And he was damned close to making sure he got killed in the effort.

She watched the fighter plunge, still firing, until it seemed that all three ships would collide, leaving nothing to mark their destruction but a mass of debris that would drift for aeons.

"Pull up, Dax," she whispered urgently. "Pull up!"

Only when the *Evening Star* veered sharply right did she realize she hadn't once spared a thought for her own destruction. The seeming suicide of the man in that extraordinary craft had consumed her to the point of

forgetting her own ship was on a deadly course. But
Roxton had followed Dax's orders to the letter. And
Dax's ruse had worked; the Coalition ship had never
gotten off another shot at them.

But had his life been the price? Was that why he had
insisted on taking a fighter out alone? Had he truly intended to commit suicide, to sacrifice himself in the
hopes his ship and his crew could escape?

She couldn't see, the Coalition vessel was far out of
her field of vision now. She wanted to ask, but she
doubted Roxton would answer her, even now. Then she
realized she would probably know all too soon of Dax's
death; the comlink was still on.

Even as she thought it, Roxton's voice blasted the
sudden stillness.

"Dax, we've lost sight of you. Come in!"

Silence. Califa sank down into a chair; she had no
choice, her knees were suddenly too wobbly to hold her.

"Dax, come in!" Roxton's voice had risen, taking on
a note of anxiety. And the silence continued. Califa shivered violently.

"Dax!" The anxiety had become desperation. Califa
wrapped her arms around herself, as if that could stop
the hollow ache inside.

And the silence settled down over her like the deadly
cold of space.

Chapter 11

She had seen people die before. Many of them. In her Coalition career she had been responsible for more deaths than she cared to think about now. She had seen shipmates die, sometimes before her eyes, sometimes in the seemingly distant explosion of a dying vessel. She had even faced death herself, more than once.

So, she told herself sternly, there was no excuse for this silly shaking. Dax was dead. He'd died heroically, if foolishly. His sacrifice had enabled his ship and crew to escape, to live. So get on with it. Don't waste the gift.

She heard the muted sound of voices, very subdued now, as the crew went about the business of putting distance between the *Evening Star* and the Coalition vessel. And the scene of Dax's death.

She tightened her arms around herself, hoping to stop the tremors that gripped her. Get on with it, she repeated silently. Even though Dax's sacrifice had not been intended to keep her, personally, alive, it had. The fact that in saving his ship from a Coalition attack, he had also saved a former Coalition officer, he would no doubt have found reason for cynical amusement.

And his mouth would have curved into that wry, mocking smile he so often turned on her.

She bit her lower lip, trying to stop the annoying quiver that had overtaken it. But then all she could think of was the feel of his mouth, the way his tongue had caressed her lip where her teeth were now digging in. The way that caress had sent ripples of heat through her, the way her body had surged in response with a swiftness she'd never known was possible. The way his low groan had made her think, just for an instant, that he might be as out of control as she was.

She shivered again. The only times she had ever felt anything even remotely like that were under the power of the controller. Yet she was certain he hadn't been using it, had never used it; his shock at the blue system and its purpose had been genuine. That was something for which she supposed she should have been grateful; had she been in the hands of someone who knew the system, she would no doubt have been his controlled whore for days now.

But not Dax. Perhaps she was a fool, but she couldn't convince herself that, even had he known what power he held over her when he held the controller, he wouldn't have used it. Not that way.

But how could these sensations, so powerful and frightening, so much more than simple desire for a physical mating, be real, when she had never, ever felt them before? Had she so changed? Or had they done something to her, along with the collar, something to make her susceptible to such feelings?

Or was it, simply, Dax?

The thought sent another shiver through her. A year ago, she would have laughed at the absurdity of that idea. Laughed at the idea that any one person could rouse such feelings in another. Just as she had, smug in her superior knowledge, laughed at Shaylah's belief in bonding.

The whole idea of one man, one woman, bonded for life was nothing more than a foolish myth from a destroyed world. The few couples she knew of who had been together for years, Shaylah's parents for one, she wrote off merely as settling for the familiar as one grew older.

She understood lust. She had seen it around her every day, had, as everyone in her world did, indulged in it on occasion, although not nearly so often as some thought. She had never believed there was more.

Until she had seen Shaylah look at Wolf.

The sound of the voices coming over the comlink was suddenly too much. The absence of one voice left a gaping hole, and she couldn't bear to listen anymore. She ran to the panel and shut it off. Then she sagged against the bulkhead, her brief burst of strength fading away.

Eos, had she been right, in her joking assessment? Was there something about the men of Trios that brought women to this pass, to this foolish wondering? Was it the knowledge that these men believed that there was one woman meant to be their bonded mate that was so tempting? Was it a need to prove them wrong, that mating should be done freely, between anyone who wished, whenever they wished, as Coalition law stated? Was it a matter of pride, a wish to be a woman so enthralling that they forgot their own beliefs in their need to have her? Or was it more subversive, some hidden wish to believe in such foolishness, and to be that one woman?

Perhaps it was some oddity, some quirk affecting only Arellian women such as Shaylah and herself. Some quirk that—

That didn't matter anymore.

She sank down to sit on the top step. Dax was dead, and how he had made her feel was less than meaningless now. She had to shake off this ridiculous freeze that had overtaken her. She had to face the immediate future. And what would happen to her now, in the hands of a crew who would wish her dead, without Dax to control them.

Without Dax.

She bit down harder on her trembling lip, bringing tears to her eyes. She knew the pain was what had done it; except for the night they'd collared her, she hadn't cried since she had been nine, and had realized the truth about her mother. And she certainly wasn't crying over the death of a cocky, arrogant, suicidal skypirate.

With the self-discipline learned in her years in the Coalition, a trait put to unexpected use when she had become their slave, she tried to steady herself. She blinked rapidly to sweep away the excess moisture that was making her eyes sting. She drew herself up straight, taking deep breaths, to stop this preposterous shaking. Then she stood up.

She knew she was facing death. The crew wouldn't hesitate to kill her once Roxton—or Rina—told them who she was. She didn't doubt that the first mate would. Rina? She wasn't sure anymore. But even if the girl was able to forgive her, Rina couldn't stop the crew if they were bent on murder.

She wasn't, Califa realized numbly as she walked back to stare out the observation port, even sure that she cared.

What did she have to look forward to, were she to escape? A life on the run, forever trying to hide, when the collar that marked her as slave made it impossible? When Dax had been here, it had been something to worry about in the future; she had been so distracted by him that it seemed unimportant. But now, when the days stretched out emptily ahead, it loomed larger.

She sank into a chair, her eyes fastened not on the stars and planets that dotted the expanse, but on the black nothingness between them. She sat there for a very long time, trying to make her mind as blank as that darkness, as unfeeling as the vacuum she stared at. She sat until her body began to protest the long stillness. She ignored it, forcing herself to embrace the numbness she'd felt before, to expand it, to welcome it, until what was left was a vague feeling of thankfulness that she had not had to watch Dax die.

"Why did you do it?"

She whirled, her hand going up to press against her chest as if it could calm her startled heart. For an instant she stared, disbelieving. Then she leapt to her feet, pure joy flooding her, a sensation she had never known in her life. She wanted to run to him, but couldn't seem to get her frozen legs to move.

"Dax," she whispered helplessly.

He stood at the top of the stairs, his gaze fastened on her intently. She wondered briefly, inanely, how long he'd been there this time, watching her. She'd been so lost, it could have been hours.

He wore a black flight suit that fit him like a second skin, molding the taut, leanly muscled body. The belt with its disrupter and dagger was gone, but the business-like knife was still in his boot. A small but nasty gash marked his temple, but it had been cleaned, and had stopped bleeding.

"Why, Califa?"

She was so stunned by his sudden appearance that she

barely registered that he had used her name. "I . . . Eos, Dax, what happened? They kept calling . . . I thought you were dead!"

"Sorry to disappoint you," he said in mock apology.

She drew back, stung. For a moment, in her joy, she had forgotten how things had been left between them. At her reaction to his mocking words, his eyes narrowed, and then, to her surprise, he seemed to relent.

"The cruiser captain's nerve broke at the last moment. He dodged to starboard. Gave me enough room to slide by."

Room he wouldn't have had had the Coalition captain been as blindly determined as most of them were, Califa thought, her knowledge based on long experience with the by-rote tactics of the officers the Coalition favored with promotion.

Room he wouldn't have had had the Coalition captain possessed the same boldness and courage—or the same death wish—as the skypirate.

"Why didn't you tell"—she stumbled over the word "me" and then went on hastily—"Roxton? That you were alive? I'm sure everyone thought what I did."

"She took a hit that wiped out my communications."

She. That amazing ship. "That fighter," she began. "I've never seen anything like it."

Suddenly, unexpectedly, he grinned. Instinctively, Califa recognized the remnants of the adrenaline high she'd once known so well.

"I should hope not. She's one of a kind."

"I've never heard of a fighter that small carrying a photon gun. The kind of power that takes—"

"She's got it, little snowfox. And more."

She suppressed a shiver at the name he'd given her; when he said it, it was as if there was something intimate between them. And she was not a tiny woman; she wasn't used to being called a little anything. But if everything was relative, then next to Dax she *was* little, she supposed. In strength if not in sheer size. Yet now, he was more like a youth with his first air rover, she thought. And never had he looked more smugly male. But she was so thankful he was alive at all, she couldn't find it in her to care.

"Where did you find . . . her?"

"I didn't. She's mine, mine and Larcos's. He helped me build her."

Califa gaped at him. "You built it? Yourself?"

"Every bit. That's where we've been for nearly a year. In a storehouse on the back side of Alpha Two."

"Alpha Two? Except for the outpost, and the Legion Club, that planet's practically uncivilized. And the back side is virtually uninhabited."

He gave her that crooked grin again. "Exactly. And nobody bothered us. Got some repairs and modifications done to the *Evening Star,* and built the fighter." He shook his head. "Larcos is a fabrication wizard. And he came up with some materials . . . I didn't dare ask how or where."

"Larcos is a designer, as well as an engineer?" The lanky young man hadn't impressed her as the kind who could conceive of such a ship. No, dream it; that was the only way a triumph like that fighter could become reality.

"No." His voice seemed to cool suddenly.

"Then who?" she asked, wondering what had brought on the chill; he'd seemed happy enough to talk about the fighter. When he looked away, the obvious answer to her question struck her. "You?"

"I . . . helped design it." She'd been right; the softening she'd sensed was fading, the harshness returning. Even the fighter was suffering in the change, Califa thought. No longer *she* but *it*. She tried again.

"You should be proud," she said, even as she wondered who had helped him in the design. "It's an incredible ship."

"It held together."

But it had been hit. As he had been hit. Her gaze flicked to his temple, where some traces of blood still remained, then back to his face. "Communications wasn't the only thing damaged."

He saw her glance. "Piece of debris caught me."

She cringed inwardly at his words; they gave rise to bloody images of how much worse the damage—to ship and to pilot—could have been.

As if he'd read her thoughts, Dax's mouth curved into

that wry, mocking smile she'd thought never to see again, and for a moment the softer Dax was back. "I was a little dizzy for a while. Drifted around out there a little. That's what took me so long to catch back up with the '*Star*.'"

Something tightened inside her at his casual dismissal of his own near death. Drifted around. With a Coalition cruiser still in proximity, and now with an even bigger reason to hunt him down; no Coalition officer would take being outflown and outwitted by a skypirate with any kind of grace. That Dax had survived the attack itself was a wonder. That he'd survived the aftermath was a miracle.

"That run you made was . . ."

She hesitated. Crazy, demented, suicidal, all the words she wanted to use were sure to destroy whatever there was of that leniency she had sensed in him, and it was tentative enough as it was. But at the same time, she wanted to shake some caution into him.

"A calculated risk," he said with a shrug, sounding so casual that Califa felt that knot inside her tighten further.

"And if you had . . . miscalculated?"

"The *Evening Star* still would have made it."

That knot was becoming unbearable. Did he not care at all for himself? He seemed to get such amusement from life, did he not feel any urge to preserve his own? The words came out incredulously, and almost against her will.

"And you would be dead."

He shrugged again. "I thought he might break."

The knot snapped, unraveling with all the ferocity of her tangled emotions.

"You thought he might break!" she exclaimed. "And on that piece of absurdity you risked your life?"

He blinked, as if startled. He opened his mouth, but Califa wasn't about to let him spout some other piece of lunacy. As happened far too often with this man, the emotions she usually kept tightly under control broke loose, tumbling out in a spate of words.

"Do you think your crew would have welcomed your sacrifice? Do you truly believe they would think it an even trade, their lives for the life of the man they esteem above all others?"

Amazingly, Califa saw a tinge of color stain his cheeks. But she didn't, couldn't stop.

"What about Roxton? That man loves you like a son! And Nelcar? Why else would such a gentle man commit himself to the life of a skypirate, if not out of reverence for the man who leads him, the man who saved him from a life too grim to be borne?"

He found his voice then. "The men understand—"

"Understand? That their captain—and no matter how you deny it, that *is* what you are—will take any opportunity to risk his life? That he takes insane chances that he calls '*calculated risks*?' "

He folded his arms across his chest, as if in protection against her tirade. Califa's mind skated briefly over the fact that he could have stopped this at any time, simply by walking away, or ordering her locked up again. She would think about that, later, but right now she was too incensed to think at all.

"So you think the men understand, do you?" Her voice dropped to a low, cutting sound. "What about Rina? Do you think she understands?"

He paled, and Califa knew her thrust had struck home. She had a hunch it had been Rina who had cleaned the wound at his temple, and had no doubt peppered the doctoring with her opinion of his recklessness. For all his fierceness, for all his bravery, Rina was the one person Dax could not defend against. Roxton he held a deep affection for, and perhaps others, but that pixie of a girl, that determined imp . . . that rarest of all beings, a child of his own world, a Triotian, held the one weapon he could not fight: his own heart. Califa felt her anger begin to fade.

She stood watching him, all the while her treacherous mind wondering what it would be like to be the recipient of such unfaltering devotion. All her doubts that such a thing existed were shaken by the evidence before her eyes; Dax loved Rina. And Califa had no doubt that he would continue to love her, for his lifetime. With no blood relationship between them. With no lust between them. With no bond between them except the most tenuous; that of survivors of the same destroyed world. Yet he would have died to save her.

"She worships you, Dax," she whispered.

He shook his head sharply, an instantaneous disavowal of the words. Did he truly not see it? Califa wondered. Or did he not want to see it, to believe it? Because he felt he didn't deserve it? She wasn't sure where that idea had come from, but something in her responded to it as if she were certain it was true.

"She does," Califa insisted. "And I don't know if she could survive another loss like that of her parents."

"Roxton would take care of her." He sounded as if he were trying to convince himself as well as her. "She'd be fine."

"As fine as you would be, if something happened to her?"

Her question made him wince as if she'd sliced him with the razor edge of his own blade. But he recovered quickly.

"Nothing's going to happen to her."

His stubbornness rekindled her ire. "That," she bit out, "is a promise you'll not keep. Not if you continue to indulge in the kind of insanity you did today."

He stiffened. "Insanity? We're both standing here, aren't we? The *Evening Star* is intact, barely damaged, and we're putting distance fast between us and that cruiser."

"Only because you have the luck of the gods."

"I gave up believing in gods. You make your own luck."

"By daring fate to strike you down?"

"By doing what has to be done!" he snapped.

"You had to go out there? You couldn't just get the *Evening Star* clear?"

"They attacked us."

"And when did you begin subscribing to the Coalition dogma that first blood must be avenged?"

He looked almost uncomfortable. "I don't bend to any Coalition dogma."

"So what was this, then? Some kind of foolhardy sky-pirate tradition?"

Exasperation crackled in his voice then. "What did

you expect? That we would turn tail and run? You're not a fool, Califa. Why do you think we haven't been attacked before now, after that raid on Boreas?"

She was too startled by his saying she wasn't a fool to give him an answer. He went on without one.

"Because we're in a position of strength, that's why. Many have tried to take us, both Coalition and our own kind. None have succeeded, and for their efforts have paid a high price. It makes us stronger, and makes the next one who looks at the *Evening Star* as a sloeplum for the picking think twice before attacking us."

"I understand that," she admitted. She did, she knew he was right, but it did little to ease her agitation over his seeming lack of any concern for his own life. "But must you do it by constantly risking yourself so recklessly? Do you really know how slim your chances were that a trained Coalition captain would lose his nerve and run?"

She knew instantly she'd gone too far. Dax's expression went utterly flat, his eyes frosty.

"Perhaps not," he said, in a voice colder than the chill that had dimmed the vivid green of his eyes. "But you do. You know to exactly what lengths a Coalition captain would go, don't you?"

She'd lost him. "Dax—"

"Which brings me back to my original question. Why did you do it?"

She didn't pretend to misunderstand; she knew exactly what he meant. But that didn't mean she had an answer for him. She didn't. She didn't know if she ever would.

"Does it matter?" she asked wearily.

"Does it matter why a former Coalition officer committed treason to save a skypirate's vessel? It might."

She couldn't look at him, couldn't face the coolness in his eyes, which was somehow worse than the anger. "I don't know why. I didn't think, I just did it."

"You didn't think before warning Roxton of the tactics the cruiser would use? Tactics you yourself had devised, that have been taught to what? Hundreds? Thousands?"

"Including you, it seems."

"Yes. Including me. Even on Trios, you were known.

Well known. Your texts are required study in our flight school."

She looked away, lifting her hands to rub her temples. Paradoxical, she thought; he was the one who had taken a blow to the head, but it was she who had the headache.

"Why did you do it, Califa?" he repeated.

"I told you I don't know. Why do you persist in trying to get yourself killed?"

"I don't—"

"Don't you? Isn't that what all this craziness is about? Fifteen-foot leaps across rooftops? Taking on a squad of guards singlehandedly? Or going up against a fully armed war cruiser alone?"

"Calculated ri—"

"Damn you!" She whirled. "And your calculated risks! Even the Coalition at its most asinine moments wouldn't have considered what you do risks. It's suicide, nothing less. The odds just haven't caught up with you. Yet."

"I've survived five years—"

"If you survive five more *days*, it will be a miracle. So will it be if you don't take us all down with you."

"I see."

"You see what?" Califa snapped. She was tired, drained, and beginning to feel a growing resentment that she had let this man do this to her.

"That's your concern," he said coldly. "You were trying to save your own ass, not the *Evening Star*."

She never even blinked at the coarseness. "I told you, I didn't think about it." She gave him a sideways look that she hoped matched his for coolness. "I should have, though. If I *had* thought about it, I would have grabbed the chance to retrieve the controller." Instead she had sat here mourning a man who would throw her own pathos back in her face. "I was a fool to give it to you. A fool to trust it to a man so determined to get himself killed, and leave me to the mob."

For a moment he didn't speak. Then he asked, very softly, "Why did you give it to me?"

"Because I *am* a fool," she grated. "I thought it might show you— Never mind. There's no point in trying to explain reason to a man who's suicidal."

"I'm not—"

"I begin to think all Triotians are slightly touched."

He went rigid then. Califa was too exhausted to care. "If you recall," he said icily, "there aren't enough of us left alive to make that judgment."

"There are enough left to prove my point," she muttered. "Who else but a bunch of suicidal partisans would dare think their little rebellion had a chance against a conquering machine like the Coalition?"

Dax went as pale as if his injury had truly drained away his lifeblood. He stared at her, eyes wide, his expression unreadable. When he spoke, his voice was oddly hoarse.

"What did you say?"

"I said Triotians are genetically crazy. Did I hurt your feelings?" Califa asked sarcastically. "Sorry. Perhaps you should think of the feelings of those you leave behind when you go off on one of your wild, brollet-brained—"

He moved then, swiftly, his hands shooting up to grab her shoulders in a grip so fierce it hurt.

"What did you say about a rebellion?"

She shifted, trying to free herself from his painful grasp. It had no effect. His eyes were boring down into hers, his gaze so intense it took all her nerve to hold it, and to answer him with a coolness she was far from feeling.

"I realize it's hardly worth the name, but—"

He cut her off with a string of sharp, urgent questions. "What rebellion? Where? What partisans? Are you saying there are other Triotians? Alive?"

It came to her then. *That's where we've been for nearly a year. In a storehouse on the back side of Alpha 2.* And there was nowhere inside the system more remote. More out of touch. She stared up at him.

"You . . . don't know?"

His expression gave her her answer. Eos, he didn't know. *Are you saying there are other Triotians? Alive?* She caught her breath. Had he thought himself and Rina the only survivors of their devastated world?

She thought of his reaction when he had deduced that Wolf was alive, or had been less than a year ago. Had it been, not just the shock of finding a friend—and your king—had survived, but learning you were not the only ones left of your people?

She didn't know what possessed her to do it. Didn't know what made her think he might let her. But she lifted one hand and gently rested it on his chest, over his heart.

"You're not alone, Dax."

And she felt her own heart quiver at the pounding of his beneath her fingers.

Chapter 12

Dax's jaw clenched as he stared down at her. He felt her fingers flex against his chest, and wondered if she could feel the hammering of his heart. He never thought of moving her hand, his shock was too great. His words came as if fired from a thermal cannon, each one enunciated with painful precision.

"Tell me. Now. All of it. Everything you know."

"I don't know much. It all began shortly before"—she gestured at the collar with her free hand—"this."

"Tell me!"

She let out a long breath. "There were always rumors that a small number of Triotians had survived. Some believed them, some didn't. But then . . ."

"Califa," he said warningly as she trailed off.

"All right, but you've got to see that by the time I heard this, I was already a slave. I don't know how accurate it is."

He tried to say "Tell me" again, but couldn't form the words. Instead he tightened his already inescapable grip on her shoulders. Califa took a long, deep breath, and started.

"There were no signs of any survivors outside the Coalition boundaries around the capitol of Triotia for years. Everyone thought the entire population had been wiped out."

"Or enslaved," Dax ground out bitterly.

Abruptly he let go of her; he didn't want her to see that his hands were shaking. An expression flashed across her face that looked oddly like pain, but he couldn't dwell on it now. An incredible thought had come to him, an idea so overwhelming he could barely breathe. It made his already aching head pound.

Dare. Could he be—

He broke off his contemplation; he couldn't wonder, couldn't even wish, or hope would inundate him, and hope was not something that went well with reason or logic. Which was what he desperately needed now. He resisted the urge to rub at his throbbing temple.

"Yes," Califa said at last, sounding reluctant. "That's what they assumed. But then the raids began."

"Raids?"

"Small ones. Acts of sabotage, an occasional theft, an assault on a supply caravan, nothing that couldn't have been just the usual resistance to Coalition annexation."

He no longer had to worry about hope; rage flooded him instead at her use of the Coalition euphemism. "Annexation?" he said, in the quiet tone his men knew meant trouble. "I believe you mean invasion. Or perhaps conquest? Subjugation?"

Califa flushed, the color showing harshly on pale Arellian skin. "Old habits are hard to break," she explained in a small voice.

And some new ones, too, Dax thought. Like spending too much time thinking about this woman. Like giving a damn about why she had looked hurt a moment ago. Like—

"Never mind," he snapped.

She wet her lips, and Dax's hands curled into fists. Never had he felt so at the mercy of an unruly body as he had since this woman had boarded his ship. Even now, amid the chaos in his mind, that simple movement of her tongue, stealing out to slide over soft, full lips as his own had once done, had the power to disorient him. And distract him.

"Go on," he muttered.

"No one had ever seen them. There was never any warning. They never made a sound, and left no traces. They clearly knew the terrain, and they had weapons and transport. At first it was thought to be just resistance," she said carefully. "But then they captured a communications station. They took a base transmitter and hand-held comlinks. And they left the station's crew alive—and talking."

"It is not our custom to indiscriminately murder anyone who gets in our way." His tone was vicious, but he couldn't help it; he never remembered being so on edge as he was at this moment. And his head was getting worse.

"No. So there were witnesses left, to describe their attackers."

"It would have been figured out eventually anyway, even if they'd slaughtered the lot of them. Triotians wouldn't feel the gaining of a little time worth the destruction of that much life."

Califa looked at him, as if his words puzzled her. "Even the lives of their enemies?"

"Triotians considered no people their enemy." He laughed, a short, harsh, unhumorous sound. "Perhaps that was our downfall."

Her eyes took on a contemplative look. After a moment she said, "Shaylah said your own laws and innate kindness were used to destroy you."

Dax's eyes narrowed. "Your friend was wise as well as brave, I see."

Califa nodded, an unexpected softness coming over her face as she let out a barely perceptible sigh.

Dax would give a great deal to know how a woman such as that could call a slave owner friend. Had she known another Califa? Dax wondered. Or guessed at her existence? Had she, too, seen the fleeting glimpses he thought he had seen, of a gentler, vulnerable woman, like the one who worried about Rina? Like the one who had berated him for his recklessness?

Like the woman who had betrayed the training of a lifetime to warn a skypirate?

"The thing I didn't understand," Califa said when he didn't speak, "was why they waited so long. The fall of Trios was five years ago. But some said it took them that long to regroup."

Dax was yanked out of his speculation. "When the Coalition murdered our king," he said, voice taut, "they did more than destroy a figurehead. His death would have taken the heart out of our people."

"Shaylah said he was ... different."

"She spoke the truth. King Galen ruled with the aid of a council of the wisest elders. He was beloved, and he loved and respected his people. Every Triotian knew they would be treated fairly, so they were free to make the most of themselves and what they had."

Califa stared, then slowly shook her head. "It sounds . . . too perfect to be real."

"Perhaps it was," Dax said, bitterness tingeing his voice. "Or perhaps we lounged too long in our own euphoria, forgetting what it took to arrive there. Forgetting that others had not yet fought the battles we had fought, and ultimately discovered the uselessness and waste of them. We foolishly thought that every world had to find its own way, so stayed impartial."

Since she had made a career out of those kinds of battles, and later of teaching others to fight them, Dax knew there was little she could say. Cursing his tangled emotions around Califa, he forced his still stunned mind back to dealing with the shocking news she had delivered.

"Weapons, transport, communications," he murmured. "So it is truly a rebellion?"

Califa's expression became unexpectedly gentle, and only then did Dax realize he'd sounded like a child struck by the wonder of the impossible coming to pass.

"Yes," she said, her tone as gentle as her expression. "They're fighting back, Dax. I don't know how many, but it's enough for them to send three tactical wings, from what I heard. They recalled some forces from leave. And—"

At her sudden stop, Dax focused on her once more. The gentleness had been replaced by a taut wariness.

"And what?" he prompted, suddenly equally wary.

"I . . ."

"You've already told me enough for them to execute you," he pointed out. "Don't stop now."

"It's not them I'm worried about."

She drew back the moment the words were out, as if she hadn't meant to say them.

Dax's jaw clenched. "If I'd wanted to execute you," he ground out, "I would have done it the moment I found out the truth."

" 'It is not our custom to indiscriminately murder anyone who gets in our way?' " she quoted.

"It's not our custom to kill the messenger, either. What were you going to say, Califa?"

She hesitated, then warned him. "I heard it in the slave quarters on Carelia, before they threw me into the prison. I don't know if it's true, it was only rumor—"

"I'd sooner trust the accuracy of the telerien than any official sources. Go on."

"They said the Triotians were succeeding. So well that Legion Command had decided to send General Corling back to Trios."

Dax went cold, barely having time to wonder at the iciness that swept him before it was replaced by the rushing heat of rage.

Corling. The mastermind of the downfall and conquest of Trios. The vicious, brutal officer who had destroyed the world that had been the source of much of the goodness and beauty in an entire system. The man who had used deceit and treachery to slaughter a people who had welcomed him under a banner of peace.

The man who had murdered a king. Who had thrown a queen to his barbarous, raping troops. And who had personally condemned a royal prince to the worst kind of slavery.

Dare. Dear God, if he had survived, if by some miracle he had gotten back to Trios, surely he was dead now. Corling would know now he should have killed Dare when he had the chance. From what Dax had heard of the man, he would have made the extermination of the last living member of the royal family his primary goal.

But could anyone except Dare have done this? Could anyone other than the brilliant, dauntless, audacious Dare, the man who had apparently survived five years of torment, degradation, and punishment and still managed to escape, could anyone less than the rightful king of Trios have accomplished this?

Dax shuddered under the pressure of his whirling thoughts. His head was beginning to pound viciously. His mind felt muddled, vague, but he realized he must be in reaction, with the last of the adrenaline of the battle fading, and the shock of what he'd learned battering him. Everything seemed a little distant, fuzzy around the edges, as it had after that piece of the fighter had clipped his temple.

He swayed on his feet. Califa reached for him, to steady him. He meant to wave her off, but had to admit that he needed the support.

"You'd better rest. I'll help you to your quarters," Califa said, her voice sounding soft and gentle in his ringing ears. As if she meant it, as if she cared that he was about to keel over.

Perhaps she did, he thought dazedly. She'd saved them, hadn't she? She'd warned them, reminding him of a long-forgotten flight school lecture, based on her own teachings, that had set out the course of action the Coalition ship would take. He tried to turn to look at her, but the floor seemed to be moving.

"Maybe you'd better just sit down."

She sounded truly worried now. It made him feel good, that tone of concern. Which was silly. She was a Coalition officer. He hated her.

No, she was a slave. She'd been betrayed by the Coalition, too. She'd been punished enough, hadn't she? And she'd trusted him with that thing, the controller, which was like trusting him with . . . what? Her soul?

So he didn't hate her. Did he?

He felt his knees start to give way. He tried to stop it, but then he was falling. Sort of. Califa was there, helping him, softening the drop. He knew it was her, he could see the black of her hair, the blue of her eyes, although he wished she'd hold still so he could look at her. Brave little snowfox. He liked to look at her.

"I'll go get Nelcar."

"No," he said, pleased that his tongue still worked. His hand wasn't as cooperative, though; it took a moment for him to find and grasp her hand. "Don't go."

She seemed to be staring at him, then at their joined hands. "Dax?" she whispered.

"Don't go," he repeated. "Stay with me."

He heard a sharp intake of breath. "I'm right here. I won't leave you."

She sounded confused. Why? he wondered. She had to know how he felt. He'd kissed her, hadn't he? After their song? Yes, he knew he had, he couldn't have imagined that fierce rush of hot sensation. How could you imagine something you'd never felt, never even known was possible?

But he'd been angry with her, afterward. Very angry. Because she'd scared him. Or something had. Why? He couldn't seem to remember. If he couldn't remember, it couldn't be very important, could it?

He tried to tell her that, but his mouth didn't seem to want to work. So he squeezed her hand instead. When she squeezed back, satisfaction welled up inside him. He could rest now. He let the blackness come.

Califa felt oddly suspended. The crew treated her as they always had, which told her they didn't know the secret she had let slip with her own foolish tongue. Roxton, Nelcar, and Rina had clearly not informed the others. They were no doubt awaiting a decision from Dax.

And Dax wasn't talking. To anyone, from what she could gather.

Nelcar had told her he was recovering, that the effects of the blow to the head, delayed by the adrenaline flow that had kept him going, had been alleviated after a full day's cycle of sleep. When she had asked about him, Nelcar had looked at her rather intently before he answered. She had supposed, because of his knowledge of her past, he was pondering whether to tell her anything. But then he had surprised her with his quiet words.

"He talked about you. While he was half conscious."

"He ... did?"

Nelcar nodded. "He said your name and something like 'sings like an angel, can't be evil.' "

Califa's breath caught. Hope leapt up to lodge behind the lump in her throat that had stopped her breath, and the combination tightened her chest unbearably.

"Then he went under for good," Nelcar said. "Rina and I had to wake him every few hours, to make certain he hadn't slipped into a coma."

That explained the young man's obvious exhaustion. "But he's awake now?"

"He's awake, but he's not talking," Nelcar had said. "He won't say a word, to me or anyone, except to tell us to get out and leave him alone."

That conversation had been three days ago, and Dax still wasn't talking. Not to Roxton, or to any of the crew. Not even to Rina. He never left his quarters, and the ship seemed somehow empty without his vital presence. Califa caught herself looking up at every set of approaching footsteps, and scanning the lounge every time she entered. It was as if, she thought ruefully, she missed him. Eos, she thought, shaking her head at her foolishness, the man was half inclined to kill her, and she missed him.

But he had spoken of her. Even in pain, half delirious, he had been thinking of her. She tried to fight down the pleasure that thought gave her. She had too much else to think about.

Roxton had come to her, after he had helped to carry the unconscious Dax to his quarters. She had half expected him to accuse her of being responsible for Dax's state, but he had gruffly informed her Nelcar had told him it was a result only of his injury from the fight catching up with him.

He had also told her that she was to restrict herself to quarters and the lounge for meals until Dax regained consciousness and decided what to do about her. And until then, he had added grudgingly, her secret would be kept.

But that decision had never come, even when Dax had regained consciousness. He was still cloistered in his quarters, refusing to talk. His silence was weighing on them all, but most of all on Rina. In one day the girl had lost both her confidants; she wouldn't talk to Califa, and Dax wouldn't talk to her.

Califa sighed, trying to stop herself from beginning to once more pace the small quarters she still, to her surprise, shared with Rina. She'd expected to be moved, but Roxton must have decided that would raise too many questions. And apparently they trusted her with the girl; for that much, she supposed she should be thankful, although it was clear Rina hadn't made up her mind about Califa.

She lost the battle to stop her pacing. She was on her second circuit when the door opened. She turned, grateful for any distraction, only to retract the thought when she saw Roxton's glowering expression.

He came in without a word, waiting until the door slid shut behind him. Then he crossed his arms over his chest and glared at her.

"I want to know what happened on the observation deck."

Califa tensed. She'd been afraid of this. "What ... happened?" she said, stalling.

"Something must have. What did you tell him that's got him holed up in there, ripping himself apart?"

She couldn't tell him. Dax had kept his birthplace a secret, even from Roxton, for years, and for good reason; she couldn't give him away.

"Nothing," she said.

Roxton swore pungently. "I've seen him, woman, and I've seen eyes less tortured on a corpse. He's on the edge of breaking. What did you talk about?"

Califa bit her lip. "I ... The battle, mostly. And his fighter. He was fine, then he passed out."

"Nothing else?"

He wasn't going to be satisfied, Califa realized. She would have to give him a little more. But she would not betray Dax's secret, not when he had kept her own.

"I did yell at him," she admitted.

Roxton blinked. "You what?"

"I yelled at him. For being so reckless. So careless with his life." She gave him a slightly wan smile. "He got very angry at me."

Roxton looked at her for a moment, assessingly. As if he hadn't expected such an admission from her. Was it that she admitted to her actions that puzzled the older man, or that she had cared enough to chastise Dax?

After a moment he sighed, and the crusty first mate disappeared, to be replaced with the grizzled old man who loved Dax like a son.

"Well, that's nothing I haven't done myself. I've never managed to make him angry, however. He merely laughs at me."

"Too bad he takes so little heed."

"Yes." He relaxed enough to uncross his arms. "I don't understand. I haven't seen Dax like this since I first picked him up on Clarion."

Califa lifted a brow quizzically. "You picked him up?"

Roxton nodded. "Found him in a taproom, pickled, trying to start a fight with three Omegans who outweighed him five times over."

Califa's mouth quirked. "Sounds like he hasn't changed much."

She won a slight smile from the man. "No, not much."

"You stopped the fight?"

Roxton snorted. "No one stops an Omegan who wants to fight. Just ask Hurcon. I merely distracted them until we could slip out the back."

She'd begun this as a distraction herself, but now she was too curious not to ask.

"Why did you step in, if you didn't know him?"

"I'm not sure. There was something about him . . ."

She certainly couldn't argue with that, Califa thought. Then Roxton's eyes narrowed as he looked at her.

"Perhaps I'd just had enough of bullies."

He said it pointedly, the allegory to the Coalition clear. Califa didn't bother to protest.

"And then?"

"After he sobered up, he was like this. Silent, refusing to eat, even sleep, looking like something was chewing him up inside. Finally we talked. We found we both had nowhere to go, and no one left there anyway. Dax suggested we take something back from those who had left us that way."

"And so you became skypirates."

"Yes." His mouth twisted into a wry smile as he tugged on his beard. "But I almost killed him, first."

"After saving him?"

"I was angry. No," Roxton corrected, "I was furious. He took every coin, all the funds we had and risked it on a single toss in chaser. And an honest toss, at that, if you can believe it."

Califa smothered a smile. "He won, I presume?"

Roxton's mouth twisted again, but this time into an affectionate grin. "Of course he did."

"So you were rich?"

"In a manner of speaking. He won this ship."

Califa blinked. "He what?"

"And enough money to outfit her, and make a few changes. One toss of the dice and we were in business."

Calif shook her head in amused wonder. "Are you certain those dice weren't rigged?"

He nodded. "They were the other man's, the owner's. Besides, Dax doesn't need to cheat. He has the devil's own luck."

Califa sobered. "Even that kind of luck runs out, Roxton. He'll get himself killed, if he keeps on like this."

The beard took a fierce tugging this time. "Do you think I don't know that? Do you think I haven't tried to get him to stop, to take care, to stop acting . . ."

"Suicidal," Califa suggested when his voice trailed off.

"Exactly," Roxton agreed, his tone grim. "I try to rein him in, but he's so damn stubborn."

"I've noticed."

Roxton chuckled humorlessly. "I suppose you have." He studied her for a long, silent moment. Then, shaking his head, he asked, "Are you sure you were a Coalition officer?"

She stiffened, but there didn't seem to be any threat in his words. "Quite."

"You don't seem like one."

"I'm not. Not anymore. Nor will I ever be again."

The man's eyes narrowed shrewdly. "And if it weren't for that collar they slapped on you?"

Califa straightened, meeting Roxton's gaze levelly. "I would still never be again."

"Had your eyes opened, have you?"

"As have all of you. It was just harder to see from the inside."

Roxton looked startled. "Well, now," he said, stroking the beard this time, "I hadn't thought of it that way. But I suppose that could be true."

Califa felt a small spurt of hope at his words. If Roxton could see that, could Dax? Later, when the shock of all she'd told him ebbed, could he see that she was, in her own way, a victim of the Coalition as well? Because if he could believe that, he might be able to one day believe that she had truly changed, that she—

The opening of the door cut off her thoughts. Rina came in, barely sparing a glance for either of them. Califa guessed from the slump of the girl's shoulders that Dax was maintaining his ominous silence. Rina's distress was clear on her young face. Califa's heart ached for the girl; she wished she could try to comfort her, but she was far too uncertain of her welcome. Roxton seemed willing to at least consider her side; Rina, on the other hand, was full of young, volatile emotions that ran hot easily, and were slow to cool.

"He's still not talking?" Roxton asked the girl gently.

"No." Rina's voice quavered as she sat down on her bunk. "He just sits there, staring out the viewport. He won't talk, he won't eat, he doesn't even sleep."

Califa thought of Roxton's story. "Is he drinking?"

Rina glanced at her, as if considering whether to answer her. Finally her concern over Dax won out.

"No."

"That's something, I suppose," Roxton said.

Rina slammed a small fist down on her bunk. "It's nothing!" she exclaimed, fighting tears. "I even told him I was going to take the fighter out this afternoon, to be sure it was fixed."

"Blast it, Rina," Roxton exclaimed, "you know he would never let you fly that—"

"I know. That's what I mean," the girl interrupted. "He never even blinked. He should have been furious."

Roxton closed his mouth on whatever the rest of his sentence would have been. His grim expression told Califa just how serious the situation was. Yet still there was a softness in his eyes when he looked at Rina.

"He knows I would never let you do such a thing. Besides, he can never be truly angry with you, little one."

Roxton's wry words came back to her. *I've never managed to make him angry, however. He merely laughs at me.*

She looked from Rina to Roxton. Perhaps there was something she could do. Something she seemed to be very, very good at.

"If neither one of you can make him angry," she said grimly, "I'll wager I can."

Chapter 13

Califa spared a brief moment, as she stood in the passageway, to wonder at the irony of the fact that Dax's door—and everyone else's on the *Evening Star,* for that matter—had no lock, while a Coalition captain's quarters required a voice and retinal scan to get in. That as much as anything, she thought, underscored the differences between the world she'd left behind and the one she found herself in now. The skypirates were far more open and trusting than the Coalition had ever been. Somehow Dax had managed to instill the Triotian respect for privacy in this varied crew.

And outside of Rina and Roxton, who were practically family to him, no one had dared violate it.

Until now.

She took in a deep breath. She wasn't quite sure why she was doing this. Wasn't sure why she should care if he stayed barricaded in brooding silence indefinitely; at least if he wasn't speaking, he wouldn't be ordering her returned to Coalition custody. Or her execution. If she did this, she could easily wind up infuriating him to the point of making a decision she personally would long regret—if she survived.

But she couldn't help feeling she had to. He obviously still intended to tell no one of his origins. Only she knew the truth of why he was in such torment, so it followed that only she could induce him to talk.

And she told herself that the memory of a kiss, and the fact that he had thought of her even in near-delirium, had nothing to do with it at all.

Before she could change her mind, she took that last step forward. The door opened with a quiet whoosh. As she stepped inside it closed behind her with the same soft sound.

The clutter of the room contrasted distinctly with the neatness she'd noticed before. An untouched meal sat on the table, boots were haphazardly thrown on the floor, and a trunk sat open against the wall, contents tossed in a jumble.

He was on his bunk, propped up by a thick cushion at his back, one knee raised. He was, as Rina said, staring out the viewport into the endless darkness. A flicker of irritation crossed his beard-stubbled face as the door opened, but he didn't look in that direction. His eyes closed for a moment, and she heard a short, compressed breath escape him. Then his lashes lifted and he resumed staring literally into space.

Califa was grateful he hadn't looked up. It gave her a chance to catch her breath, and deal with the two things that had hit her with the impact of a disrupter. First, he had discarded his shirt along with his boots, leaving an expanse of sleek, golden chest and flat, ridged belly bare to her view. And second, in his hands was the knife from his boot.

He was toying with it, holding it at both ends with his palms, the pommel of the handle resting against his right palm, the deadly sharp point against his left.

Califa steadied herself. "Planning on slitting your throat?" she inquired pleasantly.

He jerked convulsively at the sound of her voice, his head snapping around to stare at her in shock; obviously, she was the last person he'd expected to find standing there. In nearly the same instant he swore, low and harsh, as he yanked his left hand away from the knife. Blood pooled up on his palm where his sudden movement had sent the blade digging in.

He stared at the blood for a moment, then curled his hand into a fist. He refused to look at her again, closing his eyes once more as blood welled up through his fingers.

Nelcar had left a can of healer's spray on the table. Califa picked it up, and the clean cloth that sat on the tray of uneaten food. She knew if he thought about it he would resist her; she didn't plan on giving him that much time.

She quickly crossed the distance between them, sat on the edge of the bunk, grabbed his hand, and pressed the cloth against his palm before he had a chance to jerk it away.

"It will take you forever to bleed to death this way," she said in conversational tones. "If you're going to do it, do it right. Go for the throat."

He swore again, and tried to pull his hand away. Quickly she grasped his little finger and bent it back. "Hold still," she ordered.

He seemed startled at her strength—and her commanding tone—but tried again to pull away. She bent his finger back further, until he winced.

"I said hold still."

His right hand curled around the grip of his knife. She saw the motion when he lifted it, saw the flex of taut muscles in his bare arm, knew the power there. He could kill her with a flick of his wrist. Her pulse sped up, but she schooled her voice to an amused calm.

"Changed your mind about killing the messenger?"

For an instant he was motionless, knife readied. Then, slowly, he lowered it. He sank bank against the cushion, letting out a long, weary breath. He closed his eyes again.

"Just get out," he muttered.

"In a minute."

Eos, Califa thought as she checked the bleeding beneath the cloth she'd pressed to the wound, Roxton had been right. She'd seen that the moment Dax had looked at her. She, too, had seen eyes less tortured on a corpse. He looked like a man utterly drained of all will and drive and life force.

He let her clean the cut, and apply the combination disinfectant and cell renewal formula. She glanced at him as she worked; the only sign of his shoulder injury was a slight reddening of golden skin, and the mark on his temple was now only a red line beneath the neuskin graft Nelcar had done.

She tried not to let her eyes stray anymore. It was a difficult task; his muscled chest was a tempting view. So was the flat expanse of his abdomen, bisected by the trail of dark, soft hair that arrowed downward. Triotians, she thought, were too damned beautiful for anyone's equilibrium. And somehow this one, this unusual dark-haired one, was even more tempting to her than Wolf's golden beauty had been.

When she finished he repeated his earlier words, still not looking at her.

"Now just get out."

She shrugged, as if it meant little to her. "You want to wallow in it a while longer? Fine. I understand."

His eyes snapped open. "In Hades you do."

"That's *why* I do," she corrected, forcing herself to meet his eyes. "I've been in Hades, Dax. For the last year."

He let out a short, angry breath. "And you think because of that you understand? You understand nothing of this."

He was talking. He was angry, but he was talking. It was what she'd hoped for, Califa told herself. She chose her words with care.

"Perhaps not, exactly. But I know how it feels to have your world stolen from you. To lose all who were once your friends and companions. To be hunted, like a wild creature, solely because of who you are. Or because of what they've made you become."

He muttered something under his breath, something she couldn't hear. But he didn't order her to get out again. She steeled herself, thinking this spilling of guts an agony beyond any she'd ever experienced. But she was driven by the need to ease his pain. She had learned the hard way about the relief of sharing the load with someone; by the time she had finally realized it, she had no one there to share with.

"And I know how it feels to be helpless, to be able to do nothing, when everything within you is screaming out to fight, to do something, anything. And you can't."

"But I could have!"

It burst from him as if from a disrupter, a sudden blast of words that had become explosive under too much pressure for too long. And instantly his expression went rigid, and he turned his face away from her.

"You could have ... what?"

He remained silent, staring anew out the viewport.

"Dax—"

"Get out."

"It's going to tear you apart if you don't—"

"Get out," he repeated, his hand once more clenching around the handle of his blade.

"Well, that would solve your problems, wouldn't it?" she said, eyeing the knife with a disdain that wasn't entirely feigned. "You wouldn't have to talk to me, or decide whether to turn me in to the Coalition, or execute me. You could just say you lost your temper. What's one slave more or less?"

His eyes flicked to her then. "Damn you to Hades," he ground out. But his fingers relaxed around the knife's grip.

"I told you, I'm already there." And I didn't think it could get any worse, she thought. But it had, the moment she'd laid eyes on this man. She made herself ask again. "You could have what, Dax?"

Again he looked away, stubbornly silent.

"You have to talk to somebody," she insisted. "And since I'm the only one who knows you're Triotian—"

"I'm not."

That stopped her for a moment. "What?"

He turned his head. Califa met his gaze with an effort; it was hard to look at those eyes and remember how blazingly alive they had once been.

"I gave up my right to be called Triotian long ago."

She frowned. "You mean when you became a skypirate? I know Triotian laws about theft and piracy are strict—"

He grimaced. "They're more than strict. Only murder and rape are considered worse. It simply isn't tolerated. But those laws haven't had to be enforced for decades. There was no need. There hasn't been a murder, or a rape, and only minor property disputes, settled by the council."

"And the council deals with ... piracy as well?"

"They've never had to. No real Triotian would ever stoop to such activity, even if the penalty wasn't banishment."

"Banishment?"

"Forever. The worst possible punishment for a Triotian, beyond even death."

What must it feel like, Califa wondered, to belong to a world so beloved by its people that exile was indeed a fate worse than death? Was that how Dax felt? He'd become a skypirate when he'd thought there was nothing else left for him. And now he was faced with the possibility that he'd been wrong, but living with the fact that what he'd become would be an abomination to the world he'd thought dead.

"We're truly in the same straits, aren't we?" she whispered. "Our worlds still exist, but we can no longer be a part of them because of what we are now."

He stared at her. "Maybe you do understand."

"How did you wind up where Roxton found you?"

He didn't question her knowledge. He only laughed, a harsh, tortured sound that sent a chill down her spine. "Simple. I ran away."

Califa blinked. "Ran away? From what?"

He lifted his knife, and it took all of Califa's nerve not to draw back. He ran a thumb over the blade. Califa held her breath, the room so quiet she could hear the sound of his thumb scraping over the razor edge.

"From my father," he said at last. "We had an argument. A fight, really. The last in a long line of fights."

"About?" Califa prompted when he stopped; she said it gently, she didn't want him to close up on her again.

"He is . . . was an artist."

Califa noted the change in wording, and wondered if he knew his father was dead, or had just assumed the worst. And if he wasn't sure . . . She knew it must have occurred to him that his family could be among the few survivors. Perhaps that thought was what was tormenting him so now.

"An artist?" she prompted.

"A sculptor. As was my mother. And my sister. All somewhat celebrated on Trios. But he was an unbending authoritarian, as well. He expected me to follow in the family tradition, no excuses."

Califa blinked. "You're a sculptor?"

"Hardly." He gestured toward the silver dulcetpipe

that lay discarded on the table. "My only artistic talent is music, and that is minuscule."

"Hardly," she echoed, remembering the miracle he had wrought on that delicate instrument the other night. "That is what you fought about?"

Dax nodded. "He wanted me to pursue music."

"And you wanted . . . ?"

He glanced out the viewport once more, then looked back at her. "I wanted to fly. That's all I've ever wanted to do."

She thought of him docking the shuttle in flight, of the *Evening Star* dancing to his command, and of the dark fighter responding like some shadowy warbird to a master's hand.

"If what I've seen is an example," she said softly, "you had no choice. You were born to it."

He let out a long breath, and Califa sensed some of his tension had gone with it. When he looked at her then, his expression was less rigid, as if her understanding had in some way helped.

"My father didn't see it that way. We compromised, when I was younger. I went to The School of Arts for him, and flight school for me. He allowed it mainly because Dare was also there, and it was an honor to attend with the royal prince." A ghost of a smile flitted across his face. "And also because Dare nagged him into letting me go. He needed me, he said, to push him into doing his best."

That was a thought worthy of the best warriors of the Coalition, she thought. And it did not surprise her that it had come from the man she'd known as Wolf, the man who had unknowingly taught her so much about slavery, about surviving while still holding on to that little bit of yourself they allowed you to keep.

"So you learned together."

"Yes. We were . . . competitive. And well matched." His mouth quirked. "Dare's father once said that whatever advantage Dare had in skill, I made up for in recklessness."

She knew he was remembering her own lecture to him on the subject, and she smiled wryly. "An observant man. What did your father think of this?"

"My father was certain I would outgrow my need to fly, and settle down where he thought I belonged."

She studied him for a moment. "But instead, you decided where you thought you belonged."

It wasn't a question, and his expression told her of the accuracy of her guess.

"The chance came for me to take over a wing of the Triotian air defense. The Wing Leader was going to retire. I went to Dare's father and asked to try for it."

She blinked. "You went to the king?"

Dax shrugged. "He was like an uncle, almost. Dare and I were always together. He got used to having me underfoot all the time, when we were children, even at the palace."

Califa felt a twinge of self-castigation at the image of two boys, both with the golden skin of Trios, one blond, one dark, laughing with the joyous exuberance of youth. A joy that would be forcibly taken away from them far too soon.

She had never thought deeply about slaves before, they had just been there, a part of her life. But now she thought again of Wolf, and what had been taken from him; family, boyhood friends, his very world. And of Dax, who had lost nearly as much, and who because of it had wound up living a life that went against all he'd ever known. And all because of the monstrous machine she had supported. Perhaps it was just punishment that she now be enslaved in turn by that same machine, she thought wearily.

She dragged her mind back to the present; she had gotten through to him, she didn't dare stop now.

"So King Galen gave you the job?"

He chuckled, and for the first time it sounded genuine. "King Galen never *gave* anyone anything. But he agreed to let me try for it. I had to beat two men and one woman with more time in the wing in a fly off."

"Which you did, of course."

Unexpectedly, he grinned. It took Califa's breath away, and sent her blood racing. She wished she could keep him amid these happier memories forever, if it would bring that life back to his eyes.

"Of course," he agreed. "I'd been tested against the

best. If I'd learned flying against anyone but Dare, I never would have pulled it off. The woman was a great pilot. But I got the position."

"Your father must have been upset."

"That," Dax said dryly, "is an understatement. He was furious. I'd backed him into a corner. There was no graceful way to turn down an offer from the king."

"So you fought," she said softly. And then wished she hadn't; the temporary lightness faded from his expression.

"Yes. We fought. Loud and long and ugly." A dark, grim look shadowed his eyes. "My mother had to separate us, before we resorted to blows. She told me to give him time to calm down, to get used to the idea." His jaw clenched. "She was always the peacemaker, even though she liked the idea of my flying no better than my father."

"What happened then?"

"I decided I would do exactly as she said. If he needed time to calm down, I'd give it to him. Lots of it. I knew of a ship heading out to Clarion. I'd always wanted to see the Clarion Starworks that built the ship I'd learn to fly on."

And the *Evening Star,* Califa thought, and Dax nodded as if she'd spoken before he continued. She had to do little prompting, as if now that the words had begun to flow, he couldn't stop them even if he wished.

"So I went. My plan was to hitch a ride on a transport heading back, after my father had calmed himself."

"Didn't that make him angrier?"

"He didn't know. I told no one, except my sister." His eyes went dark with pain. "My little sister. She was the only one who understood. The only one who told me to do what I wanted to do, not what anyone else expected of me."

Califa could almost feel the anguish radiating from him. "You loved her very much, didn't you?" she asked, her tone exquisitely gentle.

"Everyone did. There was much to love about Brielle." His mouth twisted then, harshly. He gave her a forbidding look. "Dare could have told you that."

Califa blinked. "What?"

"They were bonded. She was his mate."

Califa smothered a gasp. Then, as the memories tumbled into place, she exclaimed, "The woman who was with him ... she had dark hair, so they thought she wasn't Triotian ..."

Her voice trailed away. This was why he had reacted so fiercely to that part of her story. He had known then that his sister was dead.

"Eos, Dax, I'm sorry. Had I known, I would have tried for more gentleness in the telling."

"There is no gentle way to tell a thing like that. But I already knew she must be gone. Dare would never have taken up with your Shaylah unless Brielle was long dead. It is not the Triotian way."

He looked away then, staring at the viewport as if he hadn't spent days doing so. Afraid he would retreat into that silence again, she tried to get past the ugly revelation.

"Had your father calmed by the time you returned?"

"I don't know," he said flatly. "I never went back."

Califa gaped at him. "What? Why?"

He looked at her then, his eyes hot with anger. When she'd first come in she would have given much to see that look; now, when it was directed at her, it made her shiver.

"Because between the time I left Trios and the time I arrived on Clarion, the all-mighty, all-powerful Coalition had attacked. By the time I found out about it, there was nothing left but rubble and bodies. I had no place to go back to. And no one. My short temper had cost me my world."

Califa could think of nothing to say, nothing that could ease such pain, nothing that could change the fact that in Dax's eyes, she stood for the power that had done this to him. She felt that unaccustomed moisture sting her eyes again, but she refused herself the indulgence of trying to hide it. There was nothing she could do to change what had happened, just as there was nothing Dax could have done.

But I could have!

His poignant exclamation, when she had spoken of being able to do nothing, echoed in her ears.

"That's what you meant," she breathed in sudden understanding. "You think you could have done something, if you'd been there."

"I could have fought, at least." His gaze had shifted once more to the viewport, and his hand gripped the knife handle so tightly his knuckles were white. "But while I was sulking, my family—my whole world—was fighting. And dying."

"Dax, there was nothing you could have done. Corling had ten full tactical wings. It was over in a matter of hours."

"I should have been there. It was my place."

"You would have died with them."

His head snapped around. "Yes!" He took a short breath. "Yes, I would have died with them! I *should* have died with them!"

Califa's eyes widened in realization. "You wish you had, don't you? Eos, you're still trying to join them, even now. Your recklessness, and crazy changes . . . you *want* to die!"

His eyes were alive with a fire she would never have wished there. "I should have been there. Every damn day I remind myself I should have been there. And if I forget, just looking at Rina reminds me." He was panting now, his chest rising and falling in quick movements. "And now . . . now I know they're alive, God, some of them are alive, and still fighting, and I . . . I can't—"

His words broke off with a choking sound, and he turned his back on her. Guilt rang in every word of his impassioned declaration, and Califa knew he would indeed welcome death, to end the agony he felt for not having been there to fight for his home. And she had only made it a hundredfold worse, with her news that some of his people struggled on, while he was out breaking their highest laws.

She saw a shudder ripple through him, then another. For a moment she thought he was crying, but she heard no sounds.

He was in the dark, all alone. When he talked, his voice sounded funny, all thick . . .

Rina's words came back to her, making so much more sense now, so much brutal sense. She wondered if he had ever cried for all his losses. Even she had managed that, the night she had realized she had truly been cast into slavery, and it had been only that release that had enabled her to go on. But she doubted that Dax would allow himself that; guilt rode him harder than any slave master.

He shifted slightly, and the faint glow from the viewport reflected off his skin. His back was broad and strong, the gold Triotian skin like silkcloth stretched over taut muscle, smooth and unbroken. Unbroken except for an odd set of faint, crisscrossed lines that began just below his shoulder blades and continued down to his narrow waist.

Whip marks.

The answer came to her on a rush of nausea; these were the scars he bore for Rina. The scars from the flogging he had willingly endured in order to ease the mind of a child who was too young to accept probability as an answer. An image leapt into her mind, of Dax chained, his back stripped bare for the lash, the silent—for she was certain he would never scream—endurance as they struck him again and again.

This man shamed her. His emotions ran true and deep, and he made a mockery of the way she had lived most of her life, skimming along on the surface, never seeing reality, or feeling it. For so long she had held herself above such things with a smug superiority, until she had lost touch with any true emotions she'd ever had. Until she had lost what little feeling she had for anyone. And until she had lost her last—and truest—friend.

The brutal reality of her enslavement had torn that facade from her. She was pared down to the core of her being, and had only her pitiful skills to rebuild with. If she were ever able to become half the person this man was, she would count it a job well done.

She saw him shudder again, and the sudden knotting of something deep inside her nearly made her reel. She moaned despite her effort to hold it back. And she couldn't help herself; she reached out to him. He stiffened beneath her fingers, the muscles of his arm going rock hard at her touch.

"Dax, please," she whispered, not certain what she was pleading for, only knowing that she couldn't bear to see him hurt like this anymore. He was torturing himself, and for something he'd had no more control over than she'd had over her own mind and body for the last year.

Driven by an instinct she didn't understand but had no urge to question, she bent and pressed her lips to his shoulder. He flinched.

"Don't."

It was muffled, but she heard it nevertheless. And she heard the undertone of desperation, the entreaty of a man so close to breaking that one soft word would send him over.

"I can't help it," she said softly.

She never knew if it was her tone, or the admission of helplessness that broke him. She only knew that he turned to her then, misery and grief turning his expression into a haunting mask she would never forget. And then he was reaching for her, clutching at her as if she could save him from drowning in a morass of pain and guilt and grief.

She could save no one, she admitted. Not when somewhere a long time ago she had lost herself. But she could hold him, now, when he needed it and could ask it of no one else.

She slid down to lie beside him and cradled his head against her breast.

Chapter 14

Not for the first time, Dax wished he could weep. But although he had often shuddered with the force of his grief, that final release was denied him as surely as any other kind of release. Tears, mating, death. All comforts denied him. He understood why; he was deserving of no release from his anguish, no comfort.

Yet he was finding comfort, he thought through a haze of exhausted emotions. Comfort in an unexpected place. Comfort in the gentle arms of the woman who had once been part of the force that had caused his despair.

She held him, crooning soothing words that he knew weren't true, that he couldn't have done anything, that he should quit torturing himself. But somehow her voice, or the feel of her embrace, eased his pain. He allowed it, because he seemed to have no choice. She held him, stroked his hair, murmured reassurances he knew he didn't deserve, but he let her. And after a long time, the shudders stopped. He drifted, too exhausted for sleep yet feeling too lethargic—and, oddly, sheltered—to move.

He'd told no one, not even Rina, what he'd told Califa. He'd never expected to tell anyone. He'd expected to go to his death holding in his ugly secret. A death that was long past due, as Califa had guessed, for in truth he had died that day five years ago, when his home had been destroyed; his body just hadn't gotten the message yet.

Yet he had told her. He'd been unable to stop, just as he'd been unable to stop himself from reaching for her, as a man caught by the vacuum of space reached for oxygen. How had she done it? How had she found the key, the words to unlock the surge gates and make him pour out his soul to her?

He told himself it was because there was no one else, no one who knew he was Triotian except Rina. But he knew there was more to it than that. This woman had drawn him since he'd first seen her. Even before he'd realized her beauty, back in that cell she'd shared with Rina, he'd been struck by her strength and her nerve. And he'd soon learned she managed, as no one else could, to make him forget years spent learning patience and lose his temper faster than anyone ever had.

And now he was sure of something else he'd suspected; her toughness was a bluff, as much an act as the slavelike submissiveness. Califa's brusque, mocking exterior masked something entirely different, a gentle, vulnerable, giving woman capable of caring for a troubled girl she'd just met. And comforting a man who literally held her life in his hands and had threatened her with that power. He wondered what had made her bury that woman so deeply; even a year of slavery couldn't have built a facade that impenetrable.

Even through those walls, she had affected him like no woman ever had. She had made him feel, made his senses waken, made him wonder if he should try again ...

No sooner had he thought it than he became sharply, fully aware of the body that held him. He felt the length of her legs entangled with his, the gentle curve of her hip where it pressed against his belly, the incredible softness of her breast beneath his cheek. She was cradling him as a mother cradled a child, but suddenly there was nothing of the wounded child in his feelings.

He edged closer to her, and she shifted to accommodate him. That simple movement sent heat flaring through him, tightening his body with a speed that took his breath away. He'd fought his growing hunger for this woman for what seemed like aeons. He wasn't sure he could fight it any longer, wasn't sure he wanted to, even knowing it was very likely that nothing had changed, that his body was still as stubborn as his father had once accused him of being.

He hesitated. If he touched her, would she pull away, fearful that he might only want to use her as she had been used before? Or worse, would she allow it, perhaps out of pity? For an instant he wished he'd held back that outpouring of emotion, that purging confession. But he knew he couldn't have; she'd been right, it had been tearing him apart.

"Dax?"

Her tentative, wary tone told him she'd felt the sudden stillness of his body against hers. Had she sensed as well the change in his mood? With her clever perceptiveness, did she know what he was thinking, what he wanted? Did she doubt it was real, after the harsh words exchanged between them?

He wouldn't blame her. His reaction to the revelation of her past life had shocked him, the more because of how he'd begun to feel. But the shock of learning the truth about his home had lessened the importance of that. Lessened it enough to where his need, his desire for this woman overcame it.

Slowly, he raised himself up on one elbow to look at her. The moment their gazes locked, he heard her quick intake of breath, saw her eyes widen, and wondered what was showing on his face.

"I owe you thanks." He was aware of the huskiness of his voice but unable to stop it. "As you said, I needed to talk."

Her tongue crept out to wet her lips, and Dax felt his body clench at the memory of that softness and how it tasted.

"I . . . You're welcome." Her voice was tentative, wary.

"We both hold each other's secrets now, don't we?"

She drew in another audible breath. "It makes trust an easier thing, doesn't it?"

"Does it?" he asked softly. "Do you trust me, Califa?"

"I . . ." She trailed off as he watched her intently. At last, with a rueful twist of her mouth, she said, "More than I should."

Somehow that answer, that she trusted him despite her doubts, forced him to rein in senses that were reeling with the vivid, erotic images that had been pounding at him since he'd come out of his emotional fog and become aware that the woman who held him was the woman he'd been fighting his response to since she'd come on board.

"I told you before to get out," he said gruffly. "I'm glad you didn't then, but I think you'd better now."

She looked blank for a moment. He resisted the urge to take that slender hand that had been gently stroking his hair and drag it down past his belly to feel exactly why she should leave now; he settled for shifting his hips so that his hardened shaft nudged her thigh.

She blinked. "Oh."

His mouth quirked. "Yes, 'oh.' You got what you came for, Califa. You'd better leave before you get more."

For a long moment she looked at him, and Dax could almost see the memory of that kiss, that hot, urgent kiss, come alive in her mind. Just knowing that she was thinking of it sent another burst of heat blazing along nerves that had come cracklingly alive, teasing him with need.

He should make her leave, he thought. He couldn't go through this again. Couldn't drive himself to the brink of insanity, knowing there could be but one result. But then she lifted a hand to his face, smiling slightly as she felt the stubble he'd neglected to use the eliminator on this week.

"And if I were to . . . want more?"

"Califa," he said warningly, but his hand went out to stroke her cheek in turn, the backs of his fingers gentle on skin that seemed too soft to be real.

"I know," she answered softly. "This is probably a great mistake. But . . ."

"But what?" he prompted when her voice trailed away.

"I can't help wondering . . ."

He groaned, low and harsh. "Neither can I," he muttered.

And then he was lowering his mouth to hers, with the desperation of a man who didn't know if he was winning or losing the battle he'd been fighting.

In the first instant he knew that what he'd half convinced himself of wasn't true; the first time hadn't been a fluke. He'd kissed women before after a long period of enforced celibacy, and it had been nothing like this.

What was it about this woman, about her particular combination of intelligence, nerve, and beauty that so got to him? That made him want to forget all the reasons—and God knew there were many—he shouldn't be doing this, and made him want to pray that this time would be different?

He thought there was a chance; he couldn't remember ever being this hot, wanting so much, needing so much. At the least, he knew he could pleasure her, and if that had to be all there was, he would have to be content. That he'd never considered that enough before didn't occur to him.

When she parted her lips for him, he plunged his tongue forward eagerly, seeking her honeyed warmth. He slid his hands up the length of her rib cage until he could feel the soft curves of her breasts nestling against his palms through the fabric of the flight suit that barely contained them. She made no protest as he cradled the warm weight of her.

He let his thumbs caress her, circling, as his fingers and palms flexed over her flesh. He waited until she moved, arching slightly, as if urging him that last small but crucial distance, before he moved to rub the rising peaks of her breasts. She made a tiny sound in her throat, a smothered cry that made his body nearly cramp in response; God, she was killing him, simply by responding to his touch.

He sucked in his breath when he felt her hands move over the bare skin of his chest, and gasped aloud at the darts of fire when she mimicked his actions and her fingers found and stroked his nipples.

He captured her face between his hands as he slid one leg across hers to lift himself over her. He deepened the kiss, and after a moment her tongue rose to meet his, tasting then retreating in a dance that made a shiver race down his spine, oddly chill against the rising heat of his body.

He threaded his fingers through the short cap of her hair; it felt like the silkcloth fiber he'd thought of when he'd been studying her that night as she sat alone on the observation deck. His own hair fell forward, and he felt the sensuous tug as her fingers matched the actions of his own, as if she'd again been waiting for his move before she felt free to make her own.

The idea made him freeze. He lifted his head, his eyes heated as he gazed down at her. Her hands fell away, as if she were afraid of what he would do now.

"Not in this, snowfox," he whispered hotly. "There is no leader in this."

Her eyes widened. "But—"

"If you are here because you feel you must, that it is ... your place, because of *that*"—he snarled as he flicked a finger at the collar—"then go. Now."

"No," she whispered. "It's because, for the first time since ... even before the collar ... I *want*. Truly want. I didn't know I could."

Something let go inside him, some last remnant of doubt or hesitation. "I want, too, Califa. So touch me. As you wish, not at my lead."

She hesitated, as if she'd forgotten what to do with such freedom. Then she lifted her hands once more, tangling them in his hair.

"I've wanted to do this," she said. "It's like the mane of an Arellian steed, thick and long and sleek to the touch."

Dax nearly blushed, but his embarrassment at her fervent admiration did nothing to cool his heated blood. Nor did the image her words called to mind: her riding him as she perhaps had once ridden the famous steeds native to her home world.

"And this," she continued, sliding her hands down over his shoulders, slowly, as if savoring the feel of his skin as he had savored the feel of hers.

At the thought, he was seized with the need to touch more of her, and without the interference of cloth. He reached for the fastener of the flight suit she wore, and tugged it down. It parted easily, driven partly by the swell of her breasts. But when he moved to push it off her shoulders, he felt her go very still.

If she had changed her mind he could stand it, he supposed. He'd certainly had enough practice at frustration. In fact he didn't even know why he was doing this, when he was so painfully certain of what the end would be, except that he seemed to have no choice.

"Califa?"

She bit her lip. He leaned down to kiss her, forcing her to stop the savaging of that tender flesh.

"What is it?"

"I . . . I'm scarred, you know. Badly."

One corner of his mouth lifted wryly. "I have a few of those, myself."

"Not like this."

"And you think it matters?"

"I never did, before. I was still who I was. I would have sliced the throat of anyone who said otherwise," she admitted honestly.

He gave her a lopsided smile. "Did I mention a snow-fox also fights like a demon when cornered?"

She looked at him for a long moment. She lifted one hand as if to touch the corner of his mouth that had quirked upward. Then she let it fall back.

"When I was . . . made a slave, it mattered. I had always accepted that, about slaves. That it lessened their value. I never thought about . . . Eos, I just never thought."

He didn't want this reminder of who she'd been, what she'd done—and Dare. He didn't want to think about it now, when his blood was running hot and the woman who'd driven him nearly mad with sudden, reawakened cravings was in his arms.

"There is no place for those thoughts in this, either," he said, his voice taut as he shifted once more, until she instinctively parted her legs for him to slip between. "No place for anyone else. Only us."

He heard her sharp intake of breath as his weight came down upon her. She hesitated, then reached for him again.

"Only us," she agreed in a whisper.

And then she was kissing him, her slender body arching beneath him to reach his mouth. The movement compounded the pressure on his already aroused flesh, and he groaned low in his throat.

He kissed every bit of pale skin he unveiled as he slid the flight suit down her body. She wore nothing underneath, and the knowledge that she'd probably had nothing to wear did nothing to cool the fire that leapt to life in him again. He caressed her, cupped her breasts and lifted them, watching with heated pleasure as her pink nipples peaked under his gaze. He heard her low moan, and looked up to see her eyes had closed as she lay there, open to his hungry gaze.

"Califa." She moaned again, but her eyes remained closed. "Open your eyes, snowfox. I have to . . ." When she still kept her lashes lowered, he broke off for a swift flick of his tongue over one taut nipple. She gasped, and her eyes shot open. "I need to see your eyes," he said hoarsely. "I need to know that you want this."

A look of understanding crossed her face. She smiled, a smile so nearly tender it made his knees weak; if he'd been standing, he thought, he would have been hard-pressed to stay that way.

"It is not the slave you hold," she promised him, "but the woman." Her smile changed to one of wonder, and its effect on him was no less potent. "A woman who has, it seems, much to learn. Teach me, Dax."

The sound of his name in that tender voice, made his body clench around a white hot shaft of need. The feel of her, soft and willing beneath him, wanting him, shattered the restraints that had held him in check since he'd first kissed her and realized just how potent this woman's effect on him was. Once unleashed, he responded as he had learned to in the past five years; recklessly, fiercely, without hesitation.

Not even the thought of the dismal ending to this that he expected could slow him. Neither did the faint, distant realization that she indeed trusted him; she made no move to hide her scarred leg from his eyes as he tugged the flight suit the rest of the way off her body.

He saw the scar, it would have been impossible not to, as it streaked its way down the outside of her left leg, from midthigh to knee. It was wide, jagged, and made him ache to look at it, knowing what pain it had caused. As if he could ease that long-ago pain, he leaned down and trailed his lips over the mark that made the skin beside it seem even softer and more delicate by comparison.

He heard her gasp, felt her tense, but he kept on. She was a fighter, his snowfox. She had withstood an injury

that would have killed many, and had forced herself to
adapt until the damage was barely noticeable. He had
been right when he'd admired her nerve in those first
moments; she was every bit as brave as he'd thought
her then.

"You are beautiful, snowfox," he murmured as he
blazed a path back up her thigh with his mouth, lingering
at anyplace that made her catch her breath, teasing the
dark triangle of soft curls with his fingers as his hands
traced other paths, caressing, stroking, fondling.

"Dax," she moaned, as her body came alive under his
touch, her legs moving restlessly, the muscles of her belly
contracting with need. Her hands slid over him, down
his back. He felt her fingers pause over the faint scars,
then trace them with a gentle touch, as if she, too,
wished to soothe away old pain.

She said his name again as she pressed his weight to
her, palms flat against the small of his back. He was
fully, painfully erect, caught between their bodies, and
the added friction made him shudder. Her fingers slipped
to the edge of his pants, and his breath caught at her
whispered plea.

She didn't have to ask; if he didn't get free of the
constraining cloth, he was going to die of the pressure.
He quickly rolled away and sat up long enough to shed
the rest of his clothes. Then he brought himself to his
knees between her parted legs.

He watched Califa's eyes as she looked at him, saw
her gaze skate up and down his body. He couldn't begrudge her, he'd looked hungrily enough at her once
he'd rid her of the flight suit. Yet it made him uneasy.
Nervous, perhaps. The realization made him draw back
for an instant; even in this, she was different. Never before had he worried about such a thing with a woman.
He'd come to accept that females found him attractive,
even though he guessed that it was his reputation that
made up for what he lacked in the traditional Triotian
golden beauty.

Yet his reputation as a skypirate held no such at-
traction for Califa. Indeed, except for getting her out of
that prison, he'd done nothing but complicate her life.
A life that was already not even her own, not while she

wore that collar. She had no reason to lust after the infamous Dax, for there was no one for her to boast to afterward.

With the others, he hadn't known, hadn't cared why. It had been enough that they had been there of their own free will. And if they chose to ignore the facts and instead boast of something that had never happened, in a way that only enhanced the other reputation he seemed to have acquired, for his prowess with females, there was little he could do about it. Little that his remaining pride would allow, at least.

Perhaps it was this realization that made him pause, wondering if even now, while he sat here, the swollen, jutting proof of his raging need obvious to her, she would change her mind. And when his eyes traced the slender lines of her body, up the long legs, lingering at the invitation of that sleek, dark delta of curls, over the slight feminine swell of her belly and the full, soft curves of her breasts, to come to a stop at the dull gleam of gold that banded her throat, he knew he had to give her that chance.

Cursing himself for a fool, he choked out the words. "You're sure? You want this?"

"Oh, Dax." It was a moan that was almost a pained laugh. "You don't understand, do you? I'm no innocent, I wasn't, even before. But I've *never* wanted like this."

She held her arms out to him, and with a groan he went into them, biting back a cry of pure pleasure as naked skin touched naked skin. He'd never known such need, never been so tightly wound, so achingly hard. He began to touch her again, first blazing trails with his hands, then following with his mouth. Her instant, heated response inflamed him further, because he had no doubt of the genuineness of it.

As she writhed beneath his ministrations, he allowed himself a brief moment of hope. Perhaps it hadn't been something wrong with him, all this time. Perhaps it simply hadn't been this woman. Then he buried it, knowing the chance was less than slim, and concentrated on what he knew was possible; he set about wringing every possible sign of desire from her, until she was clinging to him, her fingers digging into his flesh as she nearly wept his name.

"Dax, please! I can't bear it, I—Oh!"

This as his mouth found the heart of her, his tongue parting the dark curls and stroking until he found that tiny knot of nerve endings that made her go rigid against the hands that lifted her for the intimate caress.

He drove her to the edge, retreated, then began again. Only when, in desperation, she slid her hand down his body and curved her fingers around him, did he pause.

For a moment, he remained motionless, savoring the feel of her hand as she stroked him, base to tip and back, and then again, until he shuddered. Surely his body wouldn't betray him now, not when he felt he would explode at her next touch, at the next movement of her fingers. And then she did move, a slow, downward stroking that went beyond the length of his rigid shaft until she was cupping him in her palm, the feel of that delicate grasp on rounded flesh drawn tight with want threw him out of control.

He came down on her fiercely, his mouth on hers, his chest crushing her breasts, his thighs separating hers urgently. She opened for him, welcomed him, with an eagerness that seemed almost taunting in the light of what he knew as the futility of it. Yet even knowing he was dooming himself to even more torment, the pull of the pleasure he'd already felt, so much stronger than any he'd ever known, drew him on irresistibly, and he plunged forward.

He heard her gasp as he thrust into her soft heat, heard her cry out, and echoed it as her flesh closed around him, searing him until his arms shook with his effort to hold himself steady.

The look of startled, wondering pleasure on her face stripped away his doubts about what he was letting himself in for; for that look, he would suffer a lot more than the temporary, if painful, ache of frustration.

"Why surprised, snowfox?" he murmured. "It's supposed to be this way."

He began to move, rocking his hips against her, inching deeper with each forward motion. She was moaning his name, begging him not to wait. And then he couldn't wait. With a quick jerk of his hips he sheathed himself to the hilt, and a guttural sound of pleasure broke from his throat.

She tilted her hips, as if to better feel the length of him buried within her. Her hands were gripping his shoulders, using his body as purchase for the rippling movement of hers. She was driving him mad, her slick, wet flesh coaxing, caressing his, until he couldn't believe his body would not accede to the demand of hers.

But he'd known the moment he'd entered her that it would not. For he had been so close, so near to erupting that just the feel of her body accepting him, of that tight yet yielding passage closing around him, should have sent him spiraling into climax. But he only ached, that painfully familiar driving, pulsing ache, different only in the fact that now, with Califa, it was more powerful, more excruciating then it had ever been in his life. And he—or she—could do nothing to end it.

But he could end her ache. He could ease the need he felt in every movement of her body, in every touch of her hands, in every ravening kiss she gave whatever part of him she could reach as she lay there beneath him, and in every breathless word she uttered.

"Dax ... I don't ... I ... Eos, what are you doing to me?"

What I can't do for myself, he muttered silently. Putting the hope for himself that he'd briefly, foolishly held back in the dark cavern of his mind where the rest of his demons lived, he concentrated on Califa, on his snowfox, on her warm, slender body and the way it responded to him. He began to move slowly, driving himself into her and then withdrawing with long, slow, controlled motions. He moved for her, not himself, shifting his position, changing the angle of his hips so that his own rigid flesh slid over the most sensitive part of her with every thrust.

She was quivering, and with awed amazement of her cries gave him the strength to go on, to ignore the fact that her wet heat was searing him to ashes, even as his own body denied him. And then he felt it, in the instant before she cried out his name yet again, that rippling, flexing convulsion of inner muscles, gripping him, making him want to scream at ferocity of the strangling pressure that would not release. He did cry out, as he buried himself deeply in her quivering body in a final, futile effort.

But Califa was quaking in his arms, moaning his name over and over, clinging to him as he instinctively knew she had never clung to anyone. She was nearly sobbing as her body continued to convulse, crying out her shock and awe and wonder. And for that sound, that undeniable knowledge that he had shown her something she had never known before, he would have suffered worse than this.

Chapter 15

She was looking at him, still seeming dazed, yet at the same time troubled. The slight crease between her brows had appeared the moment he had withdrawn from her sated body and she had realized he was still fully erect, that sweat beaded his brow, that her slightest movement was agony for him.

"Dax?"

He sagged back on the bunk beside her, trying to slow breathing that was still accelerated, and the pulse that was still racing toward a climax that would never come.

"Sshh. Just rest," he managed to get out.

She needed to rest, he thought, able to smile inwardly despite the persistent hurt that had settled in his groin. It would recede, eventually, he knew. The ache would fade, the strained tautness of his flesh would ebb, leaving behind another layer of the gut-level tension he'd learned to live with. It was just a little worse this time, he told himself.

He pulled her closer against his side, his still distended shaft brushing against the silkcloth smoothness of the skin of her naked hip. He tensed involuntarily.

All right, he admitted caustically, *a lot worse.*

Califa began to raise up on one elbow to look at him. She fell back, as if her muscles were refusing to obey. He smiled at her, but she frowned back.

"Dax—"

"Sshh," he repeated.

"But you didn't—"

He put a finger to her lips. "Believe me, I know." He tried for some nonchalance in his shrug. "It's all right."

"But—"

"Don't worry about it, snowfox. It's . . . something inherent in Triotians." In this one, anyway, he thought in pained ruefulness. "Besides, it was worth it, just watching you come apart in my arms."

That, he judged by the sudden rush of color to her face, had sufficiently distracted her. "I ... I've never been like that. I didn't know it was possible, to feel like that."

Dax's mouth curled in purely male gratification. He was surprised at how good he felt, in spite of the fact that his body was so achingly tight he wanted to curl up and groan. Yet despite the pain, he knew he would do the same thing again; just looking at her, soft and naked beside him, made him want to start now. He might not have reached the ultimate pleasure, but he had never felt so much in the process.

"It's supposed to be like that," he said.

She snuggled closer, a small movement that had a much bigger effect on him; strangely, it was more in the area of his heart than his groin.

"I never believed that," she admitted, still sounding amazed by the pleasure that had overtaken her. "Shaylah did. It was what she was waiting for." She paused, an odd look coming into her eyes, one almost of revelation. "I never knew what my mother was seeking, with all her matings. I only knew she never found it. I think it must have been this."

Dax was torn between that smug satisfaction that he had so thoroughly achieved his goal, the lingering throb of his unsatisfied body, and a shock at realizing this was the first time she'd ever mentioned anything about her family.

"Your mother?"

She looked at him, her expression suggesting she would take offense at the question were she not been so replete. He couldn't stop that satisfied smile from forming again.

"Even slaves have them." She sounded as if she were trying to be irritated, but the contented laziness of her expression, lashes half lowered, detracted from it a bit.

"I know. I just wasn't sure Coalition officers did."

Her lashes lifted sharply. She eyed him, as if unable to believe he'd made a joke about it. He wasn't sure he quite believed it himself. Somehow his priorities had definitely shifted; her past still bothered him mightily, but it seemed to have paled in significance beside the knowledge that a small part of his world had survived and was fighting back.

He couldn't think about that now. He'd been wrestling with it for days, closed away in here, and he wasn't any closer to resolving anything.

"Is she still alive?"

"I don't know."

Her tone was sharp enough to sting, her expression suddenly cool, and he felt as if she'd slammed a door in his face. Dax drew back a little, telling himself that just because he'd poured out his entire life to her didn't mean she was going to do the same. Nor did the fact that she'd just gone to pieces in his arms.

"I'm sorry," she said suddenly, contritely, as if she'd read his thoughts. "I don't talk about her much. I don't even think about her much."

"I'm sorry," he said, uncertain what else to say.

"Don't be." She grimaced. "It's quite mutual."

"What about your father?"

She laughed then, humorlessly. "That's *why* I don't think about her."

Congratulations, he told himself ruefully. You've surely managed to shatter the mood. "Califa, I didn't mean to—"

"It doesn't matter." She lifted one slender, bare shoulder, as if to emphasize her words. The movement made the soft flesh of her breast rise as well; Dax tried to ignore the stab of heat that resulted. "I have no idea who he is. Neither did she."

Dax's brows furrowed. He was more and more wishing he hadn't pressed. She went on as if she hadn't seen his expression. As if it truly mattered little to her. Or as if she owed it to him, in return for his own confessions. He didn't like that thought.

"My mother was . . . the personification of the Coalition view on mating. She had many men. They never stayed long. My father could have been any one of three or four of them."

He truly didn't know what to say to that.

"When I was small, and there was one I liked," Califa said, as calmly as if what she was describing was—as perhaps it was, Dax thought, in her world—normal, "which usually meant anyone who acknowledged my existence, I would pretend that he was the one. Then Trayon came."

"Trayon?"

She nodded, smiling, so wistfully Dax felt his throat tighten. "He was different. He liked me. He really liked *me*. I knew, because sometimes he would come when my mother wasn't even there, to see me."

So she'd had someone to care for her, at least for a while, he thought. An old, familiar jab of guilt prodded him; his father had been a stiff-necked, authoritarian man, but Dax had never doubted his love. Even their arguments never shook that belief. Perhaps it was why he'd left so easily, because he knew that, since his father truly loved him, they would eventually make it up. But instead, he'd wound up having to live with the knowledge that the last words they'd ever spoken had been harsh and angry.

But Califa hadn't even had that. "This Trayon," he said, his voice a little unsteady, "he was good to you?"

Her eyes glowed. "He taught me to sing."

Such a small thing, really, he thought. Yet from that look in her eyes, and the fondness in her voice, it was perhaps the brightest memory in a grim childhood.

"That's when I decided it must be him. That he had to be my real father."

"Was he?" Dax asked, feeling he already knew the answer.

The fond light faded from her eyes, to be replaced by bitter remembrance. "No. When I told my mother, she laughed and said I was very wrong. That she might not be sure who my father was, but she could be sure it wasn't Trayon. I didn't understand. I insisted that if she didn't know, it could be him. She thought I was calling her a liar."

"But you were a child," Dax protested instinctively. "You didn't know—"

"Exactly. So she made certain I did know. She sat me down and told me more about the facts of mating than any child should ever know." He felt a shiver ripple through her. "Then she made me ... watch. The next time she had one of her men. So I could see exactly why she could be sure."

Dax's stomach knotted painfully. The persistent ache of his arousal had faded as her grim story had come out. Shame replaced it; she had had so little, and he so much, and he had taken it for granted. And so he had lost it all. But Califa had apparently never had anything or anyone tender and loving in her young life, except the kindly Trayon.

Unable to stop himself, he gathered her up into his arms and cradled her to him, much as she had cradled him when he had been racked with a pain too great to bear alone. For an instant she stiffened, resisting, but then went pliant against him, her cheek pressed against his chest, her hand resting on his side over his ribs.

"Your mother," he said gruffly, "deserved to lose you."

Califa made a low, remorseful sound. "I'm not sure she did. In the end, I think she may have won."

"What do you mean?"

"I believed what she told me, that mating was merely a physical need, and that no one male could satisfy a woman for long. That the only way to protect yourself from hurt was never to give yourself away."

She sighed then. And she pulled away from the encircling shelter of his embrace. She faced him, but didn't look at him. As if heedless of her own nudity, or feeling modesty was unimportant compared to what she had to say, she didn't try to cover herself. When she spoke, it was in the tone of a confession, of one expecting punishment for some wrongdoing.

"I'm sorry, Dax. I should have told you this before we ... mated. Perhaps you would have changed your mind. Perhaps you will regret it, now."

"I could never regret it, snowfox," he said quietly. Even though it had been agony as well as bliss, even though it complicated his life impossibly.

"You may. I've ... been too like my mother. Thinking mating was as the Coalition decreed it, a casual thing, between two beings possessed of a mutual urge, nothing

more. Were you to ask someone who knew Major Claxton, they would tell you she was not above sampling.
Widely."

The surface meaning of her words disturbed him. It
was so foreign to what he'd been raised to believe. Not,
he admitted with a flash of bitter self-contempt, that he'd
done much in the way of living up to those beliefs himself. But something else about the words disturbed him
even more.

"Would what they would say be true?"

She looked startled. He smiled wryly. "I know a little
of reputations." And, he added silently, I have a feeling
yours is as ill deserved as mine.

"Would what they would say be true?" he asked
again.

Her answer, spoken almost embarrassedly, was what
he'd half expected. "I ... tried to adopt my mother's
view, but I ... couldn't. Major Claxton gave the appearance of fully enjoying the mating freedom sanctioned by
the Coalition, but ..."

"Appearances can be deceptive." And who knew better than he? He lifted a brow at her. "You speak of
Major Claxton as if she were someone else."

"I ... She is. It's as if she is someone I knew, or
was pretending to be. But then all the trappings, all the
pretense was stripped away. I don't know what's left. I
only know that I don't ever want to be her again."

"And there's the difference," Dax said, his voice low.
"You said we were in the same straits, but ... you never
want to go back, and I ..."

Califa lifted her head to look at him then. "And you
would give anything—everything—to go back."

He let out a long breath. "Yes. I think I would."

"You've lost so much more than I," she said.

Only, Dax thought, because I had so much more to
lose. When she went on, she as much as confirmed his
thought.

"The only true regret I have is Shaylah. I never ...
appreciated her until it was too late."

"It is ... hard to lose a friend," Dax said. Califa met
his gaze, then looked away, and he knew she knew he
was thinking of Dare.

"But he knew how you felt, did he not? That you . . . cared for him?"

"He knew that I loved him as a brother," Dax said.

Califa's eyes closed for a moment, the semicircles of her lashes dark on her pale cheeks. She looked as if she were in pain, and shame laced her voice when at last she spoke.

"I never told Shaylah how I felt. We were friends, and yet . . ." She sighed. "You were right, when you said I was jealous. I am not proud of that. When I was hurt, and my active career ended, she kept on. She became a hero, won medals, and I . . . envied her."

"Envy is not the same as jealousy. You can envy someone and still like them."

"I did," Califa said, almost fiercely. "I even . . . loved her, I think, as the closest thing to a sister I'd ever had. But my envy kept me from telling her, and now . . . I've lost the truest friend I ever had, because she saw the truth about the Coalition long before I did."

"Why?"

Califa blinked. "What?"

"Why did she see it so much sooner?"

"I don't know." Califa's brow furrowed as she considered the question. "Perhaps because her parents were . . . different as well."

"You mean what you said about her parents being bonded." Califa nodded. "I've wondered about that. You said she was Arellian, like you."

"She is."

He shook his head in surprise. "Only a few of the outworlders who request it are granted permission for a Triotian ceremony."

"I know. Shaylah told me they had to apply, and remain on Trios for observation while the council decided."

"Not many would think it worth all that."

"Her parents did. They wished to be bonded before Shaylah's birth. I think they are why she looked at things differently. She only joined the Coalition for the same reason you fought with your father. All she had ever wanted to do was fly."

Then she would be a good match for Dare, Dax

thought, feeling a stabbing pang of regret for Brielle. He had long ago accepted his sister's probable death; Califa's confirmation of the fact had merely put the seal on the knowledge. But it hurt to think of her gone forever, that little tease she had been as a child, always getting him into trouble by making faces at him until he laughed while his father lectured him, getting him into more trouble than whatever he'd done to deserve the lecture in the first place. God, she had loved Dare so much ...

But if Dare had found a measure of happiness, with a woman such as Califa had spoken of, then Dax would be the last to begrudge him. Dare had more than paid the price for it. Perhaps he had already paid the ultimate price, and his Shaylah with him. He wondered if they had ever overcome the fact that she belonged to the force that had enslaved him.

"And why did you join the Coalition?" he asked, thinking perhaps there was a clue here, some answer that might help him understand her.

Califa studied him for a long moment, as if searching for any trap in the question, examining it to see what damage answering it could do. Not the response of a Coalition officer, or of a female in a trusted lover's bed. But Califa was neither of those; she had wanted him, had allowed him to mate with her, but trust was not a word for what flowed between them. No, her response was that of the slave, who had learned in the hardest of ways the cost of the wrong answer.

"I needed ... to belong somewhere," she said at last. *The Coalition was all I had. It was all I ever had.*

He could almost hear her saying the words that day, not as excuse—there was none, she'd admitted—but explanation. And after what she'd told him today, the words now made a poignant sense. He had been surrounded by relations and friends for most of his life. What made him qualified to judge why a lonely child, subjected to a haphazard kind of emotional abuse he could never have imagined, had grown up to find comfort in belonging somewhere, even the Coalition?

And was it not one of the basic tenets of Trios that anyone, if they had compelling enough reason in the eyes of the council for a crime, deserved a second chance?

It was a thought that hadn't occurred to him before. There was no Council of Elders left. He doubted if any of them would have survived the Coalition's bloody purge—

"Dax?"

The tentative call from outside in the passage came in a familiar voice. Dax felt Califa stiffen, saw a look of dismay cross her face, and suddenly became aware of what Rina would see if he didn't answer and she opened the door. They were sprawled naked on his bunk, arms and legs entwined, their clothes scattered on the floor. That was not a part of Rina's education he wanted to provide just yet—and certainly not so personally. The cruelty of what Califa's mother had done struck home with even more force.

"Hold, Rina," he called. "A moment."

At the look of sudden relief Califa gave him, Dax suddenly realized all the ramifications of what had happened here. Beyond Rina's reaction to discovering them together, there was the crew to think about. Were they to learn he had taken the Coalition slave to his bed, they might consider her fair game for them all, although he supposed they would not touch her for as long as they thought she was his.

And as long as they didn't know who she really was.

He leaned forward to gently kiss her forehead. "You are free to speak or not, as you wish, about what has happened between us. I would not force you one way or the other."

She looked startled, but so was he; such tenderness was hardly his rule after another of the matings that proved so frustrating for him.

He rolled out of the bunk and reached for his pants. He bent to pull them on, then paused when a movement caught the corner of his eye. Califa had also stood up, reaching for the flight suit. Their gazes locked, and for an instant they stood there, each one openly scanning the other's nakedness, as they had not done in the heat of their joining.

"I was right," Califa muttered.

"Right?"

"Triotians are too much for anyone's equilibrium."

She didn't sound happy about it, which enabled Dax to grin instead of blush. "At the moment," he said casually as he quickly dressed, including his shirt this time, "I've come to favor blue-eyed, black haired Arellians."

When he was finished, he straightened and looked at Califa, who was fastening the front of the flight suit. She had to tug at it to get it to close over her breasts. And now that he knew exactly how those soft, full curves felt in his hands, Dax felt his body tighten.

Damning the stubbornness of a body that couldn't seem to get the message that it was nigh on to crippling itself in this vicious cycle of unrelieved desire, he yanked his gaze upward to her face.

She finished and met his eyes. He lifted a brow. She took a quick breath, and nodded. Dax walked to the door and opened it himself. Rina peered into the room anxiously.

"Did you think she would kill me?" Dax teased the girl as she came in and the door closed behind her; may Rina never know how close that is to the truth, Dax swore silently.

"It was on my list of possibilities," Rina admitted, staring at him. "Right after you killing her."

Dax grinned, and indicated Califa with a sweeping gesture. "As you can see, we're both alive."

At his grin, Rina's eyes widened. Her gaze shifted from Califa to Dax, and back again. Califa kept her eyes lowered. After a moment Rina turned back to Dax.

"Are you ... all right?"

There was a galaxy of concern in her young voice, and Dax felt the tug of guilt. It was past time to stop indulging himself in his own sorrows. "I'm fine, little one. I just had ... some things to think about."

She looked slightly placated, but no less curious. "What things? They must have been pretty awful, for you to go demented like that."

Dax's keen ears picked up Califa's quick intake of breath, and senses that still seemed highly attuned to her registered her sudden tension.

"I'll tell you, when I've worked them out," he promised Rina. Then added, "I'm sorry if I worried you."

Rina looked up at him. "I didn't know what to do."

The quiet helplessness in her voice ripped at Dax. He hadn't heard her sound like that since he'd found her huddled in that cave. He hugged her suddenly, fiercely.

"You didn't have to do anything, little one. It's not your job to be my keeper."

"Someone needs to be." She returned his embrace with the strength that sometimes surprised him. Then she released him and stepped back to look at him. "But I didn't do a very good job. Nor did Roxton. You wouldn't speak to either of us."

He hadn't been capable of speaking, Dax thought. He'd been mired in a swamp of shock, pain, and guilt so deep he'd barely been aware of anything but his own misery. Nothing had had the power to get through to him. Except the woman whose words had cast him into the morass in the first place.

Without realizing it he had looked at Califa. Rina followed his gaze. Califa stood quietly, eyes still lowered. It reminded him of the submissive slave, and he wanted to shake her.

"I should have believed you," Rina said to Califa, startling her into looking up to meet the girl's eyes, "when you said you could make him angry."

"I seem to have the knack," she said, her voice low.

"For that as well as other things," Dax growled. Then, when he saw the hint of pink rise in her cheeks, he asked softly, "Is that why you came here? To make me angry?"

She met his gaze then, levelly, with the steadiness he'd come to admire. This was the Califa who pulled at him, who could tighten his body with a look, who had made him risk the torment he knew was inevitable just for the pleasure of holding her naked against him.

"I came to make you talk," she said. "Before the words choked you."

He didn't miss the implication that she had come to him for nothing more than that; but then he'd hardly thought she'd come with the idea of seducing him. Contrary to whatever the reputation the esteemed Major

Claxton might have had, his snowfox knew herself now, and she would not give herself so freely.

Yet she had. To him. And despite the agony his perverse body put him through, she had given him a greater pleasure than he'd ever known. For a fleeting moment he wondered whether, if his body had chosen this time to cooperate, he would have survived it.

"I suppose I should thank you," Rina said to Califa, not sounding as if she liked the idea.

"I would rather you didn't," Califa returned quietly, "if you don't truly want to."

Dax guessed the reason for the girl's hesitation. When he spoke, it was to Rina, but his gaze never left Califa.

"I've never told you what to think, Rina. I won't now. But I will tell you this. I believe Califa has come to hate the Coalition as we have. I cannot tell you to forgive her for what she was. Only you can decide that, and I'm not sure I can do that myself, yet."

Califa winced at the brutal honesty, but she didn't look away. She held his gaze evenly, her shoulders squared with the courage that called to something deep inside him.

"But neither will I subject her to danger because of it. The fact that she was a Coalition officer will remain between us, Roxton and Nelcar, those who already know it."

Califa closed her eyes as she drew in a deep, relieved breath. When she opened them again, she gave him a look that made him want to send Rina away and climb right back in that bunk with her, never mind the frustration.

Abruptly, Dax shifted his gaze to Rina.

"Understand, little one?"

The girl nodded. Then, in an unconscious mimicking of Califa's own steady, square-shouldered nerve, she lifted her head and met Califa's eyes.

"I do truly want to thank you. For bringing him back. I was afraid for him."

"I know," Califa said softly. "So was I."

Something flashed between the two females, a softening in Rina, a quiet understanding in Califa. Dax shifted his feet, uncomfortable with being the subject of conversation. And with being referred to as if he wasn't even here. Something slaves were used to, he supposed; he didn't much care for it. And this was but a tiny taste of that life. His admiration for Califa's determination in surviving it grew another notch, along with the warm feeling that had begun to expand in him when she'd admitted she was worried about him.

"Rina! What in Hades is going on?"

Dax sighed as Roxton's bellow nearly rattled the door. Then he realized he should be grateful Rina had come first; Roxton no doubt would have burst right in with no warning. He called to the first mate to come in, suppressing a wry smile as the door slid open to reveal Roxton still looking startled that he had answered.

"Well," the man said as he came in, tugging at his beard, "it's about time. Back with us, now, are you?"

He nodded. Then, contritely, responding to the relief on the older man's face, he added, "Sorry, Rox."

"Hmmph." The crusty first mate waved off the apology. "Man needs to think, sometimes." Then he glanced at Califa and grinned. "But if I'd known she'd shake you out of it so fast, I'd have sent her myself."

Dax scowled at Roxton, but it was mainly to conceal the surge of new warmth that filled him at this further proof that Califa had come to him on her own.

"Welcome back, son," Roxton said with a laugh.

"To where?" Dax realized he had no idea where they were. They hadn't really had a plan for after the raid on Boreas.

"We're in Sector Gamma Twelve at the moment," Roxton told him. "It seemed like a good place to wait."

For me to come out of my cloud, Dax thought, although his old friend didn't say it. But it was a good place, isolated, off both the shipping lanes and the usual path for Coalition patrols.

"What's next?" Rina asked eagerly, forgetting the anxiety and distress of the past days with the resilience of the very young.

Dax shrugged. He looked at Roxton. "What do you think?"

"We could lie low, for a while, if you want. We've

enough supplies to last a good long time. The crew wouldn't mind a bit of rest and revelling."

"Alpha Two it is, then."

Roxton nodded. Rina groaned. "I suppose this means I get to hide out while everyone else is having fun at the colony."

Roxton reached out and tousled the girl's golden hair. "Sorry, little one. The crew can blend in with the rowdies on Alpha Two, but you stand out like a perla among snailstones."

"Besides," Dax put in, "nothing's there but taprooms and Coalition crews on leave. Nothing for you except maybe a game of chaser, and I think you've had enough of that for now."

Rina flushed. "One little mistake," she muttered.

"Let me get this straight." They looked at Califa, who was staring at them in disbelief. "You're the most wanted skypirates in the system. They send warships after you. And you plan on parading under a squadron of Coalition noses?"

Dax grinned. "Why not? We always have."

Her eyes widened even further, and she let out a short, incredulous breath.

"It's safe enough," Roxton explained. "We go into the colony in shifts, just three or four at a time. Never the same groups, and always in different guises. No one notices, not among the din and confusion of that place."

"I know it's the rowdiest of Coalition outposts," Califa said, "but still—"

"In their arrogance," Dax said smoothly, "the Coalition never thinks to look, as you said, beneath their noses. Especially in a place where the main concern of most visitors is drinking and"—he glanced at Rina—"other things."

"There is truth in that," Califa agreed, her expression telling Dax that she knew quite well that most of those who went to Alpha 2 had two things in mind; finding a whore and a drink, not necessarily in that order. Or in the case of the infamous Legion Club there, a slave and a drink. She shivered visibly, and Dax wondered if she was thinking that, were it not for Rina's garrulousness, and hence Dax's interference, she, too, could have wound up there, servicing the very forces she'd fought alongside.

"Still," she felt compelled to caution him, "there are others who come there for the archives. Shaylah's medical officer went there every time he got leave."

He knew it was true. Perversely, the most brawling of all Coalition outposts was also home to the most extensive of its archives, a massive collection of records, documents, and microbooks from all of the worlds that had been forced into the Coalition by threat—or fact—of annihilation.

It was there, he recalled suddenly, that she had seen the dulcetpipe she had told him of, in the exhibit of treasures from the then newly conquered Trios.

"Watch yourself," Roxton warned Rina, sounding only half joking, "he's getting that look. He's up to something."

Dax pulled out of his thoughts, but not before promising himself to think over what had just occurred to him.

"Never mind," he said brusquely. He reached out and tweaked Rina's upturned nose. "Set course, navigator. We'll find something to amuse you when we get there." The girl brightened at the promise, and headed off for the bridge.

Roxton lingered, looking at Dax warily. "What are you scheming on?"

"Nothing."

"Sure. And you didn't intend to be noble and sacrifice yourself when you made that crazed strafing run on that Coalition warship."

Dax glanced at Califa; those words were too familiar. She lifted her brows in an expression of utter innocence.

"Are you two in collusion?" he asked sourly.

"I might consider it," Roxton said easily. "The lady seems to get things done."

Dax saw Califa's gaze fly to the old man's face, both surprise and pleasure displayed in her expression.

"Besides," the first mate added, chuckling, "anyone who can yell at you and get anything but a laugh has my respect."

She has mine, too, he almost said, but bit back the words. He'd meant what he'd said to Rina; he wasn't sure if he could forgive—or forget—Califa's past, especially Dare. But he did respect her. He did admire her courage. And God knew he wanted her like he'd never wanted another woman.

It came to him then, the realization of what he'd let himself in for. Having her around from now on was going to be a brand-new kind of torture.

"I'm going to get some food," he announced suddenly.

"Good idea," Roxton agreed, "but that's not going to distract me. What are you planning?"

Dax sighed; there were times he wondered how he'd ever been able to hide anything from the man. "Nothing. Yet. Just thinking."

"About?"

He shrugged. "A little shopping of my own."

"Personal?" Roxton's surprise was evident. And no wonder; Dax couldn't remember the last time he'd gone after something for himself. He wasn't sure he was going to do it now, but the idea had appeared, full blown and tempting, and he wasn't sure he could resist it.

"Does shopping mean the same thing this time as it did last time?" Califa asked, eyeing Dax suspiciously.

He grinned at her, just to see the incredulity widen her eyes. It did.

"Rina was right," she cried in exasperated tones. "You do need a keeper."

She walked out of his quarters, head high. Dax was thankful she'd done it before he'd had the chance to ask her if she wanted the job.

Chapter 16

Califa watched Rina switch the holograph disks. In a moment a new star system image replaced the one that had been hovering, all bodies in constant motion, over the table in their quarters for the past hour or so.

"How do you do that?" she asked as she watched the various orbits, and the streak of a comet that arced through the display at regular intervals. Rina adjusted the brightness of the display before she answered. The girl had apparently decided Dax was right, that Califa was as much against the Coalition as she, and had resumed talking to her. Califa felt surprisingly glad that she was no longer out in the cold with the little pixie.

"I just . . . look at it," Rina said.

Dax had told her Rina was what they called an "exact navigator," that rare person who could study a star system or a sector chart and commit it to memory for all-dimensional recall later, as if it were no more difficult than breathing.

At least, he'd told her that when he'd been speaking to her; he seemed once more to be avoiding her. She tried not to think about it, tried not to wonder if it was because she had failed to please him as he had so incredibly pleased her that night. He had said it didn't matter, that his lack of climax was a Triotian trait, but she wasn't at all certain. But then she recalled that Wolf—Dare—had had a reputation for endurance among those who used slaves, a reputation like Dax had among, according to the crew, most of the females in the system. Perhaps there was truth, then, in what Dax had said.

And he had, after all, sent the clothing she wore now, a loose shirt and comfortable, flowing trousers that fit her much better than Rina's flight suit. He'd found another of those, as well, that fit her better, somewhere in the stacks of crates and cases that were piled high in the cargo bay, awaiting off-loading at the storehouse.

But that didn't explain why he was avoiding her. Unless he was frightened by what happened between them, as she was. That seemed absurd, and she forced her mind back to Rina.

"You just look at it? That's all?"

"From all angles, for about an hour, then ..."

"You can recall it? Exactly? Without the holograph?"

Rina nodded, shrugging. "It's no great thing. It's just something I can do. Like Dax can use the flashbow."

Califa's brow furrowed. "You mean not everyone can?"

"No. It is a special weapon, beyond just its power. Few have been able to use it, those in whom the power has come down across generations."

"The power?"

"To activate the bow."

Califa was thoroughly perplexed now. "But it seemed there was just a lever he moved and it began to hum."

Rina laughed. "Yes. But if you're not one of the few, it does nothing. I tried it, and no matter what I did, I couldn't bring it alive. And I know my father couldn't, nor my mother. Dax is the only flashbow warrior I've ever known."

Something about the people she had just mentioned struck Califa. "Is it a Triotian weapon, then?"

Rina gasped, her sudden paleness visible even beneath the stain that dyed her skin. She looked about to run. Califa hastened to reassure her.

"Rina, don't. It's all right."

"You know," the girl whispered.

"Yes. I guessed, when Dax and I were talking."

"Dax?" Panic filled the girl's eyes. "You know about Dax, too?"

Touched by the girl's fear for Dax, which was so much greater than her fear for herself, Califa said softly, "And both of you know about me. It is a fair trade, is it not?"

Slowly, the tension left the girl as Califa's words calmed her fears. "I ... I guess so."

"I would never intentionally hurt you, Rina." She took a breath before adding, "Or Dax."

Rina eyed her then, speculatively. "You like him, don't you?"

"I'm not sure what I feel for him," she answered truthfully. "But it is . . . different from anything I've ever felt before." And that was already more than she should have said, she thought, reverting to the previous subject quickly. "So the flashbow is a Triotian weapon?"

After a moment, with an expression that revealed relief at no longer having to watch her every word, Rina nodded. "A very ancient one. Few non-Triotians have ever even heard of it. Roxton hadn't, nor had any of the rest of the crew. They have no idea what it is, just that Dax is the only one who can use it. I think they're a little afraid of it."

Remembering the hole in the prison wall, Califa murmured, "I'm not surprised."

"Only one in a generation has the power to fire it. The flashbow warriors are legend among Triotians. They were the ones who brought peace to us, long ago, because armed with the bow they were nearly undefeatable. Now it is"—the girl's voice caught as she corrected herself—"before the Coalition, it was mostly a ceremonial thing."

Califa was fascinated. "Is it a hereditary power?"

Rina shrugged. "No. A new one is found each generation, at the time of transition, when the child begins to become an adult. Part of the transition ceremony is the touching of the stone. The stone responds to only one, the next flashbow warrior. That one is sent to learn from the current warrior."

"Even when you were at peace?" Dax's father must have hated that, Califa thought.

"Yes. It is still an honor to be the chosen one."

"Then it can be anyone?"

Rina nodded. "Except that it is never one of the royal family. Something prevents it."

Too bad, Califa thought. If Wolf—Dare, she amended—had had that power, he might never have been taken. That having such thoughts when she had owned him would have been near unto treason, or that she herself had thought Shaylah near treasonous for harboring them, did not even occur to her.

"How does it work?" she asked.

"I don't know. No one really does. It's in the bolts, but no one understands why."

Califa blinked. "It's in the bolts?"

Rina nodded. "The bolts are made from a material found only in one place on Trios, and on no other world. That's why Dax so rarely uses it. He has only a few left."

"What is this material?"

"The material that's in the ceremonial stone. It's a strange combination of metal and rock. The scholars can't explain it, they only mutter something about a reaction with a chemical common to the metal and the rock."

Califa thought of the hole Dax had left in the prison wall. "That's some chemical reaction," she said dryly.

Rina grinned. "Isn't it? I think they just don't want to admit that there are some things they can't explain away."

Califa smiled. Then something else Rina had said came back to her. "You said they were *nearly* undefeatable? From what I've seen, that weapon should guarantee it."

"It is amazingly powerful, as much as any modern weapon," Rina agreed. "But it is also exhausting."

"He did seem a little dazed afterward."

"It is always like that. The concentration it takes is intense, and it is as if the power is drained from the warrior. If he is alone, and the fight goes on for too long, the warrior can die from it."

Yet another way for Dax to fulfill his death wish, Califa thought grimly. Then another realization came to her. No wonder guilt racked him, no wonder he thought he could have done something, when the Coalition attacked Trios. If he was indeed the Triotian flashbow warrior of legend, perhaps it was even true. But one man, no matter what wonderful weapon he was armed with, could not have held out against the full strength and massed forces of the Coalition. Especially if Rina spoke the truth; he would have died in the effort, and the result would have been the same.

And the flashbow would have wound up in some Coalition museum somewhere, Califa mused, an instrument of incredible destruction displayed no doubt beside an instrument capable of beautiful creation like Dax's dulcetpipe—

It hit her then, with the force of a blow. She knew what Dax was going "shopping" for.

Califa watched as Dax halted again, looking like some wild creature who had scented danger on the breeze. He looked around, and Califa froze in the shadows. She marveled at his finely tuned senses, to even suspect someone was close by. Especially when she knew he knew that except for the last group gone for their turn at the colony, the rest were still in the living quarters set up at one end of the big building. She had been there when Dax had left them a few minutes ago, saying something vague about a long walk to get used to being ashore again.

Ashore. She remembered the instant when she realized they were truly aground. She had watched incredulously from the lounge as they had come in over a broken, rocky plain caught between two steep hills. It had seemed inevitable that they would crash; there was no place in this rugged, boulder-strewn landscape that could be even vaguely considered as a place to land a ship the size of the *Evening Star*.

When a sudden, blinding flash of light made her jerk back from the port, she would have thought they'd hit except that there was no impact. When she'd looked out again, she'd seen nothing but soft, rolling ground and a large, square building that sat solidly backed up to a carved-out hillside.

She had come out of her shock to Larcos's laughter.

"I love watching people go through for the first time," he'd said.

"Through? Through what? What in Hades just happened? We should be plowing up rocks by now."

The lanky engineer's grin widened. "There are no rocks. At least, not here."

"But I saw—"

"—a reflection. Of a canyon on the other side of these hills."

Califa blinked. "A reflection?"

"Ever seen a mirage?" She nodded. Larcos shrugged, but his pride was evident. "Same principle. An image refracted by a layer of heated air."

"Another of your inventions?"

"Probably my best," he admitted modestly. "You could fly right over this place and never see a thing. And the rays used to project the image are enough to confuse any scanner."

So Dax's hideout was safe from prying Coalition eyes, she had thought. Yet here he was now, planning to leave that protection and set himself up for capture. Or worse.

She watched as he stood near the door of the storehouse, seeming to barely breathe. Califa could almost feel him listening, ears straining for any sound or movement. Then he shook his head, and she saw him grin, as if at his own foolishness. She knew as clearly as if he had spoken that he was hearkening back to what he'd said when they'd landed four days ago; while flying he was fine, but put him on the ground, and he was wound up and spun tight within a day.

He walked to the waiting air rover. Califa had seen the quick little vehicle earlier, next to the huge camouflage shelter that housed the *Evening Star* at the base of the hill behind them. Later, Larcos had headed back to the big ship; the lanky engineer had been awaiting the chance to install the scanner enhancer Dax had picked up on Boreas as eagerly as the others were awaiting a night of revelry. Califa had watched him go, and seen that the air rover was gone. When she discovered it later waiting near the storehouse door, she knew Dax wasn't going to waste any time making his move. And when he'd left the others, she'd known what he was up to.

Now, in the moment that his hands went to the side of the rover to lever himself into the seat, she moved out of the shadows of the storehouse.

He reacted swiftly, with a deadly precision that would have made a Coalition officer proud. He whirled, dodged to put the rover between himself and the shadows, and crouched, hand streaking to his belt for his disrupter, all in the same, smoothly continuous motion.

Reacting as quickly, she dropped flat on the rocky ground in case he fired first and verified identification from the body—a standard Coalition procedure. She opened her mouth to call to him, but before she could get the words out, she saw him straighten, release his grip on the weapon, and come out from behind the air rover.

"Good way to get yourself killed, snowfox," he said into the darkness.

She got slowly to her feet, thankful the movement hid the little shiver that rippled through her every time he used the diminutive name he'd given her.

"No," she said, tilting her head to look at him. "Landing a ship the size of the *Evening Star* in a valley the size of this one—and through Larcos's blasted screen— is a good way to get yourself killed."

"Landing isn't the problem," Dax said with a grin. "It's the taking off again."

She could see the whiteness of his teeth even in the faint light. She walked around the air rover, running a hand along the side, then tapping the controls lightly as she came to a halt before him.

"I thought the rule was only one group goes to the colony at a time."

He shrugged. "What are rules for, if not for bending? I'm a skypirate, remember?"

She drew in a deep breath, and held it for a moment. Then she said, "You're going for the Archives, aren't you?"

He stiffened. "Damnation," he muttered. "How in Hades did you—" He broke off, as if realizing what he'd admitted.

"It wasn't hard to guess," she said. "Not after the way you looked that day I mentioned them."

"You," he said, his tone wry, "are too damn observant."

Only, it seemed, when it came to him. All her life, before Dax, she'd been blithely unaware of others. Or hadn't cared. Another thing she wasn't very proud of. But she couldn't worry about it now. Now, she had to

concentrate on one thing: getting Dax to give up this
preposterous idea.

"Don't do it, Dax. The Archives are right next to the
Legion Club, and there's never less than a dozen Coalition officers on leave there."

"All drunk as slimehogs, or busy mating like brollets."

"Probably. I've . . . seen the place." And Eos help me
if he ever finds out this is where Dare was trained in
the carnal side of his slavery. "But are you willing to
stake your life on the chance that there will be no one
at the Archives?"

"I'll wait until the building's empty."

"Even if you do, it's a large building—"

"I know. I've studied it, Califa."

"If you get caught—"

"I won't."

"Eos, but you're stubborn!" she snapped in exasperation. "I know why you want to do this—"

"Do you?" he asked.

"It's some kind of symbol to you, isn't it? To rescue
some of what was stolen from your world, because you
weren't there to die for that world? To take something
back from those who destroyed it? Or is it just another
effort to finally get the job of dying done!"

"Easy, snowfox—"

"Easy? You're going to go get yourself caught or
killed, and you're telling *me* easy?"

Dax grinned suddenly, as if her anger pleased him
somehow. She saw it, and couldn't control her reaction;
she wanted to whack him, hopefully knocking some
sense into his thick skull in the process of sweeping that
infuriating grin from his face. As if he'd sensed the urge,
he spoke quickly.

"I've been doing this for a while now, Califa. I haven't
been caught yet."

"It only takes once."

"I'll be in and out before they even know it."

"It's alarmed, you brollet-brain!"

He grinned again. She glared at him. He was reacting
as if he liked to see her furious. He'd expressed his distaste for the submissive slave, but would he go so far as

to purposely infuriate her just to make sure she stayed away from the carefully cultivated meek demeanor?

"I know it's alarmed," he said. "Larcos rigged something up for me, to bypass it."

"He knows about this?" she exclaimed in disbelief. "He knows you're heading into disaster, and he helped you?"

"I just told him what I needed. He didn't know why."

"What you need," she snapped, "is a—"

"—keeper. So you've said."

"So everyone has said."

"Well, I don't. And you're not to tell anyone I've gone. I don't want anybody coming after me. This is personal."

She wasn't going to be able to talk him out of it, she thought. Just as she hadn't been able to talk him out of the raid on Boreas. Or his assumption of guilt for what had happened on Trios; she had only managed to free him of a little of the pain.

She took a deep breath. "You're determined to do this?"

For his answer, he swung his pack into the air rover.

"Eos," she muttered. She had to do something. Even coercion, if that was the only tool she had. It had certainly worked for the Coalition. The problem was, she didn't know if she held the bargaining power to do it. And learning that she did not would be a painful lesson.

"Then take me with you."

That got his attention, she thought with satisfaction as he gaped at her.

"Are you demented?"

"I'll cover the collar, as I did before."

Dax snorted his derision. "Woman, even without that damned collar, you'd be grabbed inside of five minutes. No."

"Then I'll go in the guise of a man."

He burst out laughing. "Snowfox, no man with eyes— or glands—is going to mistake you for a man. Trust me, I know."

She felt herself flush, and was thankful for the concealing darkness. This was the first time he had even alluded to what had happened between them in his quarters.

She steadied herself. "Then I'll go as a boy."

"You wouldn't be much safer that way," he said dryly. "There's more than one brothel in the colony that caters to that taste. No, Califa."

"You have to have some help," she insisted.

She saw his jaw tighten. "No. I won't be responsible for you ending up back in the hands of the Coalition."

And there it was, the answer she'd expected. The answer that the inherent nobility he so fervently denied he had forced him to give.

"And I suppose you'll use the controller to see that I don't follow you?"

"I don't have to use it, do I?" he said quietly. "I merely have to leave it here."

She sucked in a breath, then plunged forward. "And if I were to tell you that if you go, I'll follow you anyway?"

He drew back a little, startled at her words. It was a long, silent moment before he spoke. "I thought it was you who accused me of being suicidal."

"And you are, if you insist on doing this."

"So you hold your own death over my head? That kind of coercion doesn't befit you, Califa. It is a Coalition trick. I thought you'd left that far behind you."

His words stung, more than she would have thought possible. In her classes, she had taught that acceptable tactics were anything that worked. Now, all she felt was a chill nausea in the pit of her stomach. Before the collar, she had never known a man she couldn't compel, a man she couldn't manipulate. Only now did she realize she'd been a fool to attempt to use such stratagems on Dax. And she was ashamed at having tried.

But she would not take the coward's way out now. She drew herself up straight and faced him. "I'm sorry," she said tonelessly. "You're right. My apologies."

She heard his quick intake of breath. "You must have been an incredible officer, Major."

Her gaze flew to his eyes, searching for any sign of vitriol or hatred in his use of her former rank. She found none. It was he, she thought, who was incredible. And he was still about to do his damnedest to get himself killed.

Well, if she couldn't stop him, perhaps she could help him. And if it was treason, she thought grimly, what more could they do to her? When she spoke, her tone was brisk.

"How well do you know the Archive building?"

He blinked at the sudden change. "Well enough."

"Will you use the flashbow?"

He was watching her warily now. "No. I wouldn't want to have to hand it over to them, to add to their collection."

Her mouth twisted into a wry grimace. "You're not going to get caught, remember?"

He had the grace to look abashed. She shook her head, her expression exasperated, before she went on.

"Only the outside is alarmed. Do you know where the microbook sector is?" He nodded, his expression curious now. She went on in the tone of a formal briefing. "The Triotian exhibit is just next to it, toward the rear corner of the building. At least it was a year ago. But it appeared then to be a permanent place."

Realization crossed his face. "You don't have to—"

"There is a window in the microbook sector. Go in there. The storage racks and viewers take up much room, and they're big and tall enough to provide cover. There is cover outside as well, the wall runs close along that side."

"Califa—"

"Don't forget the caretaker. She lives above, and although mainly a scholar, she is also a Coalition officer. And armed. But they've had very little trouble there over the years. She may be slow to react if she discovers you. She may not even recognize you. I've heard she cares only for her museum pieces. I believe her name is Oranda. If she catches you, if you call her by name, you may be able to disconcert her enough to disarm her. That's all I can think of—"

"Stop, snowfox."

That shiver raced through her again at the name; it stopped her outpouring as no other word could have. He saw it that time, he must have, there was no other reason for him to suddenly pull her into his arms.

"I know that wasn't easy for you to do," he said against her hair. "I thank you for it."

She leaned into him, savoring the broad, solid strength of him. It was the first time they'd touched since she'd walked out of his quarters, and all her efforts at minimizing the memories melted now before his heat.

His hands slipped up to cradle her head, to tilt it back. Her breath caught, forcing her to part her lips for the air she suddenly found in short supply. In that instant his mouth came down on hers, his lips firm and warm and coaxing—and undeniable. She moaned as his tongue thrust past her lips, searching, and she heard him groan in turn when she met him with her own wet, velvet heat.

At the first taste of him she felt darts of heated sensation arrowing along her nerves. So quickly it stole her breath the heat began to pool low and deep inside her. It happened with such speed she felt the heat of mortification.

That is, she did until Dax's hands slid down her back to pull her tighter against him, and she felt the undeniable proof that his need had erupted as quickly as hers. Then, wrenching his mouth away, he muttered something under his breath. He stared down at her. He looked on the verge of saying something, but bit it back at the last second.

He released her and stepped back. "Thank you, Califa," he repeated. "It will help."

"Just come back," she said, her voice still husky with the effects of his kiss. She heard it, and struggled to regain her poise. "I don't want to have to explain to Rina what happened to you."

He smiled then, a slow, crooked smile that threatened to turn her knees to Omegan sand. And then he swung into the air rover and was gone, leaving behind a woman who was having a difficult time adjusting to being the one to sit and wait.

Chapter 17

"Damnation," Dax muttered.

He'd expected trouble, but he'd expected it at the Archive building, not in the shadowy, dingy taproom he'd been sitting in for the past couple of hours, just to prod the local telerien—that most efficient of underground intelligence networks—with some coin, to see what he could learn.

But Califa's information—proof again, if he'd needed it, that she no longer considered herself part of the Coalition—and Larcos's clever device that reflected the rays of the alarm sensors in an arc around the window she'd told him of, had given him the edge that had enabled him to get in and out without being detected.

And hidden in one side of his heavy cloak were a dulcetpipe even more ancient than his own, a holograph disk, and what Califa had told him of, a small piece of pristine white Triotian marble exquisitely carved into the lithe, graceful shape of a snowfox. He'd smiled when he'd picked up that one, thinking his comparison of Califa to the tenacious, willful, courageous, and beautiful little creature even more apt now than when he'd first made it. Then, when the second realization had come to him, he had nearly dropped the small sculpture before, shaken, he had secreted it in the pocket of his cloak.

And in the other side of his cloak was another piece that had made him shake when he picked it up. A circle of hammered metal, an odd color between silver and gold, etched with an intricate design, described on the display as simply an ornamental headband of some kind. It seemed impossible they could be so mistaken, but the Coalition was perhaps used to a more ostentatious flaunting of rank. Perhaps they had not even thought to check beyond their assumptions, thus did not know they held the Royal Circlet of the King of Trios.

King Galen. Dare's father. That wise, gentle man who had tolerated the constant presence of a boy not his own with a good-natured generosity. Dax's stomach had knotted with rage as he held the simple piece for the first time. Had they taken the crown from his head before or after they had severed it from his body?

And in that moment he had done something utterly reckless. He had pulled from his boot one of the bolts for the flashbow, and set it in the empty spot where the circlet had been. Let them label that, he had thought as he turned to make his escape.

A clean escape he was about to waste, it seemed. For across the dimly lit taproom stood two men in Coalition uniform. And one of them, unmistakably recognizable to Dax from the countless times he'd forced himself to watch the cinefilms of the destruction of Trios, featuring the bloated and victorious General Corling, was the aide who had stood importantly beside the general virtually every bloody step of the way.

"Look," said the raggedly dressed man who sat beside him, pointing surreptitiously at the taller of the two officers.

Dax had long ago learned to size up the most likely sources, and the thin, blue-eyed Arellian had immediately caught his eye. The man's coloring reminded him of Califa, and he wondered briefly if that was why he had been drawn to him. but he soon decided he was a likely enough choice anyway. And after some sizing up of his own, the man had accepted Dax's coins and in return provided a wellspring of information. Including the joyous news that, several months ago, a Coalition medical officer had been carried off in chains for questioning after it had been discovered that he had performed unauthorized surgery to unband a Triotian gold-collar slave.

"Mordred," the other man grunted, eyes focused on the tall officer.

"I recognize him," Dax murmured. An understatement, if ever there was one.

"They say it was he who pulled that puling general's orbs out of the twister."

"Corling?" Dax said, nearly choking on the name he hadn't spoken aloud in years.

"Who else? They say the same renegade captain who freed the Triotian slave kidnapped him."

"What?" Dax stared at the man, who grinned.

"It gets crazier. Half of it's probably not even true. But word is that she and the Triotian forced him to recall the forces sent to put down the rebellion on Trios. Then they stuffed him in his own shuttle and shooed him home to tell Legion Command their occupation of Trios was over." He laughed. "Damned fine job, if it's true. And she's an Arellian, too, from what I hear. Of course the Coalition denies it all."

They. She and the Triotian. She's an Arellian. God, it could only be Dare and Shaylah.

He kept a wary eye on the uniformed men, but his mind was racing. Was it really possible? Could they have done it? God knew Dare was bold enough, and from what Califa had said, Shaylah had the nerve to back him, but to pull off such a miracle? He'd wondered, before, but hearing it like this . . . a fierce shudder rippled down Dax's spine.

"The official version is different, of course," the Arellian said. "Mordred made up that one. Said that Corling fought his way free and flew his damaged shuttle all the way from where they mercilessly abandoned him to Legion Command, to warn them. They gave him a medal for it." The man snorted in laughter. "If that arrogant windsack could fly a child's air scooter, I'd be surprised."

Dax smiled slightly; it seemed Corling had lost some of his intimidation factor.

He sipped sparingly at the taproom brew. Dax knew he didn't dare draw any attention to himself, not the way Mordred and the other men were wandering around as they sipped at whatever brew they'd ordered. Fortunately the room was very dim, the only real light that of the fixture over the chaser table near the door. Still, getting up and walking out would surely draw their focus; heading for the back door would be even worse.

He forced himself to stay still, to maintain an air of mild curiosity.

"What is the ... status of the rebellion now?"

"Depends who you ask," the Arellian said. "Official"—he drew the word out with a long "oh"—"report is the Coalition is just biding its time. Others say those crazy Triotians have held them off for nearly a year now. There's even a rumor going around that that Triotian slave was a member of the royal family, that he's pulled them all together and built some kind of major weapon that has the almighty Coalition shivering in their boots."

Dare. He knew it now, with a gut-deep certainty nothing could shake. Only Dare could have done this, could have pulled together whatever remnants were left of the Triotian people. Only Dare could have held off the entire Coalition with what couldn't be more than a handful of people and his wits.

"Had a bit too much of that brew?" the Arellian asked sympathetically. "You look a bit bleached."

The man's words gave him a chance. Not a good one, but the only one so far. And he didn't think he was going to find a better one.

"Ye-es," he groaned, pulling the hood of his cloak up over his head. "Hit me kind of sudden. Help me outside, will you? Think I'm going to mess up the floor."

The Arellian made a face, but good-naturedly enough helped Dax to his feet. Dax stumbled, to maneuver himself to the man's other side, where he could put his left arm over his helper's shoulder, freeing his right. His right hand slid inside the voluminous folds of the cloak, found the slit in the main pocket, and reached through to the disrupter on his belt. He gripped it, keeping his hand there as they moved slowly toward the front of the taproom.

They almost made it.

They were nearly to the door, having drawn only an amused glance from Mordred, when a raucous voice called out to the Arellian. All heads, including Mordred's, swiveled their way as the Arellian turned to call out an equally raucous answer. And in the process spun Dax directly into the light from the chaser table.

Although he quickly ducked his head, as if at the sudden glare, Dax sensed Mordred freeze, saw his now shadowy shape lean forward slightly, as if staring. The man had seen his face, lit as if by a huntlight, and something had obviously registered.

Dax hunched over even more, groaned distressingly, and the Arellian began to hurry. For a few seconds his hopes soared; perhaps the man couldn't be sure of what he'd seen. He'd been off burning Trios to the ground, perhaps he wasn't as familiar with wanted skypirates as other Coalition officers were.

And then, with one low, hissed word, Mordred shattered more than just Dax's hopes.

"Silverbrake!"

Shock rippled through Dax at the sound of his name, unheard for so long. The man knew who he was. He wasn't reacting to the unexpected discovery of a wanted skypirate, he was hunting down a Triotian to slaughter.

"You're alive," Mordred said, the eagerness of a barkhound on the hunt in his voice.

For an instant Dax thought of simply killing the man. But if he killed a Coalition officer, the Arellian who had done nothing but give him information would be subject to the worst kind of torture to pry out all he knew about Dax. The Coalition would never believe that it was nothing.

Mordred shouted across the room to his companion.

"Sorry, my friend," Dax muttered as he whirled, grabbing his knife from his boot as he shoved the Arellian into the path of the suddenly advancing officer. As they both went down in a heap, Dax leapt to the chaser table, and with a swipe of his blade put out the light. He was across the table, down, and out the door into the dark before Mordred's first furious bellow died away.

The narrow, dead-end byway directly in front of the taproom was deserted, but there were people at the open end of the path, people who he would have to pass to get away. People who would no doubt quickly surrender his direction to an angry Coalition officer.

He glanced up, at the overhanging stone canopy that protected the doorway from the weather. This planet was a dank one, with a rainy season that lasted ten months out of the year except in the high country where the store-

house was. It was the reason for the popularity of the
colony; there was little else to do here, and if not for its
strategic position for the Coalition, it would have been left
to the small clans of gatherers that populated it.

For an instant Dax was grateful for the climate that
required protection such as that overhang; it gave him
the only chance he saw right now. It wasn't much of
one, but it was, he told himself, better than nothing.

He bent to pick up a sizable rock from the unkempt
byway and slipped it into his pocket. Then he turned to
face the canopy, set himself, and jumped. He caught the
edge with one hand, then reached himself up to grasp it
with the other as well. He pulled himself up and over,
flattening himself in the center of the slab of stone, praying that he wasn't visible from the ground on either side.

He barely made it in time. No sooner had he settled
down—in a chilly puddle, he realized with a grimace—
then the clatter of footsteps sounded beneath him. He
heard Mordred, shouting furiously.

"He can't have disappeared that fast! Lieutenant, you
go that way. I'll search around to the rear. You there!
Go to the Legion Club, tell them we've spotted a Triotian traitor! All you others, there's a healthy reward in
it for anyone who finds him!"

Dax heard the sound of running, saw the lieutenant
heading off toward the far end of the street, and Mordred around the corner of the building. The taproom
owner, apparently the one deputized to carry the news
to the Coalition, started slowly after the lieutenant, who
was still running. Not another soul moved; either not
trusting the promise of a Coalition prize, or demonstrating
a little rebellion of their own, Dax didn't know. Perhaps it
was simply a desire to stay out of this weather, he thought,
as the mist thickened into a light rain.

Dax waited until Mordred was well out of sight
around the corner, then took out the rock. With all his
strength he heaved it toward a narrow passage that ran
at right angles to the byway. It landed with a satisfyingly
loud clatter several yards ahead and to one side of the
lieutenant, who froze, then took off running toward the
sound. The taproom owner slowed down even further,
and when the lieutenant dodged down the small side

passage in search of the source of the sound, he stopped, shrugged, and turned back.

Dax waited, the chill seeping into him as he mentally counted down the time it would take Mordred to search behind the taproom and come up empty. If he misjudged, if he miscalculated the balance between the man's thoroughness and his angry need to find the man who had slipped through his fingers, he would be dead, Dax knew. He waited.

There were many possible hiding places to search. Dax knew that, he'd checked the back door himself before he'd ever sat down in the place. But how thorough would the man be? As thorough, Dax thought grimly, as he'd been when he'd helped Corling destroy Trios. He waited.

Califa had been right, he thought as he fought against shivering. Well, maybe not exactly. The visit to the Archives had been fine. It was stopping here afterward that had been the mistake. But he hadn't been able to resist the possibility of learning more of the rebellion. And hearing it spoken of so casually, so well established now as to be a routine topic in a distant, dingy place like this, had been ... indescribable. If he got out of this, he'd consider the risk well worth it.

No risk is excessive if you succeed.

He hung on to the words he'd once said to Califa, knowing that if he didn't succeed, he wouldn't live long enough to mull over his error.

And then he couldn't wait any longer. The instinct that had gotten him out of worse scrapes than this kicked in, telling him now was the time. He inched backward, until his feet touched the roof coping of the building. He listened again for a long moment, then stood and vaulted up onto the roof itself. He concentrated on silence as he moved swiftly toward the back of the building. He felt a jolt of pure satisfaction as, when he looked down over the edge, he saw Mordred just disappearing around the corner, heading back to the front at a run.

It was a long drop. He considered it, knowing he would be reasonably safe in a place the man had already searched. But for how long? And how long before, despite the taproom owner's lack of cooperation, the word got out to whatever Coalition troops were here? They'd tear the place down looking for him.

No, his only chance was to get out now, before they had every byway and path saturated with uniforms.

He looked at the next building. It was the same height, but a good fifteen feet away, whatever might be on its roof hidden in the darkness. Another building loomed beyond it, looking to be about the same distance apart. And beyond that, a clear path to the hills. Clear for now, anyway.

The gap was nothing, he told himself. He'd jumped as much on Boreas. Nearly, anyway. His stomach churned, sending its opinion on the matter.

Easy decision, he told himself. Stay here, get caught, wind up dead. Jump, fall, wind up dead. Or make it, and have a chance of escape. Decision's already made, then, isn't it? he asked; he wasn't sure of whom.

He didn't understand this. On Boreas he'd taken the jump without a second thought. He'd never worried about dying. So why was he now standing here, thinking that this was a damned stupid way to do it? Just jump, he ordered himself.

He backed up for a running start, marking the location of the numerous small puddles; he didn't want to break his neck before he ever jumped. After would be soon enough. He took a few deep breaths, listened once more for any betraying sounds. Then he ran.

The jump was fine.

The landing left something to be desired.

He skidded across the damp roof of the other building, slamming into a vent housing with enough force to drive the breath out of him. If there had been anyone left around, they couldn't have helped but hear it.

And they couldn't help but hear him gasping up here, Dax thought ruefully as he tried to control his gulps for air. He knew he had to get out of here; if anyone was in this building, they'd probably be up here any second to find out what sort of meteor had just hit them. He struggled to his feet, and staggered to the far side of this roof.

The next jump was a bit narrower. Still, he rested a moment before trying it; his balance seemed a little shaken. This time he landed more steadily, keeping his feet. He ran to the far side of this roof, and stood for a split second, savoring the expanse of the empty hill country before him.

He would have to be careful. If there was any sign of pursuit, he'd have to head away from the *Evening Star,* or he'd lead the Coalition right to her. He'd have to loose them somehow, then double back. Assuming, he amended as he stared at the sheer drop to the ground, that he got off this damned roof in the first place.

The wall was rough, uneven, with a multitude of small clefts and ridges. He supposed it was possible to climb down, but his heavy boots didn't make the prospect inviting. He'd be better off barefoot.

He groaned as the thought came to him. It was *cold,* damn it! Then, with a sigh of resignation, he sat on the edge of the roof and began to pull off his boots.

Rina watched Califa pace the storehouse room they were sharing, as she had been doing ever since sunrise.

"What's biting you?" the girl finally asked, looking up from the microbook she was poring over.

Califa stopped, turning to look at her. "Just restless, I guess."

"You're as bad as Dax," Rina said with a grin. "Nothing he hates more than being on the ground."

Better on it than in it, Califa thought, then turned quickly away before Rina could read her thoughts. Because she knew what the girl didn't.

Dax had never come back.

Califa knew the others just assumed he was sleeping in, after that long, late night walk story he'd fed them. Only she knew what his real plans had been. And only she had, just before dawning, crept to the small room he slept in here at the storehouse, to find it empty and unused.

He'd been caught. That was the only logical answer. Something had gone wrong—Eos, the whole idea had been wrong—and he'd been caught. And if he'd fought capture, as she knew he would, he was likely already dead. His head on a pike, on the way to General Corling, for him to gloat over.

Nausea at the bloody image swept her.

How would she tell Rina? Could the girl ever understand the kind of idiotic yet noble whim that had taken him to his death?

Then Califa's mouth twisted into a grimace. Being Triotian, Rina would probably understand better than she herself ever could. Self-sacrifice, even for a high-minded whim, had never been something she saw any sense in. Yet hadn't she learned in the last year, just what it meant to be driven by guilt? Hadn't the very foundation of her life been shattered, so thoroughly that she looked upon the person she'd been before as virtually a different woman?

And hadn't her life been rebuilt, with the help of a rakish skypirate, into something completely changed? Hadn't he made her face the corruptness, made her look at the truth, yet left her whole enough to excise the ugliness, to try and change?

And now he was dead. Dead because of some crazy need to atone. Because that was what he'd wished to be, dead, along with the people of his world.

"Califa?"

She came out of her waking nightmare to find Rina standing close in front of her.

"What's wrong?" the girl asked, looking anxious.

Feeling suddenly unable to stand, Califa sank down on edge of the bunk she'd tried—and failed—to sleep in last night, after Dax had gone. Rina immediately sat beside her. When the girl took her hand in concern, Califa felt a swirl of emotions well up inside her.

"Rina, you know ... You know Dax loves you, don't you?"

Rina drew back, puzzled. "Of course I do. I love him, too."

Califa let out a breath, forcing herself to calm, and the strain out of her voice. "I know you do. And I'm sure he knows, too."

Rina seemed to relax at the change. "Of course he does. I've told him." Then she made a rueful face. "I had to, to make up for what I said in the beginning."

Startled, Califa's brow creased.

"I mean, I was glad he found me, and took me out of that cave. But later, he told me Trios was gone, dead.

By then I knew he was a flashbow warrior, like I'd heard stories about as a child. They were our battle heroes, the ones who had made it possible for us to live in peace. So I blamed him for letting it happen. For leaving Trios to its doom."

"Rina—"

The girl waved a hand. "I know, it wasn't fair. That he couldn't have stopped it, not alone, not the Coalition. And I know he must have had a good reason for not being there." So he had never told her, Califa thought, not even in his own defense. "But I was a child," Rina said. "And my parents had been murdered. I didn't think about fair. I just blamed Dax, because he was there, to rescue me, instead of back on Trios, dead along with everyone else."

"Rina," Califa said slowly, "is that what you . . . said to him?"

The girl nodded remorsefully. "In the beginning I yelled at him, called him awful things. But then one day I finally stopped, when I grew up enough to realize that he was punishing himself more than I ever could."

"He still is," Califa whispered, Dax's impassioned words coming back to her.

Every damn day I remind myself I should have been there. And if I forget, just looking at Rina reminds me. And Rina's troubled face . . . *Sometimes he just looks at me and it's like something's tearing him up inside.*

Eos, the girl was part of his punishment, a daily reminder of what he'd done—or hadn't done.

"Califa," Rina said suddenly, urgently, "you don't think he believes I still think that way, do you?"

"I think," Califa answered, her tone wretched, "that what anyone else thinks doesn't matter. Not when he can't forgive himself."

"But what good would it have done for him to be there? Even with the flashbow, he would have died."

"Yes," Califa agreed softly. She said no more. She didn't have the heart to tell the girl that dying was exactly what Dax wanted.

And that it looked like this time he might have gotten it done.

Chapter 18

It was full morning before Rina found out.

Califa was sitting outside, in the shelter of the leeward side of the storehouse, staring off into the gloomy hills. She tried to distract herself, idly wondering if Larcos had a night view of that distant valley that was projected after dark, or if he just shut the system down altogether. The distraction wasn't very effective, and she was deciding how much longer to wait when she heard the shout of her name and the running footsteps.

Rina slipped on the wet ground as she came to a halt. She steadied herself, then gasped out, "Dax is gone! I got worried, he never sleeps this late, but when I went to his room, he was gone. It doesn't look like he slept there at all."

She had to tell her, Califa thought. And the others. Something had clearly gone wrong. If Dax wasn't already dead, he was in the hands of the Coalition, which only meant that he would suffer a great deal before they finally let him die. But then she doubted that. Why would he let them take him alive when he wanted to die anyway?

It was only then that she realized her reaction to Rina's words had given her away.

"You knew," the girl said, staring.

Califa sighed. "Yes."

"That's why you were acting so funny before, asking me if I knew Dax loved me . . ." Her expression changed to one of dread as her own words registered. "What's wrong?"

"I don't know, for sure," Califa hedged, unable to bluntly come out with what she suspected. It was as if some part of her clung to the hope that as long as she didn't say it, it wouldn't be true.

"Where did he go? Why?" When Califa still didn't answer, Rina grabbed her shoulders. "Califa, what do you know?"

"Yes," came a male voice from behind her, "just what do you know?"

She turned to face Roxton, who was looking at her grimly. Nelcar was close behind him, and Hurcon, none of them looking very happy. And Califa knew that now was the time.

"You might as well all hear this," she muttered, and got to her feet. The men and Rina followed her inside, where the rest of the crew was gathered. Something about their manner quickly caught the attention of the others, and the room fell silent.

"Well?" Roxton prodded.

Califa took in a deep breath. "Dax left last night. About an hour after the last group did."

"Left for where?" Nelcar asked.

"The colony."

There was a stir among them. "Why?" Rina asked, looking puzzled. "He almost never goes, not since they posted those placards of him all over half the system."

"He ..." Her voice trailed away. She couldn't tell them the whole truth, not without giving Dax away completely. And on the minuscule chance that he was still alive, she couldn't risk it. "He said it was personal."

"That 'personal shopping' he was talking about?" Roxton guessed.

Califa nodded.

"If he left last night," Larcos said, "and he's not back, he's in trouble."

Califa nodded again.

"He's probably dead," Hurcon said unhelpfully. Califa heard a tiny, smothered sound from Rina, and she could have slapped the man. But then she relented; how could she be angry at him for stating the truth? A truth she'd been thinking herself from the moment the first rays of dawning began to light the sky and she realized Dax was still gone.

Roxton ground out an oath between clenched teeth.

"Hurcon, break open that case of disrupters we liberated. Larcos, is that shuttle you were fooling with working?" At the man's nod, he went on. "Good, we'll take it. And we'll need some line, too, in case we have to do any climbing."

"I'll get it!" Rina said, turning as if to race off.

"No!" Roxton's order was sharp, strained. "You go and ... er, go and get ... get the miner's cloaks. We'll need them to disguise ourselves."

The girl hesitated, as if sensing what Califa had already guessed, that the first mate was trying to distract her until he found a way to tell her she was not going on what was obviously going to be a rescue mission. But the sense of what he'd said was undeniable, and after a moment she took off for the *Evening Star* at a run.

"We'll have to spread out throughout the colony," Roxton said, "see what we can find out. If he's hiding, they'll be hunting for him. If they already have him, they could be holding him anywhere."

"He'll be at the Legion Club," Califa said.

Roxton turned to look at her. "What?"

"He'll be at the Legion Club. The outpost headquarters is behind the club, and there's a small brig."

The others gaped at her, but Roxton merely, after a moment, nodded. "All right."

"It will be heavily guarded. For someone they want as badly as Dax, they won't take any chances."

"No," Roxton agreed, "they won't."

"The brig is a small, separate building. Solid stone, even the door. No windows. And anything that would blow a hole in it would kill anyone inside." She hesitated, then went on. "But if we could get him the flashbow ..."

Roxton blinked. "Then he could blow his way out from the inside," he said slowly. "But if there are no windows ..." Roxton looked at her speculatively. "Any suggestions?"

"There's an air hatch on the roof," she began, as her mind started racing over the possibilities. It had been a year since she'd had to turn her mind to any tactics more complex than those it took to stay alive, but she felt as if it were only yesterday. "A diversion would help," she said. "Any thermal grenades in those cases?"

"Some," Roxton said.

"There's a weapons and ordnance bunker a few yards away from the club. If you could figure out a way to launch a few of those grenades ..."

"We've got that old rail gun," Larcos said, warming to the planning. "I could rig it to catapult something that small."

"How long would it take you?" she asked.

"Fifteen minutes, if you want a second set of rails. That plasma gas is so powerful it tears the rails up after two or three shots."

"Forget the second rails." Califa said. "If we need it more than three times, it won't matter."

Larcos looked startled at her order, but when Roxton nodded, he shrugged and trotted away.

"We?" Roxton asked.

"We," she confirmed.

I'll have to get the controller from Dax's room, she thought. She only hoped she could find it. But he hadn't hidden it after she'd given it to him on board the *Evening Star,* it had been in the open, as if he were testing her resolve.

Roxton was looking at her oddly. "Why?"

"I'm the one who knows where the bunker is. And the brig. And I know the layout of the Legion Club."

"And if you're caught," he said, his gaze lowering to the collar, then back to her face, "they'll execute you right alongside him."

Califa held the old man's gaze steadily. "I'm willing to take that chance. Are you willing to make me stay here, and take the chance that I might be the one to make the difference?"

When he spoke, it was so softly the others couldn't hear him. "Why?" he asked again.

"Does it matter?"

"It might. To Dax."

Califa shook her head. "I don't think anything matters to Dax."

"What matters to Dax is why in Hades there's no sentry posted."

All the occupants of the room spun around at the sound of the mocking drawl. He stood in the doorway, hair damp and clinging, his cloak soaked at the hem, his boots muddy. And looking completely exhausted.

"Dax," Califa whispered unnecessarily, knowing delighted relief must be showing in her face yet unable to stop it. His gaze came to rest on her for a moment, and she thought—imagined, she told herself—that his expression softened a little. Then she heard Rina's glad cry, and realized the softening must have been for the girl who dropped her armful of cloaks and ran to him. He hugged her, reassuring her with calming words, barely audible over the clamor of relieved welcomes from the crew.

"What happened?" Roxton exclaimed. "What in Hades did you think you were doing?"

"We thought you were dead," Hurcon put in.

"Or worse," Nelcar said. No one laughed; they had all dealt with the Coalition enough to know that there were indeed fates worse than death.

Before he could answer Larcos came back into the room, stopping dead when he saw Dax.

"You're back!" He smiled widely. Then, his expression becoming slightly crestfallen, he looked down at the gun and the handful of parts he held. "I guess we won't need this, then."

Dax laughed, but there was an undertone of weariness to it. "Don't be so disappointed, Larc. We'll find a chance for you to play with it."

"Will it be soon?" Califa asked, when she could trust her voice not to betray her happiness at seeing him alive and whole. He lifted a brow at her quizzically. "I mean are they hot on your boot prints?"

He managed a smile. "I don't think they're going to show up here. I gave them plenty of opportunity to catch up, if they were going to."

I'll bet you did, Califa thought. You'd run up a flare so they'd be sure to find you, if you thought they might follow you here.

"What *did* happen?" Nelcar asked.

Dax's mouthed twisted wryly. "I was sitting in the taproom on the Rigel Byway, having a drink." Had he not gone to the Archives after all? Califa wondered. "I was just about to leave, when in walked two of the Coalition's finest."

Roxton whistled, long and low. "They recognized you?"

It seemed to Califa that Dax hesitated a second before he said, "One of them."

"You kill him?" Hurcon inquired, his voice untroubled.

Dax let out a breath. "No. I just got out of there."

Nelcar looked at him curiously. "How'd you get out of the colony? They must have been after you."

"I . . . er, borrowed a shuttle that was parked outside the Legion Club."

Califa gaped at him. "You stole a Coalition shuttle? From right in front of the Legion Club?"

"That's where it was," Dax explained reasonably. "Anyway, I flew it to the delta region, next to the river, set it down and got out, then programmed the self-pilot to take it on up a canyon. I took one of their hand communicators with me, so I could listen. Last I heard, they were still looking for the shuttle."

"In the mountains above the delta region?" Roxton asked.

Dax nodded. "With any luck, they're still up in those mountains now."

"And when they find the shuttle?" Califa asked. "All they'll have to do is read the settings on the self-pilot to know where you got off."

"That may take them a while." A grin flashed across his face. "I didn't program it to land."

Roxton laughed. "So when they find it, it'll be in pieces. Then what?"

Dax shrugged. "I also borrowed a rivercraft that was tied up where I set the shuttlecraft down. Sent it down current, toward the skyport. If they figure out what happened, hopefully they'll take off downriver, looking. And I left a few other diversions along the way."

She smiled despite herself; what a warrior he would have made. No, she corrected silently, in his own way, he *was* a warrior.

"That river's at the base of the mountains on the other

side of the flood plain," Roxton pointed out. "How'd you get back here?"

"I walked," Dax said dryly.

"Walked?" Hurcon yelped. "That's nearly an hour away in an air rover."

"Believe me, I know."

It was a good thing she hadn't gone with him, Califa thought. Her leg would never have stood up to such a trek. She watched as Dax leaned back and tousled Rina's blond mop of hair.

"I want a soak, a long one." He grimaced, glancing downward. "My feet are hurting."

"I'll start the water heating," Rina said, giving him a final hug before she ran off to the soaking room. She had told Califa Dax had built it himself after a raid last year had netted, of all things, a full-sized soaking plunge. The men had laughed when Dax had begun the project, but they'd all wound up using it.

"What are you all staring at?" Dax said when the silent group just stood there. Embarrassed, they began to shuffle away, going back to their abandoned game of chaser, their dropped microbooks, and unfinished meals. But Califa couldn't help noticing the odd looks she drew from a few of them, who were obviously remembering the moments when the woman they knew as a Coalition slave had taken over planning and handed out orders like an officer. And that Roxton had let her.

She lingered only until the last of them was out of earshot, then looked at the clearly exhausted Dax.

"I'm ... glad you're all right."

For an instant that softer expression was there. "Thanks." Then one corner of his mouth quirked. "But I think I'll wait until I look at my feet before I agree that I am."

"That was quite an escape."

He shrugged.

"Was the drink worth it?"

He grinned then at her accusing tone. "No. But the information was."

"Oh." She hadn't thought of that. She hesitated before asking, "Did you ... get what you went after?"

An odd expression, half jubilance, half awe spread across his face. "And more. Much more."

He looked at her for a moment, an odd glow lighting his green eyes. "Come on," he said quietly, glancing at the others. "I've got something to tell you."

She followed him as he walked toward the back corner of the storehouse, where his room was. She hesitated, then stepped inside after him; he nodded toward the door and she shut it. He took off his worn, wet, torn, much worse for wear cloak, handling it with a care belied by its appearance as he laid it gently on the bunk that sat against the back wall of the small room. Then he turned to look at her.

"I think they're all right," he said suddenly.

Califa blinked. "Who?" Then, as his meaning dawned on her, her eyes widened. "Shaylah?" she whispered. "And . . . Dare?"

He nodded, and told her what he'd learned. Shaken, Califa sank down to sit on the single chair in the room.

"Eos," she murmured in awe, "they did it."

"That's not what the Coalition says," Dax warned.

"The Coalition says what it suits it to say."

"Then you believe it?" he asked, his voice soft.

A curve that could barely be called a smile shaped her lips. "It sounds just like Shaylah," she said, almost wistfully.

"And Dare," Dax agreed.

"I'm glad he's free now. I know you won't believe this, but had I known then what I know now, I would have freed him myself, and damn the cost."

Dax glanced at the collar she wore. "Califa," he began, but broke off as his door slid open and Rina trotted in. Califa wondered what he'd been going to say.

"Your soak is ready," the girl said, looking only mildly surprised at Califa's presence.

"Thanks, little one. But I've something to show you first."

He walked over to a narrow shelf and picked up a holograph projector identical to the one Rina had in her quarters aboard the *Evening Star*. Then he bent over the cloak he'd placed on his bunk, felt within it for a moment, then straightened and walked to the small table that took up most of the rest of the room. He set the projector on the table, then slid the disk he'd apparently gotten from the cloak into the slot, and turned the device on.

Both Rina and Califa gasped, Califa with wonder, Rina with joyous recognition, as a scene leapt to life in the air above the table. A broad, flat meadow, green with Triotian grass and dotted with trees of a darker green, spread before them. At the far edge was a crystal blue lake, looking cool and inviting even in replica. In the distance rose a rank of rugged mountains, their peaks dusted with the white purity of snow. And to one side lay a city, of buildings that were not the cluttered jumble of styles Califa was used to, but as pristine as the snow, white and beautiful and sparkling in the sunlight, and seeming nearly as natural as the mountains themselves. Califa had never seen anything like it, anything or anyplace so beautiful.

"It's Triotia!" Rina exclaimed. "There, I can see the tower of the Sanctuary!"

Califa looked where the girl pointed with sinking heart. She saw the graceful spire, the arch of the welcoming doors, the elegance and grace of the building known as the Sanctuary of the Sojourner. But all she could think of was that this was where it had begun, in this temple of welcome to weary travelers, that this was where the Coalition had made their first move, as a jumpspider first injected his poison before sucking the victim dry.

Rina was looking so excitedly, Califa knew that she couldn't know what had happened there. But Dax did. It took only one look at his face to know that. But he said nothing to Rina, just let her enjoy this glimpse of her world as it had once been. And quickly turned away himself.

"I'm going to take that soak," he said, and to Califa, the pain in his voice was almost palpable.

"Where did you get it?" Rina asked, never looking away from the scene before her. And with the absorption of the young, not noticing the anguish Dax was in. "I . . ."

Words seemed to fail him, and Califa suggested gently, "Liberated it?"

His mouth twisted. "I guess you could say that." He

reached out and flicked off the machine. Rina looked at him, startled. "Take it to your room, will you? You can look at it there for as long as you want."

Rina went cheerfully enough, after giving him another fierce hug. Califa started to go after her, but something stopped her. She turned to look back at Dax; his effort to control the emotions roused by the holograph were visible. She searched her mind, trying to find words, any words that would ease his pain. There were none. So she simply went to him, and urged him to sit on the edge of the bunk with a gentle hand. Then she knelt before him and began to pull off his battered boots.

He looked startled at first, then, oddly, almost humble. He said nothing, just let her go about the task, even let her remove his knife and set it aside without comment.

He winced when she began to tug on the left boot, but when she looked up questioningly he nodded to her to go ahead. She did, deciding one quick pull would be better than a slow, inching removal. She heard him suck in a breath as she quickly yanked. When the boot came free she saw why; his foot was raw, bleeding in spots, despite the boot liners he'd worn over his feet.

Her troubled gaze flicked to his face again, but he only indicated the other boot with another nod. She repeated the process and found the same results, plus a raw spot where the hilt of the knife had rubbed his calf. She touched it gently with her fingers, as if she could mend him.

"I'll heal," he said, his voice gruff. She drew back her hand. "My boots, however, are probably shot," he added, his tone conspicuously glum, as if he were fighting off whatever had made his voice so husky.

Califa stifled the urge to help him as he stood and gingerly made his way to the door on his battered feet; she had the distinct feeling he wouldn't welcome it at this moment. She sensed he was too full of roiling emotions, and that he feared that any softness from her would snap his control. So she did nothing.

When he was gone, she looked down at the battered, muddy, scraped boots. As a Coalition officer, she'd known a thing or two about boots. Glad for something to do, she set to work.

*   *   *

It was time, Dax thought lazily. The water had gone from tepid to cool, and he'd better get out before the soothing effects of the originally steaming water were lost. Besides, just lying here gave him too damned much time to think. His mind had been ricocheting off painful subjects for nearly an hour now; from that glowing holograph of his home as it had been to the images he'd seen since of a blackened ruin, and from the thought of Dare enslaved and collared to an image of him free and fighting. And the image of the one collar gave rise to the other; Califa was far too much—and too vividly—on his restless mind. He knew, because every time he thought of her, his body would respond with the suddenness that he had almost come to expect.

As it was responding now, he thought ruefully, despite the coolness of the water. He stood up then, water streaming over him as he reached for a drying cloth. He rubbed down his chest and arms and belly, then stepped out of the plunge to dry his legs and hips. More than once he inadvertently brushed the flesh that had roused to thoughts of a blue-eyed Arellian, and he smothered a groan each time.

He'd forgotten to bring fresh clothes with him to the soaking room, and he couldn't bring himself to don the filthy ones he'd discarded, so he wrapped the cloth around his waist and started back to his room. His feet were still tender, but some healing spray would ease that, and he'd be back to normal in no time, he thought. If, he thought wryly as he glanced down his body to the betraying protrusion beneath the cloth, he could ever get *that* under control again.

He hadn't expected her to still be there. Yet she was, adding a finishing touch to his right boot, which was barely recognizable as the scuffed, muddy thing he'd left behind. The other was the same, showing the soft gleam of thorough care. That she had done it startled him nearly as much as the sight of her kneeling at his feet had. He had sensed then that the act had nothing to do with the submissiveness of the slave; if anything, it had been the once proud Coalition officer who had been tending him with such solicitude.

The moment he came in, she leapt to her feet, the single boot clutched in her hands. He took one look at her, and slid the door tightly closed behind him.

She stared at him, and he was as aware of her gaze sliding over his near naked body as he'd ever been of anything in his life. He'd never had a woman look at him with such pure need; desire, yes, even hunger, but never before pure need, untouched by any appraisal of his reputation as well as his body. It inflamed him until he knew she couldn't mistake his state of arousal, but she said nothing as her gaze flew back to his face.

"I meant to have this done," she said haltingly.

"You didn't have to do it at all."

He crossed the room toward her. She backed up a step, the backs of her knees coming up against the edge of his bunk. He advanced on her, and the boot slipped from her hands and fell to the floor with a soft thud. His hands came up to cup her face in the same instant as his distended flesh nudged her belly. He heard a strangled gasp break from her in the instant before his mouth came down on hers.

He didn't know how much of it came from the fact that he had nearly died last night, or how much from the fact that it had been Califa who had clearly been organizing a rescue effort. He only knew that no woman had ever had the power to do this to him, and that in these moments, when he was rigid with hot, pulsing need, whatever she'd done, whatever she'd been, mattered less than nothing to him.

As she opened for him, responding fiercely to his kiss, he wondered if she, too, was reacting to the fact that he very nearly hadn't survived his self-set mission. And then he realized it made no difference; all he cared about was that she was once more coming apart in his arms.

He didn't even care that she had clawed away the cloth at his hips, that he was naked while she was still clothed; his hands were under the soft, loose shirt, cupping her breasts, and for now that was enough. Especially when she arched her back to thrust those generous curves more fully against his palms, and he felt the instant tightening of her nipples beneath his fingers.

It was as if he'd never suffered through the last time.

As if he'd forgotten the excruciating tightness of a body left begging at the peak of arousal. And when she helped him strip away her clothes, revealing the slender body and impossibly smooth, pale skin, he knew it wouldn't have mattered if his body had remembered every painful second.

The moment her arms came up to wrap around his neck, he slid his hands down her naked back to the taut curve of her buttocks. Unable to wait another instant, he lifted her, urged her to wrap her legs around him. Without a moment's hesitation she did, and he let out a groan of pained relief as he lowered her onto him. That his entry was easy, her body already slick and prepared for him, told him more of the genuineness of her need than any words could have.

He took them both down to the bunk, letting the controlled fall drive him to the hilt inside her. She gasped his name, her hips bucking in his hands as she took him deep.

"Dax," she cried out. "Please, now! I—Oh!"

The last came as he began to move, swiftly. He could sense that she was on the verge of shattering, her body already close to erupting. He thrust hard and fast, and every time he wondered if he was being too rough, she arched her hips against him, demanding no less. It happened so quickly for her, and her body convulsed so fiercely, squeezing him so tightly, that for a moment he couldn't believe he wasn't going to erupt right after her. The exquisite sensations continued until they reached the level of pain, until sweat was pouring off of him, until he swore low and harsh and guttural, and yanked himself free of her coaxing body.

She moaned, still in the throes of a release he knew had been nearly violent. He collapsed beside her, his breath still coming in rapid pants, his body shuddering its protest as his rigidly erect shaft continued to ache with unsated compulsion.

Nothing had changed. Not even this woman, who had aroused him to heights he'd never thought possible, could break the barrier. And he knew with a grim certainty that if she couldn't, no one could. Ever.

Maybe it was too bad he'd made it last night.

Chapter 19

"You were right, you know."

Califa barely heard him; she was still staring in shock at the controller Dax had just handed her. He'd rolled out of the bunk, walked over to the bag that held what he'd brought from the *Evening Star,* and taken out the small power unit. Without a word he'd come back and held it out to her.

It was an image she knew she would remember forever; Dax, still naked, his strong, lean body still clearly aroused, standing there handing her back her autonomy. It drove all her questions about why he'd withdrawn from her before attaining his own satisfaction from her mind.

"Right?" she finally managed to ask.

"When you accused me of being suicidal." He sounded so odd, Califa thought, his words coming in short bursts. "I'd never thought about it. Not until last night. I realized I was worried about escaping. I'd never done that before."

"Dax—"

"And just now, I was thinking it might have been better if I hadn't."

"Eos, Dax," she whispered. Somehow hearing him voice what she herself had accused him of was so much worse.

"Ironic, isn't it?" His voice was sharp, caustic. "All this time, I've been trying to get myself killed, and instead all I've managed to do is get rich. And notorious."

"Dax, please—"

He cut her off. "So you'd better keep that. Just in case I succeed, one of these days."

Her hand shook. He turned his back on her. He

walked back to the bag, pulled out some clothing, and
yanked it on. She watched him, wondering what had
made him do this, now.

"Does this mean . . . you trust me?"

He froze, his back still to her. "It means," he said, his
voice suddenly harsh, "that you can do as you wish. It
means that *you* shouldn't have trusted *me* enough to
give me that thing. Or to tell me how it works. You
shouldn't have trusted me at all."

And without ever looking at her again, he walked out
of the room.

Califa's fingers curled around the controller. She'd
never thought to hold it again, to have in her hands the
freedom once taken from her. And yet at what price?
Why had he done this now, while he avoided answering
the question of whether he trusted her? What did he
expect her to do?

It means that you can do as you wish.

Before, she had taken that simple freedom for
granted. Since, she had craved it beyond all other rights.
Now, all she could do was wonder why he had given
that right back to her at the moment when he as much
as admitted he harbored a wish for death. She couldn't
help thinking it was because he expected they would
soon be separated, one way or another, either by her
leaving the *Evening Star,* or by his death.

And as she sat there in his bed, clutching the power
unit that gave her life back to her, she had to admit to
herself that she found either prospect grim.

They left two nights later.

Dax had put it to a vote, as apparently he always did.
All the crew had had their time in the colony, and
seemed to have had enough of revelry; they were bored
enough now to welcome leaving, especially after they
had spent nearly a year here not very long ago, when
Dax had built the fighter. Still, Califa wondered how
much of the willing vote stemmed from Dax's obvious
eagerness to get back flying again; this crew would do a
great deal to keep him happy.

His eagerness to be off made her uneasy, wondering
if it was somehow connected to her—or to the fact that

Larcos's image screen insured they were in little danger here.

Although Dax had ignored her, as he had been since he'd returned the controller, Roxton had sensed her unease.

"You don't agree?" he asked her before the vote was taken.

She was startled that he'd even asked, but more startled that the others—except Dax—seemed to be waiting for her answer. Something had changed; it was as if her willingness to risk herself to rescue Dax had made them accept her as one of them. Of course, most of them didn't know that it had been a Coalition officer giving those instinctive orders.

But Roxton knew, and it was he who had asked. So in the end she had answered honestly. "We are apparently safe here. I don't believe the Coalition will have given up the search so soon. And as a wise old warrior once said"—here her gaze roamed to Dax; that ancient fighter, Geron, had been Triotian—"if you do not move, you do not leave a trail."

It was then that Dax had spoken, although he still did not look at her.

"She speaks truly. There is a danger. I will not force you all to face it, not when I have brought it down on you."

Califa had looked at him for a long moment, seeing the tension in his body, the strain that lined his face, the shadows that darkened his eyes.

"But you will leave," she said softly, "no matter what is decided here."

It wasn't a question, but he answered as if it were. And he did it while looking at her for the first time, with an expression that left her little doubt that one of his reasons was her.

"I will leave."

He looked away from her then, glancing at Roxton before he walked to a window and stood looking out, separating himself from the others. He had given his vote; now it was up to the crew. And to a man—plus Rina—they voted with Dax.

She could have stayed. Roxton later told her that the

Evening Star flew with no one who didn't wish to be there, and that if she wanted to stay here, at the store-house, she was welcome.

"Does Dax know you're offering his hospitality so freely?" she'd asked.

Roxton had tugged at his beard thoughtfully before answering. "It was his idea."

But he'd sent Roxton to tell her. He wanted her to stay behind, but he hadn't wanted to face her to tell her. While it was true she could survive for a long time in relative comfort here, the idea didn't appeal to her at all. If she were ever to truly regain her freedom, she needed to find a way to be rid of the collar, and she would make no progress toward that while sitting safely beneath a mirage. And besides, Rina had come to her and asked her rather sweetly to please come with them.

"I'd miss you," the girl admitted. "I know I was angry with you. But you were right, I've changed from the silly child I was before my parents died, so I have to believe others can change, too."

And so she had decided. And she nearly convinced herself that those were the only reasons she had told Roxton she would be aboard the *Evening Star* unless Dax directly ordered that she not be.

This time, she was prepared for the flash as they broke through the refraction layer. And as she looked back, she had the answer to her earlier question; the image of the rocky plain was dark and shadowy as they lifted off into the night. Larcos, she thought, was a genius. And the Coalition had shipped him off to work in a crystal mine. If she'd needed any further proof of the blind senselessness of the monster she'd once been a part of, she had it now.

But she didn't need any more proof. All she needed was a way to expiate the crime of having been part of it. And she wasn't certain such a way existed. She fingered the collar, thinking wearily that perhaps she should just try to hunt down Dare, and hand him her controller. If she let him use her as she had let him be used, perhaps that would be enough.

But when she tried to think of it, when she tried to form the image in her mind of the magnificent golden man she remembered, all she could see was Dax. And suddenly she, who had sampled the carnal variety the Coalition deemed customary, although not anywhere near to the extent most had supposed, could not conceive of such intimacy with anyone else. She was well and truly snared, she thought, and by a man who had no wish to hold her. Indeed, he seemed most eager to be rid of her.

As Alpha 2 dropped farther and farther behind, she mulled over the irony of being so controlled by the man who had never used, had never even wanted to use, the machine designed to do just that.

"We're clear," Rina said cheerfully.

Califa turned, surprised to see the girl in the lounge. "I thought you'd still be on the bridge."

Rina looked puzzled, and Califa guessed she had been sitting here, lost in profitless wondering, for longer than she'd thought.

"I have been," Rina said. "Since I already laid in the course before we took off, Dax really only needs me to get through the screen, when all the instruments go haywire for a few minutes. But I stayed anyway, until we got free enough of the planet's gravity to power down a little."

"Course? Where are we going?"

"To the Clarion shipping lanes. Before we took all those months of downtime to work on the *Evening Star,* and for Dax and Larcos to build the fighter, we knocked off some of our best prizes there."

And the Coalition had doubled the patrols because of it, Califa thought, remembering the bulletins that had come down, describing Dax as the most bloodthirsty, merciless, and evil skypirate ever to draw breath.

"We've got plenty of supplies," Rina went on, "but the funds are getting a little low. Dax wants to snag some goods we can turn around quickly, for coin. He—"

The girl broke off suddenly, her eyes narrowing as she stared out the viewport.

"That's odd," she murmured. "We've changed course."

No sooner had she spoken than the lights flashed and

the sound of the battle alert blared through the empty lounge.

"I was afraid that was too easy," Rina yelped, whirling toward the door.

Califa watched her race away, her pulse instinctively speeding up to the rapid clamor of the alarm. She hated this, being a helpless passenger, forced to only watch, when she was used to being at the forefront of the action.

And then it struck her. She no longer had to sit back and watch. The controller was in the pocket of her new flight suit, and she could go wherever she wished.

She nearly shook at the realization, the thrill of it tempered only by the thought that perhaps this, too, was one of Dax's reasons for giving it to her. Perhaps he had hoped she would take advantage of her freedom to simply walk away. And somehow, the knowledge that that meant he trusted her not to give them away did little to ease the ache the thought caused.

This, she lectured herself, was no time for foolish emotions. She'd never even seen the bridge of the *Evening Star;* it was past time. She took off after Rina.

It was a destroyer.

She could see it, dead astern, through the grid of viewports across the back of the bridge. The huge ship was closing, but slowly.

"Surrender," she heard Roxton mutter. "Not damned likely."

The first mate was standing behind Larcos, who was sitting before the cluster of scanners to one side of what was obviously the command chair. Obvious not only by its size, placement, and the array of controls within easy reach, but by the fact that Dax sat there, long legs stretched out before him in a casual attitude that belied the tension she could see in his face.

And the guilt.

He knew, as she and no doubt everyone on board knew, that were it not for his little excursion, they could have made it out of Alpha 2 space virtually unnoticed; there was nothing of value for the Coalition to guard on the vast expanse of the planet outside the colony itself, and they cared little who came and went. But Dax had made them care. They knew their most wanted skypirate had been there, and as Califa had suspected, they hadn't given up easily.

But she also knew that if he let it, guilt over getting them into this could cripple him, make him unable to make the decisions necessary if they were to survive this. Which was doubtful enough, she thought, looking once more at the motionless ship that hung off to starboard.

She gathered, from Roxton's comment, that the traditional demand for surrender had already come.

"Shall I fire, sir?" Hurcon's voice crackled over the comlink; the Omegan must be manning one of the weapons stations.

Dax didn't answer. He didn't even move. Roxton glanced over his shoulder at him, then answered Hurcon himself.

"Not yet. Wait for the order."

The answer came back, sounding disgruntled. "Copy."

Roxton started to turn back to the scanners, then stopped when he saw Califa. His gaze flicked to the enormous ship menacing them, then back to her.

"Another message coming in," Larcos said, reaching to activate the ship-to-ship audio. Roxton turned to listen.

"We repeat," came the words, booming in typical Coalition amplified volume, as if sheer loudness could frighten them into acquiescence, "this is the Coalition Destroyer *Hellring*. We order you to surrender immediately or you will be obliterated."

Califa drew back, surprised. A second demand was rare. She glanced at Dax, but he still didn't react. Roxton gave him a worried look, then shifted his gaze once more to Califa. He gestured to her to join him. She came forward, sensing Dax's sudden stiffening as she passed him; apparently he hadn't even realized she was there, a sign of how deeply distracted he was. Rina sat at the helm position, glancing at Dax periodically, her face displaying her worry. Califa gave her a reassuring smile as she passed, although she couldn't see anything to feel reassured about.

She looked at the scanners Roxton indicated, and her

brows furrowed. None of the destroyer's weapons systems were active except the minimally destructive disrupters. She hadn't felt a hit at all, even a mild disrupter blast. She lifted her gaze to the first mate's face.

"Have they fired at all?"

He shook his head, and her puzzlement increased.

"That's unusual. Very unusual."

Drawing first blood was traditional Coalition procedure; they did not believe in talking first, before the point of their superiority was made. And if the enemy vessel happened to be accidentally annihilated in the process, well, they had just speeded up the inevitable. Especially in a one-sided confrontation such as this.

The voice boomed out again. "This is your last chance. Surrender or be destroyed."

Califa shook her head. "A third demand for capitulation without a shot yet being fired? Unheard of," she muttered. She glanced at Dax, then back to Roxton. "The Coalition does not consider patience a virtue. There's something wrong here."

Roxton glanced at Dax again. When he caught his attention at last, he gestured at Califa questioningly. After a second of silence, Dax shrugged.

"Do as you will," he said. "If anyone knows what we're up against, she does."

So for the second time, Roxton asked her, "Any suggestions?"

"I don't know," she said, turning to stare out at the hulking, dark ship as if she could divine her captain's intent. "By rights, she should have blasted us to bits by now. If she'd been refitted within the last two years, as most destroyers have, she'll have a new coil gun. If she does, we're certainly within range."

"The way they're closing," Larcos said, "they'll be able to use a hand-thrown grenade soon." He turned to look at Dax anxiously. "We're barely at quarter speed. Aren't we going to turn her loose yet?"

"No."

Dax's voice was flat, inflectionless. Califa had no idea what he was thinking. Or was he too bogged down in guilt to think at all? Somehow she couldn't believe that; he wouldn't let his crew be killed without a fight.

"Much closer and they'll be within tractor range," she warned. "A Diaxin class destroyer's beam will pluck us up like a sloeplum."

Something glinted in his eyes then. "I know."

So he was thinking, Califa thought. He had some plan. She only wished she knew what the destroyer captain was planning; his actions so far made no sense.

"Why?" she murmured, almost to herself. "Why would he think a ship as heavy as a destroyer could corral a ship so much lighter and speedier in the first place? Why would he even try?"

"Why indeed?" Roxton agreed.

"The logical thing to do is just blast the *Evening Star* out of existence before she can use her greater speed and escape. Whatever the destroyer captain is doing, it goes against all Coalition practices for engagements with a known enemy."

A known enemy.

Even as she said it, it hit her, with the stunning clarity of Larcos's mirage. They knew. They knew they had Dax, and they wanted the glory of a personal capture.

That officer, he was talking about how he was going to be the one to capture you, take your head and present it to General Corling on a pikestaff.

Rina's words rose to haunt Califa with their cruel accuracy. Despite his grandfatherly looks, Corling was a bloodthirsty man, and nothing less than Dax's head on that pikestaff would satisfy him. Califa's stomach lurched as the vision formed in her mind, Dax's beautiful body decapitated, his head paraded for all to see and exult over, his thick, long hair matted with his own blood, his vivid green eyes dead and staring.

"Better Corling's head on a pike," she muttered. She spent no time mulling over the fact that she had just uttered treasonous words. Nor did she ponder the fact that the thought of treason against the Coalition had no power to disturb her anymore.

"You think that's it?" Roxton whispered, and it took her a moment to realize he'd heard her muttered imprecation. And understood it quickly. "You think they want Dax?"

"Why else haven't they blown us to debris?" She

turned on Dax then, thinking this silent act of his had gone on about long enough. "Whatever this plan of yours is, you'd better not put it off much longer."

An odd expression, a combination she could only describe as wistfulness and pain, flickered across his face.

"It's not my plan."

She stared at him for a moment, but his eyes had gone cool, calculating, all emotion vanished, and she could read nothing more. "In a minute," she said, "it won't matter who's plan it is, because it will be too late."

For a long moment he didn't answer. Then, when Larcos called out a position report on the destroyer that put them barely over a minute from tractor range, he moved at last. Swiftly.

He flicked a button on the comlink beside him. "Qantar, are you set?"

"Yes, sir." The taciturn man's voice was as flat as his chronically emotionless expression.

"From my mark, then, count down from ten. You move on three," Dax said. "We'll move on zero."

"From your mark," Qantar confirmed.

Dax got up then, and walked to the helm position. With a gentle hand on Rina's shoulder, he gestured for her to leave with a movement of his head. She hesitated, then got up. Dax sat down, settling into the chair with all the ease and contentment of a man for whom this was the true reason for flight; steering a ship with your own hands.

"About time," Larcos exclaimed, and when Califa glanced at him she saw a grin cross his face as he watched Dax's hands gracefully fly over the helm controls. Califa heard a building hum, even thought she felt a barely perceptible vibration in the ship itself, and she suddenly pictured a proud, swift, Arellian steed, held back, its every muscle trembling as it waited for the signal to run.

"Qantar?" Dax called, loud enough to reach the comlink he'd left on.

"Ready when you are."

Dax looked at Larcos. "Forty seconds to tractor range," the engineer read out.

"Mark!" Dax ordered sharply.

Ten. Nine. Califa held her breath as the beats counted down in her head. Seven. Six. Dax's right hand shifted, hovering over the throttle control. Four. She felt nothing as they passed three, but in the next split second heard Qantar shout "Away and clear." Two.

On the next beat Dax hit the throttle control. The *Evening Star* leapt forward like that golden steed let loose. Califa waited, sure that when faced with the possible escape of his prey, the *Hellring*'s captain would cut his losses and blow them out of existence.

The anticipated shot never came.

"They bit!" Larcos exulted. "They're locked on to the *Y*-class. Qantar got it off perfectly."

"A *Y*-class fighter?" Califa asked.

Larcos nodded. "An old one. We were going to junk it anyway, once we were sure the new fighter worked. And Dax sure as Hades proved that!"

Califa turned to stare at Dax, but he was intent on the helm, sending the *Evening Star* on an wild, evasive course that would, with the ship's agility, make it very difficult to hit with anything smaller than a torpedo—

Her eyes widened. The *Hellring*'s torpedoes hadn't been armed. True, it took only seconds to have them ready to fire, but those were seconds the destroyer didn't have, not against a ship as fast as the *Evening Star*. And not when they'd been distracted by the launch of a fighter.

"They've released the fighter," Larcos said.

The captain knew now he'd been had. He'd go to full throttle now, as Dax had, and hope to get back within torpedo range.

"How close is the *Y*-class to the destroyer?" Dax asked, never looking up from the controls he was manipulating with such dexterity.

"Still a ways, but they're going to have to fly right over it to get to us."

"Calculate the time they'll be in closest proximity," Dax said, making another adjustment.

"Approximately two minutes."

Dax nodded. "We'll give them something to chase, then." He looked up for an instant, and the reckless, brilliant grin he wore took Califa's breath away. "Don't let me let them get too close, Rox."

"Aye-aye, Cap'n!" Roxton answered, a grin that nearly matched Dax's creasing his bearded face.

Then, incredibly, he slowed the ship. And straightened her course. To the Coalition ship it must look like they had suddenly lost power, and were barely limping onward. No doubt the Coalition captain wouldn't be surprised; they'd probably never seen anything move as fast as the *Evening Star,* and would figure she must have burnt out her engines.

"She's picking up speed. She'll be over the fighter in ... thirty seconds."

"You copy that, Qantar?"

"Got it, sir. Thirty seconds."

Dax looked up at the others, still wearing that joyous grin. "Want to watch?" he asked, with all the enthusiasm of a boy showing off his first air-scooter.

"If it works," Larcos said, a little grimly.

"You did it," Dax said. "It'll work."

Color tinged the lanky engineer's cheeks. Califa watched in mystification as Dax fired the port thrusters to bring the *Evening Star* around, facing back the way she had come. In the dark distance, they could see the hulk of the destroyer; Califa had no idea where the tiny fighter was, it was long since too far distant to see.

Larcos began counting down under his breath. "Right ... about ... *now!*"

And in that instant Califa knew exactly where the fighter was. She knew because it exploded, sending what had to be a furious rain of huge chunks of debris at the destroyer. Even from here they could see the huge ship rock. Califa stared; it had taken more than just the fighter itself to do that.

Dax fired the thrusters again, turning them back around, then hit the throttle. The *Evening Star* leapt forward again, and in moments the damaged destroyer was falling far behind.

"It worked!" Larcos chortled happily.

Roxton grinned, clapping the engineer on the back. "You never stop amazing me, son," he said. "Who would ever have thought all that old liquid fuel we found on Boreas would ever come in so handy?"

"It was Dax's idea," Larcos insisted. "I just built it."

Califa had had enough of being in the dark. "Built what?"

"The time delay switch on the thermal grenade that was on the *Y*-class."

She stared at him, remembering the ferocious explosion. "A grenade," she said carefully, "did not do that."

"No," Roxton agreed mildly. "The liquid fuel did."

"Liquid fuel?"

Roxton nodded. "It's what they used ages ago to power the crystal transport rigs in the mines. Guess they didn't know what to do with it after all this time."

"But Dax did," Larcos said, grinning again. "He had Qantar set the thermal grenade in a sealed box. Then he pumped the fighter cockpit almost full of fuel, and gave it time to build up a lot of vapor inside."

"He figured the destroyer would lock on to it, then either take it aboard, or release it and fly past to take up the chase again when they realized we were getting farther and farther away."

It would work, Califa thought, almost numbly. The cockpit would be, or course, tightly sealed against the vacuum of space. The grenade would destroy the box that held it, provide the spark to ignite the vapor, and the gas would expand explosively. And it had, stopping a Coalition ship five times their size.

She turned to look at Dax. Eos, but he was brilliant, she thought. And she didn't even stop to wonder at the fact that the emotion that flooded her then was pride.

Chapter 20

"I hear they doubled the price on your head."

Dax stopped in his tracks. He shrugged, without looking back. He didn't have to look, he'd seen her this morning, and knew too well how she looked. The black hair that had been so shortly cropped before had grown out a little, falling in wisps around her face, and somehow emphasizing the size and pale blue color of her eyes and the silkcloth texture of her skin.

"So I heard," he muttered. Roxton had come back with that piece of information after a trip down to Clarion in the shuttle. And apparently he'd wasted no time in passing it along.

"I also heard it's only double if they take you alive."

Roxton, Dax thought grimly, talked too much. At last he turned around to face her. He leaned back against the door to his quarters, trying to appear as if her presence didn't disturb him. As if they had never made love just the other side of this door. And trying not to think of himself, naked and sweating and desperate in her arms.

"That's the rumor. I doubt it, though. They've never cared before if I was dead or alive."

"The *Hellring* did. Why?"

The uneasiness that had been plaguing him since that encounter came back full force now. It was a very good question.

"I don't know."

"It doesn't fit, Dax. They *shouldn't* care. Oh, they'd take you alive if they could, for the glory of dragging you before Legion Command, but it's not like the Coalition not to blast their prey to Antares if they refuse to surrender. They knew it was you, Dax, they had to, after spotting you in the colony. It's completely against procedure to give the most wanted—and slipperiest—skypirate two chances to give up, let alone three. This time they wanted you alive. Why?"

It dug at him again, that one piece of knowledge he'd kept from them all, the one thing that could put this all in a different light. It would explain why they sent a destroyer after him. But it still didn't explain why they hadn't just atomized the *Evening Star* outright.

"You know, don't you? What is it, Dax?" she whispered.

God, she read him so well. No one had ever been so attuned to him, so aware of his thoughts. It reminded him of his parents, and their almost eerie accord, and that scared him more than he cared to admit.

As did the need to talk, to someone, about what had happened. But there was no one he could talk to, no one who he dared share the truth with. Except the woman who already knew. The woman who haunted him day and night. The woman he'd tried so hard to stay away from, knowing he didn't have the strength to endure the fierce rage of wanting she kindled in him. The woman he'd tried to send away by returning the infernal device that held her in thrall, knowing that if she stayed, he would weaken yet again.

The woman who stood here now, simply watching him with those eyes, the pale blue no longer icy as solicitude warmed her expression.

And he found he could no more resist that warmth than he could resist his desire for her. With a sharp, jerky motion he opened the door to his quarters and waved her inside. She hesitated. He didn't blame her. Every time they were alone, this thing between them threatened to blast out of control, and the last time he'd surrendered to the need, he hadn't exactly been the most caring of lovers afterward.

"Just to talk," he said, his voice gruff as he fought down the memories.

After a moment she warily stepped inside. He shut the door. Silence spun out, so charged that Dax thought if he tossed crystal dust in the air it would glitter along a line stretched wire-taut between them.

"They weren't after a skypirate," he said suddenly.

Califa blinked. "What?"

"They may have been, partly, they might have put it together, probably did later, but . . ."

She ignored the fact that he was rambling, dancing around the point. "Put what together?"

"Who I am."

Her silky brows drew together. "But you said someone recognized you."

"Yes. His name is Mordred."

She smothered a gasp. "Corling's aide at the conquest of Trios?"

He nodded. "The same."

"What's he doing here?"

"He appeared to be on leave, like most Coalition officers who come to Alpha Two."

She looked thoughtful. "I remember hearing something . . . that he used to like . . ."

She trailed off, and Dax finished it for her in acid tones. "Little girls? I heard that, too. And there's no place in the Coalition better able to cater to that kind of taste than Alpha Two."

She grimaced. "It was he who recognized you?"

"Yes."

"Odd. I wouldn't think someone as high up as he is would be bothered about something as . . . mundane as a skypirate. Not enough to order out a destroyer, anyway."

"He wasn't after a skypirate," Dax repeated.

Califa gave him an exasperated look that he found, perversely, enticing.

"Then who was he after?"

Dax took a long, deep breath. "He was after a warrior not accounted for after the fall of Trios."

Although he wouldn't have thought it possible, she seemed to blanch, her already pale Arellian skin going even whiter.

"But you weren't there!"

He smiled, a bitter, tight little curve of his mouth. "I know. But I'm sure they had all our records before they were through. And I'm sure he'd study carefully anyone he thought had slipped through their fingers. He probably knows what I look like better than my own—"

He broke off, laughing with harsh rancor at himself. Even after five years he'd almost said his mother.

"At least your mother would know you," Califa said. At the unexpected words he lifted his gaze to her face. "Mine didn't," she said with a shrug. "I went back to Arellia once. I wanted to brag, I suppose, that I'd made it through the academy in spite of her saying I never would. She didn't even recognize me."

He let out a long, sighing breath. "Ah, Califa, how do you do it? You always seem to know just what to say to distract me. Or make me think about things I never have before, or never wanted to. Or to make me—"

"—furious?" she suggested, sounding only half joking.

"That, too," he admitted wryly.

She smiled tentatively, but the expression faded as she asked, "How can you be sure? That Mordred recognized you as Triotian, and not just"—the smile again, stronger this time—"the infamous skypirate?"

Dax had to look away from that smile, it was far too tempting. "Because," he said, staring down at the gleaming toes of the boots she'd shined, "he used ... my family name. I ... haven't heard it in five years."

"Oh."

She sounded as if she could think of nothing else to say, and he supposed that, in truth, there was nothing else to say. But he knew she wouldn't give up for long, and he was right. Immediately she began to analyze, with that quick, trained mind of hers.

"How good a look did he get at you?"

"Good enough. Short, but in full light."

"Still, how sure can he be?"

Dax felt heat creep up his cheeks. Most times he could shrug off his own impulsiveness with a laugh, but somehow it was more difficult with Califa. Her stare as he explained that Mordred was no doubt positive, because he by now must have learned of the flashbow bolt Dax left behind in the Archives, made him decidedly uncomfortable.

"You left the bolt in place of that holograph disk?"

"No. Something else. More important, though they didn't know it."

She just looked at him.

"I know, I know," he said. "It was stupid."

"Probably," she agreed. "But I'm not sure you'd be capable of resisting that particular temptation."

That's not the only one I can't resist, he thought sourly.

"Actually," Califa said, in musing tones, "I'm not sure anyone would be. Especially any Triotian."

That surprised him. He'd realized how completely she'd turned her back on the Coalition when she'd appeared on the bridge to help them. She'd given them information about the destroyer's weaponry that could only be considered treasonous, yet she'd never hesitated. But for her to realize that as a Triotian, albeit a very wayward one, he'd truly had no choice, at least not at that moment, but to leave the bolt in place of the royal circlet, was more than he'd ever expected.

"Thank you. I think. From you that's high praise."

"If you want praise, then take it for that little escape plan of yours."

His expression changed, cooling suddenly. "I told you, it wasn't my plan."

"But Larcos said—"

"It was Dare's. I just adapted it a little to the circumstances."

He saw that she remembered then the story he'd told her, of the *Sunbird*'s encounter with the skypirate Cryon and his ship the *Wanderer,* and how Dare had blown up the *Sunbird*'s own shuttle to incapacitate the bigger ship so they could escape.

"Are all Triotians inherently so ... inventive?" she asked. Dax only shrugged. "I wonder," she went on, her eyes going distant as she pondered the idea, "what would have happened if Trios had not so long lived in peace, so long that they were far too generous to strangers. If they had had enough weapons, and leaders like you and Dare, perhaps even the might of the Coalition could not have overpowered them."

He knew she hadn't meant it as an accusation, but the old guilt goaded him. "But they didn't. They had none but the simplest of weapons. The rest were stored away in caves up in the mountains outside of Triotia, where they'd been for years. They were taken by surprise, tricked by their own goodness, and their legendary"— he spat out the word—"flashbow warrior was off sulking, while they died."

In a motion so quick he couldn't move in time to stop her, Califa darted forward and grabbed his knife from his boot. He tensed, his eyes flicking from the gleaming blade to her face. Then, startlingly, she reversed the blade and handed it to him.

"You're *still* sulking," she ground out. "Here. Take it. Slit your damned throat and get it over with. If you won't give yourself the mercy of a quick death, then give it to me. And Rina. And all the others who will mourn you when it's finally done."

His breath caught in his throat. On some deep level, his mind was clamoring that she was right, that he'd been clinging to his guilt like a child clung to a broken favorite toy. But on another level, that quick, instinctive level they called gut-reaction, all he could take in was that she'd said she'd mourn him.

"Perhaps we could even get word to your old friend," she went on, never letting up. "Perhaps when you are finally dead, when you finally atone for the heinous sin of survival, even your king will mourn."

Shaken by the slicing truth of her words, Dax tried to speak. "Califa, I—"

"Do you think he will?" Her tone had shifted suddenly, as if she were now merely considering an interesting question. "Will the king care what happened to the boy he grew up with? Will he—"

She broke off suddenly, her eyes widening. She dropped the knife. As it clanged on the floor, she looked away from him. Foreboding welled up in Dax, sweeping his chagrin at the truth of her battering words before it. He'd come to recognize that action of hers, and it told him she'd made one of those connections that always seemed to be right.

"That's it," she whispered, and the dismay he saw cloud the clear blue of her eyes told him he was right;

she'd come to some conclusion, and she didn't much like it.

"What?" he prompted, and the way she looked away then told him he probably wasn't going to like it, either.

"They want you alive . . ." she began, then stopped, biting her lip.

"We already deduced that," he said gently, trying to ignore his body's instantaneous reaction to the reminder of the softness of her mouth.

"It makes sense. It's just what they would do."

"Califa . . ."

"Don't you see?" She began to pace, short, quick steps. "Roxton said he'd heard talk that confirmed what you'd heard, that the rebellion forced Corling to withdraw and has been holding off the Coalition for months now. Whatever they're doing, whatever weapon they have, the Coalition hasn't been able to budge them for nearly a year. They can't risk that kind of news getting out, it would undermine their position everywhere. And they must know the story is already getting out."

He knew all that; he'd prodded Roxton for as much information as he could get without drawing the old man's lively curiosity. The news had only added to the tangled mass of his emotions, a quandary he was having to work harder and harder to ignore.

"But what has that got to do with why they want me alive?"

"They're desperate. They have nothing to bargain with."

Something knotted up deep in Dax's belly. "What does that mean?"

At last she turned and met his gaze. "They want you alive . . . to get to Dare."

The knot tightened. "What?"

"If they have all the Triotian records, they must have learned you and Dare were . . . close. They think they've got their lever. That's why you're no good to them dead."

"Are you saying," he asked, pronouncing each word with precise care, "that they think if they take me alive, they can use me to . . . negotiate something with Dare?"

She nodded. He stared at her.

"That's insane. Dare would do anything in his power to rescue a fellow Triotian—"

"Not just a fellow Triotian," Califa said.

Dax shook his head. "No. Any Triotian would be equally important to us all."

"The Coalition would never understand that. To them, the anonymous one is easily sacrificed for the whole."

"Dare may have to adopt that stance, since he's at war. But no matter what, he would never deal with the horde that destroyed Trios."

"Not even for his oldest friend?"

Dax's throat tightened, making his voice gruff. "He might have. Once. But I doubt I mean anything to him now." He beat down the emotion that threatened to engulf him, and forced his mind to work logically. "What do they think they could get out of him? Surely they don't think he'd ever let them back in?"

Califa shrugged. "I don't know. Maybe an agreement to keep silent. Or to refuse any refugees from other Coalition-owned worlds." Her mouth curved in a bitter, knowing smile that made him think yet again how far she'd come. "Or perhaps they just hope to trick him, as they tricked his father."

"Then they'll find themselves in deep trouble," Dax said. "Triotians are peaceful by choice, but we were warriors once, and we can be again. And Dare has the finest tactical mind I've ever known." He gave her a sideways look. "Except, perhaps, for Major Califa Claxton of The Coalition Tactical School."

She blushed, as much now, at his praise of her mind, as she ever had at his praise of her beauty, even when she'd been naked beneath him. This time it was he who turned away, to fight the fierce arousal that swept him even amid the chaos of feeling her revelation had brought on.

He walked over to his bunk and stood there, staring out the viewport. He sensed rather than heard Califa follow him. She came to a halt close behind him, close enough that he swore he could feel her warmth.

"He won't bargain," he said flatly. "Not with them. Not for me."

"Don't be so certain that everyone paints you with the same dark brush as you yourself do."

"He won't," Dax insisted. "Even if he doesn't hold me to blame, he would never risk his people for the sake of his own personal feelings. I know that. And he knows I would never expect it, even if things—if I—were different. In war, you do what you have to to preserve what is left."

"But would it be easy for him?"

Dax suppressed a shiver. "No. Even if he ... hates me now, it would not be easy for him to condemn me. He is not that kind of man. But he would do it, if he felt he must."

He heard her sigh behind him. "Then I suppose you'd best avoid capture."

He nearly laughed. He turned around then, and she seemed startled by his expression.

"Always straight to the heart of it," he observed, smiling at her.

She looked at him, perplexed. "You are a very confusing man," she muttered.

He did laugh then. "Ah, little snowfox, it's only fair. You've confounded me since I first saw you."

He felt the heat building between them, and knew what would happen if they stayed so close much longer. As if she realized it, too, she backed up a step.

"What will you do now?" she asked.

He battled the urge to grab her and kiss her into once more melting in his arms, summoning up every painful, aching memory of his inevitable frustration to do it. He tried to concentrate on her question.

"Do?"

"You can't continue to risk running into Coalition patrols, not when you've become such a priority to them. They'll be looking for you everywhere." Her brow furrowed. "In fact, you probably shouldn't linger here much longer. Clarion is a vital cog in the Coalition machine, with the Starworks shipbuilding facility here. You won't go long unnoticed."

"We're skypirates," Dax said simply. "We can't help but risk running into Coalition patrols. And it wouldn't be fair to ask the crew to give up going after prizes just because I've managed to move to the top of the Coalition's most wanted index."

"They would give it up for a while. For you."

"Perhaps. If I asked it of them."

She read his expression—as usual—accurately. "But you won't."

"It would not be fair," he repeated.

"Eos!" she exclaimed. "Are you still looking for fairness in a cosmos ruled by the Coalition? Wasn't it you who told me that anyone who trusts the Coalition is a fool?"

"What would you have me do?" he shot back. "Run and hide? Perhaps go back to the storehouse and reside there until I die of old age? I'd die of boredom first."

She studied him a moment, perversely calming in the face of his burst of temper.

"What would you do," she said at last, "if there was no one else to consider? If it were only you?"

He felt his shoulders sag; he'd wrestled with that thought far too often to feel anything other than weariness at thinking of it now.

"Dax?" Her voice was soft, coaxing. And almost against his will, he gave her the truth.

"When you first told me there were Triotians alive, I thought I ... I wanted ..."

"Wanted what?" she prompted, her voice so very gentle he couldn't refuse, even knowing his words would sound like those of a lost child.

"I wanted to go home."

"Oh, Dax," she said, her tone laced with pain. For him. He knew it was for him, and he couldn't bear it. He spoke quickly, denying the moment of weakness.

"It doesn't matter. I would not be welcome. If they've not already stripped me of my citizenship, it is only because they haven't had time to think of it yet."

"What if you're wrong? You could at least try, couldn't you? Surely they wouldn't—"

"I would, were I them," Dax said grimly.

Califa covered the safe distance she'd put between them in a single lithe stride.

"That's because you are harder on yourself than anyone else could be. Even Rina sees that."

He stiffened. "Rina?"

"Do you think she doesn't remember what she said to you, when you first found her? That she blamed you for not fighting for Trios? Did you never wonder why she stopped?"

He shook his head. "I was just glad she did. It hurt too much to hear the truth from one so young."

"She stopped because she saw you were punishing yourself more than she ever could." She took a breath, as if to steady a voice that had begun to quaver. "But even Rina knows now that you couldn't have stopped the Coalition. And that you had a reason for not being there."

He stared at her. "She knows?"

"Not what the reason was, just that you must have had one. Such is her faith in you, Dax."

He closed his eyes against a sudden stab of pain. "Too bad it's misplaced."

Suddenly, unexpectedly, she threw her arms around him. "Eos, Dax. Or I'll swear to your God, if it will do any good. Can't you ever forgive yourself?"

Before he could stop himself, his arms went around her in turn. He pulled her close, and lifted one hand to smooth the silk of her hair.

"Tell me something, snowfox. Have you forgiven yourself, for all you did as a Coalition officer?"

He felt her go rigid in his arms. Then, so softly he could barely be sure he'd heard it, she whispered. "No."

A low, pained laugh rumbled up from his chest. "What a miserable pair we are, snowfox."

For a long time they just stood there, taking an odd sort of consolation in their mutual predicament. It was only gradually that Dax became aware of the shirt, of the increasing softness of her body pressed against his, of the warmth that had begun as comfort changing to heat of an entirely different sort. It had never happened between them this way before, slowly, gently. It was like watching the sun come up over the mountains and spill down over the meadows of Triotia, a first touch of warmth followed by a growing flood of heat and golden light.

He let his hands slip to the back of her head, his

fingers threading through her hair as he tilted her face back. She looked up at him, and he could see the warmth he was feeling mirrored in her eyes. But when he began to lower his head, his lips already parting in anticipation of savoring the taste of her, she drew back.

"Califa?" His voice was rough, already husky with arousal.

"I . . . can't, Dax."

He drew back then, brows furrowing as he studied her. A possible answer came to him, and it was as if a sudden snow had struck his sun-filled meadow.

"I see," he said, his voice reflecting the chill that had swept him.

"Dax—"

"So tell me," he said in that same cool voice, "was the controller the only reason you mated with me before? In the hopes I would—what, be so appreciative that I would give it back? And now that you have it back—"

Fury flashed in the ice-blue eyes. She pulled back fiercely, yanking herself out of his grasp. He saw her move, and barely saved himself from a ringing blow by grabbing her arm.

"Damn you to Hades," she grated. "You accuse me of willing whoredom."

He saw her point, and released her wrist. He looked at her for a moment, then chose his words with care. "You must admit it seems . . . indicative that you should choose now to deny what happens between us."

"You mean what happens to me," she corrected.

His brows lowered. "I am as much in your power in this as you are in mine," he said. "So why, Califa?"

"Why won't I mate with you? You must ask?" She shook her head incredulously. "You say you are in my power as I am in yours. Do you think then that I enjoy seeing you in such pain?"

Dax froze.

"You think I could welcome even the incredible pleasure you give me, when I know it leaves you in agony?"

"I didn't think you—"

"Noticed? Eos, help me! How could I not? If this is indeed some Triotian trait, then I'm astounded your race has survived at all. No wonder you don't believe in mating outside of bonding, if this is what your people go through."

"Califa, it doesn't matter—"

"So you've said. I can't agree. I can only think how I would feel, if you took me so close and then left me wanting."

He swallowed tightly, knowing he owed her some kind of explanation, knowing it was amazing she hadn't demanded one before now. Yet he couldn't find the words to admit this last, ultimate flaw.

"It pleases me to give you pleasure," he began.

"And no matter how much it delights my body to have you do so, my mind cannot accept that you do it at such cost."

"It is . . . worth it. To watch you unravel, and know that I have given that to you."

"God!" It burst from her, and he didn't know whether it was unconscious, this use of the imprecation of his world, or if she thought it would have more effect on him. "Don't you understand, Dax? I can't do this! It's too much like I was before, mating without thought to what it was costing my partner."

She whirled away from him, her arms wrapping around herself as if she were about to shatter. When she went on, her voice sounded nearly taut enough to shatter as well.

"I detest the part of me that was able to use slaves in that way, and now you're asking me to . . . to use you, to gain my own pleasure, while you suffer?"

He stared at her, at the gleaming cap of her hair, at the fragile nape of her bent neck. That this was her reason had never occurred to him.

"Besides," she said, her voice low and choked, "I can't help wondering if . . . it's me. If I'm lacking, somehow, that I don't have what is necessary to pleasure you in return."

"God, little snowfox," Dax said as he reached for her shoulders and pulled her back against him. "It's not you, it was never you. It's me."

She shook her head, as if she didn't believe that anymore. He drew in a quick breath, and knew that he owed her this.

"Listen to me," he said. "Triotians are ... different. In mating as well as other things. You know that we believe in mating only inside a bonded or soon to be bonded relationship."

"Shaylah told me of this. I thought it merely another legend."

"It is one of our oldest beliefs. It is not a law, in that it is not inscribed with the other laws that make the Triotian creed. But it runs so deep that to some it is far beyond a mere belief. It becomes a physical thing. A bodily limitation."

He felt her go very still. Then, slowly, she turned to look at him. "Are you saying it is so with you?"

He sighed, knowing he was about to surrender the last and most deeply buried of his secrets to this woman. And knowing he had no choice.

"I'm saying," he told her, "that I've broken virtually every Triotian law on the tablets. I've run away. I've stolen, I've gambled dishonestly, I've committed arson, kidnapping, and piracy. I've denied my origins, and when pushed, I've killed. There isn't a damned law I've missed. Except the one that isn't written down."

He lifted her face then with a gentle finger beneath her chin.

"My mind may have let me run wild, snowfox, but my body won't let me break that last law. I don't know why. It has developed a will of its own, and the fact that I want you more than I've ever known it possible to want a woman means nothing. No matter how far or how long I go in mating, I never attain release."

She was staring at him, wide-eyed. "But I heard the crew ... they were talking of some Daxelian female, and of others ..."

He gave a weary, halfhearted chuckle. "Do you remember when I said I knew something of reputations? That appearances can be deceptive?"

She nodded, still staring at him.

"Well, mine is as ... deceptive as yours was. Oh, I'm not saying that I haven't, as you said, sampled my share. There were certainly enough females who seemed eager to bed an infamous skypirate. But I soon learned it was ... futile."

Her brows lowered slightly. "But those women, the crew said they bragged . . ."

"I know. I don't know how it started. But once the reputation was there, it seemed to take on a life of its own."

" '*Seems every female in the system wants to be able to say they've mated with the most celebrated skypirate of them all.*' " she quoted softly.

Dax shifted uncomfortably. "Who in Hades said that?"

"I don't remember. But it was Rina who told me you once said that some women wanted wild creatures for pets, to show them off."

"It felt that way sometimes," he admitted ruefully. "I think those women . . . fed it all, somehow. The notoriety just kept growing. I can only guess that each one thought she was the only one to fail."

"And so they lied," she said slowly, "to protect their own pride. That's why you believed me about . . . my reputation for free mating."

"I know it sounds crazy, but—"

"No. It doesn't sound crazy at all," she said softly. "I believe I know just how they felt."

He gripped her shoulders then. "No, snowfox. You must believe this. That no matter the end, making love with you has given me more pleasure than I've ever known before."

He used the ancient Triotian love words without thought; there was, he realized, no other words that truly fit what passed between them. He stared down into her eyes as if he could force her to believe him.

"Even before I left Trios, before my body began to betray me, I never knew such pleasure existed for me. If you deny me the pain, you deny me the pleasure as well."

It was an incredible statement. He knew it, and saw the same knowledge in her eyes. He spoke the only words he thought might convince her.

"I swear it, snowfox. On what is left of my world, I swear it."

"Oh, Dax."

She sagged against him, and for a moment he thought

she was weeping. But then he knew he was wrong; his snowfox would no more allow herself that than he could. But she had believed him, against all logic, and he was holding her again in the way he'd sworn never to do again.

And as they went down to his bunk together, he saw that his oath not to touch her was but a mote of crystal dust before the intensity of his need for this woman. He needed her as he had never needed anything, and every sign that she needed him as well sent surging bursts of heat through him.

He hunted down those signs, coaxed them out of her with his hands, then his mouth. He caressed every inch of her as he tugged away interfering cloth, until she was quivering, until, when he gently urged her thighs apart, she opened herself eagerly for his intimate kiss.

She cried out in shocked pleasure as his tongue replaced his stroking fingers and he tasted the sweet heart of her. She arched upward, moaning his name, and the honeyed sound of it rang in his ears as he felt her body gather itself for flight. As she writhed under his caresses, he knew that every word he'd told her was true.

And by morning he had made his decision. He could not go on like this. Califa had been right, he was still sulking, still brooding over his failure. It was time—past time—to put it to rest. He knew there was only an infinitesimal chance that he would succeed, either in the task he had now set for himself, or the result, but he had to try. He couldn't rest until he did.

And if that rest was of the permanent variety, so be it.

Chapter 21

The crew sat in the lounge, gaping at Dax as if he'd lost his mind.

"Let me get this straight," Nelcar said. "You're going to go—purposely—to the Coalition's worst labor camps, in the hope a handful of Triotians might still be alive?"

Dax nodded. All eyes save Roxton's, who was busy on the bridge—Dax already had his answer, no doubt, and Califa had little question as to what it had been—swiveled to Rina, who looked as astonished as the rest of them. When she realized they were all looking at her, she shook her head.

"It's not my idea!" Then she focused her gaze on Dax. "You're not doing this for me, are you?"

"No, little one. It's for me."

Califa watched him as he watched his crew. Would he tell them, at last, that he was Triotian? Was what she suspected true, that the driving force behind this reckless mission was his hope that somehow it would be enough penance, and his ticket home, if not to forgiveness?

He'd said little to her this morning when they'd awakened in each other's arms, merely asked her to join the crew in the lounge, because he had something to say to them all. She'd sensed he'd reached some kind of decision, but she had never expected this. But the moment she had heard his words, she had understood. Perhaps better than he did.

"I know you all have your own reasons for hating the Coalition," Dax went on. "As do I. I can only tell you that, in light of what is happening on Trios, there is no better way to strike back at them right now."

That much was true, Califa thought.

"The choice is yours," Dax said to them. "I expect no

one to accompany me on a mission that will bring you no profit, and will very likely endanger your lives. I freely admit this is a personal mission for me. If you wish to leave, we will part friends, and the *Evening Star* will take you wherever you wish to go."

"And if we stay?" Hurcon asked.

"Then when it is over, the *Evening Star* will be yours." A chorus of gasps met that announcement. "You may elect a captain of your own choosing, and do with her as you will."

"But what about you?" Larcos asked. "Suppose we pull this off, and rescue those few Triotians that may be left alive, and get them to Trios. Are you saying you will no longer fly with us? What will you do?"

He will either be back home, or dead, Califa thought, knowing that somehow this had to come to an end for him, and that those were the only two alternatives he would accept.

"I will ... decide that when it is done. But in any case, the *Evening Star* will be my payment to you."

Raucous discussion broke out, until at last the taciturn Qantar got to his feet.

"I would speak."

That itself was such a shock that the room fell silent.

"Most of you know my story. The Coalition has taken all that mattered to me in life. My woman, my children ... I would have welcomed death, indeed was courting it when Dax found me and convinced me to join you."

He looked around at them, his eyes lingering on Rina, then Dax, for a fraction of a second longer than the others.

"Yet of all the planets the Coalition has crushed, Trios, that most splendid of worlds, has suffered the worst of their viciousness. Her people are hunted down and killed with no more thought than slimehogs. Yet she resists valiantly. As my people never did." He shifted his gaze to Hurcon. "As Omegans never did." Then to Califa. "As Arellians never did. For that alone, she has earned my respect. And my help, if I can give it. I fly with Dax."

He sat down then, reverting into his stony-faced si-

lence as if he'd never given the eloquent speech. The
crew was nodding furiously; Dax looked a little stunned.

"A vote!" Larcos called out.

Dax held up his hand. "There is one more thing you
have the right to know before you vote. The Coalition
will not just be looking out for us. They will be actively
hunting us down. If they discover what we are doing,
they will throw all the forces they can spare into the
chase."

"The way I look at it," Larcos said, "those Triotians
who are fighting have done a lot to keep the Coalition
off our backs. If we can pay them back a little, I'm all
for it."

"I hear they're particular about their laws and such,"
Hurcon said warily. "What if they decide to toss us in
prison because we're skypirates, no matter what we
bring them?"

"Trios has no laws governing the behavior of outsiders
while not on Trios," Dax said, his voice carefully emotionless. "Only Triotians, or those guilty of an offense
against the royal family, must pay the price for violating
their laws, wherever the crime is done."

To Califa, his words sounded ominous. Not because
of what he'd said of those guilty of an offense against
the royal family—which most certainly would include
her—but because of what he wasn't saying. What would
he do, if this chance failed, if they found his offenses
too severe, and found it necessary to punish him?

Surely they wouldn't, she told herself. If he succeeded,
if he found any survivors, and was able to bring them
home, surely the council—or at the very least Dare—
would forgive him and welcome him. And perhaps, she
thought, she could help make sure he succeeded.

When Larcos called for a vote this time, Dax nodded.
To a man they repeated Qantar, until Califa thought the
words "I fly with Dax" would ring in her ears forever.
To an observer who didn't know, Dax would no doubt
appear unmoved, but Califa saw the tightness of his jaw,
the rigid straightness of his body. And she knew he
hadn't expected this.

Purposely, it seemed to Califa, he left her for last. She

was about to speak, to echo the others in their stirring pledge, when he spoke to her first.

"Since you are not by choice a member of this crew, if it is your wish, I will take you to wherever you wish and you may walk away."

Califa felt a chill start to creep up her spine. Why was he speaking like this, so formally? And after the night they'd spent together ... True, the end result for him had been the same, but she had watched him carefully, and had come to believe that, despite the pain, he had spoken the truth about the pleasure.

"However," he said, still in that same, detached tone, "you may have information that would be helpful, such as knowledge of the location of the labor camps."

That was exactly what she had thought to offer him; she knew of three camps where it was rumored Triotians were, or had been, held. But something in his tone made her hesitate. It must be simply that he was taking care before the crew not to treat her any differently, she decided. She would—

"I have a bargain for you. If you will share that knowledge as your part, if you will help where you can, I will swear to you that I will find someone capable of removing that collar."

Califa smothered a gasp. She felt as if she'd been slapped in the face, and more humiliated than she'd ever been in her days as a slave. He was bargaining with her. He felt he had to negotiate with her for the help she had been about to freely offer.

He was looking at her, his eyes reflecting a touch of puzzlement, as if he didn't understand what had stunned her so. "What do you say, Califa? Your freedom for the information I need?"

She had heard it said that when she was at her most furious, her eyes made glacial ice look warm. She guessed that was what they looked like now, as she raised them to his. Wariness flickered across Dax's face, and she knew he had seen the change.

"I say," she said with a precise enunciation that matched the frost in her eyes, "that you are a fool to bargain for what you could have had for free. But I will hold you to it, have no doubts."

She turned on her heel and strode out of the lounge, but not before she caught a last glimpse of Dax, who was looking very much like a man who has just realized the size of his mistake.

Dax was exhausted from battling the heavy gravity of Omega, but he had no choice but to keep going. The drugged guards would soon be waking, and they had to be long gone by then. He shifted his burden, and heard a softly voiced apology out of the dark from somewhere near his left ear.

"Sorry to be so much trouble."

"Never mind," he said.

She wasn't much trouble, really, this pale, broken woman who clung to his back. She'd been in the darkest of the dank, grimy cells, her ability to walk long lost to the torturous instruments of her captors. She'd been barely recognizable as Triotian, her once golden hair now turned to silver, her golden skin turned sallow. But her eyes had given the truth to Califa's promise that there was at least one Triotian being held here; they were the deep, soft green of the Triotian forest.

Califa. She had been by his side every step of the way, as she was at this moment. She had spent hours forcing herself to remember any bits of hard information or rumor she'd ever heard about captive Triotians and where they were being held. She had given him detailed layouts of every labor camp she knew of, always with the caution that her information was old, coupled with the assurance that the Coalition moved slowly to change.

While it had been Dax's idea to use Nelcar's potion to drug the guards, it had been Califa's for her to administer it, going blatantly into danger, flaunting instead of hiding the gold collar that marked her as slave, and her tempting body as well, masquerading as a new piece of Coalition property sent to provide food and drink—and perhaps more—for the guards. This was their third raid, and each time the result had been the same; the guards were so distracted they ate and drank what she brought without question.

His every instinct had screamed out against it when she had first suggested it.

"It is part of our *bargain,* is it not?" she had said icily. "That I shall help where I can?"

He wondered if she would ever thaw. He'd known immediately that he'd said something very wrong that day in the lounge, when those eyes had gone icier than he'd ever seen them. Unexpectedly, it was Rina who'd made him really see what he'd done.

"Eos, Dax, you've been mating with her, haven't you?"

That blunt assessment from this girl he'd always thought of as the child he'd found made his face heat. "I ... er ..."

"Do you think I'm blind?" Rina asked. "Anyone can see the crackle between you. Even Larcos noticed, and you know he's oblivious unless it's one of his blessed inventions. And Roxton said he'd never seen you look at a woman like that."

"Roxton," he muttered, as he had countless times before, "talks too much."

"So it's true, then. No wonder she was furious."

"No wonder?"

Rina let out a sigh of exasperation so quintessentially feminine it shook Dax's childlike image of her to the core. "Don't you get it? You've mated with her, yet you put securing her help on the same level as trading for coins. She's a slave, Dax. How do you think that made her feel?"

It had hit him then, hard. Had he been so long the skypirate then, that making sure that anyone who chose to accompany him on this fool's mission would be rewarded was the only way he could think of to entice them? He should have seen the truth after Qantar's moving, surprising speech; there were things other than profit that drove his crew, just as it was something other than profit that held them together. He hadn't had to bribe them, just to show them how what they would be doing would strike their mortal enemy.

He hadn't had to bribe Califa, either. And not just because it would be a blow against the system that had enslaved her. Because, God help her, she cared for him. She would have done it for that. But instead he had bargained with her, in a way trying to buy her as surely as if she'd been on the slave block at Ossuary. As Rina had said, no wonder she was furious.

And the knowledge that even had she refused he would have done his best to see that she was freed from the collar that marked her as slave lay silent and unspoken—and now, for her, unbelievable—within him.

Now they had, at last, reached their destination. Dax stopped for a moment to catch his breath; a difficult task in the dense, Omegan air he wasn't used to breathing. Califa was a few steps behind, as ill-adapted as he was to this high-gravity world.

He should have taken Hurcon up on his offer, he thought. The short, muscular native of this planet would no doubt have found this an easy trek. But he would ask no one else to take this, the greatest of the risks on their fool's mission. And besides, he was still rankling over Hurcon's well-intentioned warning against taking Califa with him into the heart of Coalition strongholds; the Coalition wanted him so desperately now, she might well be able to buy her life back by turning him over to them on one of these raids. A few well-chosen words to the right Coalition officer, and Dax would be on his way to Legion Command in chains.

That the thought had occurred even to Hurcon, who had no idea that she could easily know exactly the right Coalition officer to make her deal with, was disconcerting. Dax didn't want to believe it, but she was so angry with him now. . . .

He pushed away the thought. Gently, he lifted the fragile old woman into the cockpit of the fighter. It would be a tight fit, he and Califa and the woman, but they needed the adaptability; it would take the fighter's wings, adjustable to a much greater surface area, to get through the soupy Omegan atmosphere.

Califa ignored his proffered hand and climbed into the fighter without help, despite the pronounced worsening of her limp on this world. Smothering a sigh he went after her. And as usual, the moment they were back aboard the *Evening Star,* she walked away from him without a word.

Nelcar was waiting for them, and took the old woman—her name was Fleuren, she'd said on the flight up, which, unexpectedly, she seemed to take great delight in—rather tenderly into his care. But not before she had held Dax back with a gentle touch of her thin hand.

"I never thought to see another flashbow warrior," she whispered.

Dax stared at her. How had she known?

"My grandfather was one," she explained as if he'd spoken. "I felt around him the same aura I feel now. And besides"—her worn, weary face creased into a bright, dimpled grin that spoke of the beauty she must once have been—"I saw the bow beneath your cloak."

For the first time since he'd begun this task, Dax laughed. She watched him, her gaze lingering on the dimple that creased his cheek.

"Ah, yes, my grandfather was a charming rogue as well. It seems to come with the bow."

Dax grinned, more from the change in this woman than her words; she was coming alive now, knowing she was a step closer to home. He'd warned her of the unlikelihood they'd make it, but she'd cared nothing for that. If she were to die, she'd said, at least it would be in freedom, trying to go home. It was a sentiment Dax understood very well.

"Perhaps," Fleuren said as Nelcar carefully took her from Dax, "you should use some of that charm on your woman. She seems a bit . . . vexed."

Your woman. The words struck some chord deep inside Dax; he tried to shake it off.

"It takes a woman of rare courage and love to stay by a man she's furious with, through such danger," Fleuren said.

"You are a very astute woman," Nelcar said as he settled her in the cradle of his arms. Then he gave Dax a sideways look. "Perhaps he'll get lucky and some of it will rub off."

Fleuren laughed. "Oh, I'm going to like it here. Let's go, young man."

Nelcar laughed with her, and headed to the lounge that had been converted to a fairly efficient sick bay; Dax had foreseen that they would need it. Dax watched them go, then stood for a moment, rubbing at his gritty eyes.

"Vexed," he muttered, "isn't the word for it."

Then he turned to secure the fighter.

Three raids, and eight new passengers. Only two had been Triotian, there were three now counting Fleuren, four with Rina, but when he'd found others in the isolated cells that seemed to be universally designated for the captives he sought, he couldn't bring himself to leave them behind. So their compliment now included one more from Clarion, one from Zenox, a ragged Daxelian he'd ordered Hurcon to keep an eye on, and two Arellians.

It had been the Arellians they had found first, on the first raid. The Triotian who had been in the cell with them had been, they said, an old man who had died a week before.

"He was a tough old man," they'd said admiringly. "He never once gave in to them."

For a moment Dax had wondered if the entire mission would go like this, with them being just too late to save the few Triotians who had survived. It had been Califa who had made him look at the promising side.

"At least we know he *was* here. My information was old, but still accurate."

"I never doubted that," he'd said, hoping to placate her somehow.

"Good," she'd said coolly. "Then there will be no argument about my having fulfilled my part of our bargain."

He'd winced inwardly, but said nothing, because just then one of the prisoners had come forward to the bars, staring at Califa.

"You're Arellian!" he exclaimed.

"Yes."

"Then you'll take us out of here?"

The urgent plea was more than Dax could resist. Besides, perhaps rescuing a couple of her fellow Arellians might warm Califa up a bit. So the two—brothers who had been coffee growers who had had the audacity to resist the Coalition seizure of their lands—had been the first to board the *Evening Star*.

When they had discovered they had been set free by the famous skypirate, they regaled all with tales of his heroics, and stories of his generosity to victims of the Coalition, which they could, of course, personally attest to now.

Dax had quickly vacated the lounge when that talk started. He was no hero, and what pittance he'd given others was nothing compared to what they'd lost.

Now, when he'd finished securing the fighter, he walked to his quarters. He'd slept little in the past week, and he knew he would be risking making mistakes out of fatigue if he didn't get some rest. Once inside, he verified with Roxton over the comlink that they were on their way to the next stop at full speed. Then he sat down on the edge of his bunk.

This mission had been hard on everyone. Speed was essential, and Larcos had spent many long hours coaxing extra power from the ship's engines, and Rina had mapped out some wild but effective courses that cut precious time off their travel. She'd used every available astral body with enough mass to inch up their speed, dipping into the gravitational field and then bouncing out, having picked up some of the body's own speed. He was damned proud of her. And of the *Evening Star,* for holding together through all this.

He guessed they would have one more chance to use the slave ruse. After that, it was too likely that the Coalition outposts would have been warned about a slave bearing wine, warnings that even the *Evening Star*'s blasting through hyperspace couldn't beat much longer. After the next run, then, they would have to come up with something else. He tried to think, but he felt as if he were still on Omega, fighting the heavy pull of the planet's mass. When at last he toppled over, he had already fallen asleep sitting up.

Califa crept down the dark byway, the familiarity of this place hammering at her from all sides. She sensed rather than heard Dax behind her; he moved with a silence that was amazing for a man his size.

She remembered this outpost on Darvis II too well. She had postponed telling Dax of the rumor she'd heard in the slave quarters on Carelia, that there was at least one Triotian in the prison here, until last. She'd had no desire to return, and had thought, rather grimly, that if they were killed before reaching here, it would save her from it.

Besides, it made sense to come here last; of all the places she knew of that possibly held Triotians, this one was the closest to Trios itself.

She'd been surprised, when she'd brought it up at last, that Dax had remembered.

"That's where you were hurt, wasn't it?"

"Yes."

"Then Qantar and I will handle it."

She'd been surprised at his words; he had to know, as she did, that her presence, her knowledge of this outpost, could make the difference between success and failure. She hadn't expected such sensitivity to her feelings, and in an odd way she resented it; it made it even more difficult to stay angry with him.

That was a task she was finding it hard to carry out, anyway. With every raid her admiration for him grew. He seemed to have a clever plan for every situation, from distracting the guards on Clarion with an explosion that rocked the entire outpost, to blasting the power plant and blacking out the city of Zenox until well after they'd escaped. They'd rescued three more Triotians, one of them so ill he was hanging on only so he could die on his homeworld, yet another from Clarion, and a Carelian, all almost without having to fire a shot, thanks to Dax.

Once aboard, the Carelian had startled them all by kneeling before Dax the moment she recognized him; Carelians were a fierce, proud breed, and knelt willingly to no one.

"Your name is sacred to my clan," she told the embarrassed Dax. "It is my sister you gave the means to escape her captivity on our homeworld. She would wish you to know that all others held there escaped with her, as you requested."

While the others gaped, Roxton grinned. "So *that's* what you did with that code key!"

And Califa's admiration for him expanded yet again.

And then there was the matter of his apology. He'd quickly realized he'd hurt her grievously. Her surprise at his apology was matched by her surprise that he understood just why she was so angry; she hadn't expected him to. But she wasn't quite ready to forgive him, not yet. That he'd thought he'd had to buy her help still dug at her painfully.

But the realization that he'd assumed no one would help him on this chase without compensation because he felt he did not deserve such loyalty, also nibbled away at her anger, threatening to undermine it.

She gave herself a little shake. She knew she had been thinking of other things to distract her from the fact that the ordnance bunker where she had nearly died was their target. But if she didn't concentrate on this mission, all of the risks they'd taken, all that they'd miraculously succeeded at would be for nothing.

The bunker—or what was left of it—was just ahead of them. It had nearly been destroyed, that day. And, with grim Coalition practicality, the hulk had been converted to what they needed most; another prison. It was this Califa had heard, the name of Darvis II catching her attention, then the news that they had turned the ruin into a one-cell prison mainly to make existence as miserable as possible for a Triotian captive. And from what she could see now, they'd succeeded; she and Dax had circled the place, and it looked uninhabitable.

And watched by two well-armed guards who circled the building every few minutes. Perhaps word had reached here to be on guard, although thanks to Dax's penchant for rescuing anyone else they could along the way, the Coalition couldn't be sure exactly who they were after. But since Triotians were their most precious prisoners now, the guard had been intensified anyway.

At Dax's gesture, she inched a little closer. They waited, then moved forward again, each small gain of distance seeming to take forever. But the guards were watchful, and she knew they couldn't move any faster without risking discovery.

She didn't know what would happen this time; Dax had merely assured her the diversion would be there when they needed it.

They moved a little closer.

They had worked out the plan beforehand, based on Califa's knowledge of the outpost and the surrounding area. They'd come down in the shuttle, while the *Eve-*

ning Star was well out of range on the dark side of the planet. Dax had brought the little craft straight down to the planet, then, using Rina's incomparable memory as a guide, had flown to within a mile of the outpost, never once rising high enough to register on the outpost scanners. It was a hair-raising, incredible piece of flying, and Califa swore that more than once she'd heard the brush of branches against the underside of the shuttle.

They moved farther, a gain of a few feet this time as the guards both arrived at the far reach of their circling path. The two men were nearly out of their line of sight now, and Califa quickly followed Dax's lead until he stopped once more.

The shuttle sat about a half mile away, in a narrow cleft between two scarps created by one of the sudden shifts of the land this area was prone to. The hand-held comlink Dax carried could easily reach the shuttle, but the *Evening Star* was far out of its range. So Rina, grudgingly, had stayed aboard the shuttle, and when the time came, Dax would signal her, and she would relay the signal to the *Evening Star* with the shuttle's much more powerful communications system. The outpost would hear the transmission, no doubt, but it would be much too quick for them to trace where it had come from.

And hopefully, they would quickly forget all about it when that transmitted order was carried out.

They were now within a stone's throw of the barred door that had been implanted in the wreckage of the bunker. They waited, barely breathing as the guards came back. The two men exchanged a few words neither Dax nor Califa could hear, then began the circuit again.

As they approached that most distant point again, Dax lifted the comlink. Califa watched him as he watched the guards, his gaze intent as he gauged the timing. Time seemed to lock in place, to hold, as she looked at him. He was tense, yet crackling with vitality, more alive than any man she'd ever known. And suddenly all her anger drained away; what good was it, when they might die in the next moment?

He moved suddenly, flipping the comlink on and snapping out the order.

"Now!"

The prearranged double click came back at them; Rina had copied. Dax shut the comlink off quickly. Then, with a rakish, reckless grin, he reached out and cupped Califa's cheek. She nearly jumped; he hadn't touched her except accidentally since that day in the lounge, when he'd bargained with her. Then she realized he was tilting her head toward the sky.

It was silent, dark, and spangled with distant stars. Nothing unusual, nothing—

The sky above them erupted. Fiery objects rained down, looking like the most intense meteor shower she'd ever seen. But this was more massive than any natural event; the sky lit up as if with the flames of Hades.

Predictably, the two guards stared upward in shock at the blazing display. It was almost frightening, even to Califa, who at least knew it was somehow arranged; those two were stunned into immobility.

Dax nudged her then, and she tore her gaze from the blazing heavens. They ran the last few feet and ducked into the shadow of the ruin. By the time they reached the door, shouts of amazement and fear were echoing around them from the astonished inhabitants of the outpost; the noise was enough to cover the sound as Dax hit the door lock with his disrupter.

"What in Hades *was* that?" Califa whispered.

Dax grinned, that wild, exhilarated grin that never failed to make her heart race. "Larc finally got to use that rail gun of his. That's every bit of space debris we've been able to collect over the last week."

Califa stared at him as he pushed the door open. Fired from the modified rail gun into the upper reaches of the atmosphere above Darvis II, any object of size would indeed burn up as it reached thicker air. And a mass of them would do exactly what she had just seen.

Wordlessly—not the first time she'd been awed speechless at this man's resourcefulness—she followed him into the cell.

This Triotian was a young one, not even Rina's age. All this, for a child, Califa thought. She glanced at Dax. His face was set, his jaw rigid, and she knew he was thinking the same. And wondering how long the boy had been here.

He was chained to the wall by one thin ankle. He looked at them wildly, and Califa felt a vicious pang at the thought of him being held in this pit. The boy backed against the wall, shaking his head with fear. She couldn't blame him.

"It's all right," she said as she knelt beside him. "We've come to take you out of here. But we haven't much time."

"I don't believe you," he said, pulling away.

"You must hold still," Califa urged. "Or I can't break you free of this shackle without hurting you."

The boy trembled. "You're Arellian," he said. "There are Arellian officers. There is one in charge of this place. How . . . how do I know you're not with the Coalition? How can I trust you?"

"If not me," Califa said softly, "trust him."

The boy's gaze flicked to Dax, who stood watching their backs, and the broken door. "Who is he?"

"Dax?" He glanced back at her call. "He doesn't trust me. He wants to know why he should trust you."

Dax looked at the boy for a moment. "It's a wise man who is careful with his trust. But we *are* here to take you out of here," he promised.

The boy still looked doubtful. Dax moved then, swirling aside his cloak. When he raised his arm, the flashbow glinted silver in the dim light.

The boy's eyes widened. "The flashbow," he breathed. Dax nodded as he hid the ancient weapon once more. Joy leapt in the boy's face, and Califa quickly and carefully turned the disrupter on the shackle that bound him.

"Can you run?" Dax asked. "Honestly, now."

"I don't think so," the boy admitted. "Not far. I've been chained for a long time."

Califa heard Dax mutter something that she was just as glad not to have understood. Then he knelt and let the boy clamber onto his back; he was so thin, Califa doubted he would slow Dax much. But the burden would limit his fighting ability, so Califa kept her disrupter armed and ready in her hand, and when Dax nodded toward his waist, reached inside the cloak and took his as well.

They started back toward the door. Califa breathed a

sigh of relief when the shadows appeared deserted. She glanced upward; Larcos was still putting on a show, although it was less extensive now. The boy Dax carried didn't even notice; he was too busy clinging like a burr to his rescuer's back, his bony arms wrapped around Dax's shoulders, his legs around his waist.

They headed for the byway that would lead them out of the outpost. Califa could see the dark shadows of the hills beyond. They were going to make it. By Eos—or by Dax's God—they were going to make it. They'd be—

A sudden flare of light froze Dax in his tracks. The boy cried out, and Dax turned to put himself between the child and the threat. And out of the glare of the powerful huntlight came a voice Califa knew.

"Hold!" Then, in shocked tones. "Eos, it's Dax!"

Beltar. Beltar Estrille, the man Larcos had reminded her of. He must be the Arellian the boy had mentioned, the one in charge. She remembered they had, with typical Coalition perspicaciousness, promoted him to major soon after he had obtained a barely mediocre score in her tactical classes. She also remembered him as a bit gullible.

Califa stepped forward, into the light. The man's tone changed to one of bewilderment. "Califa? Califa Claxton? Is that you?"

"Yes, Beltar. It is."

Her fingers tightened around the disrupter. Carrying the boy, Dax was virtually unarmed. And Beltar couldn't help but see that. Just as he couldn't help but see that she was armed. What would he do? And how should she play it?

Before she could decide, she heard a long, low whistle.

"Eos, Califa, you've done it. You've captured the most wanted man in all the Coalition systems put together! General Corling will want to put a medal on you personally. You've just bought your career back!"

She could see nothing in the glare of the huntlight. But she could feel Dax's gaze fastened on her.

Chapter 22

"Turn out that light, will you, Beltar?" Califa asked. "It's blinding me."

The light clicked off obligingly. Dax swallowed tightly, his gaze fixed unwaveringly on Califa, although now that the glare had destroyed his night vision temporarily, all he could see was her slender shape.

"Is she one of them after all?" the boy whispered into Dax's ear.

"Sshh," he hissed. Mainly because he had no answer. Hurcon's words came back to haunt him now. He didn't think Califa would turn on him, but then he'd never expected she would be offered her life back in exchange, either. But in the Coalition, apparently handing over their most wanted man would be all it would take for them to admit they were wrong. Or at least to make reparations. It was a prize anyone would be hard-pressed to resist; for the woman whose whole life had been her career, it would be nearly impossible.

"Thank you," Califa said, sounding genial. "Now I can see again. Are any of your guards handy to turn him over to?"

Beltar snorted in disgust. "No. They're all off watching whatever that sky display is. I thought it might be a diversion, we've heard rumors that he"—he jerked a thumb at Dax—"was on a rampage, raiding labor camps."

"You always were a smart one, Beltar." Califa's tone was overloaded with admiration. The man didn't seem to notice.

"Yes, well, I suppose that's why they promoted me to commander here."

"And so young, too, to have a command."

The man preened visibly.

"Hmm," Califa murmured, looking thoughtful. "Perhaps we should lock them back in the boy's cell for now. I wouldn't want them to get loose. It might ruin your reputation."

"No, that wouldn't do," Beltar agreed hastily.

Dax could see him now, a lanky, loose-jointed man whose uniform seemed to look ill-fitted. He was smiling at Califa as he walked toward them.

"We wouldn't want to tarnish your regained honor, either," he said. "I can hardly wait to turn in this report. I always admired you, Major. Welcome back."

"Thank you, Major," Califa returned almost gaily. "It is good to be back."

She sounded so convincing Dax shivered inwardly. Was she truly so angry at him? Would she hand him over and then go back to her life, to further Coalition glory? Would she leave him to his fate and pick up her life where it had left off? Would she someday perhaps be the tactician who would defeat Trios in the end?

His stomach churned. There was a chance the boy could dart away into the shadows, and stay hidden long enough for him to get to the flashbow. But the bow was not a weapon that could be fired in haste; he would be dead long before he could activate it.

"Did you search him for weapons?" Beltar asked.

She didn't have to, Dax thought grimly. I gave her the only one that would help now.

"Of course." She waved his disrupter. "There was only this. Come, let's get him secured. I don't like him loose. He's too unpredictable. But they've mangled this lock." Her gaze flicked to Dax as she said, "We'll have to weld it shut or something. Do you have a laser torch?"

Dax felt his heart leap as she pointedly suggested what he'd done to the barracks on Boreas. Was this a signal of some kind, or was he being a fool?

"No, but this will do it," Beltar said, reaching to his belt and taking out a high-power laser pistol. "I've heard he's worse than unpredictable, he's crazy. Why, he's been raiding bases throughout the system, taking nothing but prisoners. What kind of sense does that make?"

Beltar started toward Dax, but he was looking at Califa, and Dax knew this was his only chance. He either moved now, or—

Or he trusted Califa. Trusted her not to have turned on him. Trusted her to have a plan. Trusted her, not only with his own life, but the boy's. Trusted her loyalty, as he had not done when he had bargained with her to join this mission.

When Beltar nudged his shoulder with the pistol, he went without a struggle. It was an ugly weapon, carving a victim into screaming pieces before granting him the mercy of death. Dax much preferred a disrupter; a direct hit meant instant unconsciousness.

The boy was not so acquiescent. He began to squirm, trying to break free. Dax tightened his grip. "Trust me," he whispered, praying he wasn't condemning them both to Hades. The boy went still. Such faith, he thought. *Such is her faith in you,* Califa had said of Rina. I hope to God mine isn't as misplaced as hers is.

The boy started to shake as they stepped back into the dank, dark cell that had been his world for so long. Dax tried to calm him again, but he wasn't feeling too confident himself. He saw Califa stop, keeping herself between Beltar and the door until Dax and the boy passed. She looked at him, but his eyes hadn't completely recovered from the flash of the huntlight, and he couldn't read her expression. But he knew his was rigid as the door swung shut behind him.

The clang of the slamming prison door echoed in his ears. It was a sound he'd never forget, for whatever life he had left. He'd been wrong. He'd gambled his life, and an innocent child's, and he'd lost. She had jumped at the chance to get her life back, all her fine words about hating the system she'd served for so long were—

"Here," she said in an absent tone, "give me the pistol." She held out her hand, not even looking at Beltar, instead studying the damaged lock as if to determine the best way to seal it permanently shut.

After an instant's hesitation, Beltar handed her the weapon. Califa took it, and aimed it at the door. She moved the hand holding the disrupter toward the officer, out of her way. Beltar seemed to relax, and turned to smirk at Dax.

Califa shot him.

She used the disrupter, not the laser, and Beltar never had the chance to scream. He crumpled to the ground without a sound. Dax felt his knees wobble, and wondered if he was about to follow him down. He let the boy slide to the ground, and braced himself against one of the bars as he let out the breath he'd been holding.

Califa straightened then, and reached for the door to swing it open.

The boy looked from her to Dax.

"She sounded so real" he said, his young voice tiny and scared, "like she was one of them ... How did you know?"

Dax drew himself up and put a gentle hand on the boy's shoulder. "Sometimes, you just have to let go and trust."

He shifted his gaze to Califa. He could see her now, could see her eyes fastened on him.

"And I owed her this," he added quietly, as if to the boy, but never taking his eyes off of Califa. "Because once I couldn't do it when I should have."

"Oh, Dax."

He heard the whisper, in a voice he hadn't heard from her in far too long. He wanted to grab her and kiss her, right here and now, he wanted—

"Somebody's coming!"

Dax whirled at the boy's cry, as did Califa. They heard the sounds now, distant, running footsteps. But not distant enough. She was closer to the outside perimeter of the ruined bunker, so she ran to look.

"It's a patrol," she reported grimly. "Six of them, on the run this way."

"Damnation," Dax swore, "he must have told somebody where he was going."

She glanced at the door, the only escape. "We'll never get past them, not that way. We'd have to cross open ground right in front of them. They'd pick us off like brollets. And they'll be here in a minute, maybe two."

Dax looked around the cell. The back of the original bunker had been built into the hill itself, and that portion was about all that was left. They'd simply sealed off the front with a wall and the barred door, leaving what was left of the bunker and its roof extending out into the air. It was an effective, escape-proof prison.

Maybe.

"How much farther does that hill go?"

Her brows creased. "You mean through it? To the back? Fifty feet or so. Twenty, maybe thirty feet on the sides."

Dax's gaze snapped back to the front of the ruin. The footsteps were getting closer, and they could hear shouting now. They were almost out of time. He looked at Califa.

"Can you fly the shuttle?"

Her brows lowered again. "Yes, but—"

"Back to the *Evening Star*?"

"Of course. Dax, what—"

"Get back against the back wall, as far as you can. Both of you."

His tone brooked no denial and tolerated no questions. Califa urged the boy back into the shadows until they came up against the wall of the bunker. Dax backed up a few steps himself, stopping several feet in front of them. Then he again reached inside his cloak and brought out the flashbow.

Califa knew what to expect now, but still, and in spite of their dilemma, it fascinated her. He took a bolt from his boot and slipped it into the open groove; Califa heard the faint sound as it hit the metal case. He notched the string, then flipped the lever she'd seen before. That low-pitched hum began. In the dim light of the cell, the glow of the bolt seemed eerie, magical somehow. And despite her logical turn of mind, Califa wasn't altogether certain it wasn't.

Dax took a deep breath, then slowly raised the weapon. He settled it against his shoulder. And then, oddly, he aimed it upward, toward the remaining roof of the old bunker, where it protruded far out beyond the wall and the door. She saw his finger curl around the trigger release on the bottom of the etched silver stock.

Califa held her breath, hearing the running footsteps closing in.

He closed his eyes, standing so very still she couldn't even see him breathing. It seemed to her that even the bow itself began to glow beneath his touch. And then, there in the dark, dank cell, she thought for an instant that the glow expanded, enveloping Dax himself as well as the weapon. Only then did he open his eyes.

"Turn your head and cover your ears," she warned the boy, who made an awed sound as he did so.

The soldiers were here, she could see the figures in the shadows outside the door.

Dax pulled the trigger.

The glowing bolt raced down the groove. A split second later a flash of light a hundred times fiercer than the mock-meteors, brighter than a bank of Beltar's huntlights, filled the ruin. In the same instant the accompanying earsplitting crack of sound made them sway on their feet. The thunder had barely died away before the roof began to crumble.

Suddenly realizing what he'd done, Califa ran forward to pull the dazed Dax out of the path of the falling debris. They huddled against the back wall until the rumble of sound stopped. She coughed as the dust began to settle. They were trapped, as thoroughly as if the Coalition had done it themselves. And she guessed a couple of the patrol had not escaped being trapped themselves, under the pile of rubble. She looked at Dax, who was still looking a little unfocused. But he had to have had a plan, she knew he did, or he wouldn't have asked her if she could fly the shuttle. And he wouldn't have sealed them in here like this, to die as soon as the air ran out.

Dax shook his head once, then looked at her. She saw him snap out of it, and glance toward the pile of rubble blocking what had once been the only way in or out. When he smiled in grim satisfaction, she knew she'd been right. She just wished she had a clue as to what he was planning.

When he looked at her again, she knew she was going to find out.

"Promise me that if you have to, you will take the boy and go. Get to the shuttle and get yourselves and Rina out of here."

"Dax—"

"Please, Califa. We don't have time to argue. I've got to know you'll do this, if you have to."

She hesitated, but as his eyes bore down into her she couldn't say no. Not after he'd walked meekly into this cell, passing up his one chance for escape, simply because he trusted her.

"If I have to," she agreed reluctantly. "But—"

"Get the boy into the far corner," he ordered, gesturing toward the corner opposite the wall nearest where they'd come into the outpost. "But you'll have to come back, Califa. I may need your help."

She scurried the boy into the corner, gave him a reassuring hug, then went back to Dax.

"I may need you to load these," he said.

She instinctively held out her hands to take what he was handing her. She nearly jumped when she realized they were the bolts for the flashbow. They felt so odd, cool and smooth, and much heavier than they appeared. And he'd given her eight of the nine that had been left in his boot. The other was in his hand.

"Don't stand too close until after I fire. Then just hand me the next one. If I don't ask you for it by the time the dust settles, slide it in the groove yourself."

She realized then what he planned to do.

If he has to fire too often, the warrior can die from it.

"Dax, it will take too many shots to blast our way out of here."

He gave her a crooked smile. "It's the only way, snowfox."

He lifted the bow again, slid in the bolt, notched the metallic string, and flipped the lever. As the hum began, Califa instinctively backed up.

She saw the glow leap, enveloping him yet again, and she knew he was about to fire. She turned her head, covering her ears, guessing the sound would be even more ferocious in this closed-in place.

She was right. It echoed off the walls, deafeningly, and she barely heard the boy's cry of fright. She wondered how Dax could stand it, but when she looked at him he wore that dazed look, as if he hadn't heard it at all.

Then she looked at the wall. Half of it was gone, and a sizable chunk of the hill itself behind it. Nearly three feet of it. If the hill was really thirty feet through, it would take all nine shots they had. If Dax lived that long. She smothered a tiny cry as she went to him.

It took him longer to come out of it this time, but when he did he merely held his hand out for another bolt. He loaded it, and it all happened again. He swayed this time afterward, but recovered when Califa steadied him. She turned to check the hole.

He'd gained four—no, it was almost five this time—feet. Apparently the wall had used up a larger portion of the first bolt's energy.

After two minutes, he loaded another bolt. The process seemed to take longer this time, but the resulting explosion was no less intense. Again he swayed, letting the bow fall to his side as he closed his eyes. He was breathing heavily now, sweat breaking out on his forehead. But he had gained a good six feet this time, it was truly a tunnel now, and Califa wondered if perhaps the ground was softer as they got farther from the bunker itself.

It took three minutes this time, but he loaded the bow again. She thought she saw him shiver, but he controlled it so quickly she couldn't be sure.

This time when he fired, he staggered and nearly went down. Califa leapt to his side, steadying him.

"No more, Dax," she said. She glanced at the tunnel. It went out of sight into darkness. She knew it had to be over fifteen feet now. An odd scent lingered in the air, an electric, burning odor she'd smelled once before, in the dank corridor of a prison.

"No more," she repeated. "We'll dig by hand if we have to, but you can't fire that thing anymore."

"No. Time. Air."

She could barely hear him over the ringing in her ears. "Dax—"

He shook his head. He seemed to focus a little then. "Got to get out. They may . . . hear. Guess."

She couldn't deny that; the explosions were deafening in here, they must be at least audible outside. And they *were* running out of air in here; apparently he'd done a superb job of sealing the entrance.

He took another bolt from her. Moving slowly, he loaded it. Califa backed away.

God, she thought, as if only his God could help her

now, what if I was wrong? What if it's farther than I thought? He could die, for nothing. For a miscalculation.

The lightning flashed and the thunder cracked. Another five feet of ground vanished. And Dax went to his knees.

The warrior can die, the warrior can die, the warrior can die...

The words echoed through her mind in rhythm with the ringing of her ears. But Dax struggled to his feet. And fired again. And again. And the last time, when he went to his knees he dropped the bow.

"Load," he gasped out.

"God, Dax, stop." Sweat was pouring off him now, his face was as pale as her own, and his eyes were dark-circled and hollow looking.

Promise me that if you have to, you will take the boy and go. Get to the shuttle and get yourselves and Rina out of here.

He'd known. He'd known what he was going to do would probably kill him.

"Please, Dax, stop. You're killing yourself."

"Two. More."

"You can't—"

"Load!"

Trembling, she took the next to the last bolt and slid it down the groove as she'd seen him do too many times now. She notched the metal strand, startled at the amount of pull necessary; it took her both hands. Nothing happened. She made sure the bolt was up solidly against the metal casing. Still nothing.

Then, shakily, Dax held out his hand. She lifted the bow, amazed by its weight; he'd always carried and lifted it so easily. She placed it in his hand.

The bolt began to glow.

It happened slowly this time, the glow flickering a time or two in a way that made Califa bite her lip. But gradually it grew stronger. And brighter. Brighter even than before. As if he were pouring the last of his strength into it.

As if he were pouring his life into it.

He fired.

The burst of light and the roar of sound echoed back down the tunnel. The bow clattered to the ground.

And Dax collapsed at her feet.

With a cry of terror she knelt beside him. She rolled him over, cradling his head with her arms. She lifted him until his shoulders were across her lap. His head lolled back, frighteningly limp. Already he felt cold to her.

He looked waxen, his face pale and slack. The skin around his eyes stood out like bloody bruises. He wasn't breathing, and Califa was afraid to feel for a pulse; she knew she would find none. He looked like a death mask of himself. She cradled him in her arms, and for the second time in two decades, she wept.

And then, on the tear-dampened skin of her face, she felt a cool breeze sweeping in from the tunnel.

"Give him the bow back."

Califa gulped back a sob and stared at the boy through eyes still blurry with tears. "Wha-at?"

"Give him the bow," the boy repeated. He'd crept out of the corner shortly after Dax had collapsed. "The legend says even a dead flashbow warrior will rise again if you put his bow in his hand."

A dead flashbow warrior. Califa felt a chill unlike any she'd ever known. God, she hated leaving him here, for the Coalition to find. But she couldn't carry his body. Not through that tunnel, and all the way back to the shuttle.

But the boy was right; at least they would find him with the flashbow in his hands, so they would know who had truly stolen their other Triotian prize from them. She lifted the heavy bow and set it across his torso, then lifted his too cold, limp right hand to press it around the etched silver stock. Then she bent over him, stroking one last time the thick, dark mane of hair before pressing her lips to his, weeping once more as she felt the coolness of his skin, the slackness of his mouth.

"Oh, Dax, I wish—"

She wished a hundred things, none of them possible. But one thing was. She would finish this task he'd set for himself. She would take the Triotians, including this boy, home. And she wouldn't leave Trios, no matter

what Dare did, even if he wished to execute her, until
they admitted that Dax hadn't been to blame for anything except youthful folly and hot temper.

She kissed him again, wishing she could see those vividly green eyes just once more.

"Goodbye, my skypirate," she whispered, then had to
gulp back another sob at the realization that she would
never hear him teasingly call her snowfox again.

It was a moment before she could bring herself to
release her hold on him.

"We must go," she said at last, easing his head to the
ground as she slipped out from beneath him.

"No, something's wrong," the boy said. "He should
come back."

Califa bit back a sob. "He's never coming back. We
must go, so that what he's done isn't for nothing."

The boy ignored her. "You have to load it," he said
suddenly. "That must be it."

He looked at her expectantly. Why not, she thought,
if it would make the boy happy. She searched the ground
and found the last bolt where she'd dropped it when
Dax had crumpled. Gently she slid it down the silver
groove until it was seated against the metal casing. With
a great effort, she notched the string. The boy nodded,
then reached over to flip the lever on the bow. Nothing happened.

"Now we must go," she said firmly, taking the boy's
hand. She pulled him toward Dax's tunnel, feeling the
cool breeze increasing as they got closer. She'd promised, she kept repeating to herself. He'd known this
would happen, that's why he'd made her promise. He'd
trusted her to keep that promise, and keep it she would.

"It's not right," the boy said, staring up at her, his
lips trembling now. "He shouldn't die like that, he's a
flashbow warrior, they're supposed to come back if you
give them their bow—"

"It's a legend," Califa explained gently. "Sometimes,
legends . . . aren't what they appear."

And who had known that better than Dax?

She stepped into the tunnel, barely having to bend
over, so huge was the hole the flashbow had made. It

was dark, but she had the feel of that blessed breeze to guide her. She tugged on the boy's hand again.

"No, wait!"

Califa sighed. She knew nothing of dealing with children, and she couldn't deal with a stubborn one, not now.

"Look!" he cried, yanking fiercely at her hand, pulling her back into the cell.

Dax still lay where he'd fallen. The bow still lay across his chest.

But the bolt was glowing.

Chapter 23

For the first time in her life, Califa knew she had been given something just for the wishing of it: Dax opened his eyes.

She didn't understand. She didn't care that she didn't understand. She only knew that she was on the floor of this damned cell looking down into a pair of jade-colored eyes she'd thought closed forever. Slightly glazed eyes, it was true, but his pulse was steady if not particularly strong beneath her fingers, and his breathing regular if shallow. He was still ashen, and far too cold for her comfort, but he was undeniably alive.

"I told you," the boy exulted.

"Yes," Califa whispered, "yes, you did."

At her voice some of the dazed look left his eyes. "Sn . . ." He tried again. "Snow . . . fox?"

"It's all right, Dax. You did it, everything's going to be all right."

"I . . . did?"

"Blasted that tunnel right through to the other side," the boy exclaimed. Clearly Dax's heroics had done much to help him forget, for the moment, that they were still in his cell.

Dax's eyes focused on her then. His brows furrowed, but only for a moment, as if it were too difficult for him to hold the forbidding expression.

"You were supposed to get out of here."

"She was going to," the boy explained. "When she thought you were dead. She was crying. I had to tell her to give you the bow back, so the legend could come true."

Dax never shifted his gaze from her face as she cradled his head in her lap. "You thought I . . . ?"

"You were, Dax. You were limp and cold and I—"

"Cried? You cried ... for me?"

His tone was so astonished she wanted to shake him. Then the absurdity of it hit her; he'd literally come back from the dead, and within minutes she wanted to shake him. Laughter welled up inside her and she surrendered to it helplessly.

"Is she all right?" the boy asked warily, staring at the woman who minutes ago had been weeping and was now laughing as if demented.

"I'm ... not sure," Dax said. Then, with a ghost of his old grin, "But then I never am."

Califa managed to control herself, wiping at her eyes. Dax was serious now, as he lay looking up at her.

"How long was I ... out?"

"I ..." How long had he lain there, dead to anything in this world? She suppressed a shudder. "Five minutes? Perhaps ten," she amended. It seemed like forever, she thought.

"You've got to get out of here. They're liable to discover the tunnel ..." He stopped, and turned his head toward the gaping hole as a gust of that breeze lifted his hair. "It ... really worked, didn't it?"

Califa froze. "You weren't sure it would?"

"I knew it would, in theory, but ... that many shots ..."

"Tell me something, flashbow warrior," she said conversationally, "has anyone else ever fired nine bolts in succession and survived?"

He looked suddenly wary, and she knew her tone hadn't fooled him. His next words proved it. "I think I'm in trouble if I answer that."

"What's that noise?" The boy was cocking his head, listening.

After a moment Califa heard it, too, an odd sort of scraping coming from the front of what was left of the bunker.

"They're digging!" she exclaimed.

"Yes," Dax said grimly. "Now will you get out of here?"

"You're right," she said, grabbing his shoulders as she got to her knees, "we'd better get moving."

"Califa—"

"Maybe they'll be so occupied with getting in here they won't be watching the perimeter. We can—"

"Califa, I'm not going anywhere."

She stared at him. "What?"

"I can't. I can hardly move."

"I know you're exhausted, but the shuttle's only a half mile away—"

"It might as well be on Trios. I'd never make it. And if I try, you never would. Just give me the bow. If they make it in here, I'll slow them down a little."

Califa scrambled to her feet. Dax grunted when his head, abruptly deprived of the cushion of her thighs, thumped against the floor.

"You son of a Carelian slimehog! I didn't realize what was happening before, that you *knew* that many shots would kill you. Well, listen to this, my fine flashbow warrior. Committing suicide on your own is one thing, but if you think I'm going to knowingly *help* you do it, you are demented!"

Dax blinked. The boy backed up a step.

"I went through your dying once, I'll be damned to Hades if I'll do it again. So you can just get yourself moving, oh infamous skypirate. And you'd better do it soon, or I'll toast your ass with a disrupter for encouragement!"

There was a long, silent moment. Then, incredibly, Dax laughed. "You would, wouldn't you?"

"Push me to it," she offered, still glaring at him.

He looked suddenly thoughtful. "I suppose a comment along the lines of how incredible you are when you're furious would get me toasted that much sooner?"

Califa felt the heat rise in her cheeks, but ignored it. "That," she ground out, "I can promise you. Now are you moving, or do I have to—"

Dax held up his hands in defeat. "I'll try," he said, although he sounded doubtful. Then he glanced around the small cell and grimaced. "Not my idea of a good place to die, anyway."

"Good. Now you—" She looked at the boy and suddenly realized something. Her tone softer, she spoke again. "I'm sorry, we never even asked your name."

"It's Denpar. My friends . . . used to call me Den."

"Den," Califa repeated, nodding. She lifted the flash-bow from the floor. "Do you think you're up to carrying this through the tunnel?"

The boy's eyes lit up with an almost worshipful glow. "I'll do it. I'll carry it all the way, if you wish."

"You may have to," Califa said grimly as Dax battled to get to his feet.

He hadn't, Califa soon realized, been exaggerating much. Every move was an effort that made her weary just to watch. Yet somehow she sensed that only her continual badgering was keeping him going.

"So crawl," she snapped when he fell the first time in the tunnel. "You're too tall to walk through it anyway."

He crawled. And collapsed. And got back to his knees and crawled some more. And then went through it all again.

She let him rest for a moment when they reached the outside. She couldn't resist the look of relief that spread across his face as he lay there, looking up at the night sky. Besides, she need to reconnoiter the area anyway. She headed silently toward the commotion coming from the other side of the hill.

She was back in barely three minutes.

"Looks like every hand at the outpost is digging at that pile of rubble you left them. I think we'll be all right, but we've got to get moving."

Dax nodded. He'd quit talking a while ago, to conserve his breath, Califa thought.

"I should have arranged this sooner," she said. "You're a lot more cooperative this way."

As she'd expected, he grimaced at her, his lip curling sarcastically. But he moved.

He made it to his feet again, but he was swaying dangerously. Califa quickly moved in to support him, and they started off, the boy following closely behind, cradling the silver bow in his arms as if it were the most precious of treasures. Which, since it had saved them, she supposed it was. But if they were spotted, the two disrupters would have to deal with it; she wasn't about to let Dax get his hands on that bow to fire that remaining bolt. She was too certain it would be the last. Forever.

It was a long, torturous trek, the ground was uneven, tripping up the exhausted Dax at what seemed like every other step. Twice he gathered his breath to speak, and twice she silenced him before he could begin.

"Don't even think it, skypirate. I don't want nobility from you, and I don't want sacrifice. I just want your feet moving."

She was rapidly becoming fatigued herself. Dax was a big man, and she was bearing a lot of his weight, although he tried hard to ease the load. The boy was beginning to waver, too; he'd been chained up a long time, and the flashbow was no slight weight for a thin, weakened boy.

Once Dax went down completely, a low groan her only warning. They were out of sight of the outpost, so she decided to take the risk of letting him rest for a few minutes. The boy sank wearily to the ground also, but he clung to his burden faithfully.

"We're close, Den," she assured him. "Not much longer."

He nodded, as if he, too, had adopted Dax's silence to save his breath. He was as tough as every other Triotian she'd met. She'd once thought peace brought softness, but these people were living proof otherwise. Perhaps, she thought, lifting her head to look at the stars, maintaining peace was even harder than fighting wars.

She wondered if Dax had been able to pick out the sparkling light that was Trios, when he'd first seen the sky again. She imagined that he had.

"Califa." She turned to look at him. "I don't think—"

She cut him off. "Good. When you do think, you make a mess of it." This, of the man who, no matter what he said about her or Dare, had the best, most innovative tactical mind she'd ever known. She suppressed a smile. "If you've got enough breath to talk, then you've got enough to get moving. Up and walking, skypirate. You've got a job to finish."

He groaned, but he rolled to his knees. Den had to help her get him up this time, and their progress was even slower. But at last she saw the rocky outcropping that marked the cleft.

She pondered for a moment, then decided the benefit would be worth the risk and reached for the comlink on Dax's belt.

"Rina?"

"Califa? Thank God, I thought—"

"I know. Get the shuttle fired up and ready. We're going to have to move fast, they may not be far behind us."

"Dax?" The girl's voice was shaky; she was obviously wondering why Califa was doing the talking, and fearing the worst.

"He's here. I'll explain later. Just get ready."

"Copy."

Rina was as good as her word. The shuttle was alive and ready, the side door open. Den had to help her again as she tried to lift Dax, who was barely conscious now, into the shuttle. Rina ran back to help, pulling as Califa pushed. His slack body sprawled on the floor, and Califa and the boy scrambled in after him. Califa at last relieved the boy of the burden of the bow, giving him an approving nod as he gratefully surrendered it.

"You're a true Triotian, Den. Quit isn't in your lexicon."

The boy smiled, then looked at Rina curiously. Rina returned the look, but only for an instant before she knelt beside Dax.

Califa put a hand on the girl's shoulder. "I know, Rina, but there's nothing we can do for him now except get out of here."

"But, Dax—"

"He's not injured. Not in any way we can help."

"Then what—"

"I'll explain later. You have to help me fly us out of here."

Rina pulled herself together with a visible effort. She ran back to the console of the shuttle. Califa followed. It had been a long time since she'd flown one, but it would come back to her, she thought.

Twenty minutes later she was grimacing wryly at her own arrogance; she'd never worked so hard in her life. And Dax had made it look so easy, responding with relaxed dexterity to Rina's warnings of a hillside here or an unexpected drop there. They were skating along barely twenty feet off the deck, following Rina's memory of the topography, unerring even in the dark.

When Dax had brought Rina along, she'd wondered why; it wasn't like him to allow her into any kind of danger. But she'd been safe enough, sitting unnoticed in that cleft of ground. And the entire mission would have been impossible without her.

"Now," Rina said at last, when they were far on the other side of the planet. Califa gratefully turned to the relatively simple task of getting the shuttle back to the *Evening Star.*

Rina wasted no time in getting to the question uppermost on her mind.

"What happened to him?"

"The flashbow," Califa answered shortly. "Nine shots."

Rina gasped. "No one's ever fired that many!"

"So I gathered," Califa said dryly. She nodded her head toward the boy. "You can thank him for Dax's life. He's the one who knew to put the bow back in his hand."

Rina's eyes, so like Dax's, widened. "You mean the legend is true? That if you put the flashbow back . . . ?"

"I only know what I saw." And the memory made her shiver.

Rina paled at Califa's expression. "He was . . . dead?"

"And then not. I can't explain it. The legend seems as good a way as any."

She tried to put impossible things—and the legend was only one of them—out of her mind and concentrate on getting them back.

And Rina ran back to sit with the unconscious Dax.

"Welcome back, boy. Thought you were going to sleep away the entire trip."

Dax blinked, then focused on Roxton's grinning face. "How . . . long?"

"Three days," the first mate said. "But from the look of you when they carried you off the shuttle, you needed every minute of it. Thought you'd gone and died on us."

Warily, Dax tried to sit up, and was gratified when it

was easier than he expected. He felt almost functional again.

"I hear you had quite an adventure on Darvis."

"It's not one I'd care to repeat," he said, his tone very dry.

"But you got it done," Roxton said, with as much satisfaction as if the whole thing had been his idea. "And we'll be at Trios this time tomorrow."

Dax blinked. "We will?"

"Sure." The old man tugged at his beard, laughing, yet studying Dax with an intensity barely disguised by his humor. "We weren't about to say no when your Arellian started giving orders in that way of hers. She said set course for Trios, so we did."

There were three Arellians aboard now, but Dax knew quite well who Roxton was talking about. And he knew exactly what "way" of giving orders he was talking about as well. She virtually terrorized him into making that trip from the cell to the shuttle, that walking, living Hades he could barely remember now. But she'd been right. He'd made it, when he'd never expected to.

"Now that's a smile I've waited awhile to see," Roxton said softly. Flushing, Dax looked away from his old friend's grinning face. "She's quite a woman," Roxton said.

"Yes."

"The boy—by the way, he's a distant relation of Fleuren's, we discovered—said she tricked the Outpost Commander into thinking she was one of them again, that she'd captured you to regain her Coalition honor and her position."

"She did. She had him eating out of her hand."

"You must have wondered—"

"Only for a moment," Dax said, feeling somehow he owed her this declaration of his trust. "I should have trusted her before, and I didn't. I had to then." He sighed. "That doesn't make much sense, does it?"

"On the contrary," Roxton said with a chuckle, "it makes perfect sense. And it explains why she's been hovering over you like a mother whisperbird. I finally had to force her to rest."

"She . . . has?"

"Right after she ordered us to 'get this bucket to Trios,' I think were her words." The first mate laughed again at Dax's expression. Then he got to his feet. "So, rest up, eat something, and you'll be home before you know it."

He was at the door before it hit Dax.

"Home?"

Roxton turned, the knowledge showing in his gentle smile. "Home," he confirmed.

"You ... know?"

"Ah, Dax, I've always known. You told me, that first night, when you were drunk, about your home, your father, and your friend Dare who would one day have been king." He shrugged. "But I thought that if you wished to keep it to yourself after that, it was your business."

He turned again to go, but Dax stopped him. "Rox?" His old friend turned back again. "I ..." His throat was suddenly tight, and all he could manage was, "Thanks."

Roxton stood there for a long, silent moment. At last he said, almost distantly, "I had a son once, you know."

Dax stared; he hadn't known. In all these years, he hadn't known.

"He died," the first mate went on, "when the Coalition swept over Clarion. I would like to think, had he lived, he would have made me as proud as you have."

He left then, closing the door on a stunned and embarrassed Dax.

"You look worried."

"I am," Dax conceded, his expression halfheartedly rueful, wholeheartedly apprehensive.

He looked at Califa, then glanced around the bridge. The others were intent on their tasks as they neared Trios; approaching a world which was, in essence, at war with the Coalition was not something to be done haphazardly. This was the first time he had been on the bridge since their return from Darvis II, and while he felt steady enough, he knew he didn't exactly look like the embodiment of good health, and his stamina was still a bit questionable.

Still, it felt good to be up. It seemed all he'd done

was sleep, when he should have been anticipating their arrival at Trios. But then maybe that was for the best; the anticipation he'd felt in the last hour since he'd walked onto the bridge was about to do him in.

"I didn't really . . . think this far ahead," he admitted, in a voice too low for the others to hear.

"Because," Califa pointed out with wry astuteness, "you didn't expect to *get* this far. You thought you'd be dead long before now."

Dax sighed. "Are you going to start chewing on me again?"

"Maybe."

He wasn't going to admit that she was right. She already knew that. He truly hadn't expected that they'd get this far. Or at least, he hadn't expected *he* would.

He wondered if this apparent death wish that he'd finally realized he had—that Califa seemed to have always known about—had something to do with his certainty that were he ever to reach this point, of coming home, that it would be futile. As he'd told her, he'd broken nearly every Triotian law that existed; they weren't about to welcome him with open arms no matter what he did. They might thank him for the return of five Triotians, six counting Rina, but that would hardly absolve him of five years of crimes that were among the most odious to any Triotian of blood.

No, in the end he would be left with even less than he'd begun with; even the *Evening Star* would no longer be his. Although if the crew decided to continue as skypirates, they might let him rejoin them—if he was still alive. In time of war, it was within Dare's power to order his execution, and he just might do it for a man he must consider a deserter, if not a traitor.

What would Califa do? he wondered. He'd toyed briefly, as he lay recovering from the strain of the flashbow, with an image of her staying aboard the *Evening Star,* with him. But that was no life for a woman, even one as strong as Califa, always among men, and rough ones at that. He'd seen that when Rina had taken to her so quickly; he hadn't realized the girl's need for another female to talk to.

Rina. She wasn't going to like it when she found out

she would be staying on Trios. They would welcome her, he was sure. She was a child, and had had no choice about the life she'd led.

He let out a compressed breath. Maybe she wouldn't mind it, after all. He had little enough to give her. When he was through here, he would have little enough to give anyone.

He glanced at Califa, facing at last the true source of his disquiet. He couldn't begin to describe the feeling that had come over him when Den had said that she had cried when she thought him dead. She'd admitted she would mourn for him, but that this woman, this strong, brave woman who no doubt never let herself cry, would cry for him moved him beyond words. He had faced the fact that, however undeserving he was, she cared for him. And, he had acknowledged at last, after a long time spent cradling the marble snowfox in his hands, that he cared for her. More than he was comfortable admitting.

But he had nothing to offer anyone, let alone a woman like Califa. She deserved peace, after what she had suffered, not the crazed, risky existence of a sky-pirate. He would fulfill his promise, he would find a way to free her from the collar, even if he had to bargain for it with his life. And then she would go, to build a life of her own. And she would be much better off.

He watched her as she glanced at the rank of viewports, where the glowing orb that was Trios was drawing closer.

"I wonder," she said slowly, "if Shaylah is still . . . with him."

Dax had no answer for that, but he wondered silently if whatever had happened between Dare and his Coalition captain had been a fraction as complicated as things were now between him and Califa.

"They won't just let you through, you know," she said. "Whatever they have that's holding off the Coalition will work on us, too. What will you tell them?"

Dax's mouth quirked. "That's the part I haven't thought about yet."

She gave him a sideways look. "I suggest you start,

then. We'll be at the edge of their space in a few minutes."

Dax felt his stomach knot. Why in Hades had he ever begun this? What demon in his obviously demented mind had made him think it might work?

"Why don't you turn on the identifier?" Califa suggested quietly. "And keep a frequency open? At least then they may give us a chance to prove we're not a Coalition ship before they blast us."

She was right. They rarely used the automatically transmitted, repeating code that identified them as the cargo ship *Evening Star*—skypirates didn't make a habit of announcing their presence or the name of their ship—but it might give them at least a chance to explain.

He turned to the console beside the command chair and flicked two buttons. Larcos turned to look back at him, startled, then appeared to think about it. He nodded, and turned back to the scanners before him.

Dax stopped himself from pacing, but only barely as they flew on. The crew apparently found no oddity in Califa's presence on the bridge; she had clearly established herself with them. It had been Larcos who had told him most of the men had guessed she had been in some position of command, and no doubt with the Coalition. But they had also learned this far too late for any of them to hold it against her now; she had proved herself to them time and again.

As she had to him, although he'd been nearly too damned blind to see it. He knew what he'd done in the cell on Darvis II had done much to make it up to her, but—

"Cargo ship *Evening Star*! This is the Triotian High Council! State your purpose or reverse your course!"

Dax felt himself pale, and he suddenly sank down in the command chair, all strength gone from his legs.

"My God," he whispered, shaken. "It's Dare."

Chapter 24

It was Roxton who finally answered.

"Triotian High Council, this is first mate Roxton of the *Evening Star*. We have ... er, cargo to be delivered."

The voice came back, strong, deep, and with an undertone of amusement. Dax felt a shiver ripple up his spine at the sound of the voice he'd thought never to hear again. Roxton shook his head, as if he couldn't quite believe he was standing here talking to a king.

"And I suppose you'd like us to lower our shields and allow you to land?"

Dax shook his head sharply. Roxton merely nodded and waved at him calmingly; the first mate, at least, had obviously thought about this in advance. And it was a good thing, Dax thought wryly, since his brain seemed to have stopped working; he'd never expected Dare to be their challenger. But he should have, he realized. Dare had never been one to use his royalty to shirk the more ordinary tasks, and he supposed when your numbers were so limited, even the king had to take his turn at sentry duty.

"No, sir," Roxton said respectfully. "We wouldn't think of it. Request permission to orbit and send down a shuttle."

All humor vanished from the voice, leaving nothing but the cool, tough tone of a leader.

"We neither expect, nor have we ordered any ... cargo."

"He's learned that caution the hard way," Roxton muttered. Then, louder, "With all due respect, I think you'll want this cargo."

"We are at war, first mate Roxton. What could be worth the risk of letting down our shields to a stranger?"

Roxton glanced at Dax. Dax nodded. Roxton took a breath, then answered.

"Triotians, sir."

There was a long, tense moment of silence.

"Explain." The order was short, sharp, and rang with command.

"Several of them, sir." At another nod from Dax, he added, "Two of them will need medical attention."

Another pause. Dax knew Dare would do almost anything for his people, and that the mention that two were injured was, if not quite fair, an effective lever he wasn't above using. Besides, it was true. Fleuren needed attention for her legs, and the ailing Triotian they'd picked up from Zenox still hadn't recovered enough to even give them his name.

"Who is your captain?"

Dax shook his head again. If Dare learned now who he was, they might never get down to the surface.

"He's ... readying the shuttle now. He wishes to be certain everyone arrives safely."

"Commendable," the voice said dryly, "but not the answer to my question."

"He will accompany our passengers in the shuttle, sir. You will meet him then."

"We have an ancient saying on Trios, about buying a blowpig in a bag. Are you familiar with it?"

Roxton laughed appreciatively at the words and the drollery in the voice. "I admire a cautious man, sir. I'm one myself. But I assure you, we are not a Coalition trick. All of us aboard the *Evening Star* are far too familiar with such underhanded dealings."

"While you, of course, are the finest of law-abiding citizens."

The mockery was still intense. Dax wondered if he was going to have to use the temptation of himself to punish as bait to get Dare to let them land.

"Now, there are those who might not call us such," Roxton said, "but the chances are good they would be in Coalition uniform."

"Why do I get the feeling that if you'd sailed our seas in an ancient era, there would have been crossbones on your banner?"

Roxton laughed again, and glanced at Dax. "He's quite a man, your king." Then, turning back to the communications console, "Perhaps there is need of such men in this era, sir. And who is to say who are the true pirates?"

When the voice came again, there was the slightest hint of genuine amusement. "Who, indeed? Send your shuttle. But be aware, the rumors you may have heard are true. The weapons guarding our docking port and the city are fusion cannons."

Roxton's eyes widened. He hit a switch on the panel and looked back at Dax, who glanced at Califa. Looking very solemn, she nodded. "I heard the rumors. It makes sense, for nothing less would hold off the Coalition so effectively. But how ... ?"

Dax shrugged. "Dare is good with weapons, as well. Go ahead, Rox."

The first mate swallowed, then released the switch he'd pressed. "Er ... yes, sir."

"No weapons aboard the shuttle. Flight crew limited to two." Dare was giving orders now, quickly, easily, with the air of a man who was accustomed to having them obeyed. "You have one hour. We will await your message that you are at the docking port shield. It will open for two minutes, the time it takes to traverse it. Two minutes *only*."

"Clever," Roxton muttered. "No time to prepare any tricks, were we of a mind to."

"And a final warning, Roxton, to your anonymous captain. If there is the slightest sign of trickery, or even of weapons aboard your vessel being armed, we will blast you out of the sky, and he can watch the explosion. Before he pays the price."

The communication ended with an audible click. Roxton turned to Dax.

"He's a tough man."

"He's had to be," Dax whispered.

And Dare had become everything King Galen had ever hoped he would be; this was a king who could truly lead. Who could pull a tiny bunch of survivors together enough to hold off what some said was the mightiest force in the universe. Who could do it, and win. Trios was not lost, would never be lost, not as long as Dare was alive.

His gaze flicked to Califa. She was staring at the communications console as if the contact were still open. At last she seemed to feel his gaze and turned; her expression was an odd combination of awe and fierce remorse.

"He is ... extraordinary," she said. Dax nodded. Then, so lowly only he could hear, she added, "And I was the most arrogant of fools to think that I owned him."

Dax went still. Incredible as it seemed, he'd almost forgotten. He supposed it was a mark of how far they'd come. The skypirate and the Coalition officer, he thought, a little awed himself. With a muddled past and a nonexistent future. At least together; Califa could have a chance to—

"Uh, Cap'n, we'd better get that shuttle ready—"

"Yes," Dax said, snapping out of his reverie. "Tell Nelcar to ready the small shuttle, and start moving the people."

Roxton's brow furrowed. "Wouldn't the larger shuttle be easier? With all those passengers—"

"No, Rox. You may need the larger one, sometime."

"Yes, but—"

"The moment we touch down," Dax said, cutting him off, "you get the *Evening Star* out of here."

Roxton blinked. "What?"

"The moment the shuttle touches down she's yours, and the crew's. As promised. Take her, Rox, and good running."

Roxton stared at him. "Now? And just leave you here? But you don't even know what's going to happen down there, what they're going to do."

"What I do know," Dax said flatly, "is that the moment Dare sees me, he's liable to blast you out of the sky anyway. I don't want you to be around by that time."

The entire bridge crew was staring at him now.

"You said you might fly with us again," Larcos began, his eyes troubled.

He didn't point out that if he was still alive, he'd find them, and if not, it hardly mattered.

"There's no time for this," he said. "Let's get moving."

He walked away, wondering why he'd ever thought this would be easier if he avoided a long goodbye.

He was walking to the shuttle bay when he realized Califa was at his heels. He stopped. He didn't turn, he didn't look at her, he just stared down the passageway. It was as empty as he feared the rest of his life would be. However long that was.

"Roxton will take you to Scoran," he said at last; he would keep this promise, at least. "There is a laser-surgeon there who owes me a favor. He will remove the collar."

"Dax—"

"Then Rox will take you wherever you wish to go. Or you might wish to stay on Scoran. It's a nice enough place, and distant enough to be relatively safe. With only one outpost, no one's likely to know of you there."

"No," Califa said.

"All right. You're welcome to go back to the storehouse until you decide what to do. It's not—"

"I'm going to Trios."

He stared at her. "What?"

"You heard me."

"Califa, that's demented. Dare isn't going to be happy to see *me*. What do you think he'd do if he saw you?"

"Probably kill me on sight."

"Exactly."

She just looked at him.

"I don't understand," he said when she didn't speak. "What do you hope to accomplish?"

"The same thing you do. Atonement. Reparation. And punishment, if necessary."

"Califa, no. At least Dare must give me a hearing before the council. Outworlders have no such right in time of war."

She merely shrugged.

"Don't you understand? You'd be walking into an almost certain death sentence!" He reached out and grabbed her shoulders then, as if he could force her to see what was so obvious to him.

"Of course I understand," she said, meeting his gaze

levelly. "I've learned of the wish for death from an expert."

"I ..." God, touching her had been a mistake. Her heat was rippling through him, burning him. "That's different," he managed.

"How, Dax? You feel you betrayed your world. I feel I unforgivably abused its king. I see no difference."

"No," he said. He couldn't stand that, too. He couldn't face the condemnation of his people and her death, too.

"I must. Just as you must."

He shook his head mutely, despair welling up inside him.

"Dax," she said gently, "do you think I don't understand what you're doing? That facing Dare, and your people, is the only way you can live with yourself any longer? And that even death is preferable to the guilt, if that is what they choose? That this is the only way your soul will find rest?"

He stared at her, his breath coming in gulps as she ripped every deeply buried emotion from its hiding place within him and dragged them out into the light.

"Will you deny me the same peace, Dax?"

He couldn't speak. He could only pull her into his arms and hold her, tightly, not sure which of them was trembling, then realizing it was both.

"Now, Rox," Dax ordered. "Break out of orbit, and get out of here. Fast."

"Are you saying the *Evening Star* is ours now?"

Dax swallowed. "I am. Get moving."

"Copy. Good luck, Dax."

Dax closed his eyes. No more Cap'n. God, he was going to miss that old man.

Only then did he let himself truly look at what was visible through the shuttle's small viewports.

"Triotia," he breathed, his heart seeming to draw up into a tiny, rock-hard lump.

It wasn't quite the disaster he'd expected. They had obviously been working hard in the year since Dare had beaten the Coalition at its own game. Yet the damage was heavy, the purity of the white buildings mangled by

Coalition guns. The meadow that had surrounded the
city, that had been recreated in Rina's holograph, was
nothing more than a barren plain.

He had thought he'd been prepared for this. He'd conquered the nausea that had risen in him when Larcos
had read off the grim results of the planetary scan he'd
done; tiny pockets of life all that was left on a planet
that had once teemed with plants and animals of all
kinds. But now, knowing he was about to set foot on his
battered world for the first time in years, he found he
couldn't move.

"Rina," he said, his voice unsteady.

"Right here, Dax. We're ready. The sick one's on the
cart Larcos rigged. Califa will handle that. But you'll
have to carry Fleuren." The girl grinned at him, her
excitement about being home at last overwhelming her
to the point where she seemed oblivious of the undercur-
rent of tension in both Dax and Califa. "She says she's
looking forward to that. You'll be going out first?"

"No. You'll have to begin." God, he should have
talked to her before this, but he hadn't been able to
bring himself to do it. "Rina ... They're going to feel
about me ... like you did, at first. I'm not going to be
welcomed here."

"But Trios is your home!"

"And I've broken most of its laws. You'd be wise to
point out you had little choice about going along."

"They'll get over it," she said cheerfully, "once they
know the truth. I'll start the others out first, then."

She left him wondering if the truth—whatever that
was—would make the slightest bit of difference.

He heard the bustle, the sound of voices, cries of joy
and welcome as Rina efficiently unloaded the passengers. Triotian voices. On Triotian soil. Dax shuddered
despite his effort to stop it.

At last it was only he and Califa, Denpar, who was
nervously clutching the flashbow wrapped in Dax's
cloak, Fleuren, and the man who lay half conscious on
Larcos's cart. Califa was kneeling beside him, clasping
his frail hands in hers. She'd worn the loose shirt and
trousers Dax had given her at the storehouse, and had

found another piece of cloth to wind about her slender neck, concealing the collar.

"You're home," she was telling the man softly. "On Trios. They're waiting for you."

The man stirred, eyes fluttering, then opening. "Home?" It was a weak thread of sound, but it sent another shudder through Dax. He bent over the man himself.

"Home," he confirmed, putting into his voice all the joy he would be feeling if he was as certain of his welcome as this man. And for an instant, despite the man's frailty, Dax envied him.

"I'll go first," Dax said, straightening. "With any luck, Dare will be distracted enough he won't notice you right off."

"And maybe you can have him angry enough at you by then that he won't kill me outright?"

His mouth quirked. "Did I tell you you're too damned observant?"

Before she could stop him he turned, picked up Fleuren, who'd been watching them both with wise interest, and strode down the ramp into a flood of Triotian sunlight.

It truly felt different, he thought. Different from the sunlight on any other world, circling this or any other star. He blinked, his eyes adjusting. But nothing could help him adjust to the wonderful shock of being home, of the familiar yet long-missed sight of the golden people of his world.

"Thank you, my son," Fleuren whispered, tilting her gently wrinkled face to the light.

Dax tightened his arms around her in answer; he was beyond words. Then a cry of pure joy broke from her as a young man ran toward them.

"Renclan!"

"Grandmother," the man cried, tears streaming down his face as he took her from Dax. "There are no words to thank you," he began as he lifted his gaze. "What you have done—"

He stopped, staring, his eyes widening in shock. "Dax," he whispered. "Dax Silverbrake."

Dax had known it would come, but hearing his name,

here, where he had once been so proud to carry it, hit him harder than he could ever have anticipated.

He vaguely heard the sound of Califa wheeling the cart down the ramp behind him, and the bustle as two people in the pale blue coats of medical personnel started toward her and the injured man, followed by Denpar's lighter steps as they came down the ramp. Then all he heard were the voices.

"Did you see who . . ."

" . . . Silverbrake!"

"Dax!"

"Did you see?"

"My God, it's Dax Silverbrake."

The exclamations rippled through the clusters of people like the undulations of the water in the lake that had once sat clear and blue across the meadow, when disturbed by a tossed stone.

There was a movement on the edge of the crowd as the ripples of recognition reached there. When Dax saw the height and breadth of the man who turned, saw the burnished gold of a mane of hair as long as his own, saw the chiseled regularity of his features, he didn't need the royal black and gold to tell him. Dax's gut contracted violently, and he wanted to run more than he'd ever wanted to in his life. But running was what had gotten him into this in the first place; he held steady.

And when the man turned his head, it took every bit of remaining nerve Dax had to meet those too-familiar eyes that were the exact shade of the grass in a Triotian meadow.

"Dax," Dare whispered.

Even from here, fifteen feet away, Dax heard it. It was stunned, it was reverent. And for an instant, hope rocketed through him as pure joy lit Dare's face.

Dare covered most of the distance between them in three long strides. Then, between the third stride and the next, his face changed, the joy fading. He came to a halt three feet away. Dax felt the hope that had leapt in him falter. With Dare's first words, it crumbled.

"I had hoped it was a mistake. That someone with your same name had become the scourge of the far reaches. I could not believe that a Triotian could ever willingly become such a thing as a skypirate."

Willingly? Dax wondered about that. But he wasn't going to quibble over a minor qualification that didn't really matter. Nor was he going to act the coward, not here, not again. As Califa had said, it was time to put it to rest, so his soul could rest. If Dare decided that rest was to be eternal, he would not fight him.

"It is true," Dax said steadily.

Pain, and regret, flashed in Dare's eyes. "I have not spoken your name for six years, fearing that someone would tell me something that would make it impossible for me to deny that the man I'd heard of, the merciless buccaneer, was really you."

Dax cringed inwardly, but he held Dare's piercing gaze. Dare had obviously heard the Coalition version. But then, what else would he have heard, being in Coalition hands for five of those six years, then here, in war-isolated Trios?

He made no attempt to justify it; no pretense would change the facts of what he'd done, or matter when laid up against solid, centuries old Triotian law. He'd decided, in those hours spent lying weakly in his bunk, not to even try.

"I will not deny who I am." I've had too much of that, Dax thought wearily. I'm glad it's finally over.

Dare shook his head slowly, the movement and his expression speaking of great pain. "That you, of all of us, should come to this ... Your family has always been the most celebrated on Trios, linked with the royal family even before my own family ascended the throne. You know the Silverbrakes could easily have become the royal family themselves, had they not had that aversion to all things martial."

It hit Dax hard to see that Dare apparently believed that family trait had run true in him as well. Dare knowing he had run away was bad enough; Dare thinking he'd done it because he didn't want to fight was beyond any pain he'd ever imagined in this long-awaited meeting.

"As you have realized," Dax said stiffly, "I am hardly the kind to become royalty."

No, Dare was royalty; it fairly radiated from him, Dax

thought. He wore the simple black and gold well, clothes that were emblazoned with the gold royal crest at the shirt's collar and down the side of the trousers that were tucked into high black boots. His own dark pants and boots, and the pristine but simple white shirt he'd put on, looked decidedly plain by comparison.

"You were hardly the kind to become a skypirate, either!" Dare snapped. "My God, Dax, is there a law you haven't broken?"

Dax barely kept his eyes from flickering to Califa. Only one, he thought, and that not from lack of trying.

"Probably not," was all he said.

Dare's eyes flicked over him. They were matched in height and breadth of shoulder, Dax realized, yet he had always thought of Dare as bigger, stronger.

"You bring a weapon, despite my order?"

Dax blinked. Then it hit him what Dare had seen. The knife. "My apologies . . . your highness. It is but a habit."

Dare seemed taken a little aback by the appellation. He waved a hand in negation. "Keep it. It will do you no good, in any case."

"I doubt anything will," he said with a shrug.

Dare seemed disturbed by his unconcern. "You know what your admission means," he said, his eyes dark with distress.

So this bothered him, Dax thought in an odd sort of detachment. The mood had descended upon him in the moments when Dare had asked of the laws he had broken. He had known for sure then that there was no hope for him. They might, perhaps, in view of the Triotians he'd brought home, let him live. But Dare might yet decide his life would be the price. He calculated the odds at about even.

"How long has it been," he asked, that detachment making his tone flippant, "since there's been an execution here? Centuries? Millennia?"

"Dax, this is no joke!"

"I never thought it was," he said softly.

Dare took a visibly deep breath, glanced around him, then fastened those vivid eyes back on Dax. "You've done a good thing here. Why? Did you expect to buy your way out of the trouble of breaking every Triotian law extant?"

The truth of that sliced deep, although Dax felt the pain as if from a distance. He *had* thought of it that way, as if he could buy his way back using his own people as the coin. True, he had been desperate, and rescuing his people and bringing them home had been, as Dare said, a good thing, but nothing could change his intent. Even Califa, with a chance to regain her entire life, had refused to use him as the coin to do it. He should be ashamed, would be, he thought, if he could feel anything at all; he was neither good enough for her, nor to be called Triotian. At heart he was more the skypirate than he had ever been Triotian.

As if in protective response, Dax's detachment grew. "Is that not the way of a skypirate?" he said, sounding even more nonchalant. "A price on everything, and everything to be had for a price?"

Dare went very still. He stared at Dax, as if wondering what had happened to the friend of his childhood and youth.

"Is no part of you still Triotian?" Dare asked, his voice taut.

Dare's words so eerily echoed his earlier thoughts that Dax almost smiled; that odd detachment was growing. It enabled him to turn to Den, who was staring with awe-widened eyes at his king, and hold his hand out for the bundle the boy held so tightly. He took it, then unwrapped his cloak and tossed it over his shoulder, revealing the gleaming silver.

He heard Dare's swift intake of breath, but said nothing, merely handed over the symbol of what he had once been, as if it were the answer to Dare's question. And in a way, he supposed it was.

Dax saw a tremor ripple through Dare as his hands curled around the weapon that he, even with his royal blood and great courage, had never been able to fire. The king of Trios held the ancient weapon of his people, and looked into the eyes of the man he had loved like a brother.

"Why, Dax?" he whispered, his voice unsteady.

Dax knew what Dare was asking, but chose to misunderstand. "It should not be in the hands of a skypirate. You will find a new warrior worthy of carrying the flashbow."

Dare looked puzzled for a moment, as if something out of synch had appeared in an image he thought he knew well. Dax quickly shrugged, returning to that light tone.

"Besides, I have only one bolt left. It's useless to me now, and a skypirate has no time for useless weapons."

Dare's eyes narrowed. "Do you care about nothing anymore?"

Dax didn't think he moved, and he knew he hadn't looked at Califa. But Dare's gaze shifted anyway, and Dax realized it had been Califa who had moved. When he looked at her, he saw a look of such concern on her face that he knew she had moved intentionally, to distract Dare from the words that should have been—and would have been, had he not been so oddly numb—cutting his old friend to bleeding strips.

"You!"

Dare was frozen, staring at Califa in stunned disbelief. But he recovered all too quickly, his hand streaking down for the ceremonial but still deadly dagger sheathed at his waist as he turned on the woman who had once been his tormentor.

"No!" Instinctively, instantly, Dax moved, putting himself between them. Dare stopped dead. Califa, who had never even flinched, stepped out from behind Dax.

"You cannot protect me from this, no more than I can protect you," she said softly to Dax. "I brought this upon myself."

Then she stood before Dare, tall and straight, and so dauntless that Dax thought in that moment he would have given almost anything for a future that would let him keep her with him. But Dare's reaction told him there would be no such future, perhaps no future at all.

"You . . . brought her here?" Dax asked incredulously, his furious gaze fastened on Califa, the dagger still clenched in his hand. "Do you know who she is?"

"I know."

At Dax's quiet admission, Dare's gaze shifted. His lips were parted for his rapid breathing. Dax could only imagine how he must feel, confronted by the woman— or what had once been the woman—who had been party to his years of degradation. And to find that the man he'd once considered his closest friend, his brother in heart if not blood, was not only a brigand, but had brought this woman to Trios . . . He was a little surprised they were both still alive.

"Do you know *what* she is?" Dare hissed it out, in a voice Dax had never heard before, a feral, savage voice he wouldn't have thought Dare capable of. But then, the Dare he'd known hadn't been enslaved for five agonizing years. And he hadn't been at war, either.

"I know what she *was*," Dax answered, fighting to keep his voice steady in the face of Dare's rage; odd how that strange detachment had disappeared when Dare had turned on Califa. "And I know she is no longer that person."

Dare whirled away, snapping an order that was almost violent to a wide-eyed young man who had stood unabashedly watching.

"Get them out of my sight! Lock them up somewhere, until the council can convene. He has the right to that, though it burns my soul to give it to him." His eyes flicked to Califa once more, and the wrath there had not abated. "I will deal with her myself, later."

He strode away, the clusters of people separating as their king passed.

Chapter 25

"I never thought I'd see another sunset here," Dax said as he stood looking out the window that was nearly as small as the viewport in his cabin aboard the *Evening Star.*

"Perhaps you should think about the fact that it may be the last one you see anywhere," Califa returned, her tone bitter as she paced the small chamber they'd been locked in for hours now. A narrow cot and a table that held an ewer of water were the only pieces of furniture in the room.

"It's Triotian," Dax said simply, as if that alone made it worth the possible price. Then he shrugged. "I knew what I was up against long before we landed."

Califa whirled then, facing him, her eyes wide and fearful. "But you wouldn't be up against it! Dare would have forgiven you, I could see it in his eyes, if you hadn't brought me here. God, Dax, I'm so sorry."

"Califa—"

"All I thought about was how angry he would be with me. I never thought of how furious he would be with you for bringing me here." She shook her head, self-contempt welling up inside her. "I seem to have the knack of thinking only of myself. You shouldn't have defended me. You should have just handed me over to him. As a gift. A reparation."

"As you would have done, were our places reversed?" Dax asked softly.

"If I thought it would save my skin—"

"No, Califa. Major Claxton might have been able to do that. My snowfox never could."

His gentle words stopped her pacing dead. Something had changed in him somehow, as if now that he was home at last, nothing else mattered, even the fact that the cost for his return might be his own death. Yet there was pain in his eyes, turning the soft jade dark with worry.

For her, she realized suddenly. He cared less than nothing for what would happen to him, but Dare's rage had frightened him, for her.

"Oh, Dax," she whispered.

He held out his arms to her, she ran to him. He enfolded her gently.

"I should never have let you come here," he said, his voice tight with misgiving. "You should be aboard the *Evening Star,* halfway to Antares by now."

She couldn't begin to explain the many reasons why she could never have done that, so she didn't try. She slipped her arms around his narrow waist, hugging him tightly. She tried to think of a way to ease his worry, but there was no way she could change the reality before them. The most she could do was distract him.

"They welcomed Rina," she said tentatively.

"Yes. They would. She is but a child, and she had little choice. She won't be held responsible for my actions."

"Fleuren, too. Did you see her face? And her grandson's? It was a wondrous sight."

"Yes," Dax said softly, "it was."

"It *was* a good thing, Dax."

"Yes. It is only my reasons that don't bear scrutiny."

She drew back a little, tilting her head back so that she could see his face. "You wished to atone," she said, puzzled. "Although I still deny you have anything to atone for. What is wrong with that?"

"I tried to buy forgiveness with my own people—"

"You risked your life to free them," Califa said fervently. "And you brought them home. Surely you have the right to expect—"

"I have," he said tightly, "whatever rights the High Council chooses to grant me. And doing what any Triotian of blood who was free and able should have done long ago is not going to win me any more."

"But even if you had, you could not have brought them home. The Coalition was here, and besides, you didn't even know about the rebellion until—"

"Ah, snowfox, you never give up, do you? If I had half your courage, we wouldn't be here now."

Courage. The man spoke of lacking courage. The man who had beaten or evaded the Coalition at every turn. The man who had time after time risked himself to assure the safety of his crew. The man who, if her senses could be believed, had *died* to save a boy he didn't even know—and a woman he should have hated.

"Stop it," she said fiercely, burying her face against his chest. "Just stop it."

For a very long time they stood there, holding each other, trying not to think of what would come. Califa was so full of tumbling, tangled emotions that she marvelled that the cool, controlled woman she had once been ever existed. The only solid, steady thing in her world right now was Dax, and she clung to his strength. She tightened her arms around him, wishing she could get closer.

"Califa?"

She heard the husky note in his voice as he spoke her name. And suddenly the veil of her confused emotions parted, and she realized she could feel him, hard and aroused against her belly. She looked up at him, her eyes wide, her lips parted.

"I know I don't deserve this solace, but I can't ... help it," he said, his breath catching as she moved in his arms.

"Neither can I," she whispered. "I've never needed like this before."

"Nor I." He lifted her chin with a gentle finger. "So, are we to fulfill the tradition of the condemned?" he asked with a crooked smile. "A last kiss before we meet our fate?"

His tone was mocking, but there was too much truth in his words for Califa to smile. And too much heat rising in her to say no.

"I had ... more than a kiss in mind," she whispered.

A low sound rumbled up from deep in his chest; she felt it against her breasts before she heard it.

"Are you sure?" His breath barely stirred her hair.

"It is I who should ask you that," she said with a sigh, "since it is I who receives all the pleasure."

"Not all, snowfox. There is nothing to match what I feel when you look at me as you're looking now. Or when you kiss me, when you let me into your mouth and then take mine in return. Or what I feel when you claw at my clothes, as if you were as anxious to have me naked as I am you. Or when you touch me, and all I can think of is wanting your hands on me everywhere, and wishing I could ask for your mouth in the same way."

In a few sentences, he had wrought complete havoc on her senses, and weakened her knees until she sagged against him. Whatever she'd known before barely qualified as a minor diversion in the face of the spiraling, scorching flame he kindled in her now.

If this was truly to be their last time, she wanted everything. Everything he'd said, and more. She wanted to open to him, to offer herself up as she'd never done before, and she wanted the same from him. She wanted him to give himself up to her, to do with as she would, to stroke and caress every masculine plane and muscled curve, to follow with her lips the paths blazed by her hands.

"God, snowfox." It burst from him on a low, harsh breath, and she knew her thoughts had shown in her face. She didn't care.

"Yes," she whispered. "To everything."

His mouth came down on hers, and they held the kiss amid a tangle of urgent hands discarding clothes without thought as skin ached for skin. Naked, they went down to the narrow cot together. Dax reached for her, but she pushed him back. He looked surprised, but lay back willingly when she placed a gentle hand in the center of his broad chest and urged him down.

Always before, it had been Dax who gave, Dax who ministered to her, even knowing he would never reach his own ultimate pleasure. But this time, Califa thought, she would be the one to give. She would give as she never had before, had never wanted to before, willingly, eagerly. In her life in the Coalition, it had always been she who controlled, and while a slave, she had been controlled. She was filled now with an odd combination of the two, a need to feel his dominance, yet exert hers

over him; she wanted to watch him hit the peak screaming, as he had watched her. Not because she longed to
control him, but because she truly wanted to give to this
man. It was a goal that was new to her, and she pursued
it with all the dedication and ingenuity of her tactical
mind.

It began with her intent to give him a pleasure so
great it could shatter the barrier his mind had built in
his body. She would use everything she'd ever known
about mating, and, if necessary, some of the things she'd
learned during her enslavement. Yet it soon changed,
and Califa found to her amazement that every sign that
she was succeeding, every low groan, every involuntary
movement beneath her hands, sent another burst of heat
through her own body, careening through her until it
settled low and deep and urgent. And every time her
body brushed his, she had to bite back a moan.

The taste of his mouth made her long for him to taste
hers. When she nibbled the sensuous fullness of his
lower lip, she wanted him to do the same. When she
tangled her fingers in his hair, savoring the sleek, dark
length of it, she remembered when he'd done the same
to her. When her hands slid over his chest and his nipples tightened beneath her touch, her own responded
the same way. The muscles of his belly rippled beneath
her stroking, and her own contracted fiercely, sending
another bolt of flame racing down to that growing pool
of heat and need deep inside her.

She became a wild creature, frenzied, yet never losing
sight of her goal; she wanted Dax—not just a man, but
this man, only this man—quivering in her arms as she
had quivered in his. Twice he started to reach for her,
to pull her down beside him, but she resisted.

"Please," she said at last, her voice barely above a
whisper, "let me."

His eyes widened, but then, as if realizing she meant
to fulfill the wish he'd heatedly uttered, he let his arms
fall back to the cot. Califa bent over him, savoring the
sight of this powerful man, naked and open to her gaze.
And her touch.

She touched him as he had asked, everywhere, tracing
every muscled line of him, lingering in any spot that

made him suck in his breath, teasing it until he groaned. Her fingers flicked over his nipples until the flat, brown disks puckered tightly and he moved restlessly. She let her fingers slide down his belly, tracing the dark arrow of soft hair that shot downward. She felt him tense as she neared the thicket of curls below his flat belly; he was already fully erect, and when she purposefully let her hands skate down to trace the long, hard muscles of his legs he groaned in frustration.

She hid a smile at this further sign of her success as she savored the long, hard muscles of his thighs with her fingertips, wondering if his sculptor father had ever realized that his most beautiful creation was his own son.

Someday, she thought, she'd like to tell Dax that. He would scoff at the idea of his own beauty, she knew. Other Triotians might be known for it, but he didn't see himself as one of them. *The beautiful golden ones,* he'd told her when explaining his dark coloring; he obviously didn't place himself among those, although to her eyes the only difference was the dark shine of his hair, and she wouldn't wish that changed for anything.

But they didn't have someday. They might not even have tomorrow. All they had was now, and she was going to make the most of it.

"Dax?"

He looked at her then, his jade eyes hot, wanting. "Snowfox, you're killing me. But if you don't touch me soon, I won't care."

She smiled. Her hand slid up the inside of his thigh. She heard him suck in a breath, and wondered if perhaps he didn't want this after all. But then his legs parted slightly, as if in invitation, and she knew he wanted her touch as much as she wanted to touch him.

She cupped him gently against her palm, lifting, savoring the so very different rounded male flesh, hot and tight against her skin. Dax let out a low, choking sound of pleasure, parting his legs further for her slow caresses.

Soon the temptation of other male flesh, fully erect and jutting potently, proved too much, and she let her hand move upward, fingers curling around the rigid length of him, sucking in a quick breath of her own at the scorching burst of heat that shot through her as she

imagined that length once more buried inside her, stroking to the very heart of her, driving her body to heights
beyond possibility.

It was only Dax's quick, involuntary movement, lifting
his hips to thrust himself against her hand, that enabled
her to restrain herself from giving up this quest and begging him to simply take her, as she had never begged
any man before. This was for him, as all other times had
been for her, and she would not give in. If he could
survive—God, how had he?—this awful ache, so could
she.

She caressed him slowly, savoring each of his groans,
each shiver that swept his big, solid body. She smiled
when she saw his hands clench around wads of the thermal cover beneath them, as if that were the only way
he could keep himself from reaching for her. By the time
the motion of his hips had become quick, urgent, she
was so close to breaking herself that she knew she had
to stop.

She did, but it was only to start over, this time with
her mouth.

"Oh, God," Dax moaned. "Snowfox, I know I said I
wanted your mouth, but ... I don't think I can *stand*
this!"

"I've seen what you can stand, skypirate," she said
with a mock severity tinged with a tenderness that startled even her; she'd never heard herself sound like that
before. "I've only begun."

The shiver that took him then set up an echoing
quiver in her; she wanted nothing more than to surrender to this need, she wanted to take and be taken, she
wanted to straddle him and take him in, she wanted him
to throw her down and impale her in one swift stroke.
But some heretofore unknown sense of rightness was
driving her; she needed to do this even more. She bent
to him once more.

She found a place just inside his left hipbone that had
made him jump when she touched it; when she pressed
her mouth to it, he moaned her name. She began to
retrace all the paths her hands had wandered, trailing
eager kisses over him until he was twisting beneath her
lips. When he did, she moved to trace the faint, raised

line of one of the lash marks that curved around his side almost to his belly. He went suddenly very still.

She lifted her head. "I've seen what you can stand," she repeated softly. "And I see you as you cannot. I only wish you could."

Then, without a warning to him, she moved to retrace, inch by inch, that most intimate of paths. At the first touch of her lips a throttled groan broke from him. When her tongue crept out to stroke him, his entire body went rigid. She lingered for a moment, but again the temptation was too great and she moved upward.

The feel of the satin hardness of him beneath her lips thrilled her nearly as much as the groaned litany of pleasure that was rising from his throat. But soon it wasn't enough, and she parted her lips to take him inside.

"God, snowfox!" It was a burst of sound that seemed to rip from somewhere deep in his belly. His hands left the cot and shot down to clutch at her, his fingers tangling in her hair as he held her to him as if he feared she would leave. She tasted him, stroked him, drawing him in deeper, until he was arching beneath her tender ministrations.

She felt the moment when he broke. In the instant before he did it, she sensed he would; he grabbed her shoulders, pulled her up his naked body, rolled and came up over her.

"I have *never*," he growled between panting breaths, "felt anything like that in my life."

Did he think it just some skill learned by a slave trained for pleasuring? she wondered with a stab of disappointment. Did he not sense that the difference was the feeling with which it was done?

It did not matter, she told herself. She had not begun this for anything more than to return some of what had been given to her. And than his mouth was on her, and she had no room for thought.

He did not have to wait to arouse her for further caresses; her attention to him had aroused her beyond imagining. When his mouth came down on her breast, suckling her with a fierceness that, had she been less ablaze, might have hurt, a rocket of flame and heat and sensation shot straight to that swelling pool of wet heat low inside her. He moved to her other breast and it came again, that burst of flame, and she cried out.

When he seemed about to move she moaned a protest, arching her back to thrust her breasts up to him in a plea for more of the sweet suckling. He returned to her then, his mouth at one taut crest, his fingers at the other, flicking both to a tightness that made her fairly undulate as her body responded.

Her plan had rebounded on her, searing her intentions to ashes. She had meant to arouse him beyond sanity, and had wound up doing it to herself. She had hoped to break down that last barrier that held him back from her, and had instead shattered all of her own. She was what they had tried to make her as a slave, but never succeeded; a willing, eager, ardent vessel wanting only the man who was about to take her. Yet she knew it was because it was Dax; only for this man had she, or would she ever become this purely sensual creature.

When he did take her, it was as she had wanted it, in one swift, sure thrust that drove him into her to the hilt. She cried out at the sudden, thick invasion. She could feel the pressure of his body as, lifting himself up, he ground his hips against her, each movement sending impossible rushes of shivering pleasure through her.

It was going to happen too fast, she hadn't wanted it this way, she had wanted so to make it go on and on, on this night that could be their last. But she hadn't counted on the savagery of her own response to her efforts to drive him over the edge that he couldn't jump himself, and she knew she had lost. She felt the tiny pulses begin deep inside her as he lengthened his thrusts, felt the increasing slickness of her body as it readied itself for that flight beyond any star journey she'd ever taken.

It swept over her then, fierce, hot, bursting, an explosion of sensation and light. She cried out his name as she clung to him, the only support in her spinning world. It went on and on as he continued to move, never letting up, never letting her drift back down to the dazed peace she'd known before.

He, too, knew it was their last time, she thought haz-

ily. But if he thought she could do this again ... She
had to tell him, she was spent, she couldn't possibly—

Something about the way he was moving stopped her
foggy thoughts. Always before, he had withdrawn from
her the moment he was certain she'd gained her release,
and after he had finally explained, she had realized it
was too painful for him to do otherwise. But now he
was still deep inside her, thrusting, his breath coming in
harsh, gulping pants, sweat beading up on his golden
skin.

"Dax?" she whispered.

"I ..." He thrust again, hard, deep, and the cot
thumped against the wall. "God, snowfox, I ..." And
again the driving thrust, and again, his still swollen shaft
cleaving her climax-slickened flesh with a renewed urgency that she'd never felt from him before.

It was then that she recognized the faint undertone
she'd heard in his voice. Hope. God, was it possible that
urgency had sprung from feelings that had been absent
before? Sensations long unfelt, long denied his body by
the Triotian strength of his mind?

She erupted into motion then, writhing beneath him,
adding her motion to his. She touched him wherever she
could reach, stroking, caressing. She kissed any spot of
the sweat-sheened golden skin she could reach. She felt
tremors sweep through him, heard the almost desperate,
guttural sounds that ripped from him. His eyes were
closed, his head thrown back, the cords of his neck
standing out tautly, the dark mane of his hair, damp with
sweat now, tumbling down his naked back.

She arched her hips upward. He seemed to grow even
harder, and impossibly larger inside her. Then, in the
same instant, she raised herself up and flicked her
tongue over his left nipple and slid her hands down his
back to cup his buttocks, spreading her legs as she tried
to pull him so deeply inside her that even fate couldn't
part them.

His eyes snapped open as his entire body tensed. For
an instant he didn't move but stared down at her, jade
eyes boring into pale blue. Then, with a harsh shout, his
body arched, curving like his bow, driving into the very

depths of her. Amazement, shock, and awe combined on his face.

"Oh, God, snowfox," he moaned.

For one startled instant, Califa could have sworn she saw a faint glow, like that she'd seen when he used the flashbow, clinging to him as the beads of sweat clung to his skin. And then she felt it, the rush of liquid warmth, the shudders that racked his body, echoing the pulsing of the flesh buried so deeply inside her. It seared her with unexpected, sudden heat, and to her shock her body convulsed around him once more, catching her unaware with hot, heavy pulses of pleasure that were unlike anything she'd ever felt, as if they were coming to her through the connection of their bodies, as if the incredible sensations had jumped that infinitesimal gap between them, and she was actually feeling what he was feeling.

Dax shook with the intensity of it, crying out at the sweet release as he poured himself into her, the barrier of years broken at last. It went on and on, and Califa found herself weeping at the sight of him rising above her, at the feel of him quivering against her, at the fierce, explosive force of his climax, but most of all at the look of his face, drawn tight with pleasure and joy in equal parts. She didn't know if she had succeeded in driving him to this, or if it was simply because he was home, and she found she didn't care; in some small way, at least, he was healed.

And when he at last collapsed atop her, nearly dizzy from the power of it, she didn't try to hide her tears.

They slept little that night. Again and again they came together, heedless of the guard posted outside the door, Dax still not quite able to believe that barrier was gone, and Califa marveling at the difference it made. The old Califa would never have thought that it mattered so much, as long as she got her own pleasure. This night proved to her more than anything could that the old Califa was no more.

They did not talk, not of what was to come, or of what had passed, but only words of the moment, words of need and pleasure and the incredible wonder that had happened between them. And neither spoke of the irony of finding this joy now, when it was too late for either of them.

It was only when the first rays of dawning began to lighten the darkness of the room that, reluctantly, they rose to use the ewer of water to wash. Califa felt a guilty enjoyment as she watched Dax; how could she take so much pleasure in just looking at his naked body when they knew not what awaited them? They dressed slowly.

But in the end she was glad she had clung to that small luxury, for when the summons came to their little dungeon, it was for her.

Chapter 26

The same young man who had brought them here had come for her. He was barely more than a boy, but there was nothing childish about the weapon on his belt; he said he was merely to escort her to the royal quarters, but Califa knew he was no less a guard than the man posted outside the door.

She flushed now to think someone had been there all night, no doubt listening to their long hours of passion, especially when she heard him mutter "Coalition scum," as she passed. She was glad to be out of his sight as the young man led her down a long corridor.

The royal quarters. Was she to face Dare now, alone? Would he exact his vengeance in private, since he was not, in time of war, compelled to give any of the usual Triotian considerations to outworlders? Would his retribution take the form of like for like, would he order her to submit to him as she had once let him be ordered?

A shudder rippled through her at the thought of mating with any other man, even one as magnificent as Dare. The involuntary reaction made her see the completeness of her transformation; there had been a time, when Dare had been merely the slave Wolf and she had been filled with Coalition arrogance, when she had contemplated sampling his wild, golden beauty. But instead she had saved him for Shaylah ...

And had unknowingly set in motion the events that had brought her here, their positions reversed, with she now the prisoner being led to a man who could only wish her dead.

But when the reached the imposingly carved door, and the young man ushered her inside, it was not that man who awaited her.

It was Shaylah.

She was sitting at a table, folding a piece of paper with quick, graceful movements. She looked as she always had to Califa, like the epitome of Arellian grace and beauty; tall, slender, with long legs and a elegant carriage. Her hair, gleaming black and kept long in the Arellian tradition, was swept up off her neck in an intricately entwined style that Califa had never been able to manage and had been a chief reason she had defiantly kept her hair short. Shaylah wore a flowing gown in a vivid blue that matched her eyes, much closer to the typical Arellian sky blue than Califa's own pale blue shade.

She rose instantly, and Califa saw the same progression of emotions flash across the face of this woman who had once been her friend as she had seen cross Dare's when he'd first seen Dax; first joy, then wariness, then a combination of pain and regret.

"Thank you, Gareth."

Her voice sounded the same, Califa thought. Richer, perhaps, with more depth. Older, she supposed wryly. If Shaylah's relationship with Dare had been anywhere near as chaotic as hers with Dax, it was no surprise.

The young man nodded, then, as Shaylah held out the paper she folded, he stepped forward and took it. In that instant, Califa could have easily stripped him of his weapon. She never moved. But when she looked back at Shaylah again, she saw the knowledge of both the opportunity and her refusal to take it in the other woman's eyes; Shaylah might have left the Coalition even farther behind than she had, but the training was still there.

"You wish me to deliver this, my lady?"

Shaylah smiled at the young man. "Yes. To Freylan. I believe he'll be able to find room in his class after all."

Joy lit the young man's face, and for the first time he looked as a boy his age should look. War, Califa thought, made even children old before their time.

"Thank you!" The boy barely managed to retain his dignity as he went out the door, but Califa knew from the sound of his steps that he'd broken into a run the moment the door had closed behind him.

At last they stood there alone, assessing each other, two women who had once flown and fought together, who had once been tied by the powerful bond of a mutual debt beyond repaying, that of each other's lives. It was a bond that had been lacerated by her own arrogance and ignorance, Califa thought, and she could only hope that it hadn't been severed altogether.

Then Shaylah started toward her, the flowing cloth of her gown clinging to the slender lines of her body. Slender except for the rounding of her belly. Califa's breath caught.

"You're with child," she exclaimed.

Shaylah smiled as her hand smoothed over the small mound. "Yes. A son."

"A son? So certain?"

"Yes. Alcaron, who serves as our physician, has said so. She has her own methods, and is rarely wrong."

Califa smiled then; she couldn't help herself. "A baby. It is hard to picture the woman who wanted nothing more than to fly free with a baby."

Shaylah's expression cooled, the momentary warmth vanished. "The price of my flying was far too high." Then, proudly, "And my son will be the Prince of Trios."

Califa tensed. "It is . . . all true, then? What we've heard of you and . . ."

Shaylah drew herself up straight. "I know not what you have heard, but my child's father is King Darian of Trios. My bonded mate."

Califa's eyes widened. "You are bonded?"

"We are."

Shaylah's eyes were glittering now, almost angrily. Califa understood; they'd argued so often about this in the past, she could hardly blame Shaylah for her reaction. She drew herself up straight, much as Shaylah had, and braced herself to pay a long-owed debt. She spoke formally.

"You may think this merely an effort at begging for mercy, now that I am in your power, but it is not. I owe you a great apology, Shaylah Graymist. I know that it will make no difference now, that words now cannot atone for the things I said when we . . . were friends. I plagued you mercilessly about your beliefs about life and slavery and mating. I called you foolish, naive, and back-ward. Worse, when you refused to follow the Coalition rule of annihilation of a target, I thought you faint-hearted or a coward."

Shaylah said nothing, but Califa saw the shadow of remembered hurt in those eyes so much deeper blue than her own. So Shaylah had known, all that time ago, the insulting thoughts her supposed friend had been har-boring. She had known, and had remained her friend anyway. Shame flooded Califa anew, but she made her-self go on.

"These words should have been spoken long ago. I was horribly wrong and blindly arrogant. You saw the truth, where I saw only what I wished to see. That the Coalition was the only kind of family I'd ever known was no excuse. You ... you were my closest, my only true friend, but I was too much the conceited fool to realize it until it was too late."

Califa saw Shaylah's eyes widen, heard her breath catch, but didn't pause in her self-castigation.

"It was I who was the coward, not you. It was you who possessed the true courage, not to deny what you felt. It was you who saw the truth, and acted upon it, long before the scales fell from my blind eyes."

"My God, Califa," Shaylah said in quiet awe, "what has happened to you?"

The emotion in Shaylah's words nearly broke Califa's determination. She swallowed tightly; she must get this said now; she might never have another chance.

"I have seen the truth, but it has not set me free. It has only shown me the ugliness of the life I have lived." Califa's mouth twisted into a painfully remorseful smile. "I did not treasure you when you were my friend, as I should have. But that you chose to be, in spite of my blindness, is one of the few things left in my life that I value."

There was nothing more she could say, Califa thought. It was up to Shaylah now. All she could do was refuse to flinch under the steady perusal of the woman who had been a better friend than she ever had realized.

"I'll not deny I was sometimes hurt by your words," Shaylah said after a long silence. "And that there were times when I wondered if I had ever really known you at all. But I also know I was the one out of step, the one who was seen as different. I didn't expect understanding."

"You had the right to expect it from one who was supposed to be your friend."

Shaylah lifted one perfectly arched brow. "You *have* changed, if you believe that."

"I've learned much of friendship lately, from a ... very unlikely group," Califa admitted. "I'm only sorry I didn't see it then."

"I didn't expect you to. I know my beliefs were, according to the Coalition, deviant. Slavery was the law, and bonding a myth."

Califa winced inwardly. In those few words, Shaylah had opened the two most painful subjects, but Califa knew they had to be dealt with if she were to truly atone for her unthinking cruelty.

"Shaylah, I ..." She hesitated, then grimaced. "The difficulty of this for me convinces me even more that it has always been you who has had more courage."

"I think," Shaylah said slowly, "that perhaps I just traveled the road first."

"Perhaps. But you always seemed to know what was wrong. I didn't see it, even when it was in front of me." Califa took a deep breath. "I swear to you, I never knew who ... Wolf was. If I had, I think that even the woman I was then would have had ... reservations about what had been done to the royal Prince of Trios. But now ..."

"Now?"

"Now I see that it didn't matter who he was. No one has the right to do that to another, be he prince or beggar."

Shaylah's brows went up. "Those are," she said in thinly disguised amusement, "almost Dare's exact words."

Califa studied Shaylah for a moment. The depth of devotion and pride in her eyes was unmistakable.

"You truly love him, don't you?" she asked.

"More than my life. He is everything I could ever wish, ever did wish for, in a man." Her mouth quirked.

"Sometimes, he is more than is comfortable. A king is not an easy man to live with."

"A king," Califa murmured, "and you his queen." The truth of what she had done, what she had been, struck home yet again. And the truth of something else struck home as well. She said sadly, "I know you can never forgive me, for what I did to him."

"It would be . . . very hard," Shaylah agreed.

Even now, Califa thought, Shaylah's innate kindness kept her from declaring the truth, that it would be impossible.

"There was no end to my arrogance," she said.

"It was more the Coalition's arrogance," Shaylah said. "And but one of the many things they were wrong about."

"Including bonding?"

Shaylah colored, a delicate shade of pink. "Yes. Before, I had only what I had witnessed with my parents, what they had taught me, to support my views. Now, I *know* every word of it is truth."

Califa sighed, a tiny, wistful sound she couldn't help. "I believe you," she said softly.

Shaylah looked startled, then speculative. "It's odd," she said, her tone sounding a bit too casual, "that I had never heard of Dax Silverbrake until last night. Oh, I had heard the mysterious legends of the flashbow warriors, and of the Silverbrake family—a few of their works survived the attack, and are enshrined now in the Sanctuary—but Dare had never mentioned Dax to me. I had heard of the notorious skypirate, of course. And now I find he is not only the same man, that skypirate and that legendary warrior, but he is Dare's oldest and closest friend."

"Was," Califa corrected tightly. "And not likely to be again. I heard your Dare, and he does not seem in a forgiving mood. And Dax . . . Dax feels he has done the unforgivable."

"And you do not?"

"He has done," she ground out, "what he had to do. He is the most brilliant, courageous *idiot* I have ever known."

Shaylah's eyes widened at the emphasis. Then a knowing smile curved one corner of her mouth. "You love him, don't you."

It wasn't a question, and Califa didn't answer. She wasn't sure she knew the answer. Then Shaylah's expression turned grave.

"God, Califa, do you have any idea how much trouble he's in? How many laws he's broken? In this time of war, Dare could order his death, even on Trios! Or the council could vote to banish him, branded forever an exile."

Califa shuddered. "I thought Trios too . . . enlightened for such punishments."

"In time of war," Shaylah said dryly, "enlightenment is often the first casualty."

"But Dax never—"

"You will not speak of him."

The order, sharply uttered, came from behind Califa. She spun around, caught unusually off guard. And came face to face with the king of Trios.

He looked every inch the king, but the man she'd known as Wolf, the man so determined to regain his freedom that he'd nearly severed his own hand in his efforts to escape his chains, was still visible in the fierce gaze he turned on her as he came to a halt a bare two feet away. It took every bit of nerve she had, but Califa met his stare unflinchingly. Acknowledgment of that nerve flickered briefly, reluctantly, in his eyes. It gave her the courage to try to deflect some of the anger he obviously held against Dax.

"Do not blame him," she said, her voice none too steady. "He did not wish to deal with me." That had been true enough, in the beginning. "It was the cost of bringing the prisoners home. I bargained with him, the location of the labor camps for a price."

"That does not excuse or explain his defense of you. Nor does it explain why he allowed your presence on Trios. And the words of an outworlder about a Triotian of blood mean nothing here."

He didn't say "especially you," but Califa heard the implication as clearly as if he had. He had quickly seen through her attempt to protect Dax, and she lapsed into silence before she provoked his anger again; this was the man who could ultimately order Dax's death.

"My mate," he said gruffly after a moment, "has convinced me you should have the chance to defend yourself before the council. She seems to think we owe you that favor, for not giving away our escape."

Califa's gaze flicked to Shaylah, who said nothing. *I wonder what kind of a battle that was,* Califa thought. *I should not like to try to convince this man of anything, not through this anger.*

"Shaylah is certain that you must have guessed that she had . . . rescued me."

It wasn't a question, but if he was willing to listen, she would start here.

"As soon as I heard you had escaped Ossuary," she said, "I knew. I remembered her face when she found I had . . . sent you there."

Remembered fury darkened his vivid green eyes for an instant. Then, controlling it, he went on. "I am . . . curious. Why did you not give us away?"

"I . . ." Califa hesitated, floundering a little. "She saved my life once, and I—" She broke off suddenly. "No. No, that is not why. When they came to me, I could not betray the woman who was the sister I had never had."

It came out vehemently, and Shaylah stared at her as if she'd never seen her before. In a sense, it was true; this emotional creature bore little resemblance to the cool, controlled Major Claxton Shaylah had known. But denying her feelings for Shaylah any longer would somehow be like denying Dax, and that she could not do.

Even Dare seemed surprised. But he said only, "They came to you?"

Califa's mouth twisted into a wry, humorless smile. "Several months after you escaped." She glanced at Shaylah. "After your medical officer let slip what he had really done that night you came for him, that he had unbanded a gold collar. That and the fact that I was the missing Captain Graymist's friend, and the owner of the escaped slave, was far too much evidence for the Coalition to ignore."

Shaylah's breath caught audibly. "They blamed you?"

Califa shrugged. "It is Coalition tradition, is it not? If you cannot punish the perpetrator, you must punish someone. Anyone."

Dare was staring at her, as if this put a chink in his anger, and he didn't like the fact. "And I suppose you think it was punishment enough? Or do you believe that rescuing a few of my people is payment enough?" The rage was building in him again. "There *is* no payment large enough!"

"I know," Califa said quietly.

"You know? How could you possibly know what it felt like, what it still feels like to this day, to remember, to dream of it and wake up shaking at the memories?"

"I know," she repeated. Then she reached up to tug at the cloth that concealed her throat. It slipped away, revealing the dull gold gleam of the collar and the crystal sparkle of the controls.

Califa heard Shaylah gasp, but her eyes stayed fastened on Dare. She saw his eyes widen, then narrow as he stared first at the collar, then at her face. He was shocked, but she could read nothing more in his expression. It was Shaylah who finally spoke, her voice shaken.

"This was your punishment? For not giving us away, they enslaved you?"

"A gold collar for a gold collar," Califa said simply. "Coalition justice."

When Dare spoke, his voice sounded as if his fury had been shaken, but his words belied the idea. "And this is why you expect me to believe this convenient change of attitude, now that you are in our power?"

"Dare," Shaylah said, still staring at the collar, "I know you are angry, but think of the price she has paid for protecting us. Think of the times she could no doubt have freed herself by simply telling what she knew."

"No." Califa drew herself up straight, ignoring her inner quaking as she faced this man who had so much reason to hate her. "He is right. I expect nothing. Except that you not take your rage at me out on another who does not deserve it."

"I care not what you expect," Dare snapped. "I am no longer your slave, to be ordered to your whim."

She closed her eyes for an instant, summoning an

image of Dax, firing that last bolt that would kill him. If he had courage enough for that, surely she could face this man without breaking. She opened her eyes.

"No," she said. "You are a king. And the rightful King of Trios has always been known as fair." And then, knowing what she was risking, she added, with a glance at Shaylah, "And even the man I knew as Wolf clearly knew where the true blame belonged. And did not belong."

Dare stiffened. He stared at her for a long moment, then snapped, "The High Council convenes at midsun. Someone will be sent for you."

He turned on his heel and was gone before either of the women could speak again.

Califa felt her shoulders sag, and fought of a wave of exhaustion. She wasn't up to this kind of emotional confrontation, she had gotten little sleep and—

Just why she hadn't gotten any sleep came back to her with a fierce jab of vivid, heated memory. A tiny moan escaped her.

"Oh, Dax . . ."

She didn't realize she had spoken it aloud until Shaylah said quietly, "I will try to talk to him again. He is a fair man, Califa, but he is very angry. I don't know that it will do any good."

"I cannot blame him," Califa said honestly. "Were I face to face with one of the people who had used this against me"—she flicked a finger at the collar—"I would be no less enraged."

Shaylah shook her head. "I can't believe they—She broke her own words off with a sigh. "I suppose I have been too long removed from Coalition madness."

"Madness." Califa sighed. "I lived for them, and it was always nothing less than madness."

"I know what it is like to have your entire concept of life turned upside down," Shaylah said sympathetically.

Califa studied her old friend for a moment, then said in awed surprise, "You . . . you believe me, don't you?"

"That you are not the woman you were? As I am not the woman I was? Yes, I think I do." Shaylah smiled ruefully. "However, I admit that since I discovered my pregnancy, I seem to have become quite the optimist."

For some reason, Rina's pixie face popped into Califa's mind. "I suppose you must," she said thoughtfully. "If you cannot hope for the best for your child, it would be a reason for sadness, not joy."

Shaylah looked startled, then she smiled. "That you understand that is the best evidence yet that I should believe you. The Califa Claxton I knew would never have wondered, nor cared, about such things. But then, I always suspected that Califa was mostly bluff."

Califa felt color tinge her cheeks.

"Nor," Shaylah added in a teasing tone Califa nearly wept to hear again, "would that Califa have *ever* blushed."

"No," Califa said, her voice tight with unshed tears. "No, she wouldn't."

And in that moment Califa knew that in regaining this woman's trust, she had won a prize worth more than her entire misspent life. Even if they ordered her execution, she could not regret coming here; she had regained her friend, and broken through the barrier that had imprisoned Dax, and she would change neither even if it would change her own fate.

"Come," Shaylah said. "Sit down. Tell me of Dax. I am most curious. I have never seen Dare so ... torn as he was last night, both hating and loving this lifelong friend."

So Califa told her friend of the man who had taken over her life, realizing now why Rina had so welcomed a feminine ear; the relief of sharing her chaotic feelings was immense.

But the relief did not last. The more she spoke of Dax, the more anxious she was to get back to him. She was afraid, both of what was to come and what he might do. Shaylah was quick to realize the reason for her growing tension, and with an apology, summoned the boy who had brought her here to take her back. Califa understood; she was still a prisoner here.

"Perhaps," Shaylah said, "you should spare some of that worry for yourself."

"I do not care," Califa said, and meant it. Yet when Shaylah took her hand and clasped it briefly, she welcomed the touch.

"I will talk to Dare," she promised again, but Califa held out little hope for a change in the direction of that particular fierce wind. Dare had too much reason to hate, and too little reason to forgive.

The look the man posted outside the door of their cell gave her, a combination of leer and smirk, did little to ease her doubts that anything had truly changed.

"He deserves to die, for consorting with the likes of you," the man muttered.

Califa kept her head high and kept going. When she stepped back into the small room where Dax lay on the cot staring at the ceiling, she tried to summon up some of Shaylah's optimism.

"Shaylah understands. It was she who sent for me. She will try to talk to Dare—"

"She needn't bother," Dax said. He turned his head to look at her then, and Califa felt a chill ripple through her at his expression. "I hear from the guard his decision is already made."

She blinked. "What?"

"He's picked out an executioner."

Chapter 27

Califa wondered if every Triotian left alive was crowded into the council chamber. The huge hall, still showing the damage of Coalition guns, was packed. All eyes were riveted either on the man who sat in the isolated chair between the crowd and the table at the front of the room, or on the man who stood to one side, a huge, curved sword on his belt, and an ominous-looking silver tool of some kind in his hand. Califa's eyes shied away from him as she wondered what method of execution was favored on the enlightened world of Trios.

Dax sat in silence, staring stonily forward at nothing. He had not said a word to her since that blunt statement when she had come back into the room that had been their cell. She tried to convince him that the guard, who had obviously learned that she was of the Coalition, was merely being vicious to a perceived enemy, but he hadn't even reacted.

But what had frightened her the most was what he had done when the armed escort had come for them. The guards had tensed when he bent to his boot and pulled out the knife, but he merely looked at it for a moment, then, with a flick of his hand, hurled it toward the door. The ease of the movement was belied by the solid thunk as the blade dug deeply into the carved wood. Then he walked past the still-quivering knife as if it wasn't even there.

But it wasn't until she had taken her own place, in the seat off to one side reserved for the next to appear before the council, and sat watching Dax's utterly expressionless face, that Califa realized the significance of that action.

He had given up. In jettisoning the knife he was never

without, he had jettisoned the last of his defenses. He looked like the slaves she had seen who had surrendered; his proud posture was slumped, his face blank, and his eyes were flat, cold, and as dead as the ashes of a long extinguished fire. Califa felt something tighten in her chest, a chilly little knot that ached abysmally.

There was a steady hum of talk among the gathering, which rose a bit in volume as a petite figure entered the room and walked down to a seat on the aisle in front, followed closely by Fleuren, carried in the arms of the man she had greeted as her grandson.

Rina's head was held almost defiantly high. Her expression was mutinous, and Califa felt a pang as she wondered what Rina had been up to. They had not been allowed to see her since Dare had ordered their confinement, and Califa had been worried.

The girl's carriage and steady stride faltered as she saw Dax, sitting silent and alone, unmoving, his back to the crowd, a guard at each side of the chair. But then she spotted Califa, and her head came up once more. Something flashed in those jade eyes so like Dax's, a look that was almost conspiratorial, and Califa knew the girl was indeed up to something. But there was no time to speculate as a door at the front of the hall opened, and the Triotian High Council entered, and filed down to their seats at the long table.

Some of them showed the same momentary hesitation when they spotted Dax, in particular a slender woman whose blond hair was streaked with gray, and the dignified older man who led the procession and took the seat at the center of the table. Only the youngest, a man barely into adulthood, did not react; he was too busy looking smugly full of self-importance, Califa realized sourly.

Shaylah had told her that Glendar, the last surviving member of the original council, would preside over the session; the older man in the center, who had led them in, must be him, she thought.

There were single chairs at each end of the long table, and when the five members of the council had taken their seats and the crowd hushed, it became apparent to Califa who they were for. No sooner had she thought it than Dare and Shaylah entered, side by side, then separated to take the remaining chairs, which placed them facing each other eight feet apart. Shaylah's back was to Califa, but she could see Dare's face all too clearly; she found nothing of encouragement in his handsome features. The respectful silence of the crowd pounded home the reality; Dare was their king by choice, and, incredibly, Shaylah their queen.

Neither of them looked at her, or at Dax. Nor did Dax look at them. Or at any of the council; he had shifted his gaze to the floor in front of the table and sat there staring fixedly.

The man she assumed was Glendar rose. He cleared his throat. Dax still did not look up.

In a deep voice that sounded somewhat strained, the silver-haired man called the session to order, announcing as if it were news that this special meeting had been called to address the question of multiple transgressions of law on the part of a Triotian of blood.

Then, sounding awkward, he addressed Dax.

"Be you Dax, of the family of Silverbrake?"

"I am."

The words were barely audible, and came in a voice as lifeless as his eyes. He never even raised his head. Califa felt that tightness in her chest increase.

"It is the understanding of the council that you have waived the representation allowed you. Is that true?"

"It is."

"You wish to defend yourself, then?"

"No."

He still did not look up, and Califa felt that lump grow tighter, bigger.

Glendar frowned. "I don't understand."

Dax said nothing.

"Dax," the old man said, "these are serious charges."

In that moment, the reason for the man's strain showed through, and the reason for that pause when he'd first seen him. He knew Dax, Califa thought. Knew him and liked him. Or had, once. And it was paining this dignified leader of the council to have to do this.

Glendar tried again. "You know the procedure, Dax.

You must have a defense, at the least an explanation. Theft, piracy, even murder—"

"Don't forget treason."

"Treason?" Glendar sounded startled.

Dax stared at the floor. "What else would you call it?"

Glendar glanced at the others; they looked as puzzled as he did. Except for Dare, Califa noticed. He looked merely thoughtful. Then, even as she watched, she saw a kind of understanding dawn in his eyes, as if something had just occurred to him.

"There is no such charge against you," Glendar said gently. "But the others are serious enough."

"Yes."

"Your defense, then."

"I have no defense," Dax repeated.

"Dax!" the man exclaimed. Dax never moved, his dark head stayed bent, his eyes fixed on some imaginary spot on the floor, as if he thought himself not good enough to even meet his accusers eye to eye.

Califa nearly shouted at him, begging him to stop this. Can't you see they don't want to do this? she cried out silently. Even Dare had stiffened, staring at Dax tensely. Give them a chance, another option, she pled inwardly.

Suddenly the woman next to Glendar stood up, the one, Califa remembered, who had also wavered when she'd seen Dax sitting there, so alone save for the guards beside him.

"Dax," she said gently, "we have not forgotten you. You were once of our best and brightest. We know there must be an explanation for the terrible things we have heard. Are they lies, exaggerations?"

"No."

"But surely—"

"The worst of what you have heard is true, and not the worst of what I have done."

The woman sank back into her chair, obviously shaken. Califa was shaking herself; he hadn't just given up, he was begging them to convict him. She could hardly breathe for the painful tightness of her chest; he had finally found a way to punish himself enough.

"Dax," Glendar said urgently, "you must realize, in

time of war, these charges could warrant even death, should his majesty so decree."

"I know."

"Then please, answer the charges."

For just an instant, Dax's eyes closed. Then they snapped open again, still downcast. "Guilty," he said.

Murmurs of shock rippled through the room. Califa heard Rina cry out, and saw her run out of the room. At a quick whisper from Fleuren, her grandson, Renclan, followed the girl hastily. Numbed, Califa listened as Glendar abandoned his pretense at impartiality. He left the table and walked over to bend in front of the single chair.

"Dax, please, you leave us no choice. No defense is as a conviction."

Dax remained stubbornly silent.

Glendar straightened. He took in a deep breath, and turned to face Dare.

"Your majesty? Do you wish to invoke the war authority for execution?"

Even through her numbness, Califa saw Dare, already looking stunned, pale a little. Shaylah moved, just slightly, and Dare's gaze flicked to her face. Then, letting out a long breath, he shook his head.

Califa felt relief flood her. But it was short-lived when Glendar's next words showed her the truth of what had happened; Dax had escaped death, but had been condemned back to the hell he'd been living in for the last six years.

"It shall be banishment, then," the old man said sadly, "as demanded by the laws of Trios, you shall be marked as an exile and forbidden ever to return."

Glendar nodded to the man Califa had almost forgotten, the man who stood to one side with that odd looking tool. He did something with it now, turning the handle. Almost immediately the tip, barely an inch across and shaped like an *X*, began to glow, first orange, then brightly, hotly red.

It wasn't until the man stepped toward Dax, and the two guards moved to hold his head, that she realized what was happening. She stared, in shocked disbelief.

Surely he wasn't going to let them do this, to literally brand him with that searingly hot metal?

Then he moved, brushing away the hands of the guards, and Califa breathed again. And as quickly lost that breath on a gasp; Dax had merely rejected their hold on him. He bent his head to one side, then reached up and tugged the thick mane of his hair out of the way, baring his neck to the man with the red-hot brand. He wasn't going to *let* them do it, he was going to help them.

"Damn you!" Califa leapt to her feet, unable to bear it any longer. Dax seemed to wince, but he never looked at her. The man with the glowing tool paused. Glendar opened his mouth to speak, then closed it as she shouted again.

"Damn you, Dax, look at me!"

She strode across the room, oblivious of the sudden chorus of exclamations in the chamber. The guards moved to stop her, but at a wave from Dare, they let her pass. She came to a halt in front of the chair.

"You're not going to do this, do you hear me? You're not going to just sit here and make them do this to you."

"Califa, don't."

His voice was hoarse, strained, but it was at least a sign of some emotion and she welcomed it.

"Don't what? Speak for you when you refuse to speak for yourself?"

"You can't speak for me."

She whirled on Glendar. "Is that true? No one else can speak for him?"

The silver-haired man looked miserable. "I'm afraid so, once he has declined that option."

Califa turned to look at Dare. He looked as torn as Shaylah had told her he was. But simply looking at him, thinking of something he had said earlier, gave her an idea. Desperately, she turned back to Glendar.

"What of my time before you? Will you let me use it?"

"Califa, no!" For the first time Dax looked up; she didn't look at him.

"Will you?" she demanded of Glendar.

"If you use it now," he cautioned, "you will shorten

the time allowed for your own defense. Outworlders are only granted so much."

"I doesn't matter. I have little enough to say."

Glendar hesitated, then glanced at Dare, who gave him a barely perceptible nod as Dax protested again.

"Califa—"

She whirled on Dax. "So now will you talk? Will you tell them why you refuse to defend yourself? Will you tell them the truth?"

He lowered his eyes again. "I have," he said flatly.

"May your God preserve me from suicidal idiots," she grated out. Then she spun around to face the Council. "It is true I am an outworlder. And whatever else you have probably heard of me is true. But I have knowledge you need to hear, and despite the stubbornness of this ... this Triotian of yours, you're going to hear it."

"Stop it—"

"Quiet," Glendar ordered Dax, an odd light in his eyes now. "You refused to speak, now refrain from it." Dax seemed to shut down before her eyes, as if he'd gone numb to everything around him.

Glendar looked at Califa. "Go on. I would very much like to know why the son of one of the most honored families of Trios refuses to even try to defend himself."

"Because," Califa said flatly, "he feels he deserves exactly what you are about to do to him. In fact, if he had his choice, I am sure he would prefer your king had invoked that order for execution."

Glendar blinked. "He would prefer death?"

"He's been trying for it ever since he committed that treason he spoke of."

"There is no charge of treason against him," Glendar repeated, still clearly puzzled by the use of the word.

"In your eyes, perhaps. But he has already tried and convicted himself, of the treason of not being here to die with the rest of his world."

The gasps that went around the room didn't distract Califa from seeing the look that crossed Dare's face; that of a man whose guess had been confirmed.

"But that was no treason!" Glendar exclaimed. "It was not by design that he was gone at that time, we all knew that."

"That matters not to him. He is alive, and until a short time ago, he thought all of you—including your king—dead. For that reason alone he has risked himself time and again, hoping to join you all in that death."

She turned to face the council table. "He denied his identity as a Triotian, denied his family name because he felt he no longer had the right to either. Even the Triotian child he rescued three years ago, though he loves her, has been a living, daily torture, a reminder of how he had failed. All because he lived on after his world had been destroyed. All because he hadn't been there to uselessly die along with the rest of his people."

Califa swallowed, knowing she was losing her emotional control but unable to fight it any longer. She had to make them understand.

"When he learned that some of you still lived, and of your rebellion, he tried to atone by saving those he could, and bringing them home. Some of you look upon this as an effort to buy forgiveness, but I tell you that deep down, he expected none. He expected nothing other than what you are about to do. But I tell you as well, that no matter what he has done, no matter what laws of yours he has broken, I swear to you, there is nothing—*nothing*—you can do to him that is any worse than what he's already done to himself. He has punished himself for six years, and in his mind, it is still not enough."

She was shaking now, visibly, and she couldn't help it. Dare was staring, not at the silent Dax, but at her, and there was a look in his eyes she'd never seen there before. She steadied herself and forced out the last words she felt she must say.

"If you must have vengeance this day, take it on me. I am the true representative of the Coalition here. I am the one you should hate, not Dax." Her voice broke. "Not Dax."

She knew she dare not go on; she who had wept but twice in two decades would burst into frantic tears before them all if she did.

"I would speak!"

The high, clear voice came from the crowd. All heads turned, and Glendar spoke.

"We recognize you, Fleuren, and your right to speak as an elder of the city of Triotia."

"I have reason to defend this man," she said. "You all know he rescued me from imprisonment, and brought me to the home I thought to die without seeing again. But there is more to my plea. During my imprisonment, I heard much of the skypirate known only as Dax. I heard that honest people had nothing to fear from him. I heard that only those who perpetuated the Coalition evil needed watch out for him. I learned of his generosity to those downtrodden by the very forces that defeated us, and that much of what he gained by admittedly criminal acts was given back to such as those."

She glanced at Califa, who watched the old woman through eyes suddenly brimming; she had feared no one else but she cared what happened to Dax. Dax himself sat with his head lowered, and Califa saw tiny shudders rippling through him, as if each of Fleuren's words was a blow. But he was feeling now, and that was something, Califa thought.

"And I heard of his recklessness, his carelessness with his own life for the sake of others. And when he came for me, I found it to be true."

Fleuren looked around, as if she were singling out each person in the chamber.

"It is true that Triotians rarely believe that the end justifies the method. But we have all agreed some of our cherished laws needs be suspended in time of war. I submit that Dax Silverbrake deserves no less."

Fleuren glanced toward the back of the room, as if expecting something. Then she turned back, and this time her attention was fixed on Dare.

"And as the granddaughter of one of our greatest legends, I submit also, your highness, something you all seem to have forgotten. That only a Triotian of truest heart can fire the flashbow. Dax Silverbrake can."

The clamor that circled the room was instantaneous, as was the look of realization on Dare's face. The noise nearly drowned out the disturbance at the back of the room as the two huge doors swung open.

Glendar had to shout for order as a large group

swarmed down the aisle to the front of the room, Rina in the lead. Califa's heart leapt; it was the entire crew of the *Evening Star*. Roxton, Larcos, Nelcar, even the silent Qantar.

The girl came to a halt as every guard in the room surrounded her small troop. She glanced at Califa, who smiled through her tears. The girl seemed to take heart from that, and glared up at the guard who towered over her.

"They have told me I belong here," she said, loud enough for all to hear. "That as the last one alive, I have all the rights of the Carbray family, and the rights of any Triotian. Is that not true?"

Helplessly, Glendar looked at Dare.

"Let them through," Dare ordered. "I wish to hear all of this."

Rina darted past the guard and ran to Dax. She threw her arms around him. Only then did he look up, anguish vivid in his eyes as he looked at the girl he loved like his own blood. Roxton strolled up and stood beside Califa, grinning.

"Damn you, Rox," Dax said hoarsely, "you're supposed to be a full day gone from here!"

"Shut up, Dax. You gave the *Evening Star* to us, didn't you? We'll do as we like with her. And we all voted to stay and save your worthless hide."

Califa laughed, she couldn't help it. She'd suspected something like this, when Roxton had so carefully worded his answer to Dax's order to break out of orbit and leave. And Dax was hugging Rina back. He was alive, responding. Roxton threw her a snappy salute.

Glendar scrambled to regain control. "Is there a point to this intrusion?"

"Sure is, your honor, or whatever you are," Roxton said.

"Your honor will do," Glendar said primly.

"The point is, you should be introduced to someone."

"Introduced?"

"To the man who has single-handedly done more to slow down the Coalition juggernaut than anyone. The man who has deprived them of more supplies, more ships, more men, more ammunition than they've been able to make up for. The man who made one ship as effective as a squadron against the full force of the Coalition. The man who took target after target, all of which had only one thing in common; taking them in some way hurt the Coalition. It took Califa here to figure it out for us, but every move that man made, every thing he did, while it made us rich, did only one thing for him—it was a blow against the Coalition. And maybe, just maybe, you should think about the possibility that the reason they didn't just blow your entire world completely to pieces when you first started this little rebellion of yours, was because they needed your resources. Because that man I'm speaking of took so damned much away from them."

Califa saw Dax stiffen, saw his eyes widen. Since he'd believed Trios already destroyed, he had obviously never thought of this aspect, and she could have kissed Roxton for realizing it.

Rina spoke then, never releasing her tight hold on Dax. Califa knew just how the girl felt; she wished she could grab him and hang on just as tightly.

"I remember little of Trios," she said. "What I do know, Dax has taught me. He taught me there was no other world like it, and when we thought it destroyed, he taught me that I should keep its memory alive, and honor it. He taught me there was no better place to have lived and grown up. But if this is what you see as justice, then he was wrong. And when you banish him, you banish me, for I go with him."

She released Dax then, and when the girl moved, Califa could have sworn she saw wetness glistening on his cheeks.

"But there is one more thing you need know. Dax left something with me—"

"Rina," Dax said warningly.

"No, Dax. I've never disobeyed a direct order from you, but even if you never forgive me, I must disobey this one."

The girl walked boldly up to Dare. She stopped, studying him with all the fierce concentration of youth. Dare looked disconcerted, and Califa was as proud of Rina in that moment as if she had been her own child.

"You are the king, are you not?" she asked bluntly.

Dare's mouth quirked. "So they say."

"Dax told me that on Trios, even a child can speak to the king."

The quirk became a smile. "That is true."

"Then I wish to give you something. Dax left it with me. He ordered me to hold it until this was over, until you had decided. I didn't understand when he said no matter what happened, I was to give this to you when it was done." She gave Dare a look that was bitter far beyond her years. "I see now that he meant even if you killed him."

Dare winced visibly before the fierce anger of this child. Even the council shifted uncomfortably.

"I'm not even certain what it is," Rina said. "I only know that when Dax gave it to me, he said that there are some things too sacred to be used for the paying of debts, especially debts that are beyond repaying."

She reached into the loose shirt she wore. When she pulled out a large circle of hammered metal, an odd color between silver and gold, every member of the council gasped. Dare stared, clearly stunned.

"I see that it is as important to you as he thought," Rina said. "Yet he would not use it to bargain with, even for his life. Or to save himself from *that*." She gestured at the glowing tool that would sear the mark of an exile into Dax's flesh. Then she backed up a step. "Well, I will. If you want this, you will have to—"

"Rina, no."

It was Dax, his voice short and sharp with command. Rina looked back at him.

"But—"

"No, Rina. It is the Royal Circlet of the King of Trios. It is his by right."

"If it is so valuable to him, then he can—"

"No." Dax swallowed visibly. "Please."

For a long moment Rina just stared at him. Whatever she saw in his eyes filled her own with tears. Her bravado vanished, and the hands that held the circlet trembled. Dax nodded slightly, toward Dare. With a strangled cry, Rina turned and handed the crown back to the king.

Dax slumped in his chair, letting out a long breath.

Rina looked around a little wildly, her gaze stopping on Califa. Wordlessly, driven by an emotion she didn't even understand, Califa held out her arms. The girl ran to her, sobbing as she threw her arms around her.

There was a long moment of silence as Dare sat motionless, staring at the circlet in his hands. It was Glendar who spoke at last, gently, unexpectedly to Califa.

"You have time for a few more words. Have you anything to say on your own behalf?"

Califa gave a final hug to Rina, then straightened. She walked over to stand where Rina had stood; she could do no less than match the girl's bravery. She looked at Dare, who still held the royal symbol returned to him by the man they were about to irrevocably punish.

"Only this," she said, her voice none too steady. "I do not wish to die. But I am not sure anything less can atone for what your king knows I have done."

The guards around Dax and the crew tensed when she reached into her pocket, but again Dare waved them back. Shaylah gasped, and Dare sucked in his breath when she drew out the control unit. She heard a commotion, and sensed Dax had tried to rise.

"No, snowfox! Don't."

She didn't turn. She didn't dare look at Dax, or she would weaken. With a hand she couldn't keep from shaking, she handed the king of Trios, who knew all too well exactly what she was giving him, the controller that said he now owned her as she had once owned him.

Chapter 28

Dare sat staring at the power unit as Califa walked silently back to stand beside Dax. She let one hand rest on his shoulder. Rina followed her and stood on his other side, her hand doing the same. Califa felt Dax shudder, heard his harsh, gulping breaths, and knew the man who never cried was fighting breaking down before them all.

Next to Rina stood Roxton. The rest of the crew gathered close. Renclan, looking clearly uneasy at what had obviously been his part in helping Fleuren and Rina arrange the crew's arrival through the shield, picked up his grandmother at her order, and they stepped forward to join the group around Dax. As did all the Triotians he had rescued, except for the man too injured to move. But even he had sent a representative; his bonded mate, who had long thought him dead, was there to stand with the others.

Dare's hand clenched around the controller, and Califa knew he was remembering. It was asking too much, she thought, for him to forgive. But she prayed he would accept her offer of herself in Dax's place, and not send Dax out to finish the job of killing himself.

Shaylah sat silently, her gaze flicking from her mate to Califa, Dax and the others, then back. She'd seen that look before, Califa thought suddenly. Back when they'd been in the academy together, and were planning some kind of mischief.

A long moment of silence stretched out as Glendar returned to his seat. Before he could call the council to order to vote, Shaylah pushed back her chair and stood up. Dare looked up at her, as did the others at the table. "I beg your forgiveness, Glendar," she said. *Even apologizing, she sounds royal,* Califa thought. Shaylah had truly found her place. "I find myself in difficulty here," Shaylah continued. "Not so very long ago, I was a stranger among you, without friends and mistrusted. Yet you all finally came to accept that I was not the enemy I had once been, and that my love for your rightful king was true. You have accepted me as your queen, and for that I am more grateful than I can say. But now we are faced with a woman in the same predicament. A woman I believe has changed as I have changed. A woman who is my friend. I find I cannot give a fair vote in this. I therefore must withdraw."

Califa's breath caught, then stopped altogether as Shaylah left the table and walked across the room toward her. She came to a halt before Califa, laid a gentle hand on her arm, then turned to face the council. And Dare.

Dare was watching her with a steady, unwavering gaze. The surprise that had initially shown on his face gave way to a love and pride that fairly radiated from him. Slowly, he got to his feet.

"My queen shames me," he said softly, yet in a voice that would carry to the farthest reaches of the room. "She who is not of this world has reminded me, and not for the first time, of why it came to be." He glanced at the council. "I, too, must remove myself from this vote. I cannot make an objective decision about my oldest and dearest friend."

Dare crossed the room with long, regal strides, spared a glance and a wink for Rina, then took a position behind Dax. The significance of that position was not lost on the crowd, and the murmur that had started when Shaylah had moved, suddenly swelled to a roar of approval.

The council, all except Glendar, looked at a loss; the old man was grinning widely. Then, with difficulty, he quieted the room.

"No vote, indeed," he said, but he was still smiling as he looked from Dare to Shaylah. Then, clearing his throat, he addressed the council. "I believe we have heard enough."

"Yes, but I am concerned," the youngest man said, as if loathe to surrender his time in the spotlight. He glanced at Califa. "We were certain of our queen's devotion to Trios because of her love for the king. How will we assure that this woman does not betray us in some way?"

"By seeing past the end of your nose, you young fool," Fleuren called, giving rise to a raucous round of laughter and the young man's blush. "Can you not see she loves Dax?"

Califa blushed furiously, Shaylah rolled her eyes, and Dare smothered a laugh. Dax had gone very still, staring once more at that fascinating spot on the floor.

"Is this true?" the young man asked, his eyes wide.

"Yes," Glendar asked, his laughter ill-concealed, "is it? Tell me, Dax Silverbrake, if the council votes to grant you both absolution, will you bond with this woman to assure her loyalty?"

Dax's head came up. He stared at Glendar, who unconcernedly grinned back at him. After a long, silent moment, Dax said lowly, "If that is the council's requirement."

"Requirement?"

Califa's exclamation was outraged as anger bubbled up inside her. Until this moment, she hadn't fully admitted to herself that what Shaylah had so easily guessed was true; she loved this man, and she wanted with him what Shaylah had with Dare. And to have him treat it as if it were no more than a way to get the council's vote to go in their favor infuriated her.

"I'll have no man who is *required* to bond with me!"

Dax drew back a little in his chair, staring at her. "You said you thought bonding was a myth," he said slowly. "That only fools and Triotians believe in it."

"That was aeons ago," she snapped. "Do you think I've learned nothing since then? You are an idiot, Dax whatever-your-name-is."

"Silverbrake," he said, slowly standing up, as if only on his feet could he reclaim the name he'd been ashamed to use for so long. "It is a good name."

She was still seething, as much from her own embarrassment at having Fleuren declare her feelings to the world when she hadn't even admitted them to herself as from his offhanded attitude. "It's no concern of mine whether it is or not."

"It could be," he said, looking at her intently.

"And why in Hades should it?"

"If what Fleuren says is true."

Califa bit her lip until it bled, trying to hold back tears of embarrassment. "I swear to your God, you are a fool. Do you think I give a damn about a skypirate who spends more time trying to get himself k-killed. . . ."

"You would be the fool if you did," Dax said softly. "But why else did you offer to sacrifice yourself for him? Why did you give up your chance to defend yourself for him?"

"B-because I . . ." she started, then had to stop to clamp down harder on her lip before she humiliated herself before them all.

"Shall I tell you why?" Dax said, softer still. "Because you're the bravest woman I've ever known. Because you had the heart to change your mind, your very soul, when you saw the truth. Because you have more courage than I've ever thought of having."

"I don't," she said in a small voice. "You do."

"If I had such courage," he said wryly, "you would have known the truth before now."

She frowned slightly. "The truth?"

He took in a deep breath. "That I love you."

Califa gaped at him, stunned. "You . . . do?"

"I have, for some time. Perhaps from that first moment. But I didn't feel I deserved such . . ."

His voice trailed off, and Califa saw, incredibly, a touch of color tinge his cheeks. And suddenly she knew what he was thinking of, of those moments last night when her love and the joy of being home had shattered the barriers his body had raised, and he had at long last been able to give himself to her fully.

"Oh," she said, color tinting her own cheeks.

Dax's mouth twisted. "I was kind of hoping for something similar, snowfox."

"What? Oh!" she exclaimed, heat flooding her cheeks now.

When she didn't go on, Dax reached out and took her hands. "Are you going to leave me out here all alone?"

His rueful words came at the same time as a healthy nudge from Shaylah. Suddenly feeling more shy than she ever had in her life, she lowered her gaze. "I . . . love you, too."

The cheer that went up around them brought home with embarrassing force the fact that they had done this in front of a room packed with people. Califa buried her face against Dax's chest, and he ducked his head as if he were as abashed as she was.

It was Dare who spoke first, as the cheers finally died away. He wiped at his eyes, damp from his own laughter, then looked across at Shaylah.

"Remind you of anything, my love?"

She smiled at him sunnily. "I do seem to recall another couple who became betrothed in this very room, in front of a mob of many of these very same people."

The chamber erupted into laughter again. Glendar turned to the council, who waved him off.

"Really, Glendar," the woman who had spoken before said, "do you really think it necessary to vote? Our time would be better spent preparing for a bonding ceremony!"

Epilogue

"—like nothing I've ever flown before!"

"It's your design, you should have known."

Califa glanced at Shaylah and smiled. Their mates were coming this way, after Dare's latest flight in the fighter Dax had built, sounding like a couple of kids after their first spin in an air rover.

"But you added the adjustable wings," Dare was saying as they came in.

"I needed them, for different conditions. Omegan space, for instance, where the air is so dense—"

Dax stopped when he realized both women were watching them with that indulgent look women get when their men are acting more like boys.

"Well, whatever the reason," Dare said, "it handles even better than I'd hoped."

"Good. It's yours."

"What?"

"You heard me. I'll borrow it back if I need it."

"Dax, you can't. You've given us more than enough. Yourself, returned to us, Shaylah's friend returned to her, six of our own home safe ... And we never expected to see the Royal Circlet again—"

"Don't argue. I'll win."

"I know." Dare scowled at him. "Your years as a skypirate have had some effects I could do without. If you can't win openly, you resort to trickery."

"I *always* did that. You just never caught on. You've always been too honorable, Dare."

Califa felt an amazing warmth expanding inside her as she listened to them joke. It had taken time to get to this stage, but the bond between them was stronger than ever.

They had had much to work out, and not all on Dax's part. Dare had, with great difficulty, finally told Dax about his sister Brielle's death during the Coalition's invasion. Dax had been shaken by the knowledge that she had died by Dare's own hand, but he had known his sister well, and later had told Califa he could envision her pleading with Dare to kill her before the Coalition took her alive.

"She knew if he survived, he would be so haunted by what they would do to her that he would be no good to Trios or her people."

"She must have been an incredible woman," Califa had said, more than a little awed. But no more incredible than Shaylah, Califa had thought, who took the news that Dax was the brother of Dare's dead mate with an equanimity and gracious sympathy that made her seem more royal than ever.

Califa had grown closer to Shaylah than she had ever felt to anyone, except Rina. The little pixie had come to live with them soon after the bonding ceremony, and while it was taking a while for the girl to adjust to the great changes in her life, she loved Dax unwaveringly, and had included Califa in that love without question now that she was certain Califa loved him as strongly as she did.

And Califa and Dare had reached a harmony of a sort, if not true friendship yet. He had spoken to her alone, the evening before the bonding ceremony between her and Dax.

"If I can believe that Shaylah changed so much," he had told her, "then I must believe it is possible that you have as well. It will not be easy, but you have my word I will try to forget what is past between us."

"I can ask for no more," Califa had said. "And I am not sure I could be so generous, were our positions reversed."

He had looked at her for a long moment. "I think perhaps you might surprise yourself, Califa Claxton. You have great courage. No other woman save Shaylah—and Rina—has ever faced me so fearlessly. And I have found it sometimes takes more courage to forgive than to exact revenge."

"The people of this world are most fortunate in their king, Darian of Trios," she had said, and had meant every word of it. And when she had discovered that Dare's bonding gift to them was the arrival of the laser-surgeon to remove her collar, she had wept.

Tonight, as they sat down to an evening meal, she looked at Dare anew, seeing how he watched the very pregnant Shaylah as they spoke of their soon to be born son. There was regret, but no anger in Dare's voice as he explained the child would not be named Galen, after Dare's father, because of a Triotian tradition that said a dead king's name could not be used for three generations. Despite his words, in that moment Dare appeared to be not a king, but simply a man deeply in love with his mate.

That was how Dax looked at her, now. It had taken a while for him to accept that his people truly held him blameless for escaping the fate of so many, that they in fact held him as a sort of hero for all he'd done to damage the Coalition, saw him as a lone warrior rather than a skypirate. Only when he had been able to believe in their welcome, only when he was certain he was home at last, had he been truly healed. And only then, a whole man once more, had he been able to fully embrace the joy they'd found together. She knew the extent of his healing when a small, exquisite, white marble carving of a snowfox appeared on the table beside their bed. The same one she'd seen in the exhibit on Alpha 2.

He told her he'd offered to return it to the sole surviving member of the family it had been stolen from, but the woman had refused, saying he had a greater right to it than she. Califa had wondered why, and her curiosity must have shown, because Dax had silently picked up the sculpture and turned it over. Califa's breath caught when she saw the ornate *S* etched on the base, the symbol she had learned stood for the illustrious Silverbrake family.

"Brielle," Dax said quietly. "She loved the animals of Trios. They were her favorite subject."

She ached for the pain in his voice, and for so much that had been lost here. And when Dax had turned to her in the darkness, when he had asked her to sing for him, something gentle and fragile, as Brielle had been, Califa felt she had been given the greatest of honors. So she had sung, softly, most of her pleasure in the music coming from the memories of the more and more frequent occasions when Dax would join her on the dulcetpipe, sometimes even in front of the king and queen, that "minuscule" talent he'd spoken of showing its true depth.

Shaylah's sudden, sharp exclamation jerked Califa out of her musings. Dare dropped his cup, and it shattered on the table as his head snapped around to his mate.

"I think the new prince of Trios wants to join us for this meal," Shaylah said a little breathlessly.

Dare paled. "Oh, God."

"No one to blame but yourself," Dax said to him with a grin.

"Don't get brassy, Defense Minister Silverbrake," Califa said, setting down her own cup to help Shaylah rise. "You don't want to give him any smart remarks to use on you later."

"To use on me?" Dax echoed, puzzled. Then, as her meaning hit, his eyes widened and he gaped at her. "Oh, God."

Dare laughed, his moment of panic apparently relived by Califa's revelation that Dax would soon be in the same position. He got to his feet, to follow Shaylah back into their bedchamber.

"And I'll be there, my friend," Dare teased Dax, "rest assured."

At the door, Dare turned back to look once more at Dax, who was sitting there looking as if he'd been hit by a disrupter on full stun.

"I hope you have a girl, skypirate. It would serve you right."

"A girl?" Dax choked out.

"Yes," Dare said, his voice suddenly quietly serious. "A girl with the courage and nerve and heart of an Arellian would be nice, don't you think?"

"A girl," Dax murmured, reverently now, as if a sudden vision had formed in his head.

"Who knows," Dare said. "Maybe someday, when they're grown up...."

*   *   *

Later, long after Califa had emerged from the chamber holding Prince Lyon of Trios in her arms, long after the pale but jubilant Dare had finished swearing he would never again touch his mate, long after Shaylah had teasingly told him he'd keep to that for about a week, and after the celebration that had threatened to keep the entire city up all night was finally over, Califa snuggled up to Dax contentedly.

"He's a beautiful baby," she said.

"Um-hmm," Dax said absently; he'd been contemplating the slight gleam of the flashbow in the dark, back in its case after Dare had returned it to him. Then he pulled his attention back to his mate's words. "Dare's golden hair and Shaylah's blue eyes."

"Our baby's eyes will be green," she said decidedly. "Jade, just like yours."

The words still sent a little shiver down his spine. "I don't think that's something you can promise, is it?"

"Why not?" she asked simply.

He smiled into the darkness. "Why not, indeed?"

"We've pulled off a miracle before, haven't we?"

"Yes. I suppose we have." He pulled her closer to him. "So, pull off another one, and make sure it's a girl."

She raised up on one elbow to look at him., "A mate?"

He grinned. "Dare's looking for Lyon's future mate."

Califa giggled, a new and pleasant sound he was growing quite fond of. She hadn't had much laughter of any kind in her life; it made him feel warm inside to hear it now. He leaned over to kiss her gently.

He'd meant it merely for good night, but her eager response changed his mind in a hurry. It had never faded, the spark that snapped to life so swiftly between them, and it took only moments before they were locked together, joyously chasing the rapture they'd found only with each other.

It was much later, holding her in his arms, that Dax sleepily thought of a straight, strong handsome young man with gleaming blond hair and bright blue eyes, smiling down at an equally straight and strong beautiful young woman, with Califa's ebony hair and his own green eyes.

He fell asleep with the oddest feeling that he had just had a glimpse of the future.

Journeys of Passion and Desire

☐ **CROOKED HEARTS by Patricia Gaffney.** Reuben Jones walks on the wrong side of the law—a card shark and a master of deception. Grace Russell has had to learn a few tricks herself in order to hold on to her crumbling California vineyard. In this sexy, rollicking ride through the gambling halls and sinful streets of the 1880s San Francisco, two "crooked hearts" discover that love is the most dangerous—and delicious—game of all. (404599—$4.99)

☐ **LOVE ME TONIGHT by Nan Ryan.** The war had robbed Helen Burke Courtney of her money and her husband. All she had left was her coastal Alabama farm. Captain Kurt Northway of the Union Army might be the answer to her prayers, or a way to get to hell a little faster. She needed a man's help to plant her crops; she didn't know if she could stand to have a damned handsome Yankee do it. (404831—$4.99)

☐ **FIRES OF HEAVEN by Chelley Kitzmiller.** Independence Taylor had not been raised to survive the rigors of the West, but she was determined to mend her relationship with her father—even if it meant journeying across dangerous frontier to the Arizona Territory. But nothing prepared her for the terrifying moment when her wagon train was attacked, and she was carried away from certain death by the mysterious Apache known only as Shatto. (404548—$4.99)

☐ **WHITE ROSE by Linda Ladd.** Cassandra Delaney is the notorious "White Rose," risking her life and honor for the Confederacy. Australian blockade runner Derek Courtland's job is to abduct this mysterious, sensual woman—only she's fighting him to escape his ship and the powerful feelings pulling them both toward the unknown. (404793—$4.99)

*Prices slightly higher in Canada

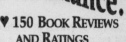